SUNSHINE

SUNSHINE

A SADDLEBROOK FALLS ROMANCE

MICHAELA JEAN TAYLOR

SUNSHINE

Editor: Britt Tayler

Cover Designer: Cindy Ras

Internal Formatting: Michaela Jean Taylor

For all the girls with stars in their eyes,
may you find a cowboy to be your biggest cheerleader.

AUTHOR'S NOTE

This book contains scenes with discussions of mature subject matter including anxiety, suicide, death, grief, cheating, and on-page panic attacks and is intended for mature audiences.

CHAPTER ONE

NOW

Winters in New York City are nothing like winters at home in Saddlebrook Falls—they're dark and biting with a wind chill that'll cut straight through to your bones. It's my second one here as a sophomore at NYU and I really thought I'd be ready for it, but it's even crueler the second time around. Snow comes down so thick I can hardly see across the street, and without a car I'm forced to walk through the storm to get anywhere.

I pull the hood of my heavy coat down as far as it'll go over my brow and trudge through the muddy slush on the sidewalk, doing my best not to slip on any patches of ice. My roommate, Chantal, already headed back to Florida for winter break, and I love evenings like this when I have the dorm to myself. Not that she's a bother to have around, but our placc is so tiny I never feel like I have enough room to spread out and relax like I want to.

As I cross a small access street, a freezing gust of wind tears through me, no longer blocked by the tall brick buildings that overtake Greenwich Village, and I curse at myself for being out in this near-blizzard in the first place. I had every intention of making it to the store earlier, but I got lost in the middle of my latest obsession—a fantasy novel that I couldn't for the life of me put down—and I never made it out to buy some much-needed groceries. By the time I finished the book and realized my mistake, I figured I could either go to bed hungry and hope the sun was back out by morning, or I could face the freezing snowfall and brave this twelve-minute walk to the closest takeout spot.

I haven't eaten anything since breakfast, so eventually my hunger won out.

A snowplow drags itself along the sidewalk in the distance, lit by the golden glow of the Christmas lights wrapped around various street signs and lampposts. I watch it spray out large clumps of snow as it goes, and I wince. It's coming right toward me—I only have about a minute before it'll reach where I'm still slugging through the snow and ice. Hurrying my careful steps, I navigate over a particularly nasty ice patch and make it to Star of India in the nick of time.

My mouth waters as soon as I walk inside, the aroma of cinnamon, clove, and nutmeg wrapping around me and shaking off some of the chill. It's been one of the many advantages of leaving my small town for college: access to so many different kinds of food. New York City is filled to the brim with eateries that offer traditional recipes from all over the world, and Indian food, I've learned, is one of my new favorites.

I'd never tried it before moving here a year and a half ago. The options for takeout at home are basically nonexistent, save for a few locally owned staples. And while I can't help but miss the comfort and familiarity of June's Cafe on Sundays or a Friday night at Mustang's Pizza with my friends, a big part of wanting to leave home for college was so that I could experience more.

There's a whole world beyond that dusty town, and I want to see it. I want to experience the bustle of a big city, and what bigger city is there than this one?

Jason's a senior at Texas A&M and has been all-in preparing for the NFL draft this spring after dedicating nearly his whole life to football. He's *good*, and as a quarterback everyone expects him to be an early pick. But even though we plan on getting married as soon as I graduate college, I don't just want to be an NFL wife. I want to make my mark on the world, find my own place in it, so it was important for me to come here, where I could be one in eight million people, and brace myself against the chaos.

I order a couple of my favorite dishes at the counter—lamb biryani and chicken tikka masala—and tip the owner before I force myself back outside to brave the cold. In just a few days I'll be on a flight to the Gulf Coast where winters are hardly a blimp on the radar, and though I don't like to admit it out loud, I can't wait to be home.

It's been four months since I've seen the sun sink down over rolling hills of green from our porch, cicadas buzzing in the nearby trees and the promise of a cool breeze caressing my skin. Four months since I've hugged my little sister, since I've felt Jason's arms wrapped around me or his lips against mine. Even though I don't regret moving so far away to escape my often suffocating hometown, I'd be lying if I said I don't miss the coastal air or the smell of freshly tilled earth from nearby farms.

Humidity so thick it sticks to you.

The sun tattooing new freckles on your skin as a wild horse whinnies.

New York City is breathtaking in its own right, the way the buildings sparkle as they stretch into the sky. People from all over the world exist together on streets that don't quite belong to anyone and yet belong to everyone. But it smells like shit most days and it never quiets, never sleeps. It took me months to get used to the lights piercing through our single dorm window at all hours of the night. I can hardly see the stars out here . . . or even the horizon, aside from a few fleeting glimpses between buildings. And the people . . . there are just so many of them, everywhere, *all the time.*

I carefully step toward the closest building to avoid another big patch of ice and hear my phone ring from inside my coat pocket. It's late and dark, and I don't want to stop moving until I'm safely back at my dorm. I usually don't venture around the city after the sun sets if I can avoid it—it's not that I'm scared, but I've heard the stories. I'm not comfortable with city life enough to know how to handle myself in a grizzly situation. Better to be safe than sorry.

But something about the ringing nags at me, and I can't help but pause my steps to dig my phone out of my pocket. I haven't heard from Jason since yesterday morning and, while it's not the first time he's gone quiet on me like this, I always feel anxious when my texts go unanswered.

By the time I wrestle my phone out with a clumsy gloved hand, I've missed the call. It's from an unknown number—one with a Texas area code. I frown, tilting my head to stare at the screen. Anyone I know at home is already saved in my phone. It's probably a telemarketer, or some other form of spam. My mom was telling me just the other day on one of our sporadic calls that Barry's business phone has been getting slammed with time-wasters lately.

I shove the phone back into my pocket, take a second to adjust the to-go bag hanging on my arm, and trudge on.

THE WALLS IN THIS BUILDING ARE PAPER THIN, AND I can hear just about everything that goes on in the dorms on either side of mine and Chantal's. The one to the left is occupied by Bernadette and Avery, who both lost the luck of the roommate draw—they can't stand each other. Chantal and I often have to play referee when they get into an argument about something because once they start, they don't know how to stop. Leslie and Danielle are on the other side of us; Leslie is a loud and generally happy transplant from Los Angeles, and Danielle is quiet and shy from upstate.

After I set my bag of Indian food on the kitchen counter, I unzip my thick coat and pull it off before I start my usual routine of fighting for space on the hooks by the door. Neither Chantal nor I have much closet space, so everything gets hung up right here in the entryway—jackets, scarves, hats, raincoats. It's a vertical pile of nylon and polyester that's always one wrong move away from cascading to the ground in ruin. I count down the days till spring as my freezing hands fumble miserably around a lime green windbreaker I don't think I've seen Chantal wear once.

Have I mentioned I hate winter?

I look around at our empty shoebox of a dorm—the entire thing could fit inside my bedroom back home. But that bedroom comes attached to a bigger house with an overbearing, meddling mother and a painfully awkward and distant stepfather, so while things might be a bit compact here, at least I can revel in the freedom of my autonomy.

I miss Annie though. I miss her so much it feels like I'm missing my right arm. My little sister is seven years younger than me, but our age difference has never gotten in the way of our close bond. She's my best friend, my soulmate, and I hate to think that I left her at such a pivotal time in her young life. The guilt of it still eats at me in the quiet moments of my new life here, and I wonder if it will ever ease. I know Annie would never want me to feel bad for hightailing it out of Saddlebrook Falls the second I could, but I know she hates the distance just as much as I do.

My phone vibrates from where it lies on the counter in the kitchen, and I quickly jump up to grab it. I don't normally get this many phone calls in a single night, but thoughts of Annie have me hoping it's her, even though it's late and I know she's likely already in bed (Mom runs a tight ship). Or maybe this time it *is* Jason. I pick it up and see the incoming call flashing across the screen—it's my mother.

I sigh. She's the last person I want to talk to right now. But it's strange for her to be calling this late. New York is only an hour ahead of Texas, but it's a school night, and those are sacred in our household. Something hums to life inside my gut, a strange but knowing awareness that I need to take this call. Without another thought, I swipe to answer and bring it to my ear. "Hello?"

"Oh, Layla!" my mother cries, and I instantly freeze.

"What?" I demand. "What's wrong?"

"Honey," she whispers, forcing the words out through a sob. Fear spreads like ice through my entire body—if something's happened to Annie . . .

But then she says it. "It's Jason, sweetheart. I'm so, so sorry."

"Mom," I demand, my tone sharp enough to cut glass. "What is it? Just say it!"

A long sigh, and then she does. "He's . . . he's dead."

CHAPTER TWO

THEN

"Layla!" my mother calls from somewhere downstairs.

I move toward my open doorway, shouting back in the general direction that her voice is coming from. "What?" I know she hates when I respond this way, that she'd much rather I make the effort to go find her than have us hollering back and forth through the house. But honestly, if she wanted a face-to-face conversation, she's perfectly capable of coming up to my room.

I hear her sigh. "Are you going to make your lunch before you leave? You're running late!"

"No," I bellow back down, "I'm going to buy lunch today."

Her response is only silence—I'm not sure if that was the answer she was looking for, but it's my first day of high school and the last thing I want to do is lug around the dorky pink lunch box that I've carried since the sixth grade.

I return to the small vanity in my room, swiping my purple

brush through my dark wavy hair. As I look at my reflection, I frown, wishing that my wild strands—a gift from my biological father, I'm told—were tamer. My mother's hair is straight and glossy, and I'm endlessly envious that my little sister inherited it. But then again, her father's hair is thin and balding, so maybe the jury's still out on who won the game of DNA roulette.

I'm wearing my new eyelet-embroidered dress with a scalloped hem and rhinestone-dusted sandals that sink me deep into my girly side, and while they make me feel pretty, it feels . . . stuffy. I'd much rather throw on an old pair of cutoffs and a loose, airy tank to battle the heavy humidity that's a nightmare this time of year. But the first day of high school only comes once, and I have a lot riding on it.

My mother's approval, for starters.

At least in a big-world sense. As she likes to remind me, this is the first day of one of the most foundational and transitional seasons of my life. These next four years of school will shape the woman who comes out on the other side, and could be the difference between future Layla being valedictorian with a cheerleading scholarship or a mediocre graduate with a fancy admission to community college.

I'm honestly more curious about future Layla's fashion sense and how many times she can get away with ditching class before she gets caught. But I know better than to try to harness Mom's expectations—especially when they're raging in full force—so I resign myself to being agreeable if not supportive of her vision.

"Layla," I hear her yell again. "Five-minute warning!"

I let out an exhale and watch through the mirror as a strand of hair blows away from my face. I've swiped on mascara and a smidge of eyeliner, and my lips are glossed in a pouty pink that enhances the blush on my cheeks. I scrutinize my face for any signs of blemishes or obvious makeup lines, but I don't see any. This is as good as it's gonna get.

I stand, snaking my arm through the shoulder strap of the lilac backpack resting on my chair, and feel it thump against my ribs. There are more books and supplies in there than I know what to do with, and the weight of it all feels like an omen on this muggy Tuesday morning. I'm looking forward to getting my locker assignment so I can shove the monstrosity inside and lock it away.

My eyes sweep the room as I mentally process through my checklist before leaving for the day and, once content I haven't missed anything, I hustle down the stairs where my mother's waiting in the kitchen.

It's only seven thirty in the morning and she's already dressed to the nines in a formal, cream-colored pantsuit, her iron-curled hair framing her small but severe face. Her hazel eyes pop from smokey, brown-shadowed lids, diamonds glinting brightly from her ears. As usual, she's dripping in tasteful luxury . . . and it makes my stomach roll with unease. She smiles when she notices me approaching from the hall. "Good morning, bug! You look darling in that dress." Her eyes sparkle as they slide down my frame. "Are you sure you don't want to go with the close-toed mules?"

My eyes drop down to my sandals, white-polished toes in formation across the top of each one.

"No?" I respond with a slight lilt of uncertainty.

She waves a hand to disregard the thought. "You look perfect, sweetheart. Do you have your cheer bag ready?"

I nod. "It's by the door."

"And you're sure you don't want to bring lunch? I'm not sure the school's options are the healthiest . . ."

"Mom," I cut her off. "I'm going to be late."

She presses her lips together and gives a curt nod. "You're right. And I need to get to the office anyway. Let's go." She grabs her purse from the console table by the door and a small leather briefcase that I haven't seen before—I roll my eyes.

My ever-so-charitable mother recently volunteered to run a new employee-retention program at my step-father's company. She's been driving herself down to his office in the city for the last week and a half to "work," like she has some whole new career or something.

And now, it seems, she carries a briefcase.

"Okay," she starts as she swings open the front door, looking back at me with a smile as I bend to pick up my cheer bag. "Don't forget that Suzanne will collect you from school later. Your father and I should be home around dinnertime." I instantly trip on her use of the word *father*, but after righting myself I decide to let it go.

For now.

"I need you to keep an eye on Annie until we get home—Miss Patsy will be here with her after school, but I know she'll worry with me out of the house." Annie's had Miss Patsy as a nanny since she was three years old—she probably won't even notice my mother is missing. But I won't tell her that. "I already cannot wait to hear about your day," she continues. "Make sure you use bobby pins to keep your hair out of your face during tryouts—those girls will be expecting your ponytail to be nice and tight."

I groan, willing her to stop with the smothering. My mother is a great mom, but my transition into high school has unleashed something inside of her that makes me crazy. It's almost as if she sees it as a chance to relive her own experience through me.

But I don't want her experience—one that left her alone and pregnant at eighteen years old, stuck in the small town she'd been in all her life. I want to be free from this place someday. I want to escape the bounds of Saddlebrook Falls and make a life bigger than anything that can be found here.

Jumping into the front seat of her silver Mercedes, I stuff my backpack onto the floor in front of me and shove my cheer bag into the back seat. My mom turns the ignition as she glances at me. "Are you nervous?"

I shake my head. "No, not at all," I assure her. But the truth is, I'm a little nervous. What if I don't know how to find one of my classes, and I have to walk in late? What if I trip and make a fool out of myself in the middle of lunch where everyone can see?

I may not carry the same expectations for my life that my mom does, but I do have some of my own. The next four years will be my chance to bloom, to expand so far out of myself that there's no option but to leave this town. I refuse to accept the path that leads me right into the throes of marriage and motherhood—there's *no* way I'm handing my life over to someone else like that.

"I remember my first day of high school," my mom says softly as she watches the road in front of her. "There's nothing like it. That feeling of new opportunity. Of having possession over the rest of your life." Her words hit me right in the chest because she's right. But it doesn't make sense, because I know with near-certain confidence that the only thing she wants me to find is a captain spot on the cheer team and a future husband.

I want a captain spot too—I'll give her that. But a husband?

I sigh again, willing the car to drive faster.

Luckily it doesn't take us long to arrive at the large brick building, its bold red letters gleaming brightly in the morning sun: SADDLEBROOK FALLS HIGH SCHOOL - HOME OF THE MUSTANGS. Instead of pulling the car through the drop-off line, my mom parks and turns off the engine.

I brace myself as I turn to look at her. Her gaze is fastened on the building, lost in thought as she takes it all in. She must notice the silence around us after a minute, because her eyes jump to me. "All right, kid, you ready?"

I nod once. "Yes ma'am." I give her a small smile to ease any worry she might feel. "Thanks for driving me, Mom."

A warm smile flashes across her face as she leans in to kiss me on my cheek. "Have a good day, honey."

"See you later," I say as I push open my door and get out, bags in hand. My mom honks once before she starts the car and backs out, and I wave her goodbye as she retreats out of the lot.

Turning around and taking in a deep breath, I make my way toward my new school.

MY FIRST DAY GOES WELL FOR THE MOST PART. I only got a little lost on my way to the science wing for Biology, but my teacher was forgiving. The school is so much bigger than what I'm used to—there are two middle schools in Saddlebrook Falls, and both of them feed into the one high school in town. There are so many new faces, kids I've seen before at Mustang's Pizza and the movie theater, and others that are unfamiliar.

In fourth period, I find my photography class full of upper-classmen. Most freshmen don't have an opportunity to pick elective classes, but since I took a pre-algebra course over the summer, I had room in my schedule for something fun. The teacher assigns me to sit next to an older boy in a letterman jacket whose notebook has *Jason* scrawled on the cover in neat, blocky letters, and I have to fight hard to hide my blush.

He's gorgeous and quiet, and the combination draws me in. I can feel him sneaking glances at me through most of the class and I'm tempted to introduce myself, but I chicken out every time I turn to find his eyes bouncing from me back to the front of the room. It's only the first day of the whole school year; I don't want to seem too eager, and I don't want to make it obvious that he's not great at hiding what he's doing.

In my last class of the day, I wait patiently for the final bell to ring. Tryouts start right after school, and it's all I can think about as our algebra teacher drones on about expectations for the year.

When the bell finally rings, I burst out of my seat and accidentally crash into the boy in front of me, my notebook falling to the ground between us. He turns to face me, a small scowl twisting his full lips, and my eyes widen in embarrassment. "Oh my gosh . . . I'm so sorry . . ." I sputter. He's tall with unruly brown hair and deep chestnut eyes that eye me warily as he eventually bends down to pick up my fallen notebook. Without a word, he hands it to me before turning around and walking out of the room.

As soon as he's out of sight, I let my shoulders slump.

That was awkward.

I make a mental note to smile out another apology tomorrow, then grab my backpack and hurry out of the room. I'm not sure who he is, but this is an advanced math class so he's probably a sophomore or junior. He looked older—his chest wide and forearms strong and corded.

I hope he doesn't take it personally.

I get to the locker room in five minutes, and spend another five changing into my cheer outfit—a simple white tank top and a pair of red Soffe cheer shorts to show my Mustang spirit. I realize after throwing my hair up into a tight ponytail that there are a ton of other girls in here, and it looks like they're all getting ready for the same thing.

I shake out my fingers and accept that the competition will be fierce today, that I'm simply going to have to give it my very best. High school football is as significant as church around here—everything shuts down for Friday night home games as people pour in to watch the Mustangs dominate on the field.

Our team is good—they've always been good. Dozens of state championship banners hang around the stadium, proudly boasting the team's mostly undefeated reign.

I don't care much about football, really, but I love to cheer. And I think I have what it takes to at least make it onto the freshman or JV team—I've been tumbling since I knew how to walk, and I cheered all throughout middle school—but I want varsity.

I want it so bad.

I pull a long red ribbon out of my cheer bag and head for the bathrooms. Just as I'm pulling it into a bow, another girl walks in and smiles hesitantly at me through the mirror.

She looks nervous, so I decide to extend her a bit of kindness. "I love your shorts," I say, eyeing the sparkly red spandex that wraps tightly around her thighs. They're a little over-the-top for tryouts, but I do love them.

She hooks her thumbs into her waistband and juts out a hip. "Thanks, do you think they're too much?"

"Not if your confidence can match them," I tell her, smiling.

Determination sets deep in her brow, and my smile widens. "Thank you—I've been so nervous all day. I think I needed to hear that." She grins. "I'm Regan."

I stretch out my hand and she takes it in hers. "I'm Layla. Are you a freshman?"

"Yeah, is it that obvious?"

"Nah. I'm a freshman, too." I wave a hand. "Stay close? Maybe we can partner up on some drills."

Her eyes widen and she nods. "Yes!"

"Okay cool. I'll see you out there!"

I sneak one last glance in the mirror and head back toward the lockers where my gym bag rests on a bench. I pull my bright white sneakers out and quickly pull them on before tucking both my things away and making my way out into the gym.

CHAPTER THREE

THEN

After a long, torturous week of cheer tryouts, everyone gathers inside the gym and settles in the bleachers facing the head coach of the varsity team. I'm sitting between Regan and David, the only boy who's trying out for the squad. He's a sophomore and made the JV team last year, and I can tell he wants varsity just as much as I do.

Coach West is a tiny woman with bright blonde hair who isn't afraid to tell it like it is. She's an undeniable hard-ass, but with the ultimate say over which Saddlebrook Falls High cheer team I'm going to make, I've been working hard to impress her all week.

I'm not worried I won't make a team, it just might not be varsity. Of the sixty students who tried out, sixteen will make each of the squad levels, which means only a dozen of us won't make a team at all.

What becomes trickier is how hard it is for a *freshman* to make the varsity team. According to school policy, at least half of the varsity team must be made up of seniors, which leaves eight spots open for the rest of us—and there are plenty of juniors and sophomores like David who have paid their dues and are vying for one of those spots.

Twenty-five freshmen are trying out, and most will make the freshman team. A few will likely make JV . . . but making it on varsity despite the rest of the competition would be a serious feat. Still, though, I feel good about my performance this week—a lifetime of gymnastics training prepared me for all of the tumbling and choreography that we worked through together.

Flying is my only area of concern . . . it's the one skill that we didn't learn in middle school.

"Listen up," Coach West booms. "I want to thank you all for showing an interest in making the Saddlebrook Falls High cheer squad. We have a tremendous cheer family here full of deeply rooted Mustang pride, and ours is a squad made up of incredible talent." Her brows rise and it lifts the red visor she's wearing over her face. "While we're blown away by the talent this year, some of you won't make the cut."

Regan tenses, and I reach out to grab her hand as I scan the sea of faces around me. Most are bunched tight in concern.

"The other coaches and I will be convening this evening to make decisions for all three squad levels. On Monday, a final roster will be posted on the bulletin board in the cafeteria." She takes a long pause to sweep her gaze across the bleachers. "Are there any questions?"

David sighs beside me, and Regan is shaking her head. "Hey," I whisper, forcing her to look at me with those wide, nerve-filled eyes. "You had a great week, Regan, and you looked amazing on the mat. Don't stress, okay?"

Her mouth pulls up slightly, but it does nothing to wipe the worry in her expression. "Yeah?"

I click my tongue, squeezing against her arm. "Would I lie to you?" The truth is Regan is good. She needs to work on her confidence, but she has a great technical foundation and hit her marks all week. She's probably good enough to make the varsity team, but I have a hunch her lack of confidence will keep her on JV.

Her smile grows. "I guess we'll know for sure on Monday."

I nod. "Yeah—only three days of torture."

She laughs. David leans over me, his eyes fastened on Regan. "You have nothing to worry about," he says in a low voice just for us. "Trust me, based on the way Coach was watching you today, it's obvious she's impressed."

My gaze snaps to him. I hadn't noticed Coach West watching her . . . maybe she will make varsity. I suddenly wonder, if it were between her and me, who Coach would choose.

But then I snuff out the thought. Regan is a genuinely nice girl and I'm not going to let my nerves or competitive drive ruin a good thing between us.

If she makes varsity and I don't, it simply means she deserves it more.

"Or she was trying to decide if I deserve a spot at all." Regan cringes, gripping my hand tighter. The rest of the students are getting up—the coaches must have dismissed the group.

David shakes his head, clearly unhurried. "No, trust me," he insists. "I know her looks; I was here last year. She likes you. I promise."

That seems to settle some of Regan's nerves, but now *I'm*

feeling them. "Let's get out of here," I say from my place between them. "I need to get home to my sister anyway."

David nods, and Regan stands. She pulls the strap of her gym bag over her shoulder and says, "Do you guys . . . maybe we can hang out? This weekend?"

I smile. "What do you have in mind?"

She shrugs.

"You guys wanna go to a party tonight?" David asks.

We both turn to look at him. "A party?" I repeat lamely. I've never been to a high school party before, and from the look on Regan's face, I can tell she hasn't either.

David smirks. "I keep forgetting you guys are freshmen. Yes, a party. It's what happens when a few dozen kids congregate at someone's house and, you know, party."

I scoff. "Riveting."

David rolls his eyes as he gives my arm a playful nudge. I look back at Regan to see what she thinks—I'm not going if she's not going. She must be thinking the same thing because her eyes widen and she shrugs once like, *Up to you, girl.*

A grin slices across my face. "Let's do it."

IT DIDN'T TAKE MUCH CONVINCING FOR MOM TO LET me go out, though I didn't exactly tell her the *whole* plan. Between bites of the fried catfish we ate at dinner, I casually slipped into the conversation that Regan and David wanted to hang out tonight. She looked at me with a spark of approval in her eye before practically shoving me out the door as soon as we finished our meal.

"Do you even know where she's going?" I heard my stepfather ask from down the hall as I changed into a comfortable pink dress.

"Oh Barry," she whined, "don't start already. It's her first weekend of the school year and she's making new friends. We should be encouraging this!"

Normally Barry doesn't have much to say about my comings and goings, taking more of a hands-off approach with his wife's daughter from a previous relationship. It suits me just fine, so I wonder why he's suddenly acting concerned. Luckily his hesitation does nothing to deter my mother, and when I hear a honk from the street I say quick goodbyes before launching myself out the front door.

David's driving an old golden minivan, and I have to do my best not to poke fun at it—I don't know him well enough to rag on what's probably a hand-me-down from his family. At least he has a car to drive. Regan waves from the front seat, rolling down her window to shout, "Get in here, bitch!"

I laugh, shaking my head as I pull the handle of the back door and slide in. The van smells like the black ice air freshener hanging from the rearview with a hint of stale french fries, and I suddenly find myself thankful for new experiences. Thankful to have two new friends who cared enough to pick me up and spend time together.

"You ready to party, freshy?" David smirks as he looks over his shoulder at me.

I smile. "Freshy?"

He dips his head. "You know: freshman, fresh meat, freshy."

I laugh. "If you say so."

The side of David's mouth rises higher. "Just be cool and blend in. Freshmen usually aren't allowed at these parties, but you're both girls and, well, you're both hot." Regan shifts in her seat, obviously pleased by the compliment. "Just don't draw too much attention, and try to have a little fun, yeah?"

Regan and I both eagerly nod before we all burst out into laughter.

Ten minutes later, we're pulling onto a curb where over half a dozen cars flank a two-story house. It looms over us, dark and stately and not at all like what I imagined when David mentioned a house party.

"Some party," Regan whispers as we all stare up at it.

David snorts. "Just wait."

We spill out into the balmy night air as the sounds of music and muffled chatter reach around from the backyard of the dark house. David leads us toward the side gate where a sharpie-written note on a piece of ripped notebook paper reads: DON'T COME BACK HERE UNLESS YOU BROUGHT BEER.

I look up at David as concern ripples through me. "We don't have any beer." How can a trio of underage teenagers be expected to get their hands on beer? It's already nearly eight, and I have to be home by ten thirty—a curfew that Barry implemented just before I made it out the door.

David shakes his head. "Connor's just fucking around. Come on." He nods toward the back of the house as he opens the gate, ignoring the sign. As if we should know who Connor is. I catch Regan's eyes but she just shrugs and follows behind.

We take the narrow pathway into the full backyard to find a couple dozen people, all obviously juniors and seniors. My eyes skim across the congregation of faces—most don't spare us a glance.

A tall dark-haired guy steps out of the house and immediately spots us, his face twisting into a wry grin as he makes his way over. "Never thought I'd see the day when you'd show up with chicks," he quips.

David sighs. "I have no problem pulling chicks, Sanders. But these girls are cool—be nice, okay?"

The guy looks me up and down before his eyes flit to Regan. His grin grows wider. "Fresh meat? You dog."

"Shut up, Connor. They're friends."

Connor throws his hands up. "All good here, bro. But keep an eye on them—some of the guys from the football team are already rowdy."

"What else is new?" David chides under his breath.

Connor laughs before he looks back at us. "There's some liquor in the kitchen—if anyone asks, tell 'em I said it was okay. Bathroom is down the hall to the right, but otherwise, everyone stays out here. My parents come home tomorrow morning, you know how it goes."

Regan and I both nod, and Connor sets off into the crowd with a dip of his chin.

"Do either of you want a drink?" David asks.

I shake my head—no way in hell am I drinking anything when I have to be home in a little over two hours. I don't trust myself to hide something like that without some experience.

"I'm okay too, thank you," Regan says, and I feel my shoulders drop in relief.

"Layla?" someone calls out from my right, and I turn to find Jason Moore—the boy who sits next to me in photography class—walking toward me with a curious look on his face. His golden-brown hair is styled to wavy perfection, and a dimple blooms from the corner of his mouth when his smile widens.

Nerves squeeze at my chest. "Oh . . . you're here," I stammer. Regan sucks in a breath next to me.

"Yeah." He nods. "I'm here. And you're here, too."

His smile is infectious, and I can't help but return it. He's been quiet in class this week, but his personality has cracked through his soft and shy exterior once or twice. I've learned he was on the varsity football team last year and he's hoping to make it again. I also happen to know from cafeteria gossip that he and his year-long girlfriend recently broke up. Both of them have been really quiet about what happened, so naturally the rumors are running rampant.

David looks back and forth between us. "You two know each other?"

"We sit next to each other in photography," Jason confirms. And then his eyes slide to David. "How do you know Layla?" There's something in the way he asks that I can't put my finger on.

David must hear it too because he hesitates before answering. "Uh . . . Layla and Regan were both in tryouts this week."

Jason looks back at me, his dark blue eyes catching mine. "You're a cheerleader?"

I nod. "Technically we don't find out until Monday, but . . . yeah. I hope so."

"Hm," he hums, that hint of a smile still teasing. "Well, I'm glad you're here. I've been working up the courage all week to ask you something."

Curiosity flares brightly inside of me. "You have?"

He nods, eyes pinned to mine. "I have. I—I was hoping I could maybe take you out sometime?"

Oh. I'm shocked. "You were?" I feel Regan look at me, and my cheeks burn hot.

Jason's smile turns soft and warm. "Very much so."

I stare at him for a long moment before answering, trying to understand how it's possible that this gorgeous specimen is interested in me. "Okay," I finally say. "That . . . would be nice."

CHAPTER FOUR

NOW

The last forty-eight hours are a total blur.

Lost in the darkest depths of a weird, bizarre haze . . . nothing feels real. It's like I've disconnected from my body and mind, forced to disentangle myself from anything resembling feelings or emotion so I don't shatter. I haven't been able to eat or sleep or get a real deep breath into my lungs since that call two nights ago, and I know I can't run on fumes for too much longer, but I just . . . I can't do anything else.

Because Jason's dead.

The man I planned to spend the rest of my life with.

He's . . . gone.

I'm suspended in time, unable to feel the ground beneath my feet or the freezing wind on my face as I exit the taxi at the airport terminal. It's like being lost in the cosmos, spinning and weightless with nothing to grab on to, nothing to hold me steady as I brace for the impact of what I know is going to crush me. But the moment the words spilled from my mother's throat and into the phone line, I slipped so far out of my body that I haven't been able to return to it, only barely having the wherewithal to get myself to the airport for this flight.

My mind is a loop of memories, every one of them featuring Jason: the striking blue eyes I thought I'd have forever to look at, the warmth of his smile I believed would carry us—carry *me*—through the hardest times. I'm stuck in a culmination of so many small moments of love and laughter and life that made whole who I was with him, the girl I became with him by my side.

Maybe I'll never be able to feel again—I'm not sure I'd mind if it means never having to face the pain I know is waiting in the periphery for me. I've spent hours staring blankly at the walls of my dorm room, stuck inside the labyrinth in my mind, a steady stream of tears slipping down my face.

Those tears are still going strong. I can tell it makes the TSA agents nervous at the airport's security line, three pairs of dark eyes watching me carefully as I pull my laptop out of my suitcase and toe off my shoes. They look at me like I might need help, debating whether they need to step in. I pray they don't . . . I wouldn't know how to explain the tears when I can't fucking feel anything.

I manage to get through security, clearing the body scanner to find my suitcase and shoes waiting on the other side. Sighing out some of my pent-up tension, I tug my sneakers back on my feet and continue toward my gate.

The flight to Texas is four hours long, and I do nothing but stare out the small square window the entire time. As the plane dips between scattered clouds, I wonder if Jason might be inside of them somewhere, watching me. Maybe he's looking for some shred of evidence of my devastation from his loss.

Maybe he's unhappy to find that all I am is numb. It gives me an odd sense of proximity to him, as if we might be able to share a secret moment together in the wide-open sky of bending light and sunset hues before this steel cage brings me back down to earth. Back to my home—our home.

I only have a small carry-on with me, so after deboarding the plane I'm able to move right past baggage claim. The humidity from what must have been a recent rainstorm caresses my face before the automatic doors even finish opening —the sun has been set for almost an hour now, but the evening air is still so much warmer than where I just came from. December can get pretty chilly here on the Gulf Coast, but nothing like the freezing cold of New York.

As I peer around the dimly lit traffic lane that veers up toward the curb I'm standing on, I watch a cluster of vehicles fight for space to pick up their loved ones standing nearby. I forget where I am or what I'm doing, so distracted by commotion that it takes me a few extra moments to realize someone is approaching me from the left, and I startle when my mother's arms wrap me in a hug.

"Oh bug, you made it," she murmurs into my hair with a voice that's frayed and tired. She pulls back, eyes sweeping over me intently, as if she might be able to pinpoint all the places I'm broken. "Are you okay? How was your flight?"

Her assessment puts me on edge. I feel another tear escape, curving along my skin until it disappears somewhere below my jaw. "Where's Annie?" I ask, ignoring her questions. All I want is my little sister.

Mom frowns. "She's at home, with Barry." She purses her lips together, brows worrying. "I figured we could have some alone time to process things."

I deflate, the claws of anxiety clutching deep inside my gut. It's an hour's drive home from the Houston airport, and the last thing I want to do is process *anything*.

Not trusting myself to speak, I simply nod.

"Come here, angel," my mother coos as she takes the handle of my carry-on and pulls me in close to her side. I've got an inch on her, so our shoulders bump in an awkward tangle. But I do my best to relent and lean in, to accept what she's trying to give me.

She'd called me a dozen times that first night, after I'd initially hung up on her in my state of disbelief. My phone rang incessantly from where it lay discarded on the coffee table. The distance combined with a lack of control shoved my mother into a tailspin. I know she didn't want to leave me alone to face the initial brunt of the news, but it took a long time before I could get myself to answer.

In some inexplicable delusion, I thought maybe I could just ignore it. Maybe if I just went to sleep and let the darkness of that cold winter night claim me, I'd wake up and realize it had all been some agonizing dream. But by four the next morning the phone still hadn't stopped ringing and I couldn't take it anymore. I needed answers.

Apparently, those would prove harder to come by.

All we know is Jason's prized red Mustang lost control on a two-lane highway and drove right off an embankment, catapulting into a deep, rocky ravine below. There'd been no skid marks on the asphalt save for his, no weather to blame. But the road he'd been on was an easy straightaway—so why did he swerve?

The unknowns only left me reeling all over again.

I'm jolted to the present when Mom shoves my blue suitcase into the back seat of her Mercedes then holds the passenger door open, guiding me in. "Let's get you home, bug," she says softly, eyes shimmering with emotion.

And ready or not, I realize it's time to face it all.

I STARE AT MYSELF IN THE MIRROR, EYES FASTENED on the black linen dress that hangs from my shoulders, on the small pearl-white buttons that stack along the front. It's one of my mother's, and though it's a little big on my thinner frame, I don't have it in me to care. Black has never been my color and I don't own anything else like this—it's much more sophisticated than the sundresses and jeans I'm used to wearing. But after today, I'll have no reason to wear something like it again, so it only made sense to borrow from my mother's closet.

I've never been to a funeral before. My grandparents are still alive and well in their retirement community down in Florida, and besides losing some of the older folks in town, death hasn't had much of an impact on my life.

Until now.

Jason would hate this dress. He'd hate how stuffy and proper it looks, the way my hair is twisted up into a simple bun at the top of my head. He loved my long hair, always wanted me to wear it down and let it flow freely along my back. I'd feel his fingertips dip underneath it as we walked together, a whisper of a touch across my neck before those fingers tugged the length of my wild brown locks. Tiny moments I'll never know again.

So much of who I am today is because of Jason, because of the way he loved me. He might've only been two years older, but as a vibrant and shimmering sixteen-year-old boy who walked right into my desperately bored fourteen-year-old life, he shaped so much about who I became.

"You almost ready, sweetheart?" Mom breezes into my bedroom, eyes finding mine through the reflection of the mirror. She's dressed in a black pantsuit with a silk black shirt and Louboutins on her feet. We both went to bed with red-rimmed eyes last night, but somehow she's been able to smooth her sadness away like footprints in the sand as fresh waves wash ashore. My eyes flick back to my own face, studying the dark shade of purple that's bloomed beneath my eyes. Sad isn't quite what I look.

Empty, maybe.

But the traces of my crying are still present: puffy eyelids that swell over my lashes; dry, salt-crusted skin on my cheeks. I decided not to bother with makeup—it would be a waste. "Yes," I say quietly back, pulling my gaze away from the mirror. "Let's go."

The drive to the only church in town is quiet. Barry navigates his brand new truck through streets so familiar to me I could traverse them with my eyes closed while my mother prods at her lipstick in the front seat. Annie sits pressed against me in the back, shoulder to thigh, with our hands clasped tightly between us. "I love you, Layla," she whispers as Barry pulls into the church lot. "And I'm here for you, okay?"

My breath catches in a sob as I look down into her hazel eyes. She's only thirteen, but somehow she's become my only real sense of ease and comfort. I want to keep her hand in mine for the entirety of the service, but I know I can't—she's a child, not a crutch. I smile down at her, pressing my free hand to the side of her face as I kiss her temple. "I love you most, Annie."

Her returning smile is a little uneasy, but I squeeze her hand in assurance as the truck rolls to a stop. I turn my attention out the window and find a swarm of people congregating near the entrance, all dressed in black. I recognize Jason's parents right away, Mrs. Moore leaning heavily on her husband as she weeps, and a heavy surge of nerves rips through me.

Barry pushes out of his door, and Annie follows him out the other side of the car. But I can't bring myself to move, my eyes locked on Jason's mother.

"You can do this, Layla," my own mother affirms. "I'll be right there beside you. And your sister, and Barry . . . the whole town is practically here, honey. And everybody loves you, just as they loved Jason."

I know she means well, but her words rake uncomfortably against my heart. "I'm fine," I force out, then push my door open. I don't wait for anyone before I start the short trek toward the steps I've climbed hundreds of times, finally tearing my gaze away from Mrs. Moore's shattered face.

Sandy Barlowe, owner of the local sundry shop, rubs a hand up and down her own arm, noticeably uncomfortable with the weight of emotions around her. Big Eddie who, until now, I've never seen in anything but a pair of worn overalls and some version of a flannel shirt, looks stiff in a starched collared shirt. Eleanor, a kind older woman who owns the flower shop on Main, is the first to see me approach. Her eyes fill with warm affection, though it's tinged in profound sadness. "Layla," she breathes out, and like a bunch of curious owls, everyone cranes their necks to look in my direction.

My eyes land back on Jason's parents, and I'm suddenly hesitant to even be here, like this is something intimate that I have no business being a part of. I nearly stumble when I reach the sidewalk, but a warm hand grabs my elbow and rights me. "It's okay, bug. One step at a time," my mother murmurs next to me.

Annie's hand slides into mine again from my other side, and I take a moment to muster the courage to continue forward. My eyes slide to the towering white church I've attended since I was a young girl—a place that holds so many memories. I'm not much of a spiritual person, but weekly attendance at service was mandatory in our house growing up, like it is for most families in this town. During high school, Jason and I would sneak eager touches from the pews in the back: a warm hand wrapped around my bare thigh, the feel of his mouth pressed just behind my ear when his parents weren't looking. It was always more bearable with him next to me, and it pleased my mother to know the boy I loved came from a god-fearing family.

Mrs. Moore's eyes catch mine, and with a shaky breath, I lean in to wrap my arms around her. "I'm so sorry," I whisper as she sobs into my neck. "He loved you so much," I tell his father, who feels stiff in our subsequent embrace. Ron Moore is currently serving his second term as mayor, and I've never seen him look anything but confident and near-regal in the way he stands tall for the people of this town. To see the evidence of his heartbreak is shocking.

He pulls back to look at me with a sincerity I've never seen from him before. "Thank you, Layla. He loved you too, you know."

I give him a watery smile. "I know."

INSIDE THE CHURCH, IT'S STANDING-ROOM ONLY. I'm pretty sure the entire town has shown up to celebrate the too-short life of their sparkling golden boy, the devastation of his loss like a crack in the very essence of what makes Saddlebrook Falls prosper. No one hesitates to make room for my family, though, as Sheriff Joe does his best to push crowds of people down the wooden pews so we can sit together near the front, right behind Jason's parents.

I'm met with so much gentle love and whispered condolences that I'm not sure how to take it all in, let alone respond —but Annie and my mother hold tightly to me, acting as barriers as best they can. And when we finally settle into our seats and the service begins, it hits me all over again that Jason's really gone.

I'll never see him again. I'll never get to admire the way the sun's warm evening light glows against his skin. Or the way his eyes glitter as they take in the view of the ocean on a trip to the coast.

I'll never again hear his low, hungry voice telling me how beautiful I am as his body moves against mine.

And I can't stop the sobs from ripping through me.

CHAPTER FIVE

NOW

Jason's celebration of life is happening at the Wild Coyote, the only dive bar in Saddlebrook Falls. Though ours is a conservative town, the people here aren't without their vices. Even on weeknights, the Wild Coyote is filled to the brim with local townsfolk eager to take the edge off.

I'm able to snag an open parking spot along the side of the old brick building. My mom and Barry decided to stay home with Annie, but they let me drive the Mercedes here myself so I wouldn't need to find a ride. I think they knew I needed a few quiet minutes alone, away from all the eyes on me, waiting for me to break.

I'm well aware that my face is swollen and raw from another day spent crying, but I don't care. I don't even look at my face in the mirror—none if it matters. Nothing in the world matters anymore without Jason. And I'm terrified that nothing ever will again.

Stepping out of my mother's car, I follow the path to the front door of the bar. The temperature outside has plummeted, but I hardly feel the chill. I didn't even bother grabbing a jacket when I left my house. I welcome the cold against my skin, hoping that it might be enough to make me feel something.

Inside, my heels clack loudly against dark hardwood floors, drawing unwanted attention from everyone who's already here. I keep my head low, my eyes locked on the ground as they trace the knots in the long wooden planks. The melancholic din greets me—so different to what the inside of this bar usually sounds like.

I can't help but notice how dark it is the farther I get, like the lights might not be turned up all the way. Or maybe that's just what it's always like. I've only been here once—Jason's best friend's grandfather owned it up until he passed a couple of years ago. I'm not sure who owns it now, but I imagine someone in Wells's family is still running things.

It struck me as an odd place for Jason's celebration of life, considering he'd probably never spent much time here either. We were too young to be in a place like this before we all left for college. Well, not counting the night Wells used a spare key to score him and Jason another round of beers after their graduation party. I'd been anxious that night, caught up my own prickling dread that they were both about to leave for college, and I'd be stuck here for another two years alone.

I imagine Jason and I would have come in here someday, long into our future, as we fought against some irritatingly warm summer night in our small first home together. Jason would throw his arm around my shoulders, holding me close as we ordered the coldest beer they had. But now it's nothing more than a daydream—a sharp, painful realization that the future I always imagined would never unfold.

Forcing myself back into the present, I wonder if maybe this was the only place that could hold so many people on such short notice. Lord knows the whole town will show up for Jason, as they did for his funeral. Everyone in Saddlebrook Falls loved him, thanks to his success on the field every Friday night and the success of his father as mayor. The Moores were practically town royalty.

I take a measured breath, finally lifting my gaze to take in everyone already here, and my eyes immediately snag on a man sitting at the bar. He's wearing a black collared shirt with the buttons undone at the neck. His hair is tousled, like he's been winding his fingers through it all day. Thick clumps of it fall across his brow, and his eyes . . . Even from here I can see the unyielding pain they carry.

But there's a flicker of . . . something, when he turns his head and those eyes find mine.

Wells.

I haven't seen him in about a year. He looks . . . different. Older. Like his edges have been sharpened, his boyish features honed into the shape of a man.

Wells has always been a force, standing well over six feet tall with a body like a brick house. It's what made him a powerhouse on the football field—he's the best offensive tackle to ever represent our team, slamming against the brute force of the defense to protect his quarterback with a wild, untamed power.

He never let anyone get past him. Never let anyone touch Jason.

A sigh spills out of my lungs as I stop walking. I didn't see him this afternoon—had he been there? There's no way he missed his best friend's funeral, right? I resume my steps, slowly making my way toward him, noticing the way the corners of his mouth fall as I approach.

"Wells," I say, watching as he takes a long pull on the bottle of beer he's holding on to for dear life. A black cowboy hat rests atop of the bar next to him.

He turns to look at me again, the red glow from a nearby neon light reflecting in his brown eyes. God, the effect is damning—he's liquid smoke. "Layla," he says back, his voice gruff and throaty.

"I didn't see you earlier."

"Yeah?" he grumbles. "Well, I was there."

He sounds annoyed. Like, of all the things he's dealing with today, he doesn't want me to be one of them. An ache pulses through my chest at his biting tone. It's old and familiar —a wound from a past life. After being so wholly numb for the past few days, I'm surprised by it.

"I haven't seen you in a while," I try.

He grunts, his eyes falling to the mouth of his bottle. "Yeah. Not since New Year's."

That's right. Last year, the three of us drove out to the beach and made a bonfire to celebrate. We got drunk on PBR and a bottle of whiskey and slept under the stars. My mother about had my head for it.

His eyes move to my cheek and I reach a hand up. I don't even realize I'm crying until I feel the dampness beneath my fingertip. I've cried so much in the last three days, I almost don't know what it's like not to. "Shit," he says, handing me a napkin.

"So," I continue, as if I'm not a broken fucking mess, "how have you been?"

He narrows his eyes at me like I've asked a ridiculous question. And I suppose I have, but seeing Wells here—it feels like something I can hold on to. Something of Jason's. Something from . . . before. And now that I have it, I don't want to let go.

He turns his gaze to focus straight ahead of where he sits, and I find myself cataloging the side of his face. It's only now, from this new angle, that I see the faint purple shadows beneath his eyes that match my own, the days' worth of stubble along his cheek. He looks like he hasn't slept since . . . well, since.

"Kasey, get me a shot," he calls out to the man behind the bar, and I look over. Sure enough, it's Wells's older brother.

Kasey gives Wells a hard look. "I think you've had enough today."

Wells scoffs. "I don't give a shit what you think. Pour me a fucking shot."

Kasey frowns but relents. He pours a finger into a lowball glass and slides it in front of Wells. His eyes are kind when he slides his gaze to me. "Layla, it's good to see you, sweetheart. You want one?"

Wells scoffs again. "Layla doesn't know how to drink whiskey."

Flashes of passing the bottle around the fire swim in my head. Wells said the same thing then, and I'd tried to prove him wrong—until I was bent over puking into the ocean, shoulders trembling from the force of it.

I ignore him, nodding my head. "Yes please." I watch as Kasey pours a second shot then places it on the bar for me.

"Thank you," I say, before I pick it up and down the whole thing.

Wells stares at me for a long moment before he picks up his own glass, spilling the contents into his mouth. His throat works as he swallows. "Layla," he starts again. "We don't have to pretend to like each other now, okay? I know we tried for Jason, but . . ." He scrubs his hand over his face. "We don't have to anymore."

I feel the insult like a knife to the chest. Wells and I didn't exactly have a conventional friendship; like oil and water, we never mixed well. But I do care about him, and he damn well knows it. Just like I know he cares about me.

"I wasn't aware my dead boyfriend was the only thing keeping our friendship alive, but point taken." I slide my empty glass back toward Kasey. "May I have another, please?"

"Of course," he says, watching me carefully as he pours me a second shot.

I refuse to look at him, but I feel Wells's gaze stuck on me as I tip this one back, too. I try not to react to the burn as it erupts in my throat—a welcomed pain to distract from the daggers Wells is throwing at me.

Something abruptly crashes behind us, and I turn to find a blonde-haired woman at the bar's entrance. She's sobbing, thick tracks of mascara running down her face, and she looks . . . disoriented. I try to place her, try to figure out who she is. Saddlebrook Falls is a small town, after all, and even though it's been a year and a half since I left for college, I'm still pretty sure I know everyone here. Plus, she looks to be about my age—so I should definitely know who she is.

Her eyes sweep the room until they land just behind me. And then her knees almost buckle. "Wells!" she howls as she begins to run toward us. I turn back to face him, surprised to find that his eyes are full of what looks a lot like . . . fear.

"I'm so sorry, Layla," he whispers, just as the woman collides into him.

Her crying turns into wails, loud and raking through my ears as she buries her face in his chest. Everyone else in the bar is quiet as they watch her fall apart, and I don't have to look at any of them to know they're just as confused as I am.

After a long moment of hesitation—his eyes still firmly planted on mine—Wells lifts his arms up and wraps them softly around the girl. "Hey, Emma," he soothes.

So, Wells has a girlfriend then? I mean, I'm not exactly surprised. If there's one thing I know about Wells—one thing the whole town knows—it's that there's always a girl within his reach. None of them last very long, but that's the way Wells prefers things. He's non-committal. Or rather: he chews up and spits out women for sport.

Why would he apologize to me about this one?

It doesn't make sense.

"I-I don't know what to do." The woman—Emma—continues sobbing into his black long-sleeve shirt. "Wh-what am I supposed to do without him?"

In a single, rapid second, my heart jumps up into my throat. I look at the girl, at the side of her face, still trying to connect the dots that I feel are right in front of me. My gaze jumps back to Wells, who's looking at me like I'm a bomb. Like he's waiting for me to detonate. "I'm sorry," I whisper, my voice lost somewhere in the confusion. "Who is this?"

His brows bunch together, all evidence of his earlier hostility gone. He looks on the verge of breaking. "This is Emma," he says, carefully.

I nod. "I gathered that already, thank you." I can hear the venom seeping into my voice. "Who is she, Wells?"

He doesn't answer. Instead, he expels a long breath as he simply stares at me. Eventually, Emma pulls her face out of his neck, wiping her eyes. She sniffs, sucking strings of snot back into her nose as she finally looks at me. Genuine curiosity flares in her eyes. "Who are you?"

Everything tilts. My vision nearly blacks as it tunnels on the two of them standing there, and the only thing I'm conscious of is the lungful of air that Wells pulls into his stupid fucking lungs. "Wells, who the fuck is she?"

Emma's eyes narrow in offense as she pulls herself back into a standing position, disentangling from him. "I'm Jay's girl-friend. Who the fuck are you?"

My eyes bounce between them. My chest begins to heave as acid bubbles inside my stomach, and the edges of my vision blur enough to make me feel dizzy. I can't stop what comes next as I lean over and vomit all over Emma's white shoes.

She looks at me, shock radiating from her face. I straighten and swipe the back of my hand across my mouth, looking back to Wells and finding his features twisted in pain.

Everything in my body feels like it's disintegrating. Like I might be melting right into this dirty bar floor. I turn around, begging my legs to cooperate with me as I break through the crowd.

But when I push through the doors and step out into the cold, I still can't find air, can't for the life of me catch a breath. I make it only four steps down the sidewalk before I fall to my knees, the concrete cutting into my skin.

"Layla, wait!" I hear Wells boom from somewhere behind me as the bar door slams open. "Fuck," he says when he finds me on the ground. "Layla." He shakes my shoulders. "Layla, fucking breathe."

I don't even realize that I'm on my side until he wraps two strong hands around my arms and effortlessly pulls me back up into a sitting position. "Layla, look at me. You have to breathe." I hear his words but they don't register. Nothing is registering. Nothing makes sense—I've been shoved into an alternate reality, thrown inside some big cosmic joke.

Jason has a girlfriend?

But *I'm* his girlfriend.

"Layla, goddamn it, look at me!" The bite of his words pierces through the fog, and my eyes snap to his. The only thing I can get myself to focus on is the panic lancing them. "Take a breath," he commands. "Come on—like this." And then his chest fills as he pulls in a deep breath through his nose before he pushes it out through his mouth.

I try to mimic him, but instead I choke out a sob. He gently places a hand on the back of my head as his thumb sweeps along my ear. "Come on, sunshine. Try again." Again, he demonstrates. And though the sobs are still ripping through me, I'm finally able to suck down a solid breath. "That's it," he whispers, his eyes softening. "Breathe."

We sit there for what feels like hours, though I'm sure it's only minutes. He continues to move his thumb along the side of my face, and I hang on to that touch like it's a lifeline. Because without it, I might just slip into the darkness and disappear forever.

"How long?" I finally ask. His body stills, but he doesn't answer me. I look at him, really look at him, and press again. "How long, Wells?"

He sighs, wiping away a tear as it falls. His lips are pressed in a firm line, and worry lines his eyes. He looks so . . . tired. "I'll tell you anything you want to know, Layla. But not here. You're freezing. Let me get you out of the cold—let me take you home."

I shake my head. "No, I don't want to go home. I can't . . . I can't." I can't face this alone. And I sure as hell can't take any of this to my mother.

He gives me another long look before he dips his head. "Give me thirty seconds," he says, pulling me up to my feet. He nudges me so I'm leaning against the brick wall and, after a brief moment of hesitation, he disappears back inside.

Sure enough, he's back before I can count to twenty-two. His cowboy hat is on his head and he wraps a black Carhartt jacket around my shoulders that smells just like him, like leather and the Texas wind.

He steers me to where his old Chevy truck is tucked into the corner of the parking lot, where I hadn't noticed it earlier when I'd walked in. Unlocking the door with a long silver key, I barely feel his hands on me as he guides me into the front seat and leans in to buckle the seat belt around my body. I don't fight him—instead, I simply sink in, resigned to let him take me wherever he wants to go.

As long as it means I get the truth when we get there.

CHAPTER SIX

THEN

I've never been on a date before, and I feel all kinds of things trying to prepare for my first one with a boy like Jason. He's so dreamy, and I have to keep pinching myself that this is happening. I still don't know what a junior would see in me.

It's been exactly a week since Jason asked me out. A week of waiting for any sort of confirmation from him that the invitation had been real as we sat next to each other in photography every day. Finding out that I made the varsity team was enough of a distraction that I didn't notice his silence until Wednesday. But he stayed quiet all week, and—besides a few smiles he shot my way—I was starting to think that I'd dreamt this whole thing up.

But then, this afternoon, he stopped me with a warm hand on my arm just as the bell rang.

"Hey, Layla," he said softly as I slipped on my backpack. I

turned around to face him, finding that wide, charming grin on his face.

"Yeah?" I asked tentatively.

"About that date . . . can I pick you up tonight? Around seven?"

The room began to spin, and I almost toppled right into a standing tripod before I managed to catch my balance. Jason was asking me out—again! Steadying myself with a deep breath, I nodded before squeaking out, "I think so."

He chuckled softly as his brows knitted together in an adorable pattern. "You think so?"

"Yeah, I . . . I usually watch my little sister after school, and I'll have to make sure my mom is home by then to take over," I rushed out, "but seven should be totally fine. Maybe I can get your number so I can text you when I know for sure?"

Oh my god, I'd thought. *Did I just ask Jason Moore for his phone number?*

His grin was lopsided as he nodded, and my heart did a cartwheel when he reached for the phone in my hand, plucking it right out of my grip before saving his number into my contacts and handing it back to me. The move was so smooth my face almost split in two with the force of my smile.

"I'll talk to you later," he murmured low before striding out the door.

And now it's five minutes to seven, and I'm coming apart at the seams with nerves. Thankfully my mom got home an hour ago, and when I asked her if it was okay to go out again tonight, she just smiled and nodded as she skirted into the kitchen where Annie was working on homework. I'd sent a quick text to Jason—a simple *We're on!* followed by my address —before launching myself in the shower to start getting ready.

I decided to wear my best denim cutoffs and a flowing pink top that falls just along the waist of my shorts, accessorizing with a few dainty gold bracelets and my favorite gold heart necklace.

I'm fumbling with my tube of pink gloss and giving my lips one last swipe when a honk sounds from outside, and the color drains from my face.

"Layla!" Mom calls up the stairs. "Is that your ride?"

"I think so!" I yell back down before squinting at the girl in the mirror. "This is going to be good," I tell myself. "Jason is cute, and he's a freaking junior. Be cool."

With a final sweep over my outfit, I decide it's now or never and hustle down the stairs. I peek out the window next to the front door and see a bright red Mustang parked along the curb.

"Who is that?" my mom asks, and I nearly jump out of my skin at the way she snuck up behind me.

"Um . . . a friend!" I say, not trusting myself to look back at her. "Gotta go, love you!"

"Layla Hayes, are you going on a date?!"

Sighing, my shoulders drop as I inevitably turn to face her. "He's just a friend, Mom. He's in my class and just wanted to hang out."

She's still wearing a work dress—beige with pearl buttons down the front—but she's taken off her shoes. Red manicured toes curl into the carpet as her hands rise to her hips. "What's his name?"

"Jason," I answer simply.

"Why didn't Jason make the effort to come to this door and introduce himself?" Her eyes move from me to the window, and I know she has half a mind to march right out there and ask him the same question.

"Mom, please," I beg, "just let me go, and I promise if there's a next time, I'll make sure he comes to the door."

Her golden eyes flit back to me, considering. "You like him?"

My shoulders rise in an honest shrug. "I sit next to him in Photography. He doesn't talk much, but he seems really nice and he's on the football team—"

"He's a football player?" Her eyes widen in delight, the corners of her mouth tipping up. I hate how much it weirds me out, because I know exactly what she's thinking . . .

Prime future-husband material.

It's almost gross, and I have the sudden urge to call the whole thing off. I'm not surprised . . . she was Saddlebrook Fall's sweetheart in her day—even crowned prom queen during her senior year—and dated a handful of football players herself. But those priorities are what got her stuck here, and I've never forgotten it.

Jason honks again. "Mom, he's waiting." I grab my purse off the table in the entryway and start to push out the door. "I have to go—I won't be late!"

"Oh don't worry about it, bug! Just be safe and enjoy yourself."

I roll my eyes as I march down the front walkway toward the sparkling sports car that revs as I get closer, and then I'm laughing, my excitement sinking back in.

JASON MIGHT BE QUIET IN CLASS, BUT HE'S FAR FROM it as we drive through the heart of town. His natural curiosity doesn't feel intimidating—he asks questions like he genuinely wants to get to know me, and I like it. A lot.

"Have you lived here your whole life?" he asks as he pulls into the parking lot of Mustang's Pizza, owned by Gus Romano who, in his prime, was a football legend here. Jason kills the ignition but turns to face me, giving me time to answer before getting out of the car.

"Born and raised," I confirm. "And I can't wait to get out."

His eyes narrow a smidge. "You want to leave?" I'm not surprised by his surprise. Most people love it here, which is probably why no one ever leaves. A few years ago, Ava Jenkins —Sheriff Joe's daughter—skipped town the day after her graduation, and the story made it into the *Gazette*. I still remember the way the sheriff's face fell when my mom and I bumped into him at Luna's Bakery. He was ahead of us in line when Nosy Maeve practically assaulted him, demanding answers in front of everyone there. Maeve is pushing ninety and leads the local bridge club, and her stance on the matter was that we all deserved to know what happened. I just wanted blueberry pie.

I think about how to respond. "Do you ever feel like . . . you can't breathe? Like the walls are slowly closing in around you and you're not sure where to turn, where to find fresh air?"

He considers. "Sometimes, on the field after a snap, if the other team's defense is good."

Not exactly what I meant, but I suppose it'll do. "I guess I feel like that here, sometimes. A little claustrophobic."

"Hm," he hums before pushing out of his door, rounding the front of the car to let me out with a soft smile.

We find a table in the back, and Gus must get wind that a football player is in his restaurant because within minutes the small, round man comes out from somewhere in the back. He pushes his thick-rimmed glasses up his nose as he grins down at us. "What a pleasure to have you here, Jason, thanks for coming in. You ready for the season?"

Jason's returning smile is warm and friendly. "Yes sir, the boys have been going hard out on the field."

"Good." Gus slaps his shoulder as his eyes move to where I sit opposite Jason. "Very good. You kids have a nice dinner, all right? I'll bring out a couple of milkshakes later, on the house."

"Thank you," Jason and I say in unison as he slips back into the kitchen.

"Does it ever get to be too much, having people fawn over you like that?" It isn't the first time I've seen townsfolk throw themselves at the feet of the football team.

"Nah." He shakes his head. "I think I'm sort of used to it because of my dad."

"Your dad?"

The corner of his mouth lifts. "Yeah, my dad—Ron Moore."

"Your dad is the *mayor*?" I bark out. How in the world did I not know this? I mean, I do my best to stay out of town politics, but as the highest-elected leader of Saddlebrook Falls, Mayor Moore is practically a deity around here.

Jason's expression turns a little shy. "I figured you knew. Everyone always seems to."

I shake my head. "I know who he is, I just didn't connect the dots, I guess."

A waitress comes by to take our order, and Jason asks for a large pizza for the both of us to share along with a couple of sodas. I planned on ordering a spinach and mozzarella calzone for myself, but decide not to say anything. For all I know, ordering for the both of us is a chivalrous move on Jason's part.

"Okay," I say when the waitress walks away. "My turn to ask questions."

Jason sits up straighter and folds his hands on the table in front of him. "Okay, shoot."

I laugh at the seriousness of his posture, and then ask, "Weren't you just dating a senior?"

His shoulders slump a little. "Yeah. Michelle. She—We dated on and off for almost two years."

"Is it off for good?" I don't mean for the question to sound so direct, but considering this is a date, I think it's a fair question.

He must agree, because he nods vigorously. "Definitely over for good."

I think about that answer. "Can I ask why?"

We're interrupted by the waitress who sets down a bottle of soda in front of each of us, and Jason uses the opportunity to take a deep breath before thanking her. "I just . . . felt like our relationship ran its course. We were friends first, during my freshman year. And then after I made it onto the varsity team last year, she told me she was into me as more than a friend. And don't get me wrong, I was into her too. But I think I started to realize she might've only been with me because of my success." He clears his throat. "Football is the single most important thing to me—I've dedicated my whole life to it. And college scouts are going to start watching me this year. I had a good season last year, but Noah King is technically the starting quarterback and I still have to prove myself. Eventually, I'd love to go pro. I think Michelle had stars in her eyes about it all."

Interesting. "You think she was using you?"

The corner of his mouth lifts, but there's no mistaking the way his eyes dim at the suggestion. "It might be a harsh way to put it. I don't think she meant anything bad by it, I just think she sort of . . . attached herself to the idea of my future. Take the jersey out of it, and I'm not sure our relationship would have been enough to make her happy."

I'm unsure why a smile crawls across my face at that, but I can't help the surprise I feel at the depth of his answer. It's so honest, so vulnerable . . . and so in line with the way I feel about this town, which is one of the main reasons my mom and I struggle so much. Finding a kind and financially successful man to settle down and have children with is her dream for me. But I don't want the white-picket-fence life without any real meaning. It's why I want to leave here someday, to travel to new places and have experiences that don't exist in Saddlebrook Falls. I want to see the world before I commit to anything permanent. Jason might be the mayor's son and headed for star quarterback status, but based on what he's saying, he doesn't want to settle either.

"Everyone at school is talking about it, you know," I say, shifting the topic a bit before I reveal anything too personal.

His eyes flash. "About me and Michelle?" I nod, and he rolls his eyes. "What are they saying?"

"There's all sorts of theories," I tease as the waitress returns to set a large pizza on the table between us. We both thank her before I continue. "One was that Michelle dumped you for a guy in college. Another is that you, um, were spotted with another girl behind the bleachers after school." It feels a bit bold to lay the rumors out there like this when I'm still just getting to know him, but he doesn't seem to mind.

Jason stuffs the end of a pizza in his mouth, chewing as he watches me. Like he's trying to figure out how I feel about it all. "People love to talk."

I shrug. "Perks of popularity," I jest.

Gus makes good on his promise to bring us milkshakes after we stuff ourselves with pizza, and soon Jason's driving me back home in his too-loud sports car. When he pulls up to the curb in front of my house, I'm surprised when he cuts the ignition and gets out of the car to walk me to the door. I wonder if my mom is watching from a window somewhere as he slips his hand into mine and leads me up the front steps.

I'm just about to say good night when he tugs on my hand and pulls me toward him, and before I know it, his lips are on mine. Nerves burst like fireworks through my body, and I'm a little caught off guard by the suddenness of it all. But then again, this is a date, right? Maybe I should have been more ready for this.

It's a quick kiss, and soon Jason's smiling down at me with those perfectly white teeth. "Can we do this again soon?" he asks eagerly.

I can't help my own smile—from nerves or excitement I'm not sure, but I did have a good time with him tonight. "Sure," I say back, and he seems pleased.

I watch as strides back down the front steps toward his car. It's not until he drives away that I force myself to wipe the dumb smile off my face and get inside, hoping like hell my mother wasn't spying.

CHAPTER SEVEN

THEN

On the third Friday of the school year, I'm happy to find Jason waiting for me outside of the gym after practice. Flyers got to practice inversions today, something I've never tried before. As one of the smallest girls on the squad, Coach gave me one of the coveted flyer positions despite my lack of experience.

I've done plenty of tumbling and stunt work in gymnastics growing up, but working those same moves while suspended in midair was much harder than I thought it'd be, and it's the first time since making the varsity team that I truly feel my own inexperience.

Luckily the girls who stood as my base today were patient, and the other flyers gave me tips and advice so that by the end of the two-hour-long practice I was exhausted, but I was hitting the right marks.

Pom-poms in hand, I walk toward a smiling Jason who leans against the brick wall of the school. He's wearing his letterman jacket, his hands stuffed casually in the pockets on each side as he nods polite hellos to the other girls who walk by. But when his eyes land on me, I see the way they light up and my stomach dips in excitement. It's enough to stop me dead in my tracks.

His smile settles into a smirk as he pushes off the wall and walks toward me, giving me a peck on the cheek as soon as I'm within reach. "Hey, Layla," he murmurs low in my ear. He smells like soap and his hair is damp from an after-practice shower, and I almost can't stand it—the way he sends my heart spiraling.

My own smile grows so wide that it's almost uncomfortable, but I can't help it—not when he's looking at me like that. Like he's been waiting all day to breathe me in. "Hi. What are you doing here?"

He pulls my bag off of my shoulder and slides it over his own before holding his hand out for me to take. "I was hoping you might want to come somewhere with me," he says as he leads us toward the school parking lot.

"Oh yeah?" I laugh. "Where?" Football games start next week so it's our last Friday of freedom for a while, but since our date last weekend the chemistry continues to burn bright between us. His attempts at photo editing have suffered from the distraction.

Everyone in class was issued a decent camera to hang on to for projects this year, and last weekend we were tasked with taking nature pictures around our houses. I spent most of Sunday afternoon trying to capture my mom's flower garden— it was a sunny day, and the coral petals from her Texas Paintbrush were almost neon in the sunlight. In class, I carefully adjusted the saturation to make the colors brighter, the green of the leaves so luminous they glowed from the computer screen.

Jason spent most of his editing time focused on me, and after turning in a dull and obscure photo of a football perched on an orange tee on his lawn, he'd been subjected to Mrs. Barajas's verbal feedback on his less-than-stellar processing choices.

He didn't seem to mind.

I'm thrilled he wants to hang out with me again tonight.

"Wells is having a few people over at his place. Nothing crazy, but I want you to come so I can introduce everyone to my girl." His smile grows, and I feel it tip right into my chest like a current.

Wells Bennett is an offensive tackle on the team. He was so good last year he became an instant starter—no other team was ever able to tackle Noah or Jason on the field with him planted there to guard them.

He's Jason's best friend, so I'm sure that helps motivate him to keep Jason safe. He also sits in front of me in math class, and every time I remember the way I crashed into him on the first day of school, I have to cool my cheeks with my fingers. That was before I knew who he was, but even now knowing, I still haven't had a single interaction with him since. I've heard plenty of stories about the Bennett family, so I've been more than happy to keep clear of him.

"Um," I say as we approach the parking lot. "Can I go home first? I need to shower and change."

I don't miss the way Jason sweeps his eyes over my body, lingering for a moment on my short black cheer shorts before he says, "Sure, can I pick you up in an hour? Is that enough time?"

"Yep," I confirm, fiddling with my ponytail. And then a fit

of bravery has me climbing onto my tiptoes to give him a quick kiss. Dating is still so new to me, but I love this part . . . like my heart might swell right out of my chest. "An hour is perfect."

He grins. "You want a ride home?"

"No thanks. My house is close and the walk helps me cool down after practice."

Jason leans in to give me a kiss this time, but his lips linger just above mine like he wants more. I giggle and push him away. "Okay, okay," he relents, handing me back my bag with a wink. "See you in an hour." I watch as he walks toward his Mustang, still reveling in the fact that *I'm* the girl he's interested in.

My walk home is quick, and I can smell something cooking as soon as I push through the door. I find my mom in the kitchen hovering over our cast-iron stove. "Hey, Mom!"

She whips around to face me, smiling brightly. "Hi, bug, how was cheer?"

"It was good—I landed a new round-off back handspring combination that I've been struggling with. We also started flying."

She smiles wider—my mom knows how hard those kinds of moves are. She was Saddlebrook Falls' varsity cheer captain in her day. "That's my girl!" She sets down the wooden spoon in her hand and reaches to wrap me in a warm hug. "You know, you are growing into quite the beautiful and capable young lady, Layla." She pulls away to look me in the eye, her hands wrapping around my shoulders. "I'm really proud of you. You keep all this up, and that handsome quarterback of yours is going to lock you down the second you graduate from school."

I roll my eyes. "Mom," I whine, "don't make it weird. I'm

not going to marry someone at eighteen—this isn't the nineteenth century, for crying out loud."

A laugh spills out of her. "All I'm saying is that you're really doing it, sweetheart. You made the varsity cheer team as a freshman, you're dating the mayor's son—I'm so thrilled to keep watching you shine."

I know better than to show it, but disappointment flares inside of me. I wish it took a little more than that to make my mother proud. But I also know the vision she has for my future is merely the by-product of her own painful history.

My father skipped out as soon as he found out my mother was pregnant with me. He wasn't from here, just a lone traveler passing through town as he made his way west. He was young and reckless, running from a life in the sticks toward something new on the California coast, but he spent almost a year in Saddlebrook Falls after he and my mom fell hopelessly in love the summer after she graduated.

In the end, when it came time to face the music, he'd left her high and dry. She didn't have a job, never went to college, and was so sure that he'd take her with him to California—take her out of this town and to the sparkling coast. Instead, he forced her to rely on the help of her parents.

When I was six, she met Barry on a trip to Vegas with her girlfriends. I'd been dropped off with my grandparents for the weekend, and by Sunday night my mom returned home with a big ring on her finger and an unfamiliar man on her arm. It caused a bit of a ruckus around town, but Barry won everyone over with his charm and deep pockets. Mom quickly got pregnant again, and Annie was born. If it weren't for her, I'm not sure my mother's marriage to Barry would be as tolerable. After she'd initially brought him home, I tried to negotiate living with my grandparents, but it wasn't long before they high-tailed it to a retirement home in Florida.

I guess we weren't their problem anymore.

"Speaking of which," I segue, "Jason's picking me up soon—I need to go shower."

Her smile slumps. "You won't be here for dinner? I'm making chicken and dumplings."

I shake my head as I move toward the hallway. "I'm sure we'll pick something up on the way. Thanks though!"

"Hold on a minute, bug. On the way to where?"

I freeze—I don't want to tell her I'm going to Wells Bennett's house. The Bennetts have a . . . reputation in this town. "He wants to introduce me to some of the guys on the team."

Her head tilts in consideration. "It's not a party, is it?"

"No, not a party. Just a few friends."

She makes a show of pursing her lips, but I already know I have her.

"Be home by eleven, okay?"

I nod. "Yes ma'am."

Jason picks me up a half hour later, tearing out of my neighborhood with a loud squeal of his tires. I slap him on the arm, knowing I'll hear about that from Mom when I get home, but I can't help but smile as he reaches to tug on a wave of my still-damp hair. He came up to my front door to get me this time, dazzling my mother with his good southern manners. But the second we turned away from the house and heard the door latch shut, he nuzzled into my neck with a small growl. "I like you with wet hair," he said low, his breath catching along the curve of my ear.

It warmed me from the inside out.

We drive to the other side of town where there's nothing but wide-open farmland on either side of the two-lane road. I've never known where the Bennett family lives, but I do know that for generations they've run some sort of horse ranch, so it makes sense that it would be in the outskirts. I don't know much about their family other than the gossip that's trickled around over the years—mostly about a cluster of rowdy and lawless boys who will do just about anything for a thrill, and their angry, drunk father who's been arrested on numerous occasions. But when those boys aren't galavanting around town in the middle of the night getting into trouble, the family mostly keeps to themselves.

Jason snakes his mustang down a windy dirt road before a wooden gate comes into view. It's propped open, fastened to the fence that lines the side of the road with an old rope. We drive through, and before long the road curves to the right toward a white house with huge windows flanked by beautiful black shutters. It's the biggest house I've ever seen, surrounded by bright green grass and a garden of colorful flowers . . . and what looks like a horse corral.

It must be a horse corral, because someone is sitting on a horse inside of it.

Half a dozen cars are parked in a row along the tree-line on the other side of the house, and Jason drives toward it to park next to an older Chevy Impala. Something about the horse in the corral snags at my attention, so I crane my neck to look out of the back windshield of the car to get a better look. I can barely see what's going on but . . . I think the horse is trying to buck the rider off of it. "Is he okay?" I ask, nerves flaring through me.

But Jason just softly chuckles, like my worry isn't necessary. "Oh yeah, everything's fine." He shoots me a quick wink. "Let's go."

I can hear whoops and hollering as we near the edge of the corral. People are crowded around watching the rider do his best to hold on, and I can't stop myself from hurtling forward, still not convinced that something isn't wrong.

As I get closer, I realize it's Wells on the horse. His face is twisted in fierce concentration as he holds tight to dark leather reins, the chestnut horse bucking wildly beneath him. His hips bounce up and off the saddle, but he sinks back into it every time the horse lands on its feet, his corded arms straining as his thighs work to keep himself seated.

"What's he doing?"

Jason smiles next to me, shoulders lifting in a nonchalant shrug. "Riding."

I turn my attention back to Wells, to his dusty black T-shirt and old backward hat. Something hangs out of the corner of his mouth as the horse continues to twist and kick, and I feel entranced by it all. I've seen plenty of horses in my life—this is Texas after all—but I've never seen anything like this outside of the rodeo competitions on TV that Barry sometimes watches.

"He's winding down," a man with a dark brown cowboy hat calls out from the other side of the corral. In the bending sunlight, he looks a lot like Wells. Maybe a few years older— one of his brothers, I'd guess. There are five of them in total, and they're all known for their bad behavior.

According to town lore their dad, Bud Bennett, lost the use of his legs in a rodeo accident over a decade ago. He became somewhat of a recluse after it happened, avoiding going into town as much as he could and finding solace from his loss at the bottom of the bottle. My mom said before his accident, you could find him at the center of barroom brawls.

After Bud's accident, his sons had to step up and run the ranch. There are whispers about what the Bennetts might *really* do here, scandalous theories of a secret drug ring or a barn full of stolen property. It's why I was hesitant to tell my mom I was coming here tonight—I knew what she'd say. But sometimes I wonder if any of those stories are really to be believed. I wouldn't be surprised if they're nothing but a convenient way for the townsfolk to peddle convenient narratives about a family they don't understand.

"Yep," is all Wells says back, eyes still focused on the horse beneath him. One of his hands stays in the air, as if to keep himself balanced.

His brother is right—the horse begins to slow, his kicks bursting less frequently and with less energy until he eventually starts trotting around the perimeter of the space. "Good," he calls back out. "Let's bring him in." He pushes off the fence to unlatch a gate that's built into it, shooting an obvious glare toward this side of the corral where a group of football players continue to jeer. I realize most of them have a beer in their hand. I don't recognize the girls with them, but they eye me curiously as Jason palms the small of my back to steer me closer.

"Hey, everyone," Jason greets. "This is Layla."

"That was fast," one of the girls says, a tall beauty in a bright green crop-top. "Michelle's body isn't even cold, and you're already parading around a new one?"

Heat burns my cheeks as Jason's grip on me tightens. "Always a flair for the dramatics, huh Stassi?"

Stassi grins. "I'm just saying what everyone's thinking."

"Knock it off, Stass," says a dark-haired boy in a letterman jacket that matches Jason's, and he hooks an arm around her. She looks at him with innocent eyes and he plants a chaste kiss on her temple. "Behave," he murmurs into her ear.

"It's nice to meet you, Layla." Another boy with a mop of blond curls greets me, holding a hand out for me to shake. "I'm Brad. And this is my girlfriend, Erin." He gestures to the smaller blonde to his left who gives me a wide smile.

"Hi," I say back, doing my best to press down the embarrassment from Stassi's words. I know Jason's breakup with Michelle was only a couple of weeks ago, but that doesn't mean what we have is any less real. It doesn't help my confidence that everyone here is clearly older than me—all probably juniors, like Jason and Wells.

Erin's returning smile is warm, though, and it helps to smooth over the nerves I feel. "Nice to meet you, Layla. I think I've seen you around—you're a cheerleader, right?"

I grin. "Yeah, I am."

Erin looks back at Stassi as the dark-haired boy leads her by the hand toward what looks like a large shed. "Don't worry about Stassi. She's really good friends with Michelle." Her eyes flick to Jason for a second before she clears her throat.

I've never felt more awkward in my life, and I debate asking Jason to bring me home. It was nice of him to want to introduce me to his friends, but I didn't ask for any of this. I steal a glance and find him looking unbothered, like none of this makes him feel as anxious as it makes me.

Something catches his attention in the distance, and I look

to see Wells approaching the group on foot with the man in the cowboy hat. The horse is gone, likely tucked back into the giant barn behind them. They speak quietly to each other for a moment before the man claps Wells on the shoulder and looks our way, that glare setting back into place as he studies each one of us. He shakes his head and then heads toward the house.

Wells's lips are pressed tight around a piece of hay. "What's Brooks's problem?" Jason asks, his hand sliding to my waist again.

Wells shrugs. "Doesn't want you all getting drunk here again. He and Kasey had to pick up a bunch of cans last time 'cause you fuckers don't have any respect."

Jason snorts. "Kasey drank more than all of us that night— they were probably his cans."

Wells flashes him a warning look. "Let's just take it easy, okay?" His eyes slide to me, like he's just realized someone new is here. His eyes drop to Jason's hand on my waist before they move back to Jason, a frown pulling at the corners of his mouth. "Jay, what the fuck?"

Great. Wells didn't even know I was coming? Jason's expression falters. "What?" He forces a smile back on his face as he looks down at me. "This is Layla. Layla, this is my best friend Wells. Forgive his rudeness." His tone dips with his own warning.

I give Wells my best thousand-watt smile. "We have algebra together, I think."

He looks at me for a beat, deep brown eyes assessing. And then he lowers his head. "Yeah."

The rest of the group has already meandered toward the makeshift building that Stassi and her boyfriend disappeared into. Jason tilts his head that way. "Let's have some fun, okay?

I'm not drinking tonight, anyway. I have to get Layla home later."

Wells still looks unconvinced, but at least his frown has disappeared. He simply nods, adjusting the worn hat on his head before wiping his brow with the back of his hand. Jason's hand slips from my waist and winds into mine, and he tugs me toward the building.

Once we get inside, I see that it's not a shed at all, it's more of a recreation room. There's a foosball table in the corner where the dark-haired boy—Ethan, Jason tells me—and Brad play. Erin and Stassi sit together on a worn sofa against the wall, watching them as they chaotically spin the little plastic men on the table. A fridge stands on the opposite wall, a dart board hanging next to it that looks like it's seen better days, and a beer pong table that sits in the middle of the room, ready for use.

Wells beelines it for the fridge, opening the door to reveal it's stocked full of beer. He grabs one, cracks it open, and takes a series of large gulps. I watch the column of his throat work with each swallow, both intimidated and a little mesmerized.

Jason dips his head low to my ear. "Sorry about Wells—he can be a bit of a grump sometimes."

I try my best to give him a confident smile, but I still feel a distant nagging that I shouldn't be here. Stassi glares at me from the other side of the room, and it's like I suddenly don't know what to do with my hands. I want to crawl into the shadows of the room, blend into the spaces where the light from the single bulb hanging from the ceiling doesn't quite reach.

The foosball game soon ends with Ethan's victory, and Jason jumps in to take Brad's place. Brad stalks off to the fridge, grabbing a handful of beers to hand out to the rest of the group. Erin and Stassi both take one, as does Ethan. Jason refuses, which eases some of the tightness in my chest. When Brad offers one to me, I shake my head. "No thank you."

Stassi scoffs, rolling her eyes. "Not as fun as Michelle, either."

Jason shoots her a dirty look, and Ethan curses low from his side of the table. Stassi, it seems, isn't going to warm up to me anytime soon.

Something brushes against my arm, and I turn to find Wells is standing next to me. He peers down at me with open curiosity before turning his focus toward the game. But then he speaks, the low timbre of his voice curling around me. "I suggest you toughen up if you're gonna hang around here, sunshine." His eyes stay rooted on the others, and I'm not sure what to make of his words, or why he called me sunshine. But before I can say a word back to him, he steps away to unfold a camping chair, placing it on the ground near the couch and settling himself into it.

CHAPTER EIGHT

NOW

*W*ells pulls his truck down an old dirt road, and my skin prickles with familiarity. I haven't been to the Bennett ranch in years. It feels like slipping into an old version of myself, when the ranch had felt like a second home, despite the anxiety that comfort inevitably led to. I may have spent a lot of time here, but it was never for Wells.

Not really, anyway.

Even after all this time, the old traces of panic claw at my throat from the complexities of it all. I didn't think he'd take me here tonight, but it's not like we have anywhere else to go at this hour where we can avoid prying eyes. The ranch is Wells's home and, all things considered, it's a safe place.

He winds his truck down the long driveway past the main house—a sprawling white two-story he's lived in all his life. He steers past a pair of cabins that I know belong to Brooks and Kasey, his two oldest brothers, before we approach a smaller cabin a bit farther in the distance. The truck slows down as Wells parks directly in front of it.

There are at least half a dozen cabins scattered around the property, and it's tradition for the Bennett children to move into them as adults. The lights inside this one are all turned off, and it feels . . . intimate. Like a step in the wrong direction.

"Don't get in your head, sunshine," Wells mutters before pushing his door open, as if he can read my mind. I can't help but watch as he unfolds himself out of the truck, his black shirt stretching across his back. He rounds the front to open the door for me, and I stare blankly at him. I'm not sure how to get out of the truck, not sure how to face what I just learned about Jay, not sure how to do anything anymore.

Wells hesitates, but then seems to make a decision as he leans over me again to unbuckle the belt. I feel the band slide across my shoulder before his hands are at my waist, gently pulling me to the edge of the seat and lifting me down to the ground. His hands are off of me the second my feet hit the dirt. But he doesn't back away.

His breath curls around my face, a heady mix of whiskey and wintergreen, and I want to lean into it. Deep brown eyes crowd my vision. "Don't get lost in that mind of yours. Just . . . come inside. Let me get you warm and tell you what I know. Okay?"

He sounds calm and steady, but I know he's worried I'll run. It's in the way his feet are planted wide, his hands raised in front of him. It's the same stance I've seen him take hundreds of times in the corral when he's working with a new mustang.

It snaps something inside of me, to be looked at that way. Like I'm a wild animal.

I swallow down a wave of anger and look past him to the

little cabin, eyes tracing the patterns of grout between uneven stones. "Fine," is all I can manage to say.

THERE ARE EMPTY BEER BOTTLES SCATTERED ACROSS the wooden coffee table. They must be old—I know Wells wouldn't have had all this to drink today and then insisted on driving me home. I sit on the green sofa in the living room, uncomfortable in my own skin as I feel him watching me. This cabin is unfamiliar, but the ranch isn't.

Wells isn't—the way his presence feels like it's everywhere.

I watch him take his hat off and hang it on a hook on the wall. And then his focus is back on me, eyes careful as they take me in like I'm fragile, like I might break at any second, and I hate it. Granted, people have been looking at me like that all day, but Wells has never treated me with much softness, and I know his reasons for looking at me like this now are so much deeper than Jason's death.

There's a stone in my stomach that rolls uncomfortably— I'm nauseous and tired. But I can't back down from this. "Tell me everything," I breathe. It doesn't come out with the force I expect, and I hate that even more.

He takes a deep breath, his eyes bouncing back and forth between mine. "Layla . . ." He hesitates. He doesn't make any moves to sit down next to me, only leans against the wall as he crosses one booted foot over the other. "Are you sure you want to hear all of this?"

The stone in my gut grows heavier at the implication. How much could there possibly be? I stare at him blankly, and nod once. "Yes," I confirm. "Everything."

He wipes the back of his hand over his brow then crosses his arms over his chest, still watching me so carefully that I might actually vomit again. But then he gives in. "Okay," he relents. "I caught Jason with another girl in his bed this past spring." I feel the blood in my veins freeze as time stops on a dime. "I don't know who she was and I never saw her again, but Jason swore up and down that you and him were on a break, that you're the one who asked for it. Something about you being in New York and needing some space to find your footing . . ." He trails off.

"That's not true," I snap. "I stayed in New York over spring break and Jason wasn't happy about it . . . we had a fight but I never asked for a break from our relationship." Chantal and I both decided to stay back that week so we could explore the city like we were tourists. After a long and hard first winter, we yearned to see the city sparkle in the sunlight.

Wells's eyes grow hard. "It's what he told me, and I . . . you were always so damn independent, Layla, it sounded legit. I believed him." He says it like it's the worst thing he's ever done, and I'm not sure how to react. "But then summer rolled around and we all came home, and it became real fucking obvious that he was full of shit. You two didn't skip a beat—I hardly saw him all summer, and I tried to tell myself that you'd just resolved whatever issues you were having, but I knew it was bullshit. I knew he lied."

"I didn't see you at all this summer." I'd wondered if Wells had even come home. After years of the three of us practically attached at the hip, it'd been weird to be home and not see him. It was even weirder that Jason hadn't mentioned him, but I figured Wells was busy here, on the ranch, or that he'd hooked himself into some summer rodeo circuit.

Now I wonder if he was trying to keep Wells and I apart. I think Jason always knew Wells and I shared this . . . I don't even know what to call it. A burden? An alliance?

I don't realize I'm crying again until I feel tears fall into my lap. Wells tracks the movement, and pain flares in his eyes. He shifts against the wall, like he's going to make a move toward me. But he holds himself back. "I'm sorry, Layla."

"Keep going," I urge through a shaky breath.

He takes a deep breath. "I kept my eye on him when we got back to school in the fall, and for a while, things were good. We were both focused on the new season, practically eating and breathing football for weeks. We didn't go to any parties other than a couple that first weekend back, and the only times I wasn't with him were when he was in class."

I brace for the impact of whatever's coming, knowing it's close. Wells feels it too, I think, because his eyes fasten to mine.

"You stayed in New York again for Thanksgiving," he declares, as if he's merely stating facts. I nod—Chantal's parents spent the holiday in Europe, and I didn't want to leave her alone. "Jay and I drove home together, but Jay went back to school early. He said something happened—a fight with his parents. It didn't make sense because he never fought with them, but he left so damn fast I didn't have time to get more out of him. I had to ask Kasey to drive me back to school on Sunday because Jay just left me here.

"I tried to ask him about it when I got back to campus, but he shrugged it off. He was acting weird that whole next week, though, staying out late and going to parties on his own. And then I noticed her . . . Emma. She'd been coming to our games and hanging around a lot during practice. Jason couldn't keep his cool, the fucking moron. It became obvious, you know?"

I close my eyes as more tears escape. There's an emotion rearing itself under the surface that I've never felt before. It's uglier than anger, more painful than hurt. Shame, maybe? Humiliation?

"I confronted him," Wells says with a deep rumble. His words are distant. Detached. I open my eyes to find his swimming with his own emotion, and I can't bear it. The rest of his words come out in a rush. "He told me that you'd broken up, but I pushed back and said I knew he was lying, that I knew he'd lied the last time, too. Things got heated, and I punched him."

"You what?" I try to picture it, Wells hurting Jason like that. After spending their whole lives protecting each other.

Wells sighs and looks down at his feet. "I told him he had to tell you, or I was going to. And that . . ." His words trail off. After a long pause, his gaze catches mine again and I can see how much he's struggling through this. "He wasn't happy about the ultimatum. And he hasn't talked to me since." And then he winces, his eyes squeezing shut. "Hadn't —shit."

My throat constricts, and I feel like I'm suffocating again. To know Jason was not only sleeping around with other girls and lying to his best friend about it, but that he also seemed to hold little remorse for his actions . . . It makes me feel sick. Nausea tumbles through me, cold and sharp, and I set my gaze on Wells's face, anchoring myself to him like he's the horizon on a stormy sea.

"Layla," he breathes, concern etched around his mouth because my chest is heaving again. I can't take this anymore . . . this pain. This loss. Fuck Jason. He isn't here to take the brunt of the anger I'm feeling, and it leaves me aching for an outlet. I need somewhere for it to go. "Layla," Wells says again, firmer this time, "what do you need?"

What do I need? What kind of fucking question is that? I need to scrub the last three hours—no, the last three days—from the walls of my mind. I need to scour this pain out of my consciousness. A lobotomy would help . . . maybe I could convince Wells to hammer a chisel into my skull. I almost laugh at the thought.

But I think a laugh does bubble out of my mouth, because Wells's face twists into confusion.

"You were always the ladies' man," I say abruptly.

His brows knit together as his head rears back. His eyes narrow on me, like he's examining me under a microscope. "What?"

I shrug. None of this matters. "You were the one who had a new girl on your arm every week. Maybe Jason learned some of your tricks."

I watch as the insult lands and his anger takes hold. It's a relief, honestly. At least it's familiar. "Layla, what the fuck?"

My gaze drops to the floor in front of me as my eyes burn with a new wave of tears. "I want to go home." I feel like I'm bleeding out, like the contents of my heart are puddling on the floor at my feet. I'm not sure I can take anything more tonight—especially not here. Not with him.

Wells doesn't move for a long time, and the silence is deafening. But then I hear him inhale softly through his nose. "It's late, Layla. Why don't you just stay here tonight?" My eyes snap up to find his, and I can see how hard he's trying to rein in his frustration. His cheeks are tinged pink and his jaw works in tandem with the hard look he throws me. "You can take the bed."

I shake my head as I stand, knowing how bad of an idea it is. The fact that he's even asking is beyond insane. "No, I—I can't, Wells. It would be . . ." I don't know how to finish the thought. It would be what? Inappropriate? To whom, Jason? My skin tightens around my body, unyielding in the way it squeezes me like a vise.

Jason is dead.

And it turns out he wasn't exactly considerate in his actions when he was alive.

"Why do you want me to?" I dare to ask. I don't even mean for the question to come out, but I'm so beyond exhausted I can't think straight.

Wells takes a step closer, his hand closing around my arm. I think it's meant to be reassuring, but his fingers are pressed tight against my flesh, as if he's anchoring himself to me as much as I have to him tonight. "Because it's cold," he says simply. "Because you're tired. You've had a terrible fucking day and an even shittier night. And because . . ." He pauses. "Because I want you to." His deep brown eyes search mine, and I realize he's nervous. "Take the bed, sunshine. I'll sleep out here. We can figure the rest out in the morning."

We.

As if this is ours to figure out.

I want to keep pushing back, but a thought stops me—if I go home, I have to face my mother. I have no doubt someone has already told her that her daughter threw up on some poor crying girl's shoes. If I stay here, I can avoid talking about any of this. At least until the morning.

And Wells . . . he's always been keen-eyed with me. It might be a temporary relief to share space with someone who actually understands the storm within my heart.

"Why do you call me that?" It's not the first time I've asked, but he's always avoided the question. I'm not sure what prompts me to try again now.

The smallest smile curls his lips, but it's weighed down with sadness. "You still don't know?" he asks, not unkind.

I shake my head. "No."

His eyes fall to the collar of his jacket that hangs around my shoulders before skimming up my neck. "Hm," he rumbles before he looks at me again. "Let's save that for another time. Come on, I'll get you settled." He drops his hand away from my arm and moves toward a narrow hallway.

I consider my options for only a handful of heartbeats.

And then I follow him into the dark.

CHAPTER NINE

THEN

Football season in Saddlebrook Falls is a near holy experience. Come rain or shine, the town shows up every Friday night to support their beloved Mustangs. Whether it's on our home turf or an away game, you can always count on a red wave in the stands to cheer on our varsity boys. Signs are posted on the doors and windows of businesses to note their closures—usually with a firm nudge to passersby that they, too, should be at the game.

There's even a Saddlebrook Falls spirit committee that coordinates the logistics for things like rideshares for people to attend away games, a volunteer sign-up to bring snacks and drinks to those away games (because everyone refuses to spend their hard-earned dollars on another school's concessions), and even to detail what's been deemed the "mascot lottery," which . . . is exactly what it sounds like. The list of eager participants who hope to be the Mustang mascot each Friday night has grown so long there's no possible way that each person will have a chance to wear the suit, so there's a weekly draw at Mustang's Pizza to identify the lucky tribute.

Ideally, the volunteers for the mascot should be young and nimble and chock-full of energy—but in our town, even old man Gerry's name is in that pot, even though last time his name was drawn he nearly needed hip surgery, thanks to all his gyrating on the sidelines. Still, his dedication to our beloved Mustangs knows no bounds, and he's confirmed that as long as he's still standing, he will support our boys.

Tonight's the first game day of the season, and it's taking place on our turf. The buzz for this game against the Tierra Vista Titans, one of our biggest rivals in the statewide division, has been next level. I peek out from behind the bleachers to see a bursting crowd in the stands, their excitement and hunger for a win palpable in the warm evening air. The nerves in my stomach set in as a handful of other girls join me in looking.

"You feel that?" asks Margot, one of the juniors.

"It's wild," Lizzie murmurs. David stands next to her, nodding as he wraps an arm around her.

"Is it always like this?" I ask, turning to look at them.

Margot's smile spreads wide. "Oh yeah," she confirms. "It's like a drug—enjoy it while you can."

And I believe her, because soon we're grabbing our pompoms and bouncing onto the field and into formation for our season-opening kickoff, and I've never in my life felt anything like it.

The stands become downright thunderous as we move through our choreography, and even as I'm twisting and flying in the air, I can hear the distinct chanting from the crowd as they roar "M-U-S-T-A-N-G-S, GO MUSTANGS GO!"

I've been to a handful of these games before, but with Annie so much younger than me it wasn't always easy for us to make it. Mom worried the games were too loud for her little ears, so someone needed to stay home with her, and with Barry's late nights at the office, we didn't have many opportunities to go.

I never realized how electric it all is, like a current zipping through my spine as the entire stadium becomes feral for the team to make their debut on the field. I wonder if they can hear the roar from where they're still tucked away in the locker room.

Soon it's time for them to make their appearance, and Lizzie and David run to the sidelines to grab the huge paper sign we painted this morning before school. A few girls lift me onto a senior named Hoa's shoulders as Lizzie is lifted to stand on Regan's a few yards away, and together we hold the top two corners of the paper sign high in the air while the rest of the girls form a long tunnel out toward the field.

The music from the marching band grows into a frenzied crescendo just as the first of the football players rips through the banner and runs onto the field. I spot Jason in his bright red jersey sporting the number 24, closely followed by Wells brandishing a crisp white 88, and I almost burst into tears from the sheer adrenaline of it.

I've never been prouder to be a part of something.

As if on instinct, I study the line of red helmets that shines under stadium lights as the guys huddle together on the side of the field. The Titans are running out from the other end zone to their own screaming fans, but I don't pay attention to any of it because my eyes land on Jason and now that I've found him, I feel like I can't peel my eyes away. He's one of the tallest on the team and the sight of him in full uniform sparks a fire in my heart.

Especially as he turns my way and I see him smile.

MY EYES HAVE BEEN GLUED TO JASON FOR THE LAST five minutes since Coach Andersen pulled Noah King out of the game after a couple of bad throws. Jason stepped in and helped the Mustangs push for a first down at the thirty-yard line as they try like hell to secure another touchdown before the Titans get the ball back. The score is tied at seventeen points each, but even if we kick for a field goal right now to gain a three-point lead, there's plenty of time left on the clock for the Titans to get a touchdown and take that lead back before the game is over.

The stands are electric in a clash of red and blue, and despite the relief of our first down, the game can literally go either way at this point—thirty yards is still a long way to the end zone. Jason rocks back on his heels and looks down the line of scrimmage for a pulse check on his teammates. I can sense his nervousness in the way he can't keep himself still, but he seems to maintain control as his pads rise and fall with a deep breath before he shouts, "Red eighty!" for the snap.

Ethan whips the ball back to Jason who captures it with ease, then he twists his body to the left to look for an open receiver. The Titans' defense is mean, and it feels like there's two blue jerseys for every red one. But Jason must spot an opening, because he hurls the ball toward the left side of the field.

Brad jumps high in the air to catch it, but he's tackled as

soon as his feet touch the ground. Still, the Mustangs gain another eight yards, and the cheerleaders around me catapult into flips and back handsprings to celebrate. I've become so focused on the game that I almost forget I have a job to do—I need to cheer for this team, for the boy on the field who is slowly capturing my heart.

In the next play, Jay underhands the ball to Ethan who charges through a blue wall of defense to gain another yard before the cluster of Titans surrounding him takes him down. The air surrounding the stadium is thick with excitement as we inch closer and closer to another first down, to a touchdown, and I want so badly to see them get it. Jason may not have started in this game, but if he's able to help clinch a win in this last quarter, there's no telling what opportunities will open for him for the rest of the season. Noah King might be a senior but his throws tonight were sloppy—the Titans even intercepted a pass in the first half of the game.

The seconds seem to grow longer as everything on the field slows down. Jason calls for the next snap and my heart jumps in my throat as one of the Titans defensemen—the biggest guy on their side of the field by far—guns it right for him. He's huge, and even from here, I can see he's determined to squash Jay like a bug. I almost cry out a warning—as if Jay would be able to hear me from where I stand on the sidelines—but Wells sees him too, and he launches himself between the player and Jason, effectively taking both himself and the rogue Titan down. With the threat of a tackle eliminated, Jason throws the ball high in the air toward the end zone.

Where Brad catches it for what might be the game-winning touchdown.

The stands erupt in absolute chaos as the boys on the field

rush Brad in a celebratory tackle, but Wells gets back to his feet and sprints toward Jason. I watch as he hurls himself at his best friend, wrapping his arms around his bulky shoulders in a giant bear hug. Jason's smile is so big it shines through his face mask and I feel the heat of his joy crash into me from all the way over here.

He's like a supernova, bright and all-consuming as it streaks across the sky. I want to capture this feeling in a jar and savor it forever. I want to run to him, to jump into his arms like Wells did. I want to give him my heart—I just hope he's careful with it.

I look up at the clock on the scoreboard and see there's only fifty-five seconds left of the game. The girls around me are gathering into a formation . . . for what, I'm not sure. I must have missed a call from one of the captains for a stunt. After scanning the three separate huddles, I realize they're setting up for a pyramid. As the smallest one on the team, I'm the center flier, so I shuffle toward the girls in the middle, grabbing their shoulders and readying myself to launch.

I brave a quick look at Jason as he jogs back to the sidelines with the rest of the offensive linemen, and his gaze lands on me for the smallest of seconds, that goofy smile still wide across his face. I shoot him one back before I refocus on the girls in front of me who put their hands together to support my weight. I take a deep breath, then step into their hold.

I'm still a little nervous every time I fly, but the toss goes well and we all stay coordinated. I can't help but squeeze my eyes shut as I fall, but I manage to keep my limbs loose enough that my landing is relatively soft. Hoa, who knows I'm still gaining my confidence with flying, whispers a quick "Nice job!"

before we roll right into a choreographed ground routine that I know by heart. But everyone in the stands is focused on the field where our kicker, Matt, is about to try for the extra point.

Everyone in the stadium collectively holds their breaths as the ball is kicked high into the air, coming back down to settle perfectly between the bright yellow goalposts at the end of the field. And once again, the crowd erupts.

The Titans end up running out of time in a scramble for their own touchdown, cementing a season-opening win for the Mustangs. For the second time tonight, I almost burst into tears as the swell of kinetic energy overcomes us all. The whole team storms the field as the clock hits zero, high on the win and the tangible magic of a Friday night game.

My eyes snag on Jason again to find him already watching me from inside the team's huddle. He's pulled his helmet off his head, and a lock of golden hair sticks to his sweat-slicked brow. His smile turns soft and as his feet begin to move this direction, I feel my heart pound from where it's currently lodged in my throat.

It takes him only seconds to reach me on the edge of the field, seconds to carefully shoulder past the other cheerleaders around me, seconds before his hands are on my waist and his mouth is on my lips for a searing, blissful kiss.

I don't hear the shrieks of the girls around me, or the heckling that comes from people in the stands. All I can feel is his smile against my mouth as he whispers, "That win was for you."

I pull back to look at him, grinning. "Pretty sure it was for the entire town."

But he shakes his head in earnest. "No, Layla . . . I wanted that win for you. That throw, the touchdown . . . it was for you."

I'm still not sure I believe him, but the notion is romantic as hell, so I relent.

And I've never been so excited in my entire life about what's to come.

CHAPTER TEN

THEN

Margot Arnold is hosting a house party tonight to celebrate last night's win against the Titans. Word about the party has been circulating all day, details about the "exclusive" invite list causing anxiety-riddled rumblings amongst the various group chats I'm a part of. I knew I'd be going to Margot's with Jason either way—perks of dating the quarterback—but I was thrilled when a text from Margot herself chimed from my phone this afternoon. It seems being a cheerleader has its perks, too.

I'm still coming down from the rush of it all—the high of my bright red pom-poms sparkling under stadium lights, of Jason's lips on mine when he couldn't wait another second. Only a month into high school, I already feel like I've *made* it, and it's all I can do to wrestle the lingering panic that it's all too good to be true. That I eventually might have to piece myself back together when this all comes crumbling down.

For now, though, I plan on enjoying the spoils.

Jason picked me up from my house an hour ago, and now we're back at the Bennett ranch sitting on stacked bales of hay and watching Kasey ride an unruly horse inside a different training corral from the one Wells was in during my first time here. Apparently, breaking wild horses is part of the gig; the Bennetts run a rescue ranch of sorts, taking in horses from all over the country that need rehabilitation before moving them on to their next homes. Jason told me that wild mustangs are dropped off here every month by the Bureau of Land Management as they work to preserve both the horses and federally-protected land.

I don't understand how taking wild horses out of their natural habitats and bringing them *here* is a good thing. It's a thought that nags at me as I watch the beautiful mare do her best to hurl Kasey off her back—I don't blame her for a second for wanting him off.

Wells sits next to Jason and me, drinking beer from a silver can. He and Jay are both sixteen and I know drinking is normal for them by now—they've probably had years of experience. But Wells didn't offer me one, and I know it's because he thinks I'm too young. He didn't offer Jason one either, I guess, but I assume that's because Jason is driving.

"I gotta piss," Jason says, breaking the silence that's not quite comfortable between us all yet as he kisses me on the cheek. "I'll be right back. Wells, you need another beer?"

Wells shakes his head. "We gotta go soon."

Jason nods. "Cool. Won't be long, and then we can leave."

"What kind of horse is that?" I ask, pointing to the black-and-white-spotted one that Kasey's riding. She's the prettiest horse I've ever seen, and my heart still snags on the sudden loss of her freedom. The way she's trapped here now.

"She's an Appaloosa," he says, taking another sip of his beer. "We just got her last week."

"What's her name?"

"Doesn't have one." I get the sense he's only obliging my sudden burst of questions in some vague attempt to make nice after how things went down the last time I was here. Wells has refrained from frowning in my direction since then, but he still hasn't warmed up to me at school.

"Well, she needs a name." I'm fascinated by her markings, by the sheer strength in her legs and the fierce spirit in her eyes as she tries to buck Kasey off the saddle. There's no doubt she's a mean one, and I feel a flare of pride at her stubborn refusal to submit. I think it's part of what makes her so beautiful. "Stardust," I whisper.

"What?" Wells asks, turning to face me, eyes blooming with surprise in a way I haven't seen before.

"Stardust. That's her name," I say with confidence. She looks like the night sky, speckled with an abundance of stars. Wells continues to look at me for a long moment before he shakes his head, his gaze moving back to his brother. "Does it hurt her?" I can't help but risk another question.

"You're gonna have to be more specific, sunshine."

I roll my eyes. "Breaking a horse," I clarify. "And I told you, stop calling me that."

He sighs. "No, it doesn't hurt her. It gives her a purpose, gives her some structure to hold on to. Something she can count on."

"Hm," I consider, watching as Stardust thrashes around. "Maybe she doesn't want that."

"What do you mean?" I keep my focus on the horse in

front of me, but I feel Wells's eyes on me again. They burn against my skin.

I shrug. "Maybe not all of them want to be broken. Maybe some of them want to live forever wild." I turn to find his brows scrunched together. There's a divot between them that looks big enough to sink a finger into. He's looking at me like I'm a puzzle, like he's studying the pieces that he's holding in his hand and trying to find where they fit. "Please don't break her."

The sun is sinking low in the sky, and golden flecks sparkle in his otherwise earthy brown eyes. After what feels like several minutes (even though I know it's only seconds), he turns to look back at Stardust, and I'm surprised when he nods.

"You guys ready?" Jason calls from the back porch where he's pulling his boots back on.

"Yeah," Wells yells back. He stands up and leaves me where I'm sitting without another look.

I push out a breath, stealing another glance at Stardust before I, too, stand from the makeshift bench, brushing pieces of the dried hay from where they've sunk into my bare legs. Jason and Wells wait for me next to Jason's Mustang, and Jason pulls open the passenger door as I approach. "Milady." He smiles at me, and I giggle before climbing in.

Wells jumps into the back seat, sitting behind me. As Jason rounds the car to get in on the other side, I turn to look at Wells. "Do you have enough room back there?"

He shoots me a look that I'm not able to read. "Yeah."

Jason gets in and starts the ignition. "Wells, do you think they have enough beer?"

"Probably not."

I turn my focus to Jason. "Am I going to have to drive you home tonight?"

He flashes me a bright smile. "Maybe."

I laugh because we both know I don't have my license yet, but there's a slight trepidation that coils in my stomach. I don't want to show it, though—the last thing I want to do is prove my own naiveté.

My gaze moves back to the road in front of us and I feel it as soon as Jason presses on the gas, like a zipper up my spine. This moment in time. The anticipation of what's to come on this early fall night as I toe the line between childhood and . . . whatever comes next. Like going to a high school party on the arm of a gorgeous, older guy.

It's a moment of *rightness*. It feels a lot like fate.

"We can go to that convenience store between here and Williamson County," Wells mumbles from behind me.

"They have beer?" Jason asks.

"Yeah."

"Do you still have Rhett's ID?" Jason looks at his best friend in the rearview, and my mind traces down the line of Bennett brothers. Rhett is the middle one. The wildest one. Story goes he's the one who burned down the old gazebo on Main a few years ago. No one's ever been able to officially prove anything, but town gossip places Rhett in a drunken rage torching the place after a girl stood him up. Folks from around town came together to rebuild it, and the surrounding grass eventually grew back, but no one forgets something like that here. An open skeleton in this family's closet.

"Yeah," Wells repeats. *Again.*

"You don't say much," I mutter as Jason pulls onto the state road that leads to Williamson County. Jason looks at me from behind the steering wheel, but I keep my focus on the view out my window for the short drive past the edge of town. Maybe it was an odd thing to say out loud, but it's true. Wells doesn't seem to ever do anything more than what's required.

We pull into the convenience store and Wells pushes through the door in the back. I watch as he pulls open the wooden door and slips inside the store.

"Be nice, Layla," Jason warns quietly.

I finally brave a look back at him and am thrown by the disapproval in his eyes. "I am! I didn't mean it as a bad thing. He's just kind of quiet."

He presses his lips together. "Just be nice, okay?" He reaches out to grab my hand, winding his fingers between mine.

I lean my head back on the headrest. "You really love him, don't you?"

His brow arches. "He's my best friend. We've been through a lot."

I sigh. "I promise to be nice."

Jason squeezes my hand and smiles. "Thank you."

The front door to the store pushes back open a few minutes later, and Wells reemerges with a case of beer in his hands. Something about the way he holds the case, the way his forearms flex with the effort of it, makes him look older. I can picture him as a man: suntanned skin and strong arms from years of football and horse training, his tall build and wide frame driving through the world with the force of a monsoon storm.

"Hell yeah, he got some!" Jason laughs next to me. He lets go of my hand as Wells slides back in. "Any trouble?" Jason asks.

Wells shakes his head. "Nah—no one knows us out here."

Jason whistles. "It's a sign, my friend. Tonight is going to be a good one."

As soon as we pull up to Margot's house I climb out of the car, suddenly nervous, rubbing my hands along the cotton of my dress to brush out any wrinkles. I look down at myself, and realize how dirty my white Converse look from all the dust at Bennett Ranch.

"You look fine," Wells mutters from behind me. I turn to look at him, watching as he pulls the case of beer out of the back seat and uses his knee to shut the door while he keeps his eyes on mine.

"I know I do," I say back, perplexed at his assessment.

He scoffs and stalks toward the house.

Jason comes around the car and takes hold of my hand as we follow Wells through the front door. There are at least a dozen people in the kitchen, some of them holding cans of beer and some with red plastic cups. Liquor bottles are lined along the kitchen's island along with various two-liters of sodas and gallons of juice. Wells sets his case of beer on the counter next to the kitchen sink and rips through the cardboard. Jason reaches in next and grabs two, stacking them together in one hand.

Wells frowns at him, but Jason doesn't see it because he's smiling at me.

He guides me through the crowd gathered in the kitchen to the back door, where other football players stand under a patio awning and next to an in-ground swimming pool.

The daylight bleeds into night as the sun hangs low on the horizon. The loud buzz of cicadas fills the air, sticky with a humidity that won't quit. Jason's group of friends celebrate when they see their quarterback. And I realize people are staring at him from all around the backyard . . . staring at him *and* me, like there's some gravitational pull that snags everyone's attention. I guess it makes sense, after last night's game— it marked the beginning of his place among Mustang royalty. He lets go of my hand to high-five his friends, leaving me to stand a bit awkwardly behind him.

Some of the other players have girls on their arms, but I don't recognize any of them. I'm relieved not to see Stassi anywhere. The group still eyes me up and down though, probably trying to figure out how a freshman like me ended up here with someone as bright and shiny as Jason. One of the girls—a redhead with curly hair and freckles dusting her face —gives me a warm smile, reaching a hand out. "Hi, I'm Haley."

I wrap my hand around hers, giving her a light squeeze in thanks. "Layla," I say back. "Nice to meet you."

She comes to stand next to me, eyeing Jason. "You're here with Jay?"

"Yeah," I respond, looking at him too. He's laughing with the guys as they recount a play from last night, his handsome face curled in delight. "We just started dating."

She smiles wider. "Nice! I'm Matt's girlfriend." She nods toward the tall blond she was just standing next to. He's the kicker from last night's game. "We've been together since last year. Matt and Jason are pretty close—I bet we'll be seeing much more of each other."

I'm thrilled at Haley's open kindness. "That sounds great

to me," I say, my nose scrunched from my returning smile. "Do you play any sports?"

She shakes her head. "No, I'm not very athletic. My parents made me play soccer growing up, but I was terrible at it. You?"

I shrug. "I cheer. I actually cheer for Jason on the varsity squad."

"Oh! That's amazing! I swear, cheerleaders have, like, the *best* bodies."

I laugh, but then my eyes are back on Jason because he's reaching for my face. His fingers slide up and across my cheeks, sending a wave of goosebumps down my neck. "Hey, are you good out here for a minute? I'm going to go get some beers for the guys."

I nod, twisting back toward Haley with a smile. "Yeah! I'm good." The guys around us follow Jason, and Haley and I are left to continue talking.

At some point, I notice Wells on the other side of the pool. He's surrounded by a group of girls, and it's obvious that they're competing for his attention. He doesn't seem fazed by it though, as he holds easy conversation with them all while sipping from a bottle of water.

Another girl—Megan—joins us, and I listen intently as they trade gossip like it's candy. I try really hard to stay engaged in the conversation, but it's honestly hard to keep up. I'm still getting my bearings on who's who, and the way Haley and Megan talk about other people makes me feel like I'm in the middle of a pop quiz I didn't study for.

The sun has fully disappeared, and Jason still hasn't come back out of the house—it's been at least a half hour since he went in there. I steal a glance across the pool to find that Wells has also disappeared. After Megan finishes telling a story about some girl who fully sat in a piece of chewed gum that someone had spit out in her chair—yikes—I politely excuse myself.

Inside, the music is turned up so loud I can't hear my own thoughts, and there are way more people here than before. Most of the lights in the house have been turned off, the living room lit only by the glow of music videos that play on the big screen TV anchored to the wall. A beer pong table has been set up down a hallway, and I spot Jason standing next to Matt on the far side of it. Both of them are holding red plastic cups as they play against two guys I recognize as Brad and Ethan. I clock Stassi and Erin standing near them, surrounded by dozens of other girls who hang around the table.

Wells is standing behind Jason, and he looks frustrated.

I push through a few people and sidle up to Jason. It takes him a few minutes to realize I'm here, but the concentration in his brow loosens when he does. "Layla." He kisses me on the cheek, his lips hot and wet against my skin. "Where have you been?"

I narrow my eyes. "Out back, where you left me."

He slaps a hand on his forehead. "Shit, I'm sorry. Matty and I got roped into a game and we keep winning . . . you know how it goes." He has the audacity to smirk at me.

A swell of irritation bubbles up my throat because I *don't* actually know how this goes. Jason is supposed to be my lifeline. He's supposed to be hanging out with *me* here, isn't he? It's obvious he's drunk. I look around and realize that everyone is drunk.

Except for Wells, who's looking back and forth between Jason and me with that frown marring his mouth.

"I want to go home," I say when I turn back to Jason. But he doesn't hear me, because Ethan just made the ball in a cup and everyone around us cheers. I watch as Jason picks up the cup, swiping the ball out of it with his finger before dropping it into the nearby water cup, chugging the contents of the one in his hand.

"Jesus," Wells mutters. He shakes his head and leans in so I can hear him through all the noise. Or maybe it's so that Jason doesn't hear *him*—I'm not sure—but either way he's so close I can smell traces of leather on his skin. "Let him finish this game," he says low, "because I don't think I can tear him away otherwise. But then we'll take you home. I promise."

Concern rips through me, the trepidation from earlier coiling tighter. "Jason drove us. He can't drive now."

"I'll drive." My eyes drop to the water bottle in his hands before they rise to meet his. He gives me a tight, barely there smile, but his eyes are hard to read. "I haven't had anything to drink. I figured this might happen."

"Oh." I'm not sure what to make of that. I don't want to be a brat, but I'm annoyed that Jason can't drive me home himself. That he didn't think of me before getting to this state. "Thank you," I mutter. Wells gives me a shrug and steps back behind Jason.

The game lasts for another twenty minutes after a standoff when both sides are down to only one cup. More and more people have crowded around the table to see the end of the game. But the more I stand here, the more upset that I feel.

Jason barely looks at me, hardly acknowledging that I'm next to him. He's so wrapped up in the competition and, honestly, I'm surprised he's even holding it together because I can see how glassy his eyes are. How he stumbles over his own feet when he attempts to throw.

Finally, a guy on the other team sinks the ball into the last cup. And before Jason can reach for it, Wells scoops it up and pushes it into Matt's chest. "You drink this, Matty. Jay's coming with me."

Jason gives Wells a confused look as Wells herds him toward the door, keeping a firm grip around his arms in what I'm sure is an effort to hold him upright. "What the hell, Wells? Party's just getting started!"

"Not for you. We're going home."

I follow behind Wells as he continues to push Jason toward the door. He tries to twist away, but Wells shoves him harder, finally getting him out into the humid night air. "What the fuck, Wells?" Jason yells as he scampers across the lawn, trying to find his balance. "We don't have to leave, we can just crash on the couch. What's the big deal?"

Wells walks away from him, shaking his head at the sky with an expression that conveys absolutely no joy. But then he stops abruptly and charges toward his best friend. "The big deal, you fucking moron, is you have a girl with you tonight. Or did you forget about Layla? You think her parents will be cool if she just *doesn't* make it home?"

I suck in my teeth at his frustration. Jason looks at where I'm standing on the front porch and his face twists in shame. "Aw, shit, Layla. I'm sorry."

I stare at him for a long minute before I push out a breath. "It's fine." And then I walk across the yard, past Jason and Wells who both watch me, and head for the Mustang. I hear the locks click when I get close, and I pull open the passenger door and climb in, slamming it shut behind me.

They argue for another minute, then Jason sprawls out in the back and Wells is in the driver's seat, giving me a long look as he adjusts the steering wheel and starts the car.

The ride to my house is silent, the only words spoken are a few directions to help navigate. At some point, Jason falls asleep, and when Wells finally pulls up along my curb, he doesn't wake.

Wells shifts the car into park and looks at me again before he speaks. "I'm sorry about him," he says, assessing me. His eyes move across my face with a determination that makes me feel exposed, and I don't like it.

"Don't stick up for him. He can face it himself."

He huffs out a laugh, and I'm struck by the lines that form around his eyes as he does, etching into tan skin. He shakes his head. "Don't be too hard on him, sunshine. We aren't used to having a girl like you around."

My brows scrunch together. "A girl like me? What's that supposed to mean?"

He stares at me for another long moment before he sighs. "Nothing. I'll wait until you get inside."

I want to press him further, but I'm also starting to sense something dangerous about Wells, and I've had enough go wrong tonight. "Thanks for getting me home," is what I settle on.

He nods, and I go through the motions of slipping out of the car and inside my house, knowing it's well past my curfew. But before I tiptoe up the stairs, I sneak a quick look out the front window and watch Wells drive away.

CHAPTER ELEVEN

NOW

My eyes snap open as my body tenses. All I can hear is the pounding of my pulse in my ears as I work to figure out what pulled me out of sleep. It takes me far too many breaths to remember where I am and what happened last night.

To remember what my life has turned into.

But when it all comes rearing back to the surface, it breaks me apart all over again, crushing against my bones and blood until my insides are a jumbled mess. Like the destruction after the meanest hurricane. The numb haze I've carried for days has finally given in against the current of my torment, and I have to stifle a shuddering breath from the impact.

As I force slow and deep breaths into my lungs as Wells instructed last night, I look around the bedroom I'm in. The king-sized bed takes up a majority of the space, and the walls are a chestnut wood-paneling with black-and-white photos of horses scattered about. There's a dark dresser with gold knobs against the wall to my left, a beautifully carved mirror attached to it.

I sit up, finding my reflection. Despite having just woken up from one of the deepest sleeps I can remember, I look like shit. My eyes are still bruised from exhaustion, and my hair is a tangled mess of curls and knots. I try not to get too caught up in the fact that I'm burrowed in Wells's bed—the last place in the world I *ever* thought I'd be. I can't help the panic that claws at me. Old, familiar pangs of anxiety rise through my limbs, and I just want to disappear until I'm a weightless, empty thing of the shadows.

A door opens on the other side of the wall, and I hear Wells's quiet voice. "What?" He sounds tired.

I realize I must have woken up from a knock at the door, and the panic inside of me sinks its claws deeper.

"Just wanted to check in on you," another voice says with a steady and hopeful tone. It's Kasey, and in an instant I'm tearing myself out of the bed. "I don't know what the hell happened last night, but it didn't look good and you left real damn fast."

"Yeah . . . it's complicated."

"Sure seemed like it."

There's a long pause before Wells finally speaks again. "I'm good, Kasey. But thanks for—"

"Wells," Kasey cuts him off. "You can't face all of this alone, brother. You can't just lock yourself in there and get drunk and expect that any of this will get better." Wells scoffs, and I hear the squeak of the swinging of the door before a loud thump sounds. "Wells, dammit, at least let me come in for a little while. I know there's a coffee pot in there. Just give me twenty minutes and I'll leave."

"It's not a good time," Wells responds lightly, but I can hear the fear in his tone. Fear about the implications of Kasey finding me here, knowing that I've spent the night. I inch the flannel comforter back over the bed and try to destroy any evidence that I was ever in it.

"You have someone in there, Wells?" *Oh shit oh shit.* I freeze, my hand on my heart.

"Get the fuck out of here, Kasey," Wells demands coolly.

"Jesus *fuck*, Wells. Don't tell me she's in there." My heart drops into my stomach.

There's a shuffle before the door shuts, and I realize Wells has pushed the conversation outside. I use the opportunity to escape inside the small bathroom across the hall, shutting and locking the door behind me.

Sinking to the floor, I cover my face with my hands and try not to let the tears fall. I should have never come here, should have demanded that Wells bring me home last night. I'm not naive to what this might look like and, even despite Jason's infidelity, I'm not prepared for the level of town gossip or scrutiny it would bring.

Five minutes pass before I hear the front door open again, a single pair of feet padding along the hardwood floor. "Layla?" Wells calls from the other side of the bathroom door.

I force my emotion down my throat as I stand to unlock it, swinging it open to find him on the other side. His hair is a mess, sticking up at all angles. A worn black T-shirt stretches across his chest and a pair of gray sweats hang loosely from his waist all the way down to his feet. The sight of Wells in sweatpants sends a jolt through my chest, and my heart beats erratically. I've never seen him look so . . . casual . . . and it feels wrong. I look back up to his face, to those tired eyes. "Is he gone?"

He nods once, his jaw jumping as he opens his mouth to answer. "I'm sorry . . . I didn't know he would come here."

"Did you tell him I was here?"

"He took a guess," he says, and I flinch. He must notice, because words keep coming, assured and determined. "Layla, it's okay . . . I told him you came here to talk, that you need a friend. He knows it was nothing like . . . like *that*."

"I need a friend?" I scoff. "You think you're my friend, Wells?" I don't recognize my own hostility, but I can't stop it from spouting out. The pressure is mounting inside of my chest, and I feel like I might rip apart at the seams with one wrong move.

His brows dip low, a deep divot slicing between them. "I'm trying to be here for you," is all he says back.

I force a breath. "I'm sorry, I—I just don't think staying was a good idea. I need to get home before someone else finds me here." Kasey might keep it to himself, but would Brooks? Would Rhett? I look up to find Wells nearly despondent, and the realization pulses uncomfortably that he's suffering too, that his suffering exists well outside of my own.

He's just lost his best friend. It's a miracle he's even capable of trying to support me at all, that he's not the one falling apart with guilt over their last interaction—when he was defending *me*. And here I am acting like he's somehow responsible for my pain. My eyes shutter and I whisper, "I'm sorry, Wells."

The hard lines around his eyes grow softer, and he looks down at the floor, at the wool socks he wears on his feet. "Me too."

I sigh, crossing my arms over my chest. "Look, I know you

mean well. And . . . thank you, for giving me the truth last night. I think I just need some time to figure out how to process all of this."

He nods again. "I understand." His eyes find mine again. "Give me a second to change, and I'll take you home."

It only takes a few minutes for Wells to throw on jeans and a heavy work coat as I wait for him in the living room. The cabin is small and there's only one bedroom, so I trace my finger along the back of the couch and try to ignore the sounds of clothing shuffling from the other side of the thin wall.

As we make our way out the door, he insists that I wear his black Carhartt jacket again. It's a chilly morning, though I have to hold myself back from arguing that I've been living in much colder weather for months. The forty-something degree temperature is a relief from the blizzards and windchill factor in New York, but it does nothing to thaw the ice in my heart. I make quick work of shrugging into it before I hurry and climb into his truck, praying no one else is out on the ranch to see me.

The drive back to my house is quiet as I stare out the window, taking in the familiar roads and buildings. The Bennett family ranch sprawls out in the countryside along the northern border of Saddlebrook Falls, and we have to drive through the center of town to get down to my neighborhood on the other side. My gaze snags on Mustang's Pizza, where I spent so many nights hanging out with Jason and our friends after football games, celebrating a win. And then on the tree-line behind the gazebo that sits right at the entrance to the park, where Jason and I snuck away so many times just to have a few quiet moments to ourselves, usually spent making out where no one could see us.

It feels like another life, lived by someone else completely. As I sit shotgun in Wells's truck, eyes glued to the glass between me and the town I grew up in, I almost can't remember what it feels like to be that girl, so young and alive. I don't think I've felt that way since Jason left for college three-and-a-half years ago.

Soon Wells pulls up alongside the curb in front of my house, a bright yellow two-story that I've lived in nearly my whole life—since Mom married Barry and our life got "back on track." He shuts off the engine and looks out his own window, working through something that has him clenching his teeth. "You know," he starts on a croak before squeezing his eyes shut and mumbling a low curse. He's uncomfortable, that much is obvious. But then he looks at me, his eyes clear, and continues. "The cabin's always open to you," he forces out, "if you need it. I can move back to the big house . . . you can have it all to yourself." His gaze jumps back to the house over my shoulder, like he knows the fight I'm about to walk into.

"Wells, you realize the optics of me staying at the ranch only days after the death of *my* boyfriend and *your* best friend, right? How can you think that's a good idea?"

His eyes harden in frustration. "I'm trying to help . . . trying to give you some fucking support here. Jason royally fucked a lot of things up when it came to you, and you shouldn't have to process through it all alone." His eyes flick back to the house before he adds, "Or with your mother."

I snort, and he sighs. It's no secret how tightly wound

Mom gets when it comes to my life and my decisions—Wells was close enough to experience a few harrowing encounters between us. His whiskey eyes find mine again. "Besides, the Layla Hayes I know wouldn't give a shit about optics or what anyone else in this town thought about her choices."

His words splinter something inside of me and I force my gaze out my window to hide the emotion. Wells doesn't know that version of me has been buried for a while now. "I just . . . I don't know what to do with any of this. And the last thing I want is to make it worse. People are already going to have a field day about Emma, you know." Saying her name sends a fresh wave of nausea through me.

A warm hand covers my own, squeezing gently. "I'm here for you," he says in a low voice. "For anything you might need. Let me be here for you."

I chance a look at him and find him watching me in earnest, his vulnerability on full display, and I can't bear it a second longer. Pulling my hand away from his, I push open the door and climb out with a mumbled, "Thanks." I drag my feet up the front walkway to the porch and look back to catch Wells's gaze through the window, watching as he shakes his head and rolls his truck away from the curb.

And then I let out a deep sigh of relief.

But that relief is short-lived because I open the door to find my mother waiting for me inside the foyer. Her gaze is sharp as she cuts me with it. "What is Wells Bennett doing dropping you off after you *failed* to come home last night?"

I roll my eyes. "Mom, drop it."

But there's that look in her eye, like she's readying for battle. "Does it have anything to do with the scene you caused last night? *Puking* on some poor girl, Layla?" She tilts her head as she looks me up and down. "You were drunk, weren't you?"

The bone-deep urge to pick up the porcelain vase at my side and smash it against the wall nearly overcomes me. "No, I wasn't drunk," I grind out. "That 'poor girl' was Jason's *other* girlfriend, the one he's been *cheating* on me with at school for the past month."

The blow lands how I expect it to. Mom's beautifully arched brows rise in shock as her mouth drops open. "*What*?!" she exclaims. "How is that possible?" She attempts to gather herself, clutching at her chest as she thinks through the implication of it all. "Jason would never do that to you . . . there must be some mistake."

I close my eyes, willing the tears to stand down. The crushing chaos in my chest I felt when I woke up this morning is quietly disappearing as I feel myself slip back into an icy numbness. "No mistake. Wells confirmed it."

Silence falls between us, and I open my eyes to her heavy stare. I can't help but wonder what she's thinking, how Lynette Perkins—the woman who's raised me with the single expectation that I find a good man to marry and have lots of children with—might feel now. Eventually, she lets out a sad sigh. "I'm so sorry, bug. I can't imagine the heartbreak you must be feeling on top of everything else. But I promise you, this will pass. You're still young, sweetheart—you'll find a man who will treat you right and give you everything you deserve—"

"I can give *myself* what I deserve," I interrupt. "I don't need a man to be happy, Mom . . . I'm not *you*." I hear the gasp she sucks in, but I've already torn my gaze away from her to stomp up the stairs. As soon as I make it into the confines of my

room, I slam my door shut and sink to the floor as silent sobs
rack my body.

CHAPTER TWELVE

THEN

On a chilly Friday in November, Jason tells me that he wants to take me somewhere to celebrate our three-month anniversary—somewhere out of Saddlebrook Falls and far enough away that I'll have to ask my mom if I can push my curfew to midnight. He won't tell me where he wants to go, and though I feign a teasing annoyance at the lack of details, I'm secretly thrilled.

It's a bye week—a much-needed break for the team who have played their hearts out all season long. With only a few weeks left in the regular season, the Mustangs are expected to clinch their first perfect record in nearly twenty years. Jason has started in every game since that first one against the Titans and continues to dominate on the field with his steadying calm and one hell of an arm.

Scouts have even been at a few of the more recent home games, sending Jason into a tailspin. On the field, he leads a strong offense, but the second he steps off the turf, those nerves take root and poke at his confidence, driving him to practice till ten, eleven o'clock most nights. If he's not practicing, he's locked inside the school's weight room. Even on the rare nights that we all hang out at Wells's, Jason spends the majority of our time together throwing balls through a tire swing near the rec room.

Needless to say, spending a little quality time with him sounds like perfection, and I can't wait. "What should I wear?" I ask from the passenger's seat of his car as he takes me home after school.

"Boots and a jacket." The corners of his mouth lift as the implication settles over me.

"We'll be outside?"

He nods. "I'd probably put a little sunscreen on your face." He looks at me with a sly grin. "Wouldn't want you to burn."

I laugh as my mind rolls through the possibilities. The beach? It's only a half-hour drive away—but that wouldn't explain a need for boots. Maybe a hike? "What kind of pants should I wear?"

This time he laughs. "You can skip the pants altogether, Layla. Trust me, I wouldn't mind."

My ears burn hot at the suggestion. We're three months into our relationship, but I haven't even let him take my shirt off yet despite his continued attempts. It's not that I'm *not* interested in taking things more physical, because I am. Very much so, actually. But I think being eager is part of the problem because I'm not sure where that eagerness is coming from.

Even when Jason and I are just making out in his car I become intensely aware of my body and the fact that I'm not sure what to *do* with it. It's an insecurity that leaves me feeling both terrified about fumbling through any attempt at *more* and also just ready to dive in and get it all over with in hopes it settles some of these bone-deep nerves.

Jason's definitely not a virgin, and I guess when it comes down to it, I'm a little scared that my inexperience might bore him or disappoint him. And I know in my heart that's not enough of a reason to give myself up, but I'm also not sure how else to feel more confident about it all.

"I'm serious!" I scold, hoping he doesn't notice my flush. "Are jeans safe?"

His smile lingers as he wraps a warm hand around the top of my bent knee. "Jeans are perfect."

The next day, he shows up at my house around noon with three bundles of flowers in hand—one for me, and the others for Mom and Annie. Annie just about topples over with excitement at her beautiful bouquet, and Mom gives me a look that confirms everything I already know about how she feels about him. And while the gesture is nice, I know it's to sweeten her up before asking if he can bring me home later than usual tonight.

"Where are you two off to, anyway?" she counters when he eventually asks.

His eyes move to mine before they jump back to her. "I was kind of hoping I could keep it a surprise, but I promise it's somewhere safe and that I'll take great care of her."

I almost snort at the thought of needing to be taken *care* of . . . like I'm a small child he has to babysit. But I know he's only saying it to appease her, so I tamp down the urge to bite back with a retort.

"Oh, I know you will, sweetheart." She waves a hand as if none of this matters anyway, not when Jason is the picture-perfect boyfriend. I might like him very much, but I still hate the way she's ready to cement him into my life forever. "Just have her home by midnight, and not a minute later, okay?"

The smile he gives her is wide and toothy. "Yes, ma'am. I will." He kisses my cheek before taking my hand and hauling me out the door.

Once we've made it into his car, I pull my seat belt over my lap and say, "The flowers were a nice touch."

The smirk he throws my way is devilish, dripping in charm. "I figured it would help steer things our way."

I laugh. "You're terrible."

He shoots me another glance, the smirk melting away into something tighter. "What do you mean?"

"The way you just played her to get what you wanted."

A beat of silence passes. "I didn't *play* her, Layla. I was just being nice."

"Yeah but . . . you did it so she'd let me stay out later."

He shrugs. "Sure, that might've been part of it. But it's hardly manipulation."

That's *exactly* what it is, but I choose to keep that argument to myself. We're only five minutes into his elaborate anniversary surprise and here I am poking at him. Guilt ripples through me at that because my frustrations have everything to do with my mother and hardly anything to do with Jason. I try to get us back to safer grounds. "So, where *are* you taking me, exactly?"

Thankfully, it seems to work—the corners of his mouth rise with the secret he's keeping. "Foxborough County."

I scrunch my nose as I work to figure out what in god's name could be waiting for us out there. Saddlebrook Falls isn't all that big, but we're still lucky to have the shops and businesses and general access that we do. None of it would rival the main drags of any big city, but we still have just about anything we might need placed comfortably within reach. Foxborough County is . . . *nothing* but country. As far as I know, it's predominantly made up of orchards and farmland and a few scattered homes occupied by the people who work them.

Jason chuckles at what I'm sure is the bright beacon of confusion shining from my face. I look down at my shoes—my trusty high-top Converse, because despite living in Texas I don't actually own a pair of boots—and hope we aren't doing anything too physical. Maybe we're picking apples or . . . having a picnic? A sneaky glance into the back seat gives away nothing except the fact that Jason is a borderline slob.

It takes us just shy of an hour to cross county lines, and not long after that I notice a glossy banner hung across one of the highway's overpasses. It takes a few seconds for the glare from the sun to shift so that I can make out the words, but when it does, I read FOXBOROUGH RODEO & FAIR – 2 MILES and I'm flooded with a heady mix of relief and joy. "A fair?" I exclaim. "You're taking me to a fair?" I haven't been to one since I was really little, when my grandparents still lived here. It's one of my better memories from those days.

Jason's smile sparkles in the sunlight shining through his window. "That all right with you?" he asks, a hint of a tease in his tone.

"Trust me, it's more than all right."

We both laugh, and I feel it again—that effervescent sense of awe that sometimes bubbles over and overwhelms me. The thrill of a new experience, and a reminder not to take any of it for granted. I'm not sure where it comes from, but it humbles me all the same.

Five minutes later, Jason pulls his Mustang into a wide dirt lot lined with what looks like hundreds of other cars. As soon as I throw open the door, the mouth-watering aroma of funnel cake and other fried treats curls around me, igniting an embarrassing growl from my stomach.

Of course, Jason hears it. His low chuckle snares my attention, and I find his blue eyes a perfect match to the sky above us. "Hungry?" he asks.

"Starved," I admit.

"Let's go eat."

I'M NOT SURE HOW IT'S POSSIBLE, HOW MEANDERING through fairgrounds gets inexplicably *better* with age. Or maybe it's that it's been so long since I've done it and I'm flooded with the memories from a much smaller Layla who explored row after row of concessions and game tents, hands gripped tight to her two favorite people. This isn't even the same fair as before, but it still siphons out a sense of homesickness that aches beneath my ribs.

I don't allow myself to fixate on it much anymore; I haven't let myself open that mental trapdoor in years. But I *desperately* miss my grandparents, and being here today is a reminder of that longing. They might have their issues with my mother and the decisions she's made, but they've always been good to me.

Before they moved to Florida, I spent many nights at their house while my mom worked night shifts at the local diner, doing her best to keep the lights on in our one-bedroom rental. I'd tuck myself tightly between them on the couch, a blanket thrown over all six of our legs as if it might cement us together forever, and we'd watch movies until I grew tired enough to fall asleep. My grandpa taught me how to ride a bike when I was five, soothing my skinned knees later that day with gentle hands while my grandma warmed cornbread in the oven. She always had something warm to eat on a dime, her favorite way to comfort.

I've only seen them a handful of times since they moved away. For so long I held on to bitter resentment over their decision to leave, but as I've gotten older I think I understand why they did it. It had been too easy for my mother to fail back then, too easy for my grandparents to pick up the pieces of her life, as they'd always done—especially after I was born. When Mom came home from Vegas with a shiny new husband on her arm, they took it as an opportunity to break free. So, no. I don't blame them for it. Not anymore.

I was just collateral damage.

"Okay," Jason says around the fried Oreo in his mouth, pulling me out of my haze of memories. "I think we've eaten enough food."

I look down at the orange-lacquered picnic table between us, at the paper cartons of fried Oreos, fried pickles, *and* the plate-sized funnel cake I insisted on, dusted with copious amounts of powdered sugar. They're all mostly empty now. Pulling the final piece of cake in half with my fingers, I shrug before tossing one side of it into my mouth. "There's always room for more." He laughs, and I feel a zing of pride that I can make him do that. "But," I add mournfully, "I'm going to need a solid half hour of digestion before we can even think about getting on a ride." My gaze moves to the Zipper in the distance, to the cages of people flipping as they orbit around the tall boom, and my stomach lurches.

Jason nods. "No problem, we have somewhere to be, anyway."

"We do?"

He plucks the other half of the cake from my fingers and drops it into his mouth, eyes crinkling as a warm grin spreads wide. "Yeah, come on."

We untangle ourselves from the bench seats and throw our trash away. The sun is high and bright in the sky as Jason grabs hold of my hand and leads me deeper into the grounds, where a small arena comes into view—just past the Wacky Shack funhouse full of screaming children—and I remember the banner on the highway. "A rodeo?" I ask.

"Yeah, it starts at noon," he says, pulling his phone out of his jacket pocket to check the time. "We have about ten minutes to find a seat."

He looks more excited than I'd expect over a county rodeo —but maybe I'm learning something new about him, a golden nugget I can tuck away for later. He pulls me into the bleachers where we walk the metal platform before spotting an open spot six rows up. We take our seats just as the national anthem starts playing over the loudspeakers.

There's an undercurrent of anticipation that buzzes as a red tractor drags an industrial-sized rake across the dirt, forming neat lines as it goes. It's not long until I notice horses being led toward the line of chutes as cowboys work to fill them one by one on the other side of the arena.

Soon the first event starts: saddle-bronc riding. The first contender makes it nearly six seconds before being thrown from the saddle, a dull thump sounding as his body hits the earth. I can't help but flinch. Coordinators throw their arms up to appear bigger as they attempt to herd the fuming horse back to safety, and within moments the second rider starts. But it's the third rider that has me gasping into the palm of my hand.

Wells.

There's no mistaking him and next to me, Jason is beaming, eyes locked intently on his best friend. "Hell yeah, Wells," he mutters under his breath. "You got this." I'm struck by the pride in his eyes, so obvious it's almost palpable. It knocks something loose in my heart to witness a display of support like this—of friendship—especially when I hold it up against the experiences I've had in my own life.

Friendships haven't always come easy to me. In middle school I often felt used and discarded; other girls would temporarily try me on just to toss me into the go-back pile when all was said and done. No one ever seemed to stick, and at times I felt downright lonely.

I guess I still ache to belong to someone the way I'm realizing Jason and Wells belong to each other.

I fasten my attention back to Wells, on the black cowboy hat he wears as he waits in the chute. I've only seen him wear that hat once, when he and Kasey were getting ready at the ranch to take their mother to Beaumont to visit her sister. It's a stark difference from his usual dirty ball cap—it makes him look so much more grown up.

An air horn sounds, and the cowboys on the floor of the arena yank open the gate. The white horse Wells straddles bursts out like a strike of lightning and my heart leaps in my throat as he begins to thrash. Wells has one hand out in the air, and even from here I can see the determination set in his jaw, his mouth nothing but a firm line. He wears black chaps over his jeans, dark fringe bouncing with the movement of the horse.

For what feels like the longest eight seconds of my life, I can't drag my eyes away from his face, bracing myself for the moment when he's bucked so hard he goes flying. But he doesn't. Even as the horse bucks harder, Wells keeps control of his body and stays rooted in the saddle beneath him, until the air horn sounds again and the crowd in the stands roars with applause.

Twenty minutes later the saddle-bronc event ends when the tenth rider is thrown into the stadium fence, and Wells makes his way to join us in the stands with a joy in his eyes I've never seen before. Something silver flashes in his hands as Jason gets up to hug him. "Dude, that was so sick," he says, slapping his best friend on the shoulder with an open palm. "You literally fucking won!"

Wells grins, and I'm stunned by the casualness of it. He seems . . . pleased. As if that horse knocked his standard-issued attitude right out of him. I'm surprised when he turns his focus to me next, his earthy brown eyes filled with that familiar edge of curiosity. "What about you?"

I stare blankly at him. "What about me?"

"What did you think?"

Jason turns to look at me too, just as a loud buzzing starts an assault against my thoughts. *What do I think?* "About you? On the horse?"

The corner of his mouth tics, and I feel a flush crawl up my neck. "Yeah," he confirms.

"Oh, um . . . I—" I stall, looking around at the people around us. "It's impressive," I fumble. "You . . . I mean. *You* were impressive." His eyes flash with something like amusement and before I can stop myself, I ask, "Can you teach me how to ride?"

His face blanks, all traces of humor gone. "You want to ride?"

"Yeah. I mean . . . not like *that*," I jut my chin toward the arena. "I'm not trying to get hurled into the dirt or anything. But, I'd like to try riding a horse, I think." My ears burn hot as Wells and Jason look at me like I just asked them to take me to Europe for the summer.

"Um," Wells starts, looking at Jason as he shrugs. It's clear I've caught him off guard. "Sure."

Jason looks back and forth between us with a layer of gratitude in his expression. Wells is one of the most important people in his life, and I know he wants us to get along. "Okay, but she's on her own. Last time I got on a horse I ended up in the mud."

Wells rolls his eyes. "That's 'cause you're a moron and you didn't listen to a word I said."

Jason laughs, his eyes dropping to Wells's hand. "Aw shit, you got one?!"

Wells turns the buckle over in his hand, that soft smile playing on his lips. "Kasey's going to freak." He looks around, a thought triggered by the reminder of his brother. "Speaking of . . . he's around here somewhere."

Jason's smile grows bright. "Let's find him and go have some fun."

CHAPTER THIRTEEN

NOW

I spend the next five days in hiding, locked in my room and content to forget about the life that goes on without me.

Without Jason.

Even knowing the truth, I still find myself missing him, wondering what it's like wherever he is . . . wondering if he's at peace.

I quietly teeter between a dangerous level of anxiety and self-loathing and a full-body numbness that blankets over it all.

I *know* I'm experiencing a catastrophic loss, not just from Jason's death but also in the smoke and mirrors of our relationship. And I'm not sure I'll ever feel ready to subject myself to the people of this town—not after what happened at Wild Coyote. I also can't bear to hash things out with my mom again. My room is the only place that feels safe, the only place I can sit with my thoughts and try to rationalize the whirlwind that has become my life.

Grief and shame burn along the corners of my mind like edges of a paper, always there but never quite swallowing me whole. I wish they would, if I'm being honest. At least it would be productive—I'd have something to show for my time beyond my swollen eyelids and the crumbs on my mattress from the crackers I eat to appease my mother, who's taken to standing on the other side of the door to listen to the wrapper crinkle as I eat.

I hear Barry leave for the office each morning, not to return home again until dinnertime. Mom moves around the house, getting Annie to and from school and doing whatever else it is she does to occupy her time. I hear her on the phone a lot, the town's gossip train in full force, especially when it comes to me.

She's worried about me—I know she is. And I love her for it. But we've never seen eye to eye, so I'm not sure what shared ground exists between us and I'm too exhausted to fight about what comes next. I expect she'll want me to take it on the chin, to grieve for an appropriate amount of time before getting back out there to start over. To find a suitor worthy of my future.

I'm not ready to hear *any* of her opinions. But as my restlessness increases, I can't bear to look at my pale pink walls or my George Strait posters or—god forbid—the collage of photos I keep taped to my mirror that are full of Jason's face.

Not for another second.

So when I hear my mother's phone ring, when I hear her subsequently slip out the back door so she can take her call out of earshot in the safety of her garden, I get dressed and scurry down the stairs, grabbing her car keys from the foyer table and booking it out the door.

I WIND MY MOTHER'S MERCEDES UP THE LONG DIRT road that leads to the ranch's main house, filling the air with dust as the tires crunch on scattered rocks. There's going to be hell to pay when I bring her car back home dirty, but I already feel a deep sense of relief in the distance I've put between me and the dark corners of my mind that have been holding me captive all week. It's the first time I've felt the sun on my skin in days, the first time I've been outside to breathe in fresh air, and it loosens some of the barbed tension that's clawed into my body.

I slow when I notice movement in one of the corrals. It's the one closest to the house that's predominantly used for the newer horses that are brought here to the ranch, the one Jason and I used to spend afternoons hanging out at, watching Wells and his brothers work.

A quick look back tells me it's Wells who sits on the beautiful roan horse, his backward hat and broad shoulders a dead giveaway. Rhett and Kasey watch him from just outside the wooden fence, both wearing cowboy hats low over their eyes. It's not until I beep the car locked with the fob that they all look my way.

I do my best not to let my nerves get the best of me as I make my way toward them, even though being here still feels wrong, somehow. I forgot how much I love the smell of the ranch. It's rich with earth and grass and—despite the obvious traces of horse shit—it's familiar in a way that a place like this can only be after it's sunk deep into the fibers of your being.

I'd probably never admit it, but it's my favorite place in Saddlebrook Falls. I've always felt so at home here, the worn buildings and wide-open fields becoming a place of refuge—even with Wells's temperamental attitude toward me.

I used to chalk it up as a place where I could hide out and avoid going home, but now as my feet lead me toward the wide corral, I think it might have always been more than that. This ranch is tucked far enough away from the rest of town that I feel like I can get an honest-to-god deep breath in when I'm here. It's a welcome reprieve from the constant scrutiny.

Not counting the night of Jason's funeral last week, this is the first time I've been here since the summer before college. But nothing's changed in the year and a half that I've been away—other than the realization that now I'm showing up alone.

It's a thought that rips through me, a cutting awareness that I'm here without Jason. My steps falter as I question what I'm even doing here . . . Maybe this was a mistake. Glancing back at the lot behind me, I find that I'm only halfway to the trio of Bennetts—if I turn back now, I bet I can make it to the car before anyone has a chance to catch me.

But as I turn back around, I find Wells staring at me. His expression is almost unreadable, but there's a curiosity there that sparks between us, and I'm suddenly moving toward him again. The horse he's riding whinnies as she turns to trot away from the fence, and I can tell she's anxious. She's probably new here, but not so new that she's trying to buck him off. It's clear they've been putting in the work with her, because despite her trepidation she leans into Wells's gentle direction as he steers her back toward the fence line.

I can feel Rhett and Kasey's eyes on me, but I keep my focus on Wells as his lips turn up at the corners. I'm relieved that he doesn't seem upset at my presence, but the relief is short-lived when I get a better look at his face.

His normally honeyed skin is pale, and the bruising under his eyes is so dark it has my stomach twisting. He isn't sleeping. "Layla," he says on an exhale before he clears his throat. "You're here."

The nerves in my stomach spike. "Yeah . . . sorry for just showing up like this, but I was hoping I could talk to you?"

His brown eyes dart to his brothers before landing back on me. "Sure." He nods, swinging a leg over the horse's back to jump down from the saddle. "Can you bring her in for me?" he asks Kasey. "I'll run her out again before dark."

I finally brave a look at the two men standing to my right and find them both watching me. Kasey nods as Rhett's brow furrows, like he can't figure out what good me being here will bring.

I don't blame him.

Wells pushes open the built-in gate and hands the reins to his brother. And it strikes me again, how bad he looks. It's obvious how much he's struggling, and I've done nothing to extend any show of support like he's done for me.

"How about a walk?" I ask, hoping to put a little distance between us and prying eyes.

He nods. "Okay."

We take a few tentative steps toward the large field beyond the corral, eventually catching a rhythm in our stride. A few minutes of silence pass between us before I find the courage to break it. "I want to apologize," I start, looking up at him.

He frowns. "Apologize?"

"Yes, about the other night. I . . . I didn't carry myself well, and I was kind of a bitch to you."

"Layla." He stops walking, and I have to turn to look back at him. There's a fierce determination set in his jaw that surprises me. "*You*, of all people, have nothing to apologize for."

I shake my head, swallowing down a swell of nerves. "I'm not the only one who lost him." It comes out as a whisper.

His head drops, and he stares at the ground for a handful of heartbeats. When he lifts his gaze to mine again, there's emotion swimming in his eyes. "Can I show you something?"

My heart thumps in my throat where words are caught. All I can do is nod.

He tilts his head toward a new direction and I trail along beside him. The silence doesn't feel as heavy as it did a moment ago, so I take the opportunity to look around the ranch as we move through it, taking it all in: the large white barn with painted black trim that looks a bit worse for wear; the three horses that graze in a second corral, all eyeing us curiously as we walk past; the way the land stretches so far in the distance I can't make out the farthest point before it tangles with the incredibly blue sky.

Wells leads us toward the open pasture to the east of the house, and it's then that I see her.

"Stardust," I whisper, eyes wide in a burst of excitement that feels almost foreign to me at this point.

Wells lets out a soft breath of laughter and it's almost rusty, like it might be his first attempt at a laugh in a long time. "There's your girl, sunshine."

She's just as beautiful as I remember, grazing in the tall grass alongside a handful of other horses. "You still have her?" I can't hide my shock—the Bennett ranch is a rescue ranch that takes in horses from all over the country, sometimes from other failing ranches or even from wild herds. The Bennetts work to rehabilitate them before ultimately selling them off. Most go to ethical dude ranches in Texas or surrounding states, but some have also been sold to nonprofits that provide equestrian therapy to mental health facilities or schools.

Wells promised me a long time ago that they wouldn't break Stardust—I saw the wild beauty in her eyes and couldn't bear to think of her submitting to anybody—but I always assumed they'd have her transferred out of here to a more permanent home. Most horses don't stay here long, save for the horses the Bennetts keep for personal use.

"Yeah." He adjusts the backward hat on his head before crossing his arms over his chest. "Kasey and I worked to transition this pasture to accommodate some of the mustangs. They normally don't come this close to the fence line . . . they like to stay out there in the hills." He points toward the distance, to a more natural landscape of small shrubs and scattered oak trees. "But I saw them here this morning, and now I can't help but think she knew you'd be here."

I look up and see a sliver of that vulnerability back. It's in the way his lips press together as he waits for my response. It knocks me off-balance—I've spent years making room for his bristling. This quiet eagerness is something new, and I can't help but wonder if it was there all along. "How long ago?"

The divot between his brows deepens. "What?"

"How long ago did you and Kasey turn this into a pasture for her? And the others," I add.

He wipes a hand over his mouth. "I don't know. Shortly after I made you that promise. Kasey only helped me because I threatened to tell our mom about his secret rodeo circuit—no one understands why I want to keep them here. But I wanted to keep my promise, and this was the only way I knew how."

My chest squeezes. "You did this for me?"

The brown of his eyes seems to come alive. "For Stardust," he amends, but the truth is all over his face, and I don't know what to make of it.

"Why didn't you tell me sooner?" I've been here so many times over the years, even taken rides out through this very pasture with him and Jason, and he never said a thing.

He shrugs. "I wasn't sure how to without making it a big deal."

I have to look away before I give him too much. Stardust lifts her head in our direction before whinnying and whipping her tail. The four other horses around her pause their own grazing to look up at her. "Hey girl," I say quietly, as if she can hear me through the wind from all the way over here. "You look so good. Are you happy?"

She simply stares back at me, and I wish she could respond. I wish I could read her mind and know if it was worth it to stay unchained, to escape any attempts the Bennetts might have made to break her. Or would extending her trust to them to be taken care of for the rest of her life have been a relief?

"She is," Wells murmurs as he watches her too. And then I feel the weight of his eyes on me again. "I'm competing in a rodeo in Fort Worth in a few days if . . . if you want to come."

I let the words sink in. "Don't you have to get back to school? The season isn't over." I can't imagine going back to NYU this soon, but I know how rigorous his football schedule is. Despite everything Wells is going through, I'm sure there's an expectation about his return to the field—playoffs start next week, only a week before Christmas. Even the holidays hardly stop the force that is college football.

He throws me an unreadable look before focusing back on the horses as his hands wrap around the wooden fence. "I'm not going back."

What? "Like . . . ever?"

He shrugs. "I don't see the point. My future is here, on the ranch with the horses. College feels like an unnecessary distraction."

"What about the draft?"

Pain lances through his features. "That was Jay's dream, not mine."

I don't know how to respond to that. There's an uncomfortable twist in my chest at the mention of Jason—making it to the NFL was all he ever talked about. But I thought Wells wanted it too. I never imagined he might only be along for the ride.

To know he never wanted any of it for himself . . . I wonder if he would have gone through with the draft in the spring, or if he would have found a way to let Jason down easy.

"Are you going alone?" I ask, shifting focus back to his invitation.

He shakes his head. "Kasey is competing too. We'll stay overnight and then drive back the next morning. We already have rooms booked, but I'm sure we can get a third one for you once we get there."

If it were anyone else going with him, I think I'd probably decline. But Kasey already knows I was at the cabin the morning after the funeral, so what's the harm in me tagging along for a quick rodeo trip? Getting out of this town for even a day would be a huge relief, and Wells must know that if he's asking me.

I think back to my earlier apology, to the whole reason I came here. Here's a chance to show him some support back.

"That sounds like exactly what I need," I say honestly.

Wells's mouth curves and I'm rewarded with a bright smile. A *real* one. It's been so long since I've seen it, I almost forgot what it's like.

He's the only one in the world who, for the most part, can understand what this last week has been like for me—because he's going through it too. Maybe if we lean into the pain together, we can make it to the other side a little lighter than if we were to go it alone.

I drape my arms over the fence and watch Stardust as she grazes, and for the first time since my world came crashing down around me, I feel a sense of hope.

CHAPTER FOURTEEN

THEN

In three and a half months of dating Jason, I've never seen him have a bad day.

Now, I realize the likelihood of a near-hundred-day streak of *good* days is probably a little far-fetched. Still, he's never worn anything darker than that easy smile he gives so freely, aside from the occasional nerves leading up to a big game. I guess I just assumed it was part of the magic of his composition: gorgeous eyes and unwavering charm, a dynamite athleticism that will probably take him pro someday, and an attitude so positive it's hard to feel anything but *good* standing next to him.

His general optimism toward life was part of the reason I fell for him so quickly in the first place. It began to chip away at my internal belief that if I don't show up to life with anything but my best, the good things around me will fall apart. I wouldn't call myself a pessimist, per se, but I *have* learned to expect the worst.

If I strive for perfection, *maybe* I can avoid the possibility of failure. I believe it's why I made the varsity cheer squad as a freshman and why my grade-point average starts with a four —I work really *really* hard for it all. But when I started spending more time with Jason, I could feel the relief of his easier frame of mind, and I couldn't help myself from leaning into it.

Today, though, his typical zest for life is nowhere to be found.

Because today, Jason is *pissed*.

I know he's blaming himself for last night's loss against Mayfield; in the last minute of the game, he threw an interception that took the Matadors all the way to their endzone, earning them a narrow win by just three points. It broke the Mustangs' perfect record and *might* affect the opinions of the scouts who've been spotted at recent games. Coach Andersen turned an angry shade of red, spit flying from his mouth as he yelled at Jason on the sidelines while the stands stood quiet, their disappointment clear.

I can't imagine holding the weight of expectation from every person in this town, an expectation to *win*. The devastation on Jason's face was completely new territory for me, seeing those handsome features that normally spark butterflies in my stomach rearrange themselves into something different altogether. It's the look he still wears today, except now it's also teeming with fury.

I hear the screen door slam from the front porch of the ranch house and turn to find the matriarch of the Bennett family. Her hand is propped over her brow as she looks down to find Wells and me carefully watching Jason shoot cannons through the tire swing. We're all silent, and I wonder if she can feel the tension roiling between us. "You kids want some lemonade?" she calls out.

Wells flicks his gaze to her before focusing back on his best friend, a small frown playing on his lips. "Sounds good, Mom," he calls back, though he seems unsure. I don't blame him, but it strikes me that even Wells is perplexed by Jason's mood.

Mrs. Bennett turns back to the house, her blue button-down flowing back from her shoulders before she disappears inside. It's a breezy late November day, breezier out here on the ranch than it was in town this morning. Wells is trying to make good on his agreement to teach me to ride a horse, having made plans with Jason and me earlier this week to spend our Saturday here, but now that we are, I feel silly about the whole thing.

It's not that I don't want to learn to ride—I do. But with Jason's foul mood and Wells's growing concern about it, I can't help but feel like this is all a major inconvenience. I watch the wind tear through Jason's shirt as he winds his arm back to launch a football through the tire swing again, and my regret presses down harder. "We don't have to do this," I say quietly, hoping I might still be able to save everyone from the burden I'm being.

Jason doesn't even glance my way. But Wells does. "What do you mean?"

I throw a pointed look to Jason as if to say, *You know exactly what I mean.* But I answer honestly, "The riding lesson."

Wells sighs, eyeing Jason who retrieves the ball he just threw for probably the hundredth time. "Jay," he says simply.

Jason glares at him. "What?"

They stare at each other, some silent conversation

streaming between them. I look down at my dirty white Converse, a quiet shame bubbling through me. I never should have asked for this.

Whatever passes between the boys must not go the way Wells hoped, because soon Jason's firing another pass through the tire swing, the tip of the ball slamming into the edge of the black rubber with a loud smack. He groans, cursing under his breath as he stalks over to pick it back up again. Another surge of dread courses through me, and just as I'm about to offer up another out for all of us, I realize Wells is watching me. "Let's just . . . let him stew in his feelings for a bit. We can get you on a horse."

I consider it. "Are you sure?"

"Why wouldn't I be?" His frown deepens. I can't help but look back at Jason, but Wells keeps going. "Layla, you want to ride a horse. And I said I'd help you do it. Plain and simple."

His words are an arrow piercing through my cloud of doubt. The screen door slams again, and we turn to find Mrs. Bennett with a tray in her hands. "I'm going to leave this right here," she hollers as she sets it down on a small table pushed up against the house, flanked by two rocking chairs. I imagine Mr. and Mrs. Bennett sitting in them on quiet mornings, warm mugs of coffee in hand. But truthfully, I'm not sure they get much use.

I've seen Mrs. Bennett a handful of times during my visits to the ranch, but she seems to keep her focus inside the house rather than outside of it. I've still never seen Mr. Bennett in the flesh, but I do hear him yelling from a second-story window from time to time. It's the five Bennett boys who actively run the ranch, Brooks and Kasey taking on the biggest roles in the operation. There's also a farrier named Hank who's here once a week to shoe the horses and a vet who comes around about as much to check up on them.

Rhett takes the lead on breaking the wild mustangs that are brought in. Wells helps when he can, but with school and football, he doesn't have as much time to dedicate to it. Sawyer has been away at college all semester but he got home last week for winter break.

Of all the Bennett kids, Sawyer is the most unlike the others with his thick-rimmed glasses and pressed button-down shirts. I heard Wells tell Jason once that his passions swing toward the conservation side of the business rather than in actual cowboying. He's also the first in the family to ever go to college.

"Thanks, Mom," Wells shouts, then says to me, "You ready? Let's ride first, and we can have some lemonade after."

I nod. "Okay."

Jason doesn't bat an eye as I move to follow Wells toward the barn that sits about a hundred yards away from the main house. He just keeps hurling that damn football through the tire over and over again, punishing himself for the mistake he made last night. I wish there was something I could do to fix it, but I think it's something he needs to work through on his own because not even Wells is having any luck.

Instead, I focus on readying myself to get on a horse, falling into step beside Wells with a swirling mix of eagerness and trepidation stammering in my chest. Inside the barn, he leads me to a stall where a beautiful golden horse with a white mane stands tall, and not for the first time I'm struck by how *big* horses are. "This," Wells says, "is Champ. He's going to be yours today."

"Champ," I recite as I watch the horse greet Wells with an

affectionate sniff over the top of the stall door. "Is he friendly?"

Wells smirks. "You think I'd put you on one that's not?"

I shrug. "For all I know, this is your way of getting rid of me forever."

His smirk slips as he fastens his gaze on me. "Why would I want to get rid of you?"

"I'm not exactly sure you like me, Wells," I say honestly. We may have developed a bit of a truce over the last few months, but I still think he'd rather I wasn't around so much. Sometimes I feel like I'm encroaching on his and Jason's "guy time," but when I've brought it up to Jason, he assures me I'm not.

"I do," Wells counters, looking back at Champ with a stormy expression. But it's there and gone in a flash. "I'm sorry if I've made you feel that way, but I like you just fine."

"Oh," I say, feeling a little bamboozled. "Okay."

His gaze moves past me to the barn door. "We'll get Champ out of the barn and I'll show you how to saddle him. You can just watch for now—today's lesson will be getting you comfortable *in* the saddle."

I nod, hiding my surprise that today sounds like only the first lesson in what might be many more. I thought I would maybe ride around the pasture, and that would be it.

He opens the door to the stall and slips a halter on Champ before leading him out. I follow behind, captivated by the way his muscles move and glide with each step. It's not until Wells is loosely wrapping the lead around a post outside of the barn that I ask, "Is he a workhorse?"

Wells flashes a smile. "He was a racehorse—one of the best Texas has ever seen."

"But not anymore?"

He shakes his head as he picks up a brush and gently glides it over Champ's hide. "No, he retired just before his tenth birthday. He was sent to a sanctuary in Tennessee, but they shut down, so he ended up here about five years ago. Brooks wanted to keep him—he's a good horse, and he helps us work some of the others."

My eyes snag on his long mane. "He won't be too fast with me, will he?"

Another smile tugs at Wells's mouth. "No. I promise he'll be gentle." He finishes brushing Champ's beautiful golden back. "In the spirit of the lesson: I brushed him to make sure his coat is free from any dirt from his ride yesterday when Kasey took him out into the pasture. We want to make sure the saddle isn't uncomfortable for him now." I nod, intent on absorbing everything. "This"—he holds up what looks like a folded blanket—"is a saddle pad. It eases the strain from the saddle." He lays it over Champ's back, the blue fabric fraying along the edges from use.

"Does the saddle hurt him?" I ask.

"No," Wells answers. "Not if you put it on right." I watch as he straightens the pad until it rests evenly over Champ's spine, just behind his shoulders. And then he hoists the saddle up and over, positioning it over the pad. He walks me through fastening all of the straps and belts that hold the saddle in place, and then he picks up a small pile of leather straps. "This is the bridle. It goes over his face."

My brows bunch together. "What does that do?"

"It's what the reins connect to. It's how you communicate with the horse while you're riding. When you make subtle commands through the reins, the horse will feel it with this and know to adjust."

I try to imagine what it would be like to be communicated with through some bizarre leather face mask. "It doesn't hurt?"

He shakes his head. "Not if you know what you're doing."

"Promise?"

Wells looks at me for a long moment. And then he dips his head once. "I promise, Layla. You're not going to hurt him, I'll make sure of it."

It eases my mind enough that, as soon as Champ is ready and inside of the closest corral, I don't hesitate to climb up into his saddle. Wells gives me a boost, shooting me a small smirk as he looks at the Converse I'm wearing. "You're going to ruin these out here, you know. If you're going to learn to ride, you'll need some decent shitkickers."

I shrug. "They're all I have."

"Hm," he hums as he takes a step back. "Put your feet in the stirrups." He points at the wide loop that hangs alongside Champ's belly. I do as he instructs and reach for the reins to ready myself for whatever comes next. "Wait." He holds a hand up. "You don't need those."

I look down at the reins in my hands, at the contrast of the dark brown leather against my skin. They're so worn with use that they're softer than I expected. "I don't?"

"Nope," he confirms. His eyes trail across Champ's back, as if taking in the size of the animal he's just put me on. "The reins are only a part of how you communicate. A horse can feel a fly land on his back . . . he can feel everything that you feel. Every emotion, every fear. You want him to trust you just as much as you want to trust him, so you need to show him that you do." He looks up at me, eyes squinting in the sun beneath that dirty backward hat. "No reins."

"So what do I do?"

He smiles as he looks down at the dark boots on his feet. It's a different smile from any others I've seen from him—it lacks the usual cockiness that he wears so well. When his face turns back up toward the sun, it strikes me how handsome he is. "Trust him, sunshine."

I look down at Champ's long neck, at his bright mane that lifts lazily with the breeze, and feel something warm bloom through me. I can't explain it, but for as much as I was trying to get out of all of this only a few minutes ago, there's a sudden feeling of rightness that this is all. . . inevitable. I nod, my gaze flitting back to Wells, realizing how much I trust him with this. "Okay."

Wells gently takes the reins from my hands and clicks his tongue at Champ, and before I know it we're moving. Champ's shoulders shift beneath the front of the saddle as Wells leads us to the center of the corral. "Okay," he says quietly, a whisper of that smile still playing on his lips. He reaches to wrap the reins once around the saddle's pommel, and he glides his hand affectionately down the side of Champ's belly before taking a step back from us. "It's between you two now. Remember: he can feel what you're feeling. Trust him."

Champ must understand the invitation because as soon as the words leave Wells's mouth, he takes off. The lurch forward takes me by surprise and I nearly fold backward at the waist, but I quickly recover and somehow keep my panic at bay. Champ eases into a slow trot, making his way toward the edge of the corral before shifting to the left to move alongside it.

"Relax, Layla," Wells calls from where he stands. I sneak a look back at him and find his gaze sharp and focused. I take a deep breath and do what I can to lessen some of the tension in my back and legs, knowing that I need to stay calm for this to work.

Trust him.

I close my eyes, letting instinct take over as my body sinks into each step Champ takes. I realize I *do* trust him. I'm not scared. Even though it's my first time being on a horse, I know Wells is watching me. *I'm safe.*

Champ picks up speed, not quite running but moving quicker as he hugs the fence line of the corral. I open my eyes again to see that we're on the opposite end, effortlessly coasting along the perimeter.

I can't help but look over my shoulder at Wells, noting the obvious approval in his eyes. It fills me up like a balloon, and I laugh.

"Something funny?" he calls out, the corners of his mouth rising higher.

"Not at all," I say. In the span of only a few seconds, I feel like I understand the Bennetts better, why they do this: there's a high in the inevitable submission . . . in trusting the horse. And it makes me wonder if it's a similar feeling to earn their trust back.

The crunch of tires on the gravel driveway pulls me from the thought, and I look to find a black pickup truck moving up the long drive toward the house—Brooks's truck. I watch as he parks next to Jason's Mustang before opening his door and jumping out. Brooks is tall and muscular, the oldest and biggest of all the Bennett brothers. He wears a black T-shirt over dark jeans and black boots, a cowboy hat riding low over his brows. I can only see the bottom half of his face, but I swear he looks this way.

The passenger door opens too, and a small woman with

curly blonde hair steps down in white cowboy boots with bright red and pink flowers on them. They're *cute*—I could definitely be persuaded to wear shitkickers if they make them like that. She opens the back door and reaches in before pulling out a small child.

He looks to be only three or four, though his little body is nearly half the length of his mom's. Brooks comes around from the other side with a car seat hanging from his hand, another boy of about six or seven at his side. It's clear this is his family, though I had no idea he had one. I know he lives in his own house on the property—the biggest one aside from the main house—but I always assumed he lived in it alone.

Wells holds a hand up in greeting, and Brooks lifts his free hand back. Before Brooks can stop him, the oldest child kicks off into a sprint right toward us. "Uncle Wells!" he hollers, his feet furiously pounding against the scattered grass.

Wells chuckles out a warm and buoyant sound, jumping over the corral's fence line and kneeling just as the boy barrels into his arms. He stands back to his full height with the boy tucked in his grip, straddling his waist from the side. "Hey, Liam," he says, his expression full of a deep affection that catches me off guard. His eyes flash back to me, checking to make sure I'm still okay.

"Who's that?" Liam asks, pointing a blue-markered finger my way.

Wells smiles wider. "That's Layla. She's my friend," he says. And it feels like a lightning strike to the chest, how easily he claims it.

"Nice to meet you, Liam," I say, grinning like a lunatic, I'm sure. The dynamics of the Bennett family intrigue me; I've never seen a family so big and full of life.

Liam's returning smile is small and shy, and he wiggles until Wells plants him back on the ground.

"Sorry about that!" the woman calls out as she approaches from the drive.

"No worries," Wells replies. "Catch anything good?"

The woman laughs, shaking her head. "You know how these boys are . . . *way* too loud for us to have any real chance of coming back with a fish." She turns to look at me, her expression curious. "Hi," she says over the distance, though Champ has naturally moved us closer to them, his interest piqued at the new arrivals. "I'm Melody, Brooks's wife." Though she seems outgoing and friendly, there's a shadow in her expression.

I wave a hand up awkwardly. "I'm Layla, Jason's girlfriend."

"Ah." Melody nods as all three of us look in Jason's direction. Liam's made his way over to him and has somehow stolen the football. Jason chases him, no humor on his face. "Everything okay with him?" she asks, unfazed by Jason's frustration.

Wells shrugs. "We had a bad game last night."

Liam pretends like he's going to bolt to the left toward a tree, and just as Jason's body moves that way he shifts to the right and squeals with joy. Jason's anger looks more forced now, like he's trying to hold on to it with everything he has. But it's clear he's fighting a smile. He recovers the fake-out and sprints to Liam, finally catching him and throwing him over his shoulder with a wide grin.

"Well," Melody says, "looks like the Liam Effect is working." She turns her attention back toward me. "I'm going to go save Jason, but it was nice to meet you!"

"I like your boots!" I say before it's too late.

She looks down at them, at the embroidered flowers stitched right into the leather. "Thanks, I made them myself."

"Wow," I let out. "They're beautiful."

She gives me a shining smile, then turns and heads for the main house. Wells shifts backward in his boots before shaking his head and climbing back over the fence and into the corral.

I almost forgot I was still on a horse.

"Ready?" he asks, looking up at me earnestly. He seems looser, like his nephew unraveled some of the tension in his shoulders. I sense Jason approaching, knowing he's also just had some of his anger unraveled, but I don't look in his direction. Instead, I focus on Wells, nodding. "Okay, I want you to stand up in the stirrups and swing your right leg over here, and I'll help you down."

"Okay," I say as I shift my weight to my feet, careful not to squeeze against Champ's belly. He shifts his weight and for a moment I'm scared he's going to bolt, but he doesn't. I do as Wells instructed and swing my leg over, immediately feeling Wells's hands fasten to my waist, warm fingers splayed against my lower ribs.

He lets go of me as soon as my shoes hit the earth and shifts his focus to retrieving the reins back off the pommel. I look at Jason, who *definitely* seems lighter. "How was it?" he asks.

I give him a small smile. "It was . . . really good, actually." I turn back to Wells. "Thank you. I already can't wait to do it again."

The look he shoots back is pure delight, and for the second time today, I'm surprised by his easy joy.

CHAPTER FIFTEEN

NOW

It's about a four-hour drive to Fort Worth from Saddlebrook Falls, and I'm squeezed in the middle of Kasey's two-door bench seat between him and Wells for the whole thing. Not that I mind—at least I get to spend the next thirty-or-so hours out of the confines of my bedroom.

Mom was *beyond* pissed when I returned home with her dusty Mercedes the other day, demanding to know where I'd gone and who I was with. It was almost as if she'd forgotten everything I'd been through in the last week and a half, thrusting us both through space and time until I was fourteen all over again and my life was hers to commandeer.

Needless to say, she didn't take kindly to my blatant disregard for her questions as I disappeared into my room, shutting the door hard behind me. I couldn't help the tears that rolled down my cheeks as I tucked myself back into bed, wondering how my life had turned into such a nightmare. But then thoughts of Stardust grazing in the pasture flitted to the forefront and I let myself become immersed in the frenzy of thoughts surrounding Wells and all that he'd done for her—all that he'd done because of *me*.

It was never a secret that Wells and I didn't have the easiest friendship. Our dynamic consisted of quiet negotiation and semi-forced compromises as it related to Jason and the space I took up in his life after we started dating. I, of course, always wanted more of it—more of *him*—and Wells didn't want to lose his best friend to me. We shared an eagerness to find a way that we could both be the Most Important Person in his life, especially after learning that working against each other only made things worse for everyone.

The only ultimatum Jason ever gave me was after a particularly petty spout of my whining about Wells in the early days of our relationship, when I felt like the too-cool and reckless best friend of the boy I liked was out to get me. Jason was undoubtedly the glue that held us all together, and without him I'm not sure any of it would have stuck.

But somewhere inside of all that, Wells was quietly working to protect something important to me. Not that horses weren't important to *him*—his family's entire livelihood revolved around their dedication to them. But something tells me Wells wouldn't have been so eager to give Stardust the freedom he did if not for that evening so long ago.

Now, as I sit so close to him, I can smell the wintergreen gum he's chewing, and I sink into the moment. It was a sheer stroke of luck that Mom had just left for the grocery store when Kasey pulled his truck up to the house, a silver horse trailer in tow. I hadn't told her about the rodeo—I knew she'd raise hell about it. So I wrote her a quick note on the back of an envelope and left it for her to find on the kitchen island before throwing my old cheer duffle over my shoulder and beelining it out the door.

For the stretch of road between Fairfield and Richland, I find myself imagining that I'm in some sort of alternate universe, one where Jason didn't die. One where he never existed in the first place. I know I'm dissociating, but for nearly thirty minutes I feel . . . content. And *man* if it isn't a relief.

We get into Fort Worth around ten, and Kasey finds a strip mall with a big enough parking lot to safely park his rig. "You guys hungry?" he asks as he expertly backs the trailer alongside the far edge of the lot.

"We should probably eat something," Wells answers, eyes bouncing to me. He's wearing an olive-green pearl snap button-down and dark jeans, his black cowboy hat resting neatly in his lap. Apparently, rodeos call for dressing up. "Not sure we'll have another chance."

Kasey shifts the truck into park and nods toward the other side of the lot, reaching for his own hat from where it's tucked between the dash and windshield. "There's a Waffle House," he says. "I could eat some waffles."

Both of them look at me like I'm the deciding factor in all this. "Sounds good." I shrug.

Inside, Kasey and Wells order the All-Star Special (Wells asks for the pecan waffle, and Kasey opts for chocolate chip) and I ask for the bacon, egg, and cheese hashbrown bowl. For another small stretch of time as we quietly sip our coffee—or, in my case, orange juice—life feels normal again. But as if on a timer, Jason's face floods my mind and I remember why all of this is anything *but* normal, and I start to feel a bubbling panic in my gut at being here.

"You okay?" Wells asks from where he sits next to me,

pulling me out of my spiraling thoughts as Kasey pretends to watch something out the window.

I nod. "Yeah, I just . . ." My heart fumbles as I work to figure out what to say.

But he seems to understand, because he nods and looks down at the table. "Let yourself feel it as it comes," he murmurs, so gently and carefully that the corners of my eyes begin to burn. Luckily I'm saved by the waitress who brings us our food, and we all quietly dig in.

We make it to Dickies Arena just before noon, and Kasey parks the trailer in a dirt lot that holds hundreds of others. I hop out of the truck behind Wells and look around at all of the people who are here to compete—the only rodeo I've ever been to was the small circuit at the county fair Jason took me to five years ago, and it was *nothing* like this.

There are horses everywhere, and at their sides are cowboys who look like they know how to rope and ride—and not just for sport. Even in December, they have sun-kissed faces from days spent beneath the wide-open Texas sky, and the dirt on their boots is proof of the hard work they put themselves through. My gaze snags on Wells and Kasey as they lead Kasey's horse, Ghost, out of the trailer, and I'm suddenly struck by the realization that they're *real* cowboys, too.

Wells's eyes catch mine, and for the first time since I've been home—since everything's changed—I see that spark in his gaze, like a burst of lightning, the same one that was there at the last rodeo I watched him compete in. I can't help the small smile that grows, a whisper of something good that I'm desperate to cling to.

I'm about to ask when his event starts but three girls cut between us from the front of the truck, their attention wholly focused on the guys. "Kasey!" one of them shrieks, a beautiful Black girl with long braids that drape across the back of her plum tank top. She throws her arms around his neck and her tan cowboy hat knocks against his, sliding back across her head and almost falling off.

Kasey lets out a huff from the impact, lips curving into a smile as he reaches up to press her hat back down. "Madison, always good to see you." He pulls back to look at her. "How's Jeremy?"

Madison shrugs. "He's still out for at least another six months, but he's working through PT, trying to keep his head up."

Kasey nods, his dark blue shirt wrinkling as he folds his arms across his chest. "Good. It's been a few weeks since I talked to him. I'll give him a call soon."

Madison smiles. "He'd like that."

Kasey turns to Wells. "You remember my brother?"

"Yeah, of course, how could I not?" She reaches to hug Wells, who leans into her embrace.

"Hello," he says, eyes catching mine before dropping to the ground.

"Good to see you," Madison says, and turns to her friends. "This is Riley and Nicole . . . I'm mentoring them this season."

Kasey whistles. "You ladies must be good if you have Maddie here overseeing your training."

Riley, a tall girl with freckled skin and auburn hair, flashes a wide smile. "Who better to learn from than the best?" Madison playfully shoves her on the shoulder.

"You riding today?" Kasey asks Riley.

She nods. "Our event is up soon. We're headed to get our horses."

"Good luck." Kasey grins.

Riley makes a point to let her gaze linger on his arms before looking back up at him. "Maybe we'll see you after?"

He gives her a small shrug and a devilish grin. "Maybe."

Madison rolls her eyes. "And that's our cue. Good luck out there, guys." She leads Riley and Nicole toward another trailer, and Kasey gives Wells a shit-eating grin. "Fucking barrel racers," he laughs, slapping an open palm against Wells's shoulder before moving to the end of the trailer to unload his horse.

Wells shakes his head. "You okay?"

I'm surprised by the question. Sure, those girls didn't notice me standing here next to Kasey's truck, but I don't mind. It's actually nice to be around people who don't know me and couldn't give two shits about the emotional turmoil I'm going through. "Definitely." I nod, then gesture toward the other cowboys meandering around parked trucks, some leading horses deeper into the arena. "So . . . how does all of this work?"

Wells's brow furrows. "The rodeo?"

"Yeah," I say. "Like, how do you know when it's your turn?"

Wells leans back against the side of the trailer, hooking his thumbs in the front pocket of his jeans. He lifts a single, brown boot to prop up against the metal trim. "There was a draw three days ago for certain events, including saddle-bronc riding. It's what determines which horse each rider is paired with and what order we go."

"Luck of the draw," I say.

He dips his head down, the corner of his mouth twitching. "Literally."

I consider this as Kasey leads Ghost out of the trailer. "Why did Kasey bring his own horse if they assigned you to one here?"

Wells turns to look at his brother. "He's also competing in the calf roping event, and he can use his own horse for that one. Ghost's his favorite."

My eyes widen. "Calf roping? Like, baby cows?" Wells huffs out a low chuckle and nods. I glare at him. "Does it hurt them?"

His amused expression falters. "It shouldn't. The goal isn't to hurt any of the animals here, just like it isn't the goal to hurt any out in a pasture or on a cattle drive. It's to showcase the everyday skills needed in cowboying."

I nod, squinting at the big arena in front of us. There's a hustle and bustle here that feels a lot more structured and formal than the last rodeo I saw Wells compete in—but that was an amateur circuit at the fairgrounds. *This* feels much more official. Many of the competitors here are a little older than the strictly early twenty-somethings at Foxborough, and they wear their best pearl snaps, bolo ties, and Kerry Kelley spurs.

"What's your draw?" I ask Wells.

"Third," he says.

"I'll be cheering for you."

His eyes come alive. "I'll try to give you something to cheer for."

And he does.

CHAPTER SIXTEEN

THEN

The Mustangs make it all the way to the state championship, and the town is bursting with excitement.

June Danvers paints the front windows of her café bright red and attempts to outline a fierce Mustang with a white window marker, but it comes out looking more like a soft pony with wings.

Gus Romano gives the team free pizza for an entire week, keeping the celebration alive each night as the boys demolish his inventory, forcing him to pull the plug on the whole thing only four nights in.

Mayor Moore hosts a pep rally right in the middle of the town square. The bridge club decorates the (newly constructed) gazebo with red and white streamers and the marching band plays somewhat sloppy renditions of "Sweet Caroline" and "Eye of the Tiger" as sweet old Maeve Meadows twirls giant mounds of red cotton candy onto white paper cones from a machine that looks like it came out of a 1980s catalog.

Jason, of course, is thrilled with all of it. "Isn't this fucking amazing?" he yells over the noise, tipsy from the vodka Ethan snuck into his punch. His tongue has turned so red it matches the letterman jacket he wears casually over a pair of nice jeans. He's loose, high on dopamine or endorphins or whatever it is that oozes when over a hundred people are fawning about your very existence.

He nearly trips over his own feet as he sways to the swelling crescendo of the band, and I can't help the laugh that spills out of me. Because he's right—this *is* fucking amazing. "Be careful," I warn, winding my arm through his to steer him toward a half-empty plastic table, adorned with a centerpiece bouquet of red balloons. Wells has been sitting there idly all night, looking increasingly impatient with the festivities.

Jason sinks into the seat next to him and slaps him on the shoulder. "Dude, isn't this fucking amazing?"

Wells frowns at him before arching a brow at me.

I shrug, knowing that he also sees the plastic cup Jason clutches tightly in his hand. Wells rolls his eyes. "Really, Jay? Right in the middle of everybody?"

Jason looks confused. "What do you mean?"

Wells shakes his head and crosses his arms over his chest, one booted foot tapping anxiously on the ground. "I think I'm going to head home soon," he suddenly declares. "Do you think your parents could take you and Layla home later?"

This has Jason's face twisting into frustration. "What the hell, Bennett? Why can't you just enjoy the limelight for fucking once in your life?"

My heart sinks at the idea he might leave early. Jason clearly can't drive, and I've never been alone with him and his parents before.

Wells scoffs. "You think I care about any of these people?" he asks. "You think I really give two shits about the people who give absolutely *zero* shits about my family?"

Jason's face falls. "Wells . . . we're going to state. Of *course* they care about you."

"Oh, they care about me now that I'm on their precious winning football team?" He glares at Jason, and my heart thumps hard in my chest. I sit in the chair on the other side of Wells, the cold plastic a shock to my bare thighs where my cheer skirt doesn't reach, and brace for the argument I know is coming. Wells has little patience for Jason when he drinks, which, to be fair, is valid. When Jason drinks, he becomes . . . someone else, someone I don't even like sometimes. But Wells is more wound up than normal, which is saying a lot. And he's right—people have treated his family poorly for as long as I can remember.

"Hey," I say quietly to Wells, and they both look my way. "Are you okay?"

He takes a deep breath, his brown eyes murky with distrust. "I just . . . I think I should go home." Something over my shoulder catches his attention, and his eyes widen in surprise. "Fucking dammit," he mutters before shooting out of his chair and marching past me with a wild look on his face.

"Oh hey, Wellsy boy," a familiar voice croons, and I turn around to find Rhett stalking toward our table. He's dripping in cockiness, his dark cowboy hat riding low enough on his brow that it mostly hides his smug gray eyes as he appraises his younger brother. "I was hoping to find you here."

"What are you doing?" Wells asks, voice low and urgent as

he steps into Rhett's personal space. Eddie and Martha Brown eye them suspiciously from the table next to us, and my stomach flips with nerves.

"Who me?" Rhett counters, his face a mask of innocence. "I thought the whole town was invited to this little shindig. Why *wouldn't* I be here to support my youngest brother?" His eyes sweep the scene before landing expressly on the gazebo in the distance as more and more people crane their necks to see. "Huh, that gazebo looks a little different. Did they rebuild it or something?"

"Rhett, what the fuck?" Wells asks, shoving Rhett in the chest. "Quit trying to start shit."

Rhett's expression shifts from bland amusement to anger in half a second, and he shoves Wells back. "What? Afraid we'll give them all something *new* to talk about?"

"All right, all right," Sheriff Joe calls out, winding himself through the growing crowd. Jason must realize this is turning more serious because he rises from his chair and moves to stand behind Wells. I stand too, but my feet are rooted into the ground as I watch Sheriff Joe lock his gaze onto Rhett. "Mr. Bennett," he says loudly over the low murmuring around us. "Always a pleasure."

"Mr. Bennett is my father," Rhett replies a bit haughtily.

"Oh yes, I know your father well."

It seems to be the wrong thing to say, because Rhett's eyes smolder as his lips press firmly together.

"Rhett, chill out," Wells tries, his own expression slipping into one resembling fear.

"Is there a problem here?" Mayor Moore steps up from somewhere to the right, eyes bouncing back and forth between the sheriff and Rhett.

"That's what I'm trying to figure out," Sheriff Joe says. "It looked like Rhett and Wells were on the verge of a physical altercation."

"I'm here to support my brother, not *fight* him," Rhett spits out, face flushed. "But I forgot how hard it is to exist in this god-forsaken town without somebody worried about what the Bennetts are doing."

"Rhett," Well snaps, his tone near pleading.

"Dad." Jason gives his father a pointed look.

Mayor Moore looks from Rhett to Jason to the sheriff before settling his gaze back on Rhett. "Look, son, we don't want any trouble, and I don't think you do either. You're welcome to stay and support our Mustangs, but if I catch a whiff of any funny business, there will be hell to pay. Am I clear?"

Rhett's expression is so thunderous it sends a shiver of nerves through me. "Crystal."

Mayor Moore nods. "Come on, Joe," he says. "Let's go find our wives—I think I saw them head toward Eleanor's flower booth."

The sheriff finally tears his eyes away from Rhett, like a dog called back to his master.

"**What the hell is the matter with you?**" Wells whisper-yells as we all make our way to the parking lot in front of Sandy's Sundries. It's one of the bigger parking lots in the vicinity of town square and where Wells parked his truck a couple of hours ago when we arrived. "Mom told you to cool it with your town escapades."

Rhett scoffs, his shoulders high and tense beneath his black leather jacket. "You think I'm going to listen to that horse shit? These people have been mocking our name since before either of us was born, Wells." He pulls a small silver flask out of the front of it and twists off the cap to take a swig.

Next to me, Jason sighs. He seems to have sobered up in the last few minutes, the loose and bubbly joy flattening. He's lucky no one smelled the vodka on him. "I don't know why it always has to be like this," he says to no one in particular.

Rhett wheels around, pinning him with a look so heated I'm nervous he might be about to hit him. "I expect you wouldn't, golden boy," he spits out.

"Jesus," Wells mutters, reaching a hand up to press gently against the center of Rhett's chest in a move that's half support, half warning. After a beat, his eyes soften. "Did you ride here?"

Rhett takes in a deep breath through his nose before letting it out in one swift *whoosh*. "Yeah." He tilts his head toward the smaller lot that's reserved for June's Cafe, where his motorcycle sits waiting.

Wells tosses his keys toward me, and I'm surprised when I catch them. "Follow me in the truck?"

"I can drive, you moron," Rhett argues, but Wells shakes his head once, firmly.

"No, especially not after that shit you just pulled. I'm not about to watch you get taken away in handcuffs."

Rhett rolls his eyes, but hands over his keys. Wells looks at me again. "Follow me?" he asks again.

"I don't—" I begin to say, unsure of how to break it to him that I'm still too young to drive.

"She doesn't have her license," Jason says for me. And it

feels like both a relief and a curse, because while the last thing I want is to be responsible for Wells's truck, I hate the way his face falls at the realization.

"Oh," Rhett says, delighted. "You like 'em younger, Jay?" He wags his eyebrows knowingly, and my face grows hot with embarrassment.

This time, Wells isn't soft about shoving Rhett's shoulder. "Don't be a dick," he says, turning back to me. "Sorry, Layla."

I shrug. "It's okay."

Wells looks at the ground as he thinks. "Okay, new plan. We're all going in my truck," he says, reaching a hand out to take his keys back from me just as Rhett reaches to take *his* from Wells. Wells clutches Rhett's close to his chest and throws his shoulder between them, his other hand clumsily wrapping around my wrist in pursuit of his own. This misstep clearly shocks him somehow, because he's quickly pulling his hand back, keys in tow, as if I've burned him.

Jason sighs again, like he might be regretting his bootleg liquor and subsequent inability to be a second driver. *Good*, I think. It's not that his drinking bothers me, it's that he's a little selfish about it, not thinking it through beyond the simple want for a drink. This isn't the first time he's put Wells—or me—in a pickle. I know he couldn't have anticipated Rhett's little parade of rebellion right through the heart of his father's pep rally, but was spiked punch really necessary in the first place?

We all silently serpentine through the café's parking lot and climb into Wells's truck. Rhett takes the front seat, and after Jason shuts his door opposite of me in the back, he holds his hand out between us, face up. Despite my flare of annoyance, I take it. I know he's looking for comfort to salve over his remorse, and I suppose as his girlfriend it's my duty to offer that to him.

But I'm still irritated.

The lack of any conversation extends the whole way to my house, and when Wells pulls up alongside the curb, the front porch light kicks on. Mom must have been watching for me. "Thanks," I say, catching Wells's eyes in the rearview mirror. He nods once before his eyes flick elsewhere, and I turn to look at Jason. "I'll see you Monday?"

His mouth ticks up with an effort to smile, but it's flat and doesn't reach his eyes. I wonder if I've done something wrong in all this. "Yeah," he finally says after a beat that feels too long. "Definitely."

Inside my mother *is* waiting for me, but she's not alone. "You're home early," she remarks, brushing Annie's wet hair from where she sits on the floor in front of Mom's legs.

I shrug, unsure what to say. "Yeah, I guess so."

"Who was that in the truck?" she asks with a tone that feels casual but I know isn't. I'm not surprised that, even in the middle of brushing my sister's hair, she was still able to not only hear the truck pull up, but inspect its occupants. "Rhett."

Her eyes jump to mine. "The wild one?"

"Aren't they all?" I volley back. It's meant to be sarcastic, but she misunderstands.

Her smile curves high. "Touché."

I try to tamp down the guilt as I climb the stairs to my room.

CHAPTER SEVENTEEN

NOW

We both stare at the bed in the middle of the motel room, arms crossed over our chests as we contemplate our next move.

After Wells got his hands on the first-place prize money for bronc-riding (dropping Kasey down to second place by mere points), we all celebrated at the Dirty Cowboys Saloon in downtown Fort Worth. Wells and Kasey snuck pints of beer to my side of the booth, careful not to let any of the staff catch on, and I was thankful for it. I hoped it might take the edge off the adrenaline that flared through me as I watched Wells take The Hammer, a beautiful Buckskin male, all the way through a tumultuous eight-second ride.

I'd seen Wells on a bucking horse a hundred times by now, but this time, something was different. Wells exuded his usual steady confidence, only there was something else beneath the surface of today's ride: a hunger for the violence of it all.

Even from a hundred feet away in the stands, I could feel

the wave of aggression that rolled through him. It wasn't directed at the horse—he was beyond careful in all the ways his body moved with The Hammer. But there was an unusual thrill in the performance, an outpouring of pent-up emotion that needed release. It'd taken a long time to dislodge the fear in my throat that I was about to watch Wells get seriously hurt— but he'd prevailed.

And dammit if the relief didn't twist something inside of me.

After getting our fill of fried chicken and cornbread—and plenty of Coors Lights from the tap—the three of us made our way to the small motel where Kasey had booked rooms for him and Wells weeks ago. They'd tried to pay for a third room for me, but the man behind the desk in the lobby said they were booked solid because of the rodeo. My buzz had me waving it off, assuring them both that it was fine. It was just for one night.

But I never considered the sleeping arrangement.

"I can sleep on the floor," Wells mutters softly, his gaze intently focused on the decorative pillows that rest against the simple pine headboard.

I turn to look at him, noting the dirt on his jeans and where it's collected along the nape of his neck, mixed with the sweat from his exertion earlier. It's clear his back is stiff, and I noticed at the bar he's leaning a little more on his right leg. He'd never admit it, but he's sore from getting thrown around on that ride today, and the floor is the *last* place he should be sleeping.

"No," I say softly, the lightness from the beer still coursing through my veins. "It's okay. I'll take the floor."

His dark gaze tracks over my face. "I'm not letting you sleep on the floor, Layla. Don't be stubborn. Take the bed."

I roll my eyes. "*You're* the stubborn one," I argue, holding his stare as I square my shoulders. Twenty seconds must pass before I let out a sigh. "We can both take the bed, can't we?" Even as the words roll off my tongue, my heart begins to pound. It's impulsive. Reckless. A terrible idea.

Surprise splashes across his face. "We *could* . . ." He looks at the bed again, at the ordinary green comforter and white pillows. "Are you sure?" he asks, sliding those deep brown eyes back to me.

I shrug, feigning nonchalance. The regret is instantaneous, but now that the idea of sharing this bed is out there, I have to commit so I don't risk making things more awkward. "I don't see why not."

He nods, the movement a little overexaggerated. I wonder if he's just as buzzed as I am. I almost hope he is. It would ease the magnitude of what sleeping next to each other would mean.

I'm his best friend's girl, after all.

Well, at least . . . I was.

That identity feels uncomfortable now after learning about the existence of Emma, and as I watch Wells fold himself to sit on the foot of the bed, leaning over to pull off his boots, I can't help the question from spilling out. "How are you?"

He looks up at me, one dusty and well-worn boot clutched tightly in his hands, and something dark passes over his face. "What do you mean?"

"You know what I mean," I say with more confidence than I feel. "How *are* you?"

He drops the boot to the floor between his feet, leaving the other on as he studies the sand-colored carpet. Seconds pass, and I'm just about to walk back the question when he finally speaks. "I miss him so damn much." It comes out in a whisper, and his face twists into a riot of emotions before he swipes a hand over his face, scrubbing at his jaw with the backs of his knuckles. "Today was a good distraction," he continues, and I think he's avoiding my gaze, looking everywhere but at me. "But . . . with you here . . ."

It's like he's thrown a bucket of ice-cold water directly in my face. "You *invited* me—" I start to say, but he quickly interjects.

"No, no—god, that's not what I meant, Layla. Fuck." His eyes are wide as they finally find mine. "I'm glad you came," he insists. "I wanted you to, I promise. It's just . . ." He doesn't finish his sentence. But he doesn't need to.

"A reminder," I say.

His eyes drop to my mouth before falling to my feet. "Yeah."

I can't say that the clarification makes me feel any better, but at least it's honest. And honesty is something I'm a bit needy for right now, after learning that so much of what I thought was my life has been a lie. Wells isn't normally so open about his feelings, so I appreciate that he's trying now. "I'm sorry," I whisper.

He shakes his head. "You shouldn't be. None of this is your fault. It's just . . . *so* fucked up." He digs the heel of his hands into his eyes, as if to block any emotion from surfacing. When he drops his hands to his lap and looks at me again, the skin around his eyes is red and his ears are flushed. "His mom came to the ranch yesterday."

My mouth falls open. "She did?" He nods, and I suddenly feel stuck, like I'm seven years old again, playing freeze tag on the playground. It takes at least four steadying breaths to find my voice, but it still comes out shaky. "What did she want?"

The question sounds harsher than intended as it rolls off my tongue. As if Georgia Moore has no right to step foot on Bennett Ranch, despite her son having been there so much it was practically his second home. But for as much as Jason and Wells orbited around each other, Jason's parents kept a safe distance from the Bennetts, just like everyone else did. I'm not even sure Wells has ever stepped inside Jason's house. I've been there for dinner countless times, but I'd never once seen Wells there.

Whatever she went to the ranch for, it must have been bad because there's no mistaking the emotion in Wells's eyes now. They shine even under the dull light of the motel room ceiling. "She wanted to know about . . . the last few weeks, before the accident. What he was like."

Suddenly my chest is like a vise and I can't breathe. My legs give out from the weight of new stabs of pain pressing through me. I sink to the floor, curling in on myself, and force more deep breaths into my lungs. "Did the police find more evidence?" I finally find the bravery to ask, though I'm not confident I can handle the answer.

Wells watches me carefully but stays seated at the foot of the bed. "No. Not that I know of anyway."

I force my eyes to meet his. "Then why?"

"She wanted to know about Emma," he says simply. "I guess she wants to understand what might have happened. If Jason was . . . depressed." The word hangs in the room around us, stealing all the air before he continues. "I think she was looking for answers."

The night Jason died, there was only one set of tire marks

on the road where his Mustang careened off the cliff, and his blood alcohol level was twice the legal limit. If there was another car involved, there's no proof of it. Everything seems to point to two possibilities: Jason was too impaired to drive and lost control, or he purposefully went off that cliff.

"What did you tell her?" I ask, my voice so small I hardly recognize it.

Wells straightens and finds a spot on the wall across the room to focus on. "I told her what I told you at the cabin, that I figured out he was cheating on you. That I confronted him. That I . . . that I punched him."

I suck in a breath, closing my eyes against a wave of nausea.

"There's more, Layla," he says evenly, looking like the weight of the world is on his shoulders. Like of all the personal hells he could be in, this is the worst one.

"What?" I croak out. "What do you mean there's more?"

He sighs. "His mom told me that she talked to Coach Jones. Apparently, the day before the accident, Coach told Jason that he was going to start Stevens in the next game. Jason had a few missteps in some of our recent games, and he was starting to slip at practice too."

"Oh my god," I whisper. Football was *everything* to Jason, more than school or his family or even Wells and me, and we all knew it. Learning that his coach intended to pull him from the starting lineup would have been . . . *devastating*. "Do you think . . . ?" I start, but promptly stop. I can't force the words out.

"What?" he asks.

I close my eyes and say the words as I hug my knees close to my chest. "Do you think he was distracted by Emma? Was that why he was messing up?"

Wells's eyes soften. "I don't know, Layla." He finally pulls his second boot off, giving himself time to think through an answer. "It's possible he was feeling the mounting pressure of not being the golden boy on campus like he was at home, which could have driven him to be impulsive. I'm not sure which one led to the other. Either way, he was struggling more than any of us realized."

My skin burns hot and I almost can't stand it anymore—combing through the web of Jason's lies is ruining me.

"But he was also really fucking careless," he adds, and it's tinged with his own hurt. His own frustration.

I nod through the burn of tears, knowing if I try to speak this dam will break. My mind spins with a flurry of thoughts. One of the things I keep replaying in my head is one of my last phone conversations with Jason. It was after Thanksgiving, when I *thought* he'd just returned to campus from his trip home with Wells. He'd been noticeably vague as we recounted our holiday weekends, but was still curious how I spent mine with Chantal. It would have been a perfect chance for him to let me in on his side of things, to share anything that might have been bothering him.

I'd handed over six years of my life to him like a sacrificial lamb. And in return he fed me lies and ultimately turned to someone else for comfort during a real time of need. I'd bet money that Emma knew he was being pulled to the bench—it's not something he would've been able to hold in and process on his own. And while I always knew the pressure was often unbearable for him, I thought I was giving him the support and encouragement he craved to round it all out. I thought *I* was on the front lines of his needs.

It's a whole new feeling of betrayal to think even *that* might have been for show. An orchestrated slow dance in a room that was crumbling all around us.

I try to fight against it, but the tears break through like the crash of a wave against the shore. It's only moments before I'm sobbing into my palms, fighting for air.

Wells is there in an instant, lowering himself to the floor next to me and pulling me into a warm and sturdy embrace. He doesn't say a word, but he doesn't need to.

He knows.

You're the love of my life, sweetheart, Jason had murmured the last time I saw him, the end-of-summer bonfire in front of us growing high enough to lick the ink-black sky.

I can't wait to call you Layla Moore.

The phantoms of our younger selves haunt me, and I can do nothing but succumb to this grief that's become so wide I'm not sure how to fill it with anything but pain and anger. Pain for the girl I once was: resilient and unwounded. Anger for Jason who set fire to it all, and then went and fucking *died* so I'd have no one to anchor any of it to.

I'll never leave you.

My skin turns to ice, and I'm not sure if the heat of fury dissipates or if the room is just cold, but I shiver against Wells's chest. He runs his wide hands up and down my arms, creating a friction that feels like a relief. "I hate seeing you cry, sunshine," he says low, the vibration of his voice against my cheek. "I don't have the stomach for it."

I huff out a small laugh as I pull back and wipe my eyes. "I'm sorry . . . There's just still so much love in my heart for Jay, for who he wanted to be, and it hurts. I believed in him, you know? I don't know the right words for how I feel. Shame, maybe? Regret?"

He tucks an errant strand of hair behind my ear. "It's okay to be mad at him, just like it's okay to still love him. He was your *first* love . . . there will always be something special that exists between you and his memory. But he wasn't perfect. Not even close. And you deserved a hell of a lot more from him."

I suck in a deep breath, keeping my eyes trained on the cotton of his T-shirt, now spotted with my tears.

"Look at me," he says softly, lifting my chin with his fingers until our eyes catch and his dark gaze burns into my skin. "This isn't the end of your story, Layla. You'll fall in love again, and it'll be with someone who can love you back and give you everything you need. You won't have to earn it."

The words crack me right down the middle. Can it really be so simple? "Thanks, Wells," I say. A long sigh spills out of me. "Look at us . . . on the ground again."

The corner of his mouth quirks. "You have a thing for crying on the floor," he says plainly.

"Name a better place," I quip.

He shakes his head. "Can't." And then his smile flattens, and his gaze tracks across my face. "Come on, let's get you to bed."

Later as I fall asleep, the room is dark and cold, but the warmth of Wells's body next to mine cocoons me. And just as I tip into the edge of empty black nothingness, I hear him say it in the midst of his own dreams.

Sunshine.

CHAPTER EIGHTEEN

THEN

In the week before the state championship, Coach West adds morning practice alongside our normal afternoon ones. There's a swell of collective nerves that knocks many girls off their game, and Coach grows increasingly annoyed by it.

"Do you understand how important this moment is for us?" she screeches from the middle of the gymnasium as we all circle around her. "It's not the time for sloppiness. It's not the time for weakness. We are Mustangs, and we will be *perfect* on that field, do you hear me?"

"Yes ma'am!" we all cry out from dry mouths, parched from running suicides after another flyer fell too early during our halftime rehearsal.

As is tradition, the state championship game is being hosted at AT&T Stadium in Arlington, and the cheer squads from both sides will be given the field for a twelve-minute performance. It's the opportunity of a lifetime to perform for an NFL stadium full of people—it should feel like a dream come true.

Except I can hardly focus on any of it because I'm too wrapped up in Jason's nerves.

The boys are playing against the Mayfield Matadors for the title—the one team we've lost to this season in the game Jason threw an interception that led to them winning. Both of our teams currently stand with 13-1 records, and while it helps to know that we beat the one team they lost to, it doesn't erase the fact that they've already beaten us.

Jason made numerous mistakes in that game, most of them small enough that they shouldn't have been such a big deal. But combined, the result was crushing. We lost our winning streak, and Jason blamed himself. Knowing the Mustangs have to face them again in the biggest game of the season hasn't been easy, but in the last couple of days, Jason's degree of tailspin has gone from bad to catastrophic.

On Wednesday he showed up to school late after running drills in his backyard all morning and earned himself a detention from his history teacher. Mr. Laurier might be the only person in this school brave enough to pull something like that against our star quarterback during the most important week of the year. Luckily, Jay was able to talk the principal into dropping it so that he could make it to practice on time.

On Thursday afternoon the cheer team worked on painting signs in the bleachers while the football team practiced, and I couldn't help but notice that Jason was having a hard time throwing the ball to his target. The whole team was growing more and more impatient with him, and by the end of practice, Coach Andersen looked ready to send him back to the bench.

"He won't *really* bench you, right?" I asked him later as we walked to his car.

He shook his head. "Nah, it's too late to pull a change in the starting lineup now." But for as convincing as he made the sentiment sound, the expression on his face was a dead give-away to the anxiety he was feeling.

Wells clapped him on the shoulder with one of his rare toothy smiles. "Jaybird, you have to relax, okay? You've got this in the bag. You're the fucking star of the school, and you're going to show *everybody* just how talented you are when we get on that field on Saturday."

Jason blew out a long breath, his shoulders relaxing for the first time all week. "I just get so nervous," he admitted.

Wells shrugged. "We all do. But you're Jason fucking Moore—that trophy is as good as ours." He gave Jason one last nudge on the arm before pivoting to his truck parked two rows over.

The words seemed to settle the tension blazing through him in the moment, but by Friday morning he was wound so tight again I thought he might spontaneously combust.

It was the day before the big game, and the cheerleaders planned Operation Mustang Pride to show our support for each player. I was assigned to bring a treat for Jason (naturally) and spent the evening before baking my grandma's famous chocolate chip cookies with Annie.

When I found him at his locker, I presented him with the Tupperware, the brightest smile I could muster on my lips. "Surprise!"

Jason turned to look at me, confusion rippling across his face as his eyes dropped to the burgundy plastic lid. "Oh," he said through a sigh. "What's this?"

"Cookies," I explained, already feeling like it might have been a mistake.

He looked . . . unsure of what to do with them. I was about to explain that they were for eating, but then he spoke again. "Thanks, babe. I just . . . I'm not sure sweets are a good idea right now. At least not until we get past the game. But save some for me?" he asked, pressing a quick kiss to my cheek and turning to walk away, leaving me standing alone with a quart-sized container of homemade cookies.

It wasn't his explanation that had my nerves spiking—it was the complete disregard for the time spent on something thoughtful for him. It was the first time in our four months of dating that I felt . . . dismissed. But I knew he was feeling the pressure of it all, that he was caught up in the web of his own mind, so I did my best to shake the whole thing off.

But it still stung.

The disappointment still nips at me now as I sit cross-legged on the hardwood floor of Hoa's living room, surrounded by a handful of other cheerleaders who are here for a sleepover. I watch as they pass around the container and eagerly pull out pieces for themselves.

"These are *so* good," Lizzie exclaims as she licks a smear of chocolate off her fingertips.

David nods enthusiastically. "You've been holding out on us, freshy. You're gonna give Luna at the bakery a run for her money."

I smile. "It's my grandma's recipe."

"Jason didn't want them?" Regan asks, eyes narrowed as

she realizes what it means that *we* are eating the cookies. I'd sent her a picture of them fresh out of the oven, so she knew what —who—they were meant for.

I shrug, trying to keep the smile on my face. "I guess not."

"Wait, these were for him?" Lizzie mumbles around another bite.

"Well, yeah, but . . ."

"Uh oh," David interjects. "Trouble in paradise?"

"No," I huff out defensively. "He just didn't want a sugar overload the night before the big game. Something *I* didn't think of." I don't know why I'm so eager to take the blame for our fumble this morning, but the thought of everyone knowing how much that rejection stung seems unnecessary.

"What's it like, anyway?" Lizzie asks curiously. "Being with him, I mean."

"With Jason?"

She throws me a pointed look. "Duh."

David chuckles. I feel the eyes of all the girls around me as I reach into the Tupperware for another broken piece of a cookie. "It's . . . really nice," I say.

Hoa laughs from where she's lying on the sofa, taking up the whole thing to herself while the rest of us are scattered on the floor. I guess when it's your house you can do what you want. "Dating Jason Moore is *nice*?" She looks at me for a long beat, and when I don't say anything, she says, "It's just that I've heard some of the shit he pulled with Michelle."

"Yeah, didn't he leave her stranded at prom?" Lizzie asks.

David's watching me thoughtfully, and I feel my cheeks burn.

"Yes," Heidi, another senior, confirms. "Brock and I had to

give her a ride home because Jason left in the middle of the dance."

"Why?" Lizzie asks.

Heidi shrugs. "Found something better," she says. "Or . . . some*one*."

"Jason's not like that," I burst out. Heidi just smirks. She's always been distant toward me and I assumed it was because I was a freshman, but now I realize it's because she's friends with Michelle.

"So." Hoa sits up on the couch. "Have you given him *your* cookie?"

Regan chokes from the corner.

"What?" I ask, confused.

"You know," Hoa continues. "Have you guys had sex yet?"

"O-Oh . . ." I stammer. I don't need a mirror to know the flush has spread to my neck. I look down at the piece of cookie in my hand, wishing I could transport myself out of this situation.

Hoa snorts. "I'll take that as a no."

"They've only been together for like . . . four months," Regan chimes in.

"Yeah, but Jason's a junior. He's more . . . experienced." Hoa tilts her head, as if appraising me. "Do you *want* to have sex with him?"

"Um, yeah," I say. "I mean . . . eventually."

She throws her hands up. "Don't do it if you aren't ready. Fuck boys, stay strong on your boundaries. I'm just saying, it's *Jason Moore*, you know?"

"Don't be surprised if he ditches you at prom," Heidi jests. "Michelle *was* putting out—look what happened to her."

"Okay guys," David groans. "Can we please talk about

something other than Jason Moore's sex life? I think I'm going to puke." I throw him a look of gratitude as he pops another cookie in his mouth.

The truth is, I know Jason expects our relationship to bloom into something more . . . *physical* . . . soon. This football season has been enough of a distraction, but after the game tomorrow, the season will be over, and he keeps reminding me he'll have a lot more time to focus on me. It's not that I don't want that kind of attention from him—it thrills me to know he wants me in that way. But I'm not sure I feel ready to take that step yet.

"What do you think the guys are all doing right now?" Lizzie asks as she pops open a diet soda.

"Probably stuffing their faces with carbs," Heidi says. Gus Romano gave the football team access to Mustang's Pizza for the evening, closing the doors to the public to allow the boys the room to spread out and eat while the coaches run through plays.

"I wonder if they like my lemon-frosted bundt cake," Hoa ponders.

David turns to look at her. "You baked them a cake?"

"I baked *Wells* a cake," she corrects. "And he said he'd bring it to their dinner tonight."

"Wells Bennett is so hot," Lizzie remarks.

A smile grows on Hoa's face. "It's like, *criminal* how hot he is."

"I heard he hooked up with Stassi under the bleachers during lunch before she started dating Ethan," Heidi announces.

"Scandalous." David rolls his eyes.

"Stassi said she saw you at his house," Heidi says, looking at me.

And just like that, everyone's attention is back on me. "Uh, yeah. She was there the first time Jason brought me."

"The *first* time?" Hoa asks. "So you've been there more than once?"

I shrug. "Yeah, a few times."

"What's it like?" Lizzie asks. "Is Bud Bennett as mean and crazy as everyone says?"

I don't think I like where this conversation is going, but something tells me David isn't going to save me from this one. He's looking at me with just as much interest as the rest of them. "I haven't seen him," I say. "But his mom is nice."

"Do you think Rhett really burned down the gazebo?" Regan asks, and I fight the urge to throw a cookie at her for participating in this nonsense.

Heidi huffs out a laugh. "Definitely. I heard it from Nosy Maeve herself."

"Yeah, but do you think Maeve *really* knows?" Lizzie asks.

Heidi shrugs. "Maeve knows everything."

I think about the way Rhett called out the new gazebo at the pep rally, like he was goading Wells about it. I have to admit, it does seem likely he had something to do with the fire.

"I'm tired," I announce as I gather the Tupperware and lid from the floor. "I think I'm going to try and get some sleep."

Regan scrambles to her feet from the corner. "Me too!" she says, following me to the den where makeshift beds have been constructed by Hoa's mom. I hear David say he's going to head out—Hoa's mom would never let a boy sleep over, cheerleader or not—and hope I didn't just prematurely end the night for everyone else. But it doesn't feel right to sit there and listen as everyone speculates about Wells's family—not when he's starting to feel like a real friend.

Regan and I tuck ourselves into the two farthest beds. "Night," I say, and turn onto my side to face the wall, feeling a desperate need for a little space to wind down before I can fall asleep.

"Night, Layla," Regan says back, shuffling under her blankets next to me.

It doesn't take long to realize the Mayfield Matadors will be taking home the state championship today.

From the first snap, Jason's obvious nerves take hold, and he doesn't even complete a pass until the end of the first quarter after Mayfield has already scored twice. The second quarter goes by in a blur, and by the end of the third, we're down 28-0.

I silently pray that Coach Andersen pulls Jason from the game to give the boys a chance to catch up, but I know how wrecked Jason would be to lose the opportunity to turn things around himself. Still, it's excruciating to watch him botch play after play as the pressure of it all wreaks havoc over what we all know is natural talent.

The entire town showed up for this with the help of the spirit committee's work organizing rideshares. Old man Gerry is even dressed up in the Mustang mascot after reasoning that he'd likely die before he ever had another opportunity. Our side of the stadium is quiet while the other side roars with applause, and the effect is devastating.

"This is a bust, huh?" David murmurs from where he's

positioned next to me. The squad hasn't given up cheering, but it's getting harder and harder to find anything to cheer for.

"We could still turn it around," I say.

He looks at me. "Layla, they're ahead by four touchdowns and there's less than eight minutes on the clock. There's no way we're coming back from this." He settles his focus back to the field, and my shoulders slump. "At this point, all we can do is hope we get *something* on the scoreboard so it's not a complete shutout."

I know he's right, and my heart utterly breaks for Jason.

I'd called him this morning from the bus and when he answered, I could hear the excitement from the rest of the team in the background. "Hey, babe!" he'd greeted with a cheerful tone, immediately quelling any fears I had about his state of mind. "How was your sleepover?"

"It was good." I smiled. "How was your night?"

"Good," he echoed. "We watched a bunch of tapes on Mayfield and ran through plays—I feel ready, Layla. I feel fucking ready for this."

"That's so great, Jay! I know you and the team are going to kill it," I encouraged. "And I'm happy I get to be there to watch from the sidelines."

"My beautiful girl," he said, and I could hear that he was smiling, too. "I'm lucky to have you."

Unfortunately, it looks like Jason's confidence and positive energy wasn't enough to sustain him on the field. Thankfully, the Matadors aren't able to get to the end zone with their next possession. But when the Mustang's defense hustles back to the sidelines and the offense moves out, I notice number 24 stays on the bench.

Coach took Jay out of the game.

Noah King, the second-string senior that Jason replaced in the first game of the season, runs out into the middle of the field with the rest of the offense, and it's the first time in a long time that the stands behind me come to life. "Fuck," I mutter under my breath, gaze focused on Jason.

Hoa shouts out a cue for us to start a cheer choreography, and I'm forced to rip my eyes away from him. By the time we finish and get back into line, the team has started the first play and Noah is looking for a receiver downfield. He sees an opportunity and throws the ball to Brad, who catches it and runs to gain twenty yards. The crowd behind me is instantly screaming, but all I can do is watch as Jason shifts and bends his head low.

Noah drives the Mustangs all the way to the end zone for a touchdown, eliminating the opportunity for the Matadors to completely shut us out. But the immediate turnaround in momentum seems to ignite some frustration in the crowd.

"You should have put Noah in two hours ago, Coach!" someone in the first few rows shouts.

"Jason lost us the game!" someone else hollers, and I can feel the blood drain from my face.

Jason turns around from the bench to look at the crowd, and I know he heard it. I know he's going to beat himself up over this for a long time, and I wish there was something I could do to help.

The Mustangs' defense runs out for the Matadors' drive, and Wells takes a seat next to his best friend. He tentatively puts an arm up around his shoulders, but Jason flinches and twists out of the touch before getting up and walking away from him.

I'm frozen in place as the rest of the game plays out. When the final whistle blows to signal the end of the fourth quarter, the blue and gold swarm of fans from the other side of the stadium seems to become a single living being, moving in a rippling tandem. Their players and coaching staff rush the field as blue confetti suddenly bursts from the sky, and all I can do is *stand* here.

"Come on, Layla," Regan says, gently wrapping her hand around my arm. I didn't even notice her approach. "It's over."

But I can't move. I scan our sidelines for Jason, knowing that I need to do something to help him process, but I don't see him. In the sea of red and white jerseys, he's nowhere to be found.

"Layla?" Regan gently asks, but I still don't turn to her. I'm suddenly lightheaded. Black spots dance along the edges of my vision, and I feel weak, like I might . . .

"Jason," I whisper as a vicious dizziness sets in. And then everything goes black.

THE FIRST THING THAT INFILTRATES THE HAZE OF unconsciousness is a low murmuring of voices.

She must not have eaten enough . . .

. . . upset about the game . . .

. . . you see him run?

The second thought that hits me like a bucket of ice-cold water is that I'm being carried; two strong arms hold my body tight, curling around my shoulder blades and behind my knees. My head rocks gently against a hard-padded shoulder, and somehow I *know* I'm safe.

. . . happened?

She just dropped right to the ground . . .
. . . call a medic . . .
We stop moving, and the murmuring around me ebbs and flows in rhythm with the pounding in my head.
What the hell happened?
. . . careful with her neck . . .
. . . a medic, goddammit!

WHEN I FINALLY OPEN MY EYES, I'M NEARLY BLINDED by the bright white fluorescent bulb that buzzes from the ceiling above. It takes a handful of breaths to realize I'm lying in a bed, in an unfamiliar room. There's a dull ache in my right temple, but I brace through the pain and turn my head to look around the room. To my left, there's nothing but a white wall with an attached counter adorned with a small silver sink. To my right, I find my mother sitting in a chair with her head in her hands.

"Mom?" I'm surprised by how weak and tired my voice sounds. It sends a chill up my spine—something really bad must have happened.

Her head whips up, eyes wide and full of worry. "Layla," she says through the woosh of an exhale. And then she stands to pivot toward the door, her purse thumping against the metal door jamb. "Nurse?"

"What happened?" I ask.

She turns back to me, moving to the side of the bed as she grabs my hand in hers. "Oh, my sweet bug. You fainted on the field."

My brows pull together and a surge of pain immediately pulses through my forehead. "I did?"

She nods. "Coach West thinks you may have been locking your knees." I groan—it's something Coach has drilled into us about standing in formation, always warning us to keep our knees soft to avoid issues like this.

A nurse in dark green scrubs and a bouncy ponytail bounds into the room. She pumps sanitizer into her hands and rubs them together as she moves to effortlessly cut in front of my mother. I wonder if she realizes that in any other circumstance, Mom would have had her ass for something like that. "Hi, Layla," she says brightly. "My name is Yawen. Do you know why you're here today?" I can only shake my head and watch as her deep brown eyes hold mine.

Her smile parts to reveal beautiful white teeth. "That's okay," she reassures. "An ambulance brought you here from the football game you were cheering at. It seems you lost consciousness and may have hit your head when you fell. Can you tell me what day it is?"

My gaze drops to the white letters embroidered on her scrub top: TEXAS HEALTH MEMORIAL HOSPITAL. "Saturday," I answer.

"Good. Do you know the date?"

"December thirteenth."

"And what team were you cheering for today?"

"The Saddlebrook Falls Mustangs—my high school team."

Her eyes crinkle as her cool hand caresses my arm. "Great job, Layla. I'm going to send a doctor in to give you a more thorough exam, but we're hopeful you can get out of here this evening, okay?"

I nod and look back at my mom as Yawen leaves, noting the pinch of worry between her brows. "Is Jason okay?" I ask.

"What do you mean?"

"When he carried me off the field," I say. "Did he look okay?"

Mom gives me a peculiar look before smoothing it away. "Yes, honey. Jason was fine—just worried about you, of course."

I nod, settling back against my pillow. "Good."

CHAPTER NINETEEN

NOW

I wake with a start, my body jerking and stomach sinking as the sensation of *falling* washes over me. But I'm not falling—I'm in bed, tucked between a heavy comforter and foreign bedsheets that smell like Irish Spring and faint hints of cigarette smoke.

On impulse, one eye snaps blearily open, and I take in the room around me: an ugly taupe wall with a vintage portrait of a rodeo arena hanging in a wooden frame, an old pine desk and chair set, and a brown leather belt with a bright silver buckle hanging over the back of it.

Wells.

With a second jolt, the memories of last night come crashing back and I quickly turn to look behind me, searching for the six-foot-three source of comfort whose tenderness surprised me last night. But the bed is empty on the other side, the comforter pulled up and tucked underneath the pillow. I reach a hand out to find it cold.

Turning back to the other side of the room, I eye the large metal door that opens into the parking lot, as if it might clue me in on where he is. Thankfully I don't have to wonder long, because just as I'm peeling myself out of bed, that metal door pushes open, and Wells walks in with a bakery bag and a carrier of coffees. "Hey," he says when he spots me, his mouth curving into a soft smile.

"Hey," I say.

"How'd you sleep?"

I shrug. "Really good, I think. I hardly remember even going to bed."

He arches a brow. "Well, it was kind of a tough night."

"Yeah . . . thanks for that," I say, and I mean it. "I cried all over your shirt."

His smile widens. "Trust me, I'm not offended."

I laugh, shifting on my feet.

And then I realize I'm not wearing any pants.

My head falls as I visually assess this new and confounding update, and I see that I'm wearing an oversized Wild Coyote T-shirt that falls mid-thigh. Then I remember.

"Here," he says, picking up my bag. "I'll bring this to the bathroom."

I throw a hand out to stop him, pressing an open palm softly against his chest. "No, it's okay," I say. "I don't think I have the energy for my usual before-bed routine. I'm just going to sleep in my clothes."

Wells's brow dips as he lowers the bag back to the ground. "You can't go to sleep in jeans, Layla." But the look I give him must be convincing enough, because he relents. "Here then." He pulls out a dark green shirt from the top of his bag and holds it out for me. "Wear this."

"Oh," I say now. "I, um . . ." I look back up at Wells and find his focus caught on my legs. "I'm sorry," I rush out as I dart away, face burning with embarrassment. "I need to give this back to you!" I march toward the bathroom, praying last night's clothes are still where I left them. I shut the door behind me with a soft thud.

"I'm just going to run a coffee to Kasey," I hear him call from the hallway. "I'll be back in five."

"Sounds good!" I shout, doing what I can to get *out* of this shirt. The back of my hand hits the wall with a loud *whack*, and I hear boots shuffle closer.

"You okay?" Wells asks. His voice echoes like it's mere inches away from the door.

"Fine! Just . . . hit my hand." I tug on my *own* shirt from where I found it folded and stacked on my jeans.

"Okay," he says. And then I hear him move away as he leaves the room. The metal door clicks shut, and I let out an exhale.

By the time he comes back in a few minutes later, I'm seated at the foot of the freshly made bed with my bag ready and waiting at my feet. "Hi," I say cheerfully, doing my best to stamp away any awkwardness that sharing a bed or wearing his shirt might produce. I take a long sip of the coffee he left behind for me and try not to make a face at how bitter it is.

His eyes bounce to mine, warm and yet . . . distant. "Hey. Kasey's ready to go whenever we are."

"I'm ready." I nod.

"Okay." He scoops up my bag and I stand to follow him out the door, but just as he reaches for the handle he pauses, turning around.

"I think you should find someone to be there for you," he says quickly, as if he's rehearsed the line all morning.

"What?" I ask, my brain working to assign meaning to the words.

"I think," he repeats, slower and a bit more carefully, "you should find someone to be there for you. And I'm not sure that it should be me."

I frown. "Why not?"

"Because I . . ." He pauses, eyes falling to the ground. "I don't think I can be what you need. Not right now, at least. And I-I need some time. To deal with everything."

Just like that, the wounds reopen.

"I—I'm sorry," I stammer, confused. "I shouldn't have gotten so emotional—"

"No," he interjects, eyes rising back to mine. A morning sunbeam lights up half his face, and I notice how tired he still looks, and I'm worried it's partly because of me. "I'm not saying that, Layla. But I think we're both going through a lot right now, and it's all really heavy and *hard* and . . . I think it might be better if we processed it apart."

I nod, hoping he can't see the shame burning bright beneath my skin. "Yeah, okay," I agree, even though the sentiment carves new fissures in my already fractured heart. "I totally get what you mean."

The lie rolls easily off my tongue, and it must be all he needs to hear because he turns back toward the door and pushes through it.

Outside, the sun blinds me, and I throw a hand up to shield my eyes as I follow behind Wells. Kasey is already waiting by the truck, sipping on his own coffee. "Morning," he says. "Ready to hit the road?"

All I can do is nod as I climb silently into the truck.

THE DRIVE HOME IS MOSTLY QUIET, WHICH ONLY increases the anxiety churning in my chest. Wells keeps his focus out the passenger window, careful to keep his legs and arms from touching me despite being smashed together on the bench seat. Thankfully Kasey doesn't seem to notice anything amiss; he's been singing along with old Hank Jr. songs since we left Dallas.

Now that we're approaching Saddlebrook Falls, my nerves have also ignited thoughts of my mother. I know she's probably furious with me for skipping town and leaving her with nothing but a note—she'll be even more outraged when she finds out that I spent a night in a motel with Wells and Kasey.

But when Kasey pulls up to the curb, I realize I might be having another stroke of luck—Mom's car isn't in the driveway.

Wells makes quick work of unbuckling himself and jumping out on the sidewalk, giving me room to scoot myself out. Just as I reach the edge of the seat, I turn around to look at Kasey. "Thanks for letting me tag along."

He smiles. "Anytime, Layla. You're always welcome."

Warmth blooms in my chest at the unexpected words. I smile back at him, then jump down onto the cement where Wells waits with his hand on the frame of the door. His face is unreadable, and my chest cools at the reminder that I might *not* be welcome anywhere with *him*, as Kasey suggested.

I grind the toe of my shoes into the ground and say, "So—"

just as he says, "Thank you—" But it makes him smile as he nods for me to go first.

"So," I start again, "for what it's worth, I appreciate that you invited me to go with you guys. And I'm sorry I got emotional last night, but I really did love getting out of town for a bit."

His earthy brown eyes stay focused on mine. "It's no problem. Thank you for coming along, and don't apologize for your emotions, Layla. There's nothing to be sorry for."

I want to press him further, ask him why he's pushing me away then. But I know it's probably not ideal with Kasey waiting patiently in the truck. So instead, I just say, "I'll see you around," and head up the front walkway, back to reality. I hear the car door shut behind me, and though I don't look back, I still notice that Kasey doesn't pull away until I get through the door.

Just as I turn around to peek from a safe vantage point behind the curtain, I'm startled to see Annie's already there with her face glued to the window.

"Was that a horse trailer?" she asks curiously.

I clutch my chest as a laugh spills out of me. "Yeah."

"Was there a horse inside?"

I smile at her. "Yep, a big beautiful white horse named Ghost."

"Wow," she breathes.

"Maybe I'll take you to see him someday," I say, though I regret the words as soon as they come out. Mom would never let Annie come with me to Bennett Ranch, and I'm not even sure *I'm* welcome there after what happened this morning.

"Mom's pretty upset with you," Annie confides, looking up at me with worry splashed across her face.

I keep an easy smile plastered to mine—I don't want Annie to worry about Mom and me. "I figured she would be," I say. "I'm sorry I left like that, but I needed a little break from my own mind. And being here sometimes doesn't help, you know?"

She considers this. "Where did you go?"

"To Dallas. For a rodeo."

Her eyes light up like the Christmas tree behind her. "A *rodeo*?"

"Yes," I laugh again. "Some of my friends are cowboys who work on a ranch. That was their horse."

You should find someone to be there for you.

And I'm not sure that it should be me.

"Since when are you allowed to be home alone anyway?" I ask, forcing all thoughts regarding Wells Bennett from my mind.

"Since I turned thirteen," she declares with pride. "But only for, like, an hour at a time. Mom just went to the grocery store."

"Ah, I see," I say. "So on a scale from one to ten, how mad is she?"

She tilts her head, as if appraising me. "Well, you didn't say where you were going. And you weren't home for church this morning."

I nod. "So, like an eleven?"

"At *least* a fourteen."

"Shit," I say, wagging my eyebrows. "That sounds pretty serious."

She giggles, and we hear a car pull up outside. "She's home," Annie says ominously. I know she worries about Mom and me getting along—she's witnessed more strife between us than I'd ever want. But as much as I want Annie to respect her parents and enjoy her relationship with them, I also feel a quiet sense of pride at the opportunity to teach her to find her own voice. To uncover her own hopes and dreams for her life.

I'd hate for her to fall into the belief that who she marries will make or break her life's success, and I want her to know there's so much more out there than simply growing a family. She's at the age now when my mother started to drill those things into my head; I can only hope she finds a way to be more accepting of Annie.

I realize my sister is holding her breath as my mother walks in the door, eyes immediately landing on me. I lurch toward her to grab the grocery bags from her hand. "Here, let me help," I say.

Mom hands the bags off without argument as she studies my face. "Where were you?"

A quick glance at Annie shows her worried expression. "I was invited to a rodeo with some friends," I say. "And, to be honest, the distraction of it sounded really good." I silently beg her to let it go. "I'm sorry I didn't tell you ahead of time."

She nods. "What friends?"

My heart stutters because I know exactly where this would go if I gave her the truth, and I hate that I have to lie about Wells and Kasey. The Bennetts are good people—they don't deserve the level the distrust the rest of the town extends toward them. But my mother is hardly one to be agreeable, and Wells did ask for space after all.

"Regan," is what I settle on. "And David." I catch Annie's expression change in my periphery, but I keep my focus trained on the way Mom's face lights up.

"Oh, how are they doing? Gosh, I haven't seen either of them in a while."

"They're good," I say smoothly, eager to end this conversation. "Anyway, I'm sorry. It won't happen again. I'm . . . going to put these groceries away." I turn toward the kitchen.

"Thank you, bug," Mom says from behind me. And I let out a breath of gratitude.

CHAPTER TWENTY

THEN

Jason broke up with me on the Thursday before my sophomore year started.

He was driving me home from the closest mall, an hour's trek from two towns over, and as he slowed his Mustang to the blinking red lights at a railroad crossing, the words spilled out of him.

"I think I need to be alone for a while, Layla."

The unexpectedness of it was so unnerving that my first instinct was to laugh. But then when I looked at him and saw his haunted expression, I realized he'd been holding on to this decision for long enough that it was eating him alive. "What?" I asked, dumbfounded.

"I just . . . I really need to give this football season everything I have. It's going to be one of the most important seasons of my life."

It took Jason *months* to get over his team's loss last year.

He'd become a near recluse until spring break when Wells forced him to go on a boys-only camping trip somewhere on the coast. I don't know what happened on that trip, but when the boys came back Jason was lighter and so much like his normal self, I'd been thankful for it.

We ended the school year strong . . . or, so I thought. In April, he took me to his junior prom, and it was one of the most romantic nights of my life. He twirled me around the dance floor, never once complaining or trying to sneak away with his friends. He made me feel like the most beautiful girl in Texas, and it was then that I realized I loved him.

Over the summer, he went on three official visits to colleges that are courting him to play for their teams, and somewhere along the way, he admitted his anxiety has been at an all-time high again. The pressure to perform can claw into him so deep, and I know he's terrified of losing any opportunity that comes his way.

It doesn't help that his parents have also increased the expectations they're putting on him, as if all that matters right now is his ability to clinch a football scholarship. According to them, a scholarship will only be earned if he helps the Mustangs win state this year. And Jason believes his chance in the NFL is based on a school believing in him enough to offer him a full ride.

It's a mounting domino effect of pressure, and the crux of it all weighs on his coming senior season.

Still, though, the excuse of his anxiety nags at me. It might hold the weight of some of his truth, but I've been careful to temper my neediness over the last year, making sure I don't ever ask too much of him. I can't recall a time that I've *ever* whined about him choosing football over me, so how has it suddenly become a push and pull between the game he loves and the girl he *claims* to love?

I wish I could say the breakup doesn't wreck me, but it does. It consumes me the entire weekend before school starts, and the haze of it doesn't lift an inch.

I throw myself into the distraction of cheer tryouts, but I know even in that gym I'm a mess. My tumbling is sloppy, my flying stiff. It's enough that Coach West pulls me aside on Wednesday after I nearly kick another girl in the face mid-toss.

"Layla," she hisses, narrow eyes sharp. "What the hell's gotten into you? You're better than this." Her words both move me and destroy me. I may have made the varsity team last year, but Coach didn't give me much one-on-one attention. Her style is to lead through the senior captains, so most of us don't have a whole lot of interaction directly with her. I always assumed I flew under her radar as one of the youngest on the team, so for her to know me well enough to notice I'm off my game—it warms some of the cold numbness in my chest.

By the end of the week, there's a layer of exhaustion that's settled over the heartbreak. Coach gives us a similar speech as she did last year and my fate on this squad is at her mercy—I won't find out if I lost my place until Monday.

Regan finds me after Coach releases us. "You in for tonight?"

I stare at her blankly. "In for what?"

"Connor's party. According to David, he throws it every year."

"Oh," I say, shrugging. "I don't know . . . I'm not really in the mood, Ray."

"Come *on*," she insists, her expression softening. "What better way to get over a heartbreak than to throw yourself into some fun?"

She has a point, which is how, four hours later, I find myself in Connor's kitchen with a bottle of whiskey and a plastic cup half full of fruit punch.

Just like last year, the crowd is heavy, and the music is so loud I can't hear my own thoughts. But after finding the bottle of liquor, I figured it was as good a time as any to see what all the fuss is about. I lift the bottle to my lips and take a greedy gulp at the same time Connor walks into the kitchen.

The whiskey burns the entire way down my throat, eliciting a wet cough that makes Connor laugh as I try to chase it down with the fruit punch. "Woah there, cowgirl. You're not used to drinking the hard stuff, are you?"

My neck flushes hot from embarrassment, but I do my best to school my face into indifference. "So?"

He shrugs, a crooked smile climbing up the side of his face. "What's the occasion?"

I wipe the back of my hand across my lips. "What do you mean?"

He nods to the bottle. "The whiskey. You celebrating something?"

If you only knew. I'm unsure how to answer, so I shake my head and twist the cap back on the bottle.

Connor studies me for a moment before he looks around the party. "Jason here with you?"

Again, I shake my head. "No. We—" I break off. I can't seem to force myself to say it out loud.

But Connor must understand because he lets out a low "Oh. I'm sorry."

I shrug, twisting the cap back off the bottle so I can take another swig. He watches me with curiosity as I attempt another large gulp of the amber liquid—I don't cough this time, but my eyes still water from the inferno rushing down my throat. I look around the kitchen for Regan, but I don't see her anywhere.

"It's his loss, though," Connor says.

"Yeah?" I ask. "How so?"

Connor's eyes sweep down my body. "I mean," he says. "Look at you."

I'm sure Connor means well—he's not a bad guy. But my body bristles at his words and I take a step back to put some space between us. "Yeah, well, I guess it's not enough," I say with a small smile. I don't mean for it to come out like that; Jason said he wanted to focus on football and that it wasn't about me. But it feels good to let out a little kernel of truth, that I feel like I've somehow failed. "I'm going to go find Regan," I say, turning toward the living room with the bottle clutched in my hand.

The effects of the whiskey start to blur the edges of my vision, and I welcome the feeling as I move through the crowd of people, looking for Regan. I'm almost at the back door when I accidentally clip someone's shoulder.

"Oops, sorry!" I shout over the booming music.

Wells.

His eyes narrow as soon as he sees that it's me. "Layla?"

"In the flesh." I hold out both arms as if to prove to him it's me.

He spots the bottle in my hand. "What are you doing here?"

I drop my hands to my sides. "Trying to distract myself," I

say honestly. I haven't seen Wells since Jason and I broke up, but I know he knows about it. How could he not?

He rolls his lips and reaches for the bottle. "Maybe we should get you home," he tries.

I pull it away. "What? I don't want to go home, we just got here."

"We?"

I nod. "I came with Regan. Which reminds me . . ." I start toward the back door again.

Wells juts an arm out in front of me and anchors himself along the side of my body, dipping his mouth close to my ear. "Layla, how much have you had to drink?"

I turn to face him, noting the flecks of gold in the brown of his eyes from the nearby kitchen light. *Beautiful*, I think. "I don't know," I answer. "What does it matter?"

"Wells!" Connor shouts from the kitchen. "Glad you came through, my man. Want a beer?"

A thought suddenly occurs to me. "Is Jason here, too?" I ask shakily.

He shakes his head. "No . . . he was at the ranch earlier though. He's pretty messed up."

"About me or about football?" I ask, arching a brow.

Wells sighs, and I feel the cool wintergreen of his breath dance along my cheek. "I don't like this," he says, eyes dropping to the bottle.

I simply shrug and push past him, making my way out the door into the warm, sticky night air.

I finally spot Regan over by the pool with Lizzie, Erin, and Brad and make a beeline toward them. "There you are," Regan says when she sees me. She eyes the whiskey warily. "Where'd you get that?"

"Kitchen." I grin. "Want some?" I hold it out for her to take, but she shakes her head.

"I'll take it," Lizzie says, and I hand it to her, watching as she takes a drink from it like it's nothing. She hands it off to Erin who does the same.

"Brad's driving." Erin smirks as she hands it back to me, and I take another long pull.

"Who's driving *you*?" Lizzie zeros in on me, and then her eyes widen at something over my shoulder.

"Yeah, sunshine, who's driving you?"

I turn around to find Wells behind me, glaring at us. This time, I take a good look at him, cataloging the black T-shirt that stretches across his broad chest, the dark jeans adorned with a bright silver buckle, and the dirty brown boots on his feet. His usual Wild Coyote hat sits backward on his head, the backstrap resting just above his brow. His lips are pressed together tight, and he doesn't look the slightest bit amused. "I don't know," I say. "Don't people just usually end up staying the night?" I remember it was Jason's plan at Margot's last year.

His jaw rolls. "You are *not* sleeping here."

"Why do you care?" I ask before taking another swig of the whiskey. By now, my mouth is almost fully numb from the alcohol, so the liquor goes down easily.

"Jesus," he mutters, shifting on his feet. "Can you please put that down?"

"Why?"

"Because you've already had half the damn bottle!" he snaps.

I look down at the bottle in my hand and sure enough, the amber liquid only reaches the middle of the black label on the front. "Seriously, what does it matter, Wells? God knows you know what it's like to want to let loose."

"Oh, let loose?" He repeats in an incredulous tone. "Is that what you're doing?" I shrug again, and he huffs out a breath. "Look, I know you're going through some shit right now, but trust me when I say that numbing it out with alcohol will make it worse."

I stare at him blankly, not understanding why he's so hell-bent on ruining this for me. Doesn't he understand that my heart is shattered? Is it so wrong for me to enjoy the effects of some fucking whiskey?

"Hey, Wells!" Connor calls from across the yard, and Wells's jaw tightens with impatience. But he doesn't look away from me.

"Please just let me—"

He doesn't have an opportunity to finish his sentence because in the span of mere seconds, I've gone from irritated to viciously nauseous. I jackknife at the waist with a low groan, and before I realize what's happening, I'm puking in the bush next to me.

Regan gasps as Lizzie lets out a whiney "Ewwwww." But I can hardly get a breath down before I heave again.

"Oh shit, is she okay?" I hear Connor ask.

"I've got it," Wells mutters as he pulls my hair back with light fingers.

"Dude, she can't puke in my backyard."

"I said I've *got* it," Wells growls.

Connor sighs and walks away, mumbling something about getting the hose. "Shit," Regan says from behind me. "I'll text David, he's supposed to get here soon. I'll ask if he can take us home."

"How did you two get here?" Wells asks, voice heated with frustration.

"We walked from my house," Regan explains shyly. "It's only a few blocks away."

I wretch again, the vile liquid spilling out of my mouth. It burns just as much on the way up as it did on the way down, and I have to cough through the fire.

"I'll take her home," Wells announces, his fingers cool as they smooth along my temple. "Brad, can you go find some water for her, please?"

"On it," Brad replies.

"I'm sorry," I whimper. I never imagined the night ending with Wells hunched around me as I threw up in a hydrangea bush. I try to focus on individual leaves to stop the ground from spinning, but it only makes me dizzier. He doesn't respond, but his fingers continue to dance on my skin, and I give myself over to the relief it brings.

"Here," I hear Brad say a few minutes later. *Thank god*, he must have found water.

"Thanks," Wells says. "Okay Layla, can you make it out front to my truck?"

I nod and climb up to my feet, wiping my mouth with the back of my hand. Shame curls tightly in my throat—this is *so* embarrassing. Wells keeps his hand on my shoulder, a soft pressure encouraging me forward. I turn to Regan, who looks a little awestruck. "I'm sorry," I say again as a tear escapes down my cheek. I really hope I didn't ruin her night, too.

She shakes her head. "You have nothing to be sorry for. Just get some sleep, and I'll call you tomorrow, okay?"

"Okay," I agree.

WELLS'S TRUCK IS PARKED A COUPLE OF HOUSES down along the curb, and when we reach it, he straightens me so I'm facing him. He scans my face, and that heaviness washes over me again for putting him in this position.

"How's the stomach?" he asks tentatively, twisting the top off the bottle of water and handing it to me.

"Um." I take a long drink. "Not great, but I think I'm okay right now."

"Okay enough for you to make it through the drive to your house?"

I nod, and he pulls open the passenger-side door. I climb onto the worn seat and he reaches to buckle me in. "Why are you doing this?" I ask as he pulls the lap belt over my waist.

His gaze jumps to meet mine. "Doing what?"

"Helping me," I say.

His eyes bounce back and forth between mine, but he doesn't say anything in response. Instead, he pulls himself out of the truck and shuts the door between us.

Okay . . . so much for that.

When he gets in on his side, I keep my focus on a mailbox outside my window. It's wooden, carved in the shape of a bird, and it makes me wish I could fly away from here. That I could escape this night, escape this week and this town and everyone in it.

CONNOR LIVES ON THE OTHER SIDE OF TOWN FROM me, but Wells makes quick work of navigating us to my house.

It's ten o'clock, which means my mom and Barry have probably gone upstairs into their room for the night. Annie's bedtime is eight, so I'm hoping I can quietly sneak in without anybody noticing me.

This is exactly why I always say no to drinking: I know my mom will have my head if she finds out. And I don't blame her. I've had a few sips here and there out of curiosity, but not enough to ever feel anything. I still don't feel like I'm ready, and spending the last year hanging out with upperclassmen doesn't mean that feeling just goes away.

I already regret my actions tonight, but being rejected by Jason hurts in a way I've never felt before, and I don't know how else to dull that ache.

"How are you doing?" Wells asks quietly as he pulls the truck up along the front of my house, studying the dark windows in the front.

"I've been better," I say through a sigh. If only I could make the trees stop spinning around us.

Wells grunts, and it sounds like he's irritated. *I deserve it*, I think. *Look at the mess I'm making.* He pushes out of his door and rounds the hood to my side to let me out. I almost stumble as I climb down, but his warm hand steadies me, and I find myself leaning into his touch.

I'm surprised when he walks me all the way to my front door like that. "This is as far as I go," he says warily, releasing my arm.

I guess it probably makes him a little nervous to bring me home in a state like this. None of this is his fault. "I'm really sorry," I say again. When he finally looks at me, his familiar brown eyes are attentive. I have to squint one of mine closed to keep from seeing four of them.

"You're too good for this shit," he finally says back.

I huff out a laugh. "I don't know about that."

"I do."

I can only stare at him as the shock of his earnestness pulls a fresh wave of tears to the surface. "I just don't understand what I did wrong," I force out, my face twisting around a low sob.

Wells moves closer to me, determination slicing through his brow. "You didn't do anything wrong," he says firmly. "Trust me."

"Then why?" I ask, desperate for a *real* answer. "Why is it too much for him to be with me?"

Wells hesitates, jaw clenching tight as if he's holding something back. I'd give anything to know what it is. "You know what I think?" he finally asks.

"What?" I rub the pads of my fingers under my damp eyes.

He moves toward me again, and it's only now that I realize how close he's gotten. I watch his throat work around a swallow, and my eyes trail up his deep olive skin until I have to tip my head back. "I think you're way too fucking good for him anyway."

Something low and instinctual pulses deep inside me, like a beacon signaling danger. His dark eyes roam along my face, and I revel in the feeling of being seen so honestly, even if it all feels like too much. It's the kind of look that means something, and I don't know how to grapple with the fact that it's Wells on the other end of it.

"I think I should get inside," I whisper. My tongue feels thick against the roof of my mouth.

His eyes flare brightly before they dim, and he pulls his gaze away. "Okay." He gives a quick nod. "Drink another glass of water before you go to bed."

"Sure," I concede, though I'm not sure I feel like risking the noise.

He takes a deep breath before he says, "Take care of yourself, sunshine."

And then he walks back toward his truck.

CHAPTER TWENTY-ONE

NOW

It's a week until Christmas, and Mom has officially gone off the deep end with decorating the house. Annie is finally on winter break from school, so I lean into spending more and more time outside of my room to soak her in. Still, though, there are unexpected moments of grief and resentment that feel like a knife twisting inside of my chest, and it's often a narrow escape back to the safety of my room where I can sob into my pillow.

The mix of learning about Jason being pulled to the bench before he died and the quiet rejection from Wells to process it together only catapults me back into a dangerous headspace. The influx of Christmas around me feels like a cosmic joke; aside from the warmth I feel in my sister's smile, I can't find a single ounce of joy to sink into.

There's no denying that getting out of the house helps. Instead of covert escapades to the Bennetts' ranch, Annie and I spend the afternoons walking through town. On Wednesday morning Regan calls to say she's home from Florida State and wants to see me. I've gotten a number of texts from her since word about Jason's accident got out, but I haven't responded to any of them. What is there to say? *Yes, my boyfriend is dead, and I'm fucking devastated. But after his funeral, I found out he's been having an affair with a girl named Emma, and it's thrown a giant wrench in our memories. Oh, and it's possible his accident might not have been an accident, because things were going wrong with his "life plan" and he never learned how to deal with the hard shit.*

Yeah, *way* too much drama to lay on anybody in a text message.

Still, I'm happy to hear from her. We make plans to get together at Luna's Bakery, and the hug she gives me in the parking lot drives me right into the crying mess I'm always on the verge of. But it only makes her hug me harder.

After we manage to get ourselves inside to order a couple of mugs of tea and freshly baked gingerbread muffins, we sit in a small corner booth where I tell her *everything*. By the end, she looks at me like everyone's been looking at me since I threw up on Emma's boots at the Wild Coyote—alarmed and full of sorrow. "Wow," she gasps, clutching her chest. "I am *so* sorry, Layla. I don't even know what to say . . ."

"It's okay." I give her a half-hearted smile. "I'm just trying to process through all the layers, you know?"

It's okay to be mad at him, just like it's okay to still love him.

She nods, and I wonder if she can sense where my thoughts have turned because she asks, "Have you seen Wells?"

I force a small laugh, void of emotion. "Yeah."

"How is he?"

I shrug. "He's . . . he's dealing with a lot, too." It's not my place to bring up any of his issues with Jason or the fight they had right before Jason died. But it's another reminder of how much shit he has to navigate on his side of it all.

Regan shakes her head. "I honestly don't know how you're even here with me right now."

"I spent a week and a half crying alone in the dark," I admit. "At some point, the distraction of getting out felt more achievable than sobbing through another day."

She clicks her tongue. "You poor thing."

I think in the end it's the pity in her eyes that gets me, and I have to excuse myself from my half-eaten muffin and our attempt at this casual hangout. "Annie's home alone," I lie, "and I really should be getting back."

I stand abruptly, and Regan awkwardly follows suit. "Okay." She nods. "Sure, whatever you need." She reaches to hug me again, and when her arms squeeze tighter around me a tear spills out from the corner of my eye. "I'll be home for a couple of weeks—let's see each other again before we go back to school, okay?"

"Sure," I mumble into the shoulder of her brown jacket, and then I pull myself away and hurry out of the bakery without another look.

On Friday, Mom and Barry head into Houston for some Christmas shopping and Annie and I decide to go to June's Cafe for a late lunch before they get home. I can tell Annie is going stir-crazy with school being out. She texts with her friends all day long but says she's not interested in seeing them. I think she doesn't want me to feel abandoned, and I love her for it, but she deserves to enjoy her break. I silently hope that, by going out into town, she might run into some of them.

It's only a twenty-minute walk. The warm winter sun gets

lost behind incoming clouds along the way, and a cold breeze begins to whip between us. We duck inside the warm café, where the smell of fresh biscuits and June's special pot roast wraps around us. June's daughter, Olivia, greets us at the front podium and brings us to a table by the window.

"Hope this is okay," she says, and sets down two menus. I notice the worry in her expression as she looks at me, so I give her my best attempt at a smile.

"It's perfect," I answer as I sit in one of the old wooden chairs. "Thanks, Olivia."

"Anytime." She turns to walk away, but something stops her. "You know," she says carefully. "I just want to say I'm real sorry for everything you're going through, Layla. You and Jason's family have been in my heart since I heard the news, and my mom prays for you every night."

Annie looks back and forth between us, nervous that I might be triggered into another breakdown. But right now, I feel . . . okay. "I appreciate that, thank you."

Her mouth tips up in a bleak smile before she scuttles back to the podium. Olivia is a couple of years older than me and graduated in Jason's class, so she knew him well enough—though I wouldn't say she was *friends* with anyone in our circle. She was much more studious and focused than any of us were.

"You okay?" Annie asks over the top of her menu.

"Yeah," I say quickly, brushing it off. "She's just being kind."

Annie looks up at me, considering. "Jason really messed up when he cheated on you."

I can only stare at her, taken aback by the bluntness of her statement. "Yeah," I finally manage. "He did."

"Is it hard to pretend like you miss him?" She sounds genuinely curious.

"I *do* miss him, Annie," I insist. "Just because he was cheating on me doesn't mean that the love I felt for him disappeared."

She hums and looks back at her menu.

I fold my hands on the table. It's important she understands. For *anyone* to understand it, really, besides Wells. "Look, under normal circumstances, finding out someone you love is hurting you like that would be unbearable. It takes a lot of time and healing to come to terms with the fact that the relationship isn't what you thought it was. But in this case . . ." I look around before my gaze settles back on Annie. "Jay's dead. He's not here for me to yell at or to help me understand how any of this happened. And that's pretty shitty, too. Because I'm stuck in this place of loving him and grieving him but I'm also so goddamn *furious* at him. It's not that I'm pretending. I just don't know how to deal with such an impossible situation.

"And it's no secret that everyone in this town loved him. He was important to people . . . but he was also flawed. I guess sometimes people don't understand that."

Annie's blue eyes grow sharp. "You could make them understand."

I give her a sad smile. "I'm not sure that'd help anything. He's not here to defend himself. And even if he did make mistakes . . . were they bad enough to try to ruin the image everyone has of him?"

She shrugs. "Honestly, I think you're making yourself responsible for other people's feelings. I know he's not here to defend himself, but that doesn't mean he didn't wreck you. Who cares about everyone else—if you want to throw a tantrum, do it. The only feelings you should care about are your own."

My mouth falls open as her words hit me like a freight train. "Damn, Annie," I mutter through the shock. "Who are you and what did you do with my baby sister?"

She laughs. "I just don't want you to be burdened by all of this forever," she admits. "And I think it's okay for you to be a little selfish."

I shake my head in disbelief. I love her so damn much, but I've always been worried she'd grow up with my mother's perspective on life. Hearing her now, I realize she's a force of her own, and it thrills me. "Thanks, Annie," I say, reaching out to touch her arm. "You have no idea how much I needed that."

June comes by our table, her purple cat-eye glasses perched high on her nose and her curly red hair stacked atop her head. "Hey, Layla," she greets. "Hi, Annie. Just you two today?"

Annie nods. "Yes ma'am." June looks back at me, and I can tell by the way her eyes squint that she's about to say something about Jason.

"Do you have any specials tonight?" I rush to ask.

Her brows arch. "Oh," she says, tucking a strand of hair into her bun. "We actually just pulled some chicken pot pie out of the oven . . ." She trails off, her gaze locked on something outside the window next to us. I turn to see what's caught her attention and find Georgia Moore and Emma walking toward the diner from the far end of the parking lot.

Jason's mother, and the girl he was cheating on me with.

"Is that . . ." Annie starts to ask.

"Yep," I say, my body already in flight mode. "Let's go." I pull my purse off the back of my chair as I stand. There's a panic climbing up my throat, and I know if I don't get out of here before they make it to the door, I'll be trapped. "I'm so sorry, June—I—"

"It's all right, dear," she says wistfully, and it's all the permission I need to book it. Annie stays close behind me, and we make it out of the diner just as Georgia steps onto the sidewalk from the other end of the building.

"Layla?" I hear her call out, but I keep my focus trained ahead. There is no way I can handle seeing both of those women without heavy emotional preparation—especially not after what Wells shared. *Is that what's happening here, too?* I think. *Is Georgia with Emma to ask her what she knows about Jason's last few days?*

I'm almost insulted that she wouldn't try to talk to me about it. It's an entirely new punch to the gut that she might think Emma would know him better than I do.

Does she?

"Layla, you okay?" Annie asks nervously, and I'm pulled out of the thought as I realize we've walked right up to the entrance of a car wash.

Sighing, I lean heavily against the brick structure and try to breathe. When I look up across the road, I spot a familiar red and white truck parked in front of Gerry's Feed Store.

Wells.

I turn to Annie. "Do you think you can walk home by yourself?"

Her face falls, and I hate it. But I need to do something, and I need to do it alone. "Are you sure?"

I try to force a smile. "I just need to talk to a friend. I'm okay though, I promise."

There's a reluctance in her eyes, but she relents. "Okay, but you'll come tonight, right?"

My heart lurches at her fear that I might disappear again. "Of course." I nod. Mom might be pissed that I'm sending her home alone, but she's almost fourteen now—the age I was when I started babysitting her. I know she'll be okay. "Mom and Barry will be back soon."

"Okay," she says, and pulls me into a hug. I squeeze her tight, watching her until she disappears down a side street.

IN A STROKE OF LUCK, WELLS SHUFFLES OUT THE door of the feed store as soon as I make it across the street. He's carrying a bag of grain over his shoulder like it's nothing, his standard backward hat propped up on his head. He makes it all the way to his truck before he finally spots me standing beside it, his brows lifting at the surprise of finding me here . . . waiting for him. Because I realize that's what I'm doing.

"Layla," he says, his movement stalled.

"Hi," I offer. My mouth stays parted as I try to form more words.

"You need something?" he asks tentatively, eyes tracking across my face like he might be able to decipher what it might be.

I wouldn't be surprised if he could—he always seems to know.

I look at the truck, at the rust-edged steel and fading red paint. "Take me somewhere?" I ask, looking back at him.

Dark brows dip in confusion. "Are you okay?"

"Anywhere," I say in answer. "Please."

He stares at me for a moment that seems to stretch time, and heat crawls up my neck at how I'm putting him in a position he specifically asked *not* to be in. But the truth is . . . I need him.

Annie's right—I need to focus on my feelings if I have any chance of working through them, and I'm not sure where else to turn.

He tosses the bag into the bed of his truck and pulls his keys out of his pocket. I watch as he twists the key and unlocks the passenger-side door, pulling it open. He turns back to face me, his expression a mix of concern and understanding.

It's all the invitation I need. I climb into the seat he's offering, throw him a look of gratitude, and try to keep my shaky hands still in my lap.

I shift my focus to the street in front of us as he gets in, but I feel the prickling heat of his gaze on me, almost expectant. "Do you want to talk about it?" he finally asks.

I shake my head. "No." At least not yet—I'm not even sure what to say.

I see a single, curt nod from my periphery, then he's turning the key in the ignition and peeling away.

CHAPTER TWENTY-TWO

THEN

It takes Jason three weeks to undo what he did.

He waits for me after cheer practice on the second Friday of school, and when I see him standing on the curb of the parking lot, my heart flips. It's reminiscent of the first time he waited for me after practice. There's a small smile on his lips, nervous but determined, and when he asks me to take a ride with him, I don't even blink.

"I'm so sorry, Layla," he says as soon as we're shut inside the silence of his Mustang. "I've just been going through a lot with my parents about college and . . . it's no excuse."

My eyes narrow at this, a lightbulb going off inside my mind. "Did they tell you to break up with me?"

He gives me a sheepish look, and I can't help but scoff. I've known his parents for almost my whole life—they've been influential in Saddlebrook Falls for years. Before Ron Moore became mayor, he used his legal and political science education to help pass legislation in Texas that protects the future of

Saddlebrook Falls's township. It saved our town from being swallowed by Williamson County when county executives were trying to dissolve Saddlebrook Falls and absorb our resources as part of their own. Georgia Moore runs our local library and sits as an appointed trustee for Readers Make Way, a statewide charity that works to strengthen literacy in children.

I've only interacted with them a handful of times as Jason's girlfriend, usually just saying hi to them when I see them around town. I've never thought much of their opinion of me, but to now realize they played a part in all this makes me . . . sad.

My hands twist together in my lap as I fiddle with my fingers. "I don't understand."

"You didn't do anything wrong," Jason assures. "It's not about you, Layla, I promise. It's just . . . with our loss at state last year and conversations I've been having with college programs, my parents know how important this season is for me. I can't fuck it up. They don't want me to have any distractions."

I brace myself for where this conversation might be going. As hopeful as I am that he's reconsidered, it also sounds like he may be about to double down. To try to get me to understand. Maybe Wells told him about Connor's party . . . maybe Jason feels *bad* for me.

"Look," he continues. "I know my parents mean well. They just want what's best for me. But Layla, you and I have a good thing here, and I don't want to stop seeing you. Maybe . . . maybe we can figure out how to make it work."

My gaze snaps to him. "Jason, it's not like I've ever tried to get between you and football—I know how important it is to you. I don't know what more I can do to show you that you have nothing but my support."

He nods. "I know, babe. You've been so great. Trust me, I know how easy you've made things for me. I guess sometimes I feel like I need to do *more*. Take you on more dates and spend more time with you. And it adds to the pressure I'm feeling, you know?"

My heart sinks at the realization that it really isn't anything I've done wrong.

"I'm worried about you," I admit.

Jason's brow arches. "What do you mean?"

I shrug. "You're such a happy and positive guy—it's why I fell for you. But all this stress might be getting in the way of that happiness."

He shakes his head. "Trust me, Layla, it's all worth it. Someday when I get drafted to the NFL and get my first paycheck as a professional athlete, we'll look back and know that all of this was more than worth it."

"Even if it costs you being happy now?"

"Definitely."

I'm surprised by how sure he is. I know going pro is his biggest dream, and I don't want to discount that, but I can't imagine sacrificing what might be the best years of my life for a career. Then again, I don't have a big dream like he does, so maybe I just don't understand.

"But," he sighs. "I'm willing to stay together as long as you promise you're okay with my main focus being on football. It won't always be like this, but right now I need to do this for myself."

I'm hesitant, knowing how hard I took the breakup in the first place. It aches somewhere deep in my gut that he'd have the audacity to break up with me if he wasn't going to follow through with it—and to frame it like that? I've already long accepted that football is his first love. I don't like knowing my place in his heart is so easily disposable as he tries to make himself feel better.

Maybe he didn't realize the strength of his feelings for me. It's what I tell myself, at least.

THINGS GO BACK TO NORMAL RELATIVELY QUICKLY, as if the whole ordeal never happened at all. Jason brings flowers to school that he plucks from his mother's garden, and he tries to take me cruising in his Mustang when he has time to spare after practice. The entire town readies itself for another football season, and the first few weeks of games go off without a hitch. Since Noah King graduated, Jason is uncontested as the starting quarterback of the season, and he looks *damn good* on the field.

For as much as Jason focuses on football, I throw myself into cheer. My flying skills have sharpened in the last year and Coach West has me working on more complex inversions. Life feels good in all aspects—except for when it comes to Wells.

After our first lesson last year, Wells has given me regular lessons in riding, grooming, and feeding the horses on the Bennetts' ranch. I don't think either of us planned on him teaching me so much but I've become insatiable in my love for the animals and really enjoy learning about all his family is doing to foster rehabilitation for their rescues. It's also obvious they need the help—other than the Bennetts themselves, there's only a handful of employees that support the entire operation—so I've spent a lot of my Saturdays helping where I can.

But after Connor's party, Wells has become . . . moodier. I try not to take it personally, but I would almost understand if it was only directed at me. I mean, it took Wells a long time to warm up to me in the first place, and after my little whiskey stint, I can understand why he'd be turned off about having me around. But his sour attitude isn't only directed at me—it's affecting his relationship with Jason, too.

"I just don't understand what his fucking problem is," Jason huffs out one Thursday night at Mustang's Pizza, tossing the wrapper of his straw in the middle of the table.

Jason's social life is more than limited, but he's been making an effort when it comes to both Wells and me. Yet Wells keeps putting Jason off, saying he's too busy with work at the ranch to hang out.

"Are you sure there's a problem?" I ask. "Maybe he really *is* just busy."

Jason shakes his head. "Nah, he's been busy with the ranch our whole lives and it's never stopped us from hanging out. It's why we usually spend so much time there, so he can multitask. Something's off." He blows out a breath and scrubs a hand over his face, and it twists something inside of me to see him so cut up about it.

Yet another thing for him to be anxious about.

I have no idea if Jason knows what happened at Connor's party, but the thought of there being distance because of me makes me nervous. Like football, Wells is another non-negotiable to Jason's happiness, and if I'm somehow responsible for ruining that, I can only imagine how Jason would handle it.

"You know, it's been a while since he's given me a riding

lesson. Maybe I can try to schedule the next one, and you could ride with us? Make a day of it?"

Jason considers. "I'm not good on a horse . . . not like he is, anyway."

I scoff. "I don't think anyone is as good as Wells. Or any of the Bennetts, for that matter."

Jason smiles, and I feel a warmth uncurling within me. "I mean, yeah. If he's down, so am I."

"Okay." I smile back, picking up the slice of pizza in front of me. If anything, it gives me an excuse to face Wells head-on and see if there really is an issue between us.

I wouldn't blame him for being upset about my behavior at that party, but I hope he'd understand the state of mind I was in after his best friend broke up with me.

On Friday morning, I spot Wells at his locker after first period.

"Hey," I say as I sidle up behind him.

He turns, a mask of disinterest on his face. "Layla."

I falter only slightly, then ask, "Do you have plans on Saturday?"

He shoves a black notebook into his locker and pulls out a binder. "Yep."

"Besides ranch work," I amend.

He sighs. "Why?"

I take a deep breath. "Because Jason is worried that you're avoiding him, and I can't help but think it's because of me. I don't want that on my conscience."

Finally, he turns around fully, leaning his back against his still-open locker as his eyes sweep over my cheer uniform. It's game day, and all the cheerleaders are dressed out for it. "How noble of you."

"Look," I try. "I'm sorry for what happened at the party. I was emotional about the breakup and I wasn't exactly putting my best foot forward—but it's no excuse for ruining your night. You shouldn't have had to deal with me like that. But don't leave Jay hanging."

His eyes narrow. But he doesn't say anything.

"Let me make it up to you?"

He pushes off the locker. "How?"

"I was thinking we could all go for a ride on Saturday? Jason even said he'd love to go, and you know how he feels about horses."

Wells gives me an incredulous look. "You think Jason getting on a horse is somehow the key to falling back in my good graces?"

I swallow. "Yes?"

He shakes his head as a low chuckle escapes him. "For the record, I'm not mad at you. *Or* him. I really have been busy, and I guess maybe I needed a little space from everything?" He scratches at his brow. "If you guys want to come to the ranch on Saturday, you're more than welcome. Can't say I'm thrilled with the idea of Jason getting on a horse, though."

I roll my eyes. "He's a big boy. He'll be fine."

Wells looks right at me. "I'm not worried about Jason. I'm worried about the horse."

I laugh at that, a smile spreading wide on my face. "Thank you, Wells," I say. And I mean it.

ON SATURDAY MORNING, JASON PICKS ME UP ABOUT an hour after I finish eating homemade waffles and peaches for breakfast with Annie. He comes to the door with flowers for her and my mom again, and I think he's a little nervous about my family's feelings about him after breaking up with me. But all things considered, he has nothing to worry about—at least not in my house.

Annie is nearly eight now, and she's convinced that Jason is my Prince Charming. Barry has only formally met Jason a handful of times and I'm not sure he even knew we'd broken up in the first place. And Mom . . . well, she's just happy to see us back on track for our "ten-year plan" which includes marriage after college and a litter of babies for me to tend to while he becomes an NFL superstar.

I really do love Jason, and I'm happy he's giving our relationship an honest shot even with so much going on in his life. But sometimes as I lie in bed at night and will myself to sleep, I can't help the thoughts that race through my mind, wondering if I've fallen into a Jason-shaped honey trap, just like Mom did with her first love. Granted, she fell for a transcontinental hippie who was always going to leave, and Jason is a good person who's simply chasing his dreams. But sometimes I feel like I have to remind myself of the independence I've always craved.

It doesn't help that I don't know what that looks like. I love the Bennetts' ranch and the rescue horses, and I hope I can keep exploring the joy it brings. I'm also still enjoying photography, having signed up for the more advanced class this year. It may not lead to anything lucrative in the future, but Mrs. Barajas says I have a natural talent and it bolsters a sense of pride within me.

I'm just not sure an entire lifetime as Jason's wife could ever be enough.

When we pull up to the ranch, the sun is high in the sky and there isn't a cloud in sight—thankfully I remembered to put sunscreen on my face after my shower this morning. We find Wells outside the stalls with three horses turned out and tacked up for our ride, and when he sees us coming, he waves.

Wells *waves*.

I've never seen him perform such an act . . . so casual and friendly despite the stiff and awkward rocking of his wrist. He's making an effort to reverse his grumpiness, and though it feels forced and unnatural, there's no denying the immediate effect it has on Jason.

"Bennett!" Jason shouts over the distance as we trudge toward the collected horses. "Is this where you've been hiding?"

Wells flashes a look at me before responding. "You know I'm always here, Moore. Family duties and all that."

I brace myself for Jason to call him out, but he doesn't. His eyes track along the horses; Wells has pulled his favorite, a beautiful brown mare named Lady. Next to her is Champ, who I've been on every time I ride, and Ghost stands tall beside him, his white coat glowing in the sun.

Jason tucks his red SFHS hat down his forehead, shielding his face from the sun. "Which one of these lucky beasts is with me today?"

Wells's smile falters. "Uh . . . Ghost. I was going to put you on Ace, but he needs new shoes and the farrier doesn't come until Tuesday."

Jason nods and walks up to Ghost, running a hand along his back. "Let's show 'em how it's done, huh, buddy?"

Wells scoffs. I walk up to Champ, careful to approach him where he can see me like Wells taught me last year. It's been almost a month since I've seen him, and he affectionately pushes his nose into the hand I hold out. "Hi, Champ," I laugh.

"Here," Wells says from behind me, and I turn to find him holding out his cowboy hat. "For your face."

"Oh," I say. "You don't have to do that."

"We're going on a longer ride and the morning sun will be beating down on us almost the whole way," he explains. "Trust me, you'll thank me later."

I take the black hat from him and stare at it as he shuffles away to mount Lady. Wells usually wears his dirty ball cap when he's on a horse and saves his cowboy hat for special occasions. I'm surprised he wants me wearing it knowing it'll get dusty.

But I *don't* want to get burned, so I fit the hat on top of my head and look at Jason. "Does this look okay?" I ask.

He looks at the hat and then at me, something dark passing through his eyes, there and gone in a breath. "Looks great," he says, and then he lifts a foot into a stirrup.

I frown, wondering if it offends him that I'm wearing another guy's hat—but it's *Wells*. I almost take it off and leave it behind, but I don't want to make things weirder than they already are. So I take a deep breath, give Champ another quick rub, and mount him.

CHAPTER TWENTY-THREE

NOW

We drive down an old country road for almost thirty minutes in utter silence as Wells chews gum with the dedication of a chain smoker, replacing the spent piece in his mouth with a new one three times along the way. If he's nervous, it's hard to tell. There's still no real sign he doesn't want me in his truck, but it does little to quiet the steady hum of nerves that swell inside me.

Finally, he slows to turn down a dirt road. It's not well-maintained—there are tall weeds and old roots that he carefully navigates through—but he seems to know where he's going. After winding through a tunnel of low-hanging trees whose branches brush against the windshield as we pass, the road opens up to a clearing of wild grass.

A meadow.

We drive through it to the other side before Wells stops and shifts the truck to park. I look around, surprised that we're stopping here, but ahead of us is a copse of trees so dense there's no way he'd be able to steer the truck through it.

"Where are we?" I ask.

"Come on," he says, then gets out and waits for me, keeping his gaze forward on what's ahead.

Stepping down into the tall grass in my sandals, I shuffle through it until I'm standing next to him. A breeze kicks up, pushing my hair off my shoulder and igniting a riot of goose-bumps along the back of my neck. Thank god I had the fore-thought to tug on my jacket earlier. My shoes, however . . .

"It's a bit of a hike," he says. And then he stalks forward, walking through the grass like it's nothing. I suppose it *is* nothing for him in his boots. But I don't complain.

I'm the one who asked for this.

I do my best to stay close enough to follow the small path he's creating with the disturbance of his long strides. He's right that it's a bit of a hike, but it's mostly flat and the cool weather helps to keep it bearable.

It must be twenty minutes before the ground beneath us begins to dip, a steep hill of overgrown trees and brush so thick there's no clear path through. Wells pauses to turn around and face me, lowering his gaze to my shoes. He looks back up at me with an unreadable expression.

"I wasn't expecting to traipse through the Forbidden Forest today," I say in defense of my gem-studded Steve Maddens.

He snorts before turning back around, bending his knees, and kneeling low in front of me. "Come on," he says.

"Uh, come where?"

He gives a pointed look over his shoulder before clearing his throat. "Climb on."

I finally realize what he's asking. "No thanks," I protest,

shaking my head as if he can see me. "I can make it." I side-step around him to march on, but he reaches out to wrap a warm hand around my wrist. His calloused palm glides against my skin and the shock of the contact is a current up my spine.

He pulls me back to face him, his eyes a kaleidoscope of browns and golds in the spotted light of the sun. "You're not making it ten feet in those poor excuses for footwear."

I scoff, making a show of looking offended even though this feels like the first easy breath I've taken since getting into his truck. "I've gotten all the way *here* with them, haven't I?"

The corner of his mouth lifts, and it's a bone-deep relief. "Because you've been walking in the path I set like an eager little bear cub," he jabs.

"*Again,* I didn't realize we'd end up in the middle of literal uncharted territory."

He shifts his weight onto one foot, his smile fading. His expression grows irritated, but I can tell he's trying to hide it. "You told me to take you anywhere."

"Yeah." I nod. "It could have been the bowling alley. Or the mall."

His eyes narrow. "Oh, I'm sorry. Forgive me for thinking you needed an escape from town and not a fucking *shopping* trip," he says. "There's clearly something going on, and I'm trying to help."

His words pierce me right in the chest because that's exactly what I asked of him.

I think you should find someone else to be there for you.

I let out a breath. "I'm sorry," I say. "For even coming to you after . . . after you asked me not to."

His face softens. "Layla, you can always ask me for help.

That's not what I meant." He swipes a thumb against the wrist he's still holding before pulling his hand back.

"What did you mean, then?"

"Just . . ." He trails off, his eyes dropping to my mouth before quickly changing course to the left, somewhere in the trees. "It's hard to explain." His eyes flash back to me before he turns around, kneeling again with his arms out wide. "Please get on," he asks again.

This time I give in. I step forward until my shins brush his jeans and press my palms to the tops of his shoulders, pulling myself up and wrapping my thighs around his waist. His leather belt digs into my skin and I shift to get more comfortable as his hands wrap beneath my knees. He straightens, and I wind my arms around his neck, keeping my hold on him as loose as possible so I don't choke him.

He doesn't say a word as he turns back to the hill and starts to descend.

He takes each step carefully, giving no indication that my added weight makes any of this harder for him. It only takes minutes before we reach the bottom, where the thick cluster of trees overhead makes it harder for the sun's warmth to break through. There's a steady humming I worry might be a nearby wasp nest until I see the river over Wells's shoulder.

After stepping through the worst of the tangled brush, he bends to let me back down. I try to slide down gracefully until my feet touch the ground, but the hem of my linen shorts snags on his belt and the material rides up to expose the skin where my leg meets my hip. I quickly yank it back down, smoothing it out just as he turns around to face me.

"A river?" I ask.

His smile is small, his dark brown eyes soft and sincere. "A river," he confirms. "Unfortunately, *not* a mall."

I almost laugh. A heady warmth slices through my anxious heart, and I don't understand it, how he somehow always leads me back to a sense of comfort. Maybe it's a trauma bond as we both grapple with the loss of Jason. Or maybe . . . maybe he's always been able to do this for people, and I just didn't realize.

In the years that I've known him, our friendship has oscillated between hot and cold and—at times—fading into nonexistence. I only wish it could have felt this sincere when the world wasn't falling apart.

"What is this place?" I ask, because there's no way he simply guessed this river was here.

"My grandfather took me fishing here when I was younger," he answers, casting his eyes back toward the moving water. "He's the only one I've ever been here with. I don't think anyone else knows it's here."

His answer catches me off guard. "No one?"

He shakes his head. "I was pretty young my first time here. Maybe six or seven? Things were chaotic at home, and as the youngest I always felt lost in the shuffle. Grandpa must have noticed because he brought me here one weekend to camp and promised me this spot was mine, that he wouldn't bring any of the others."

I try to picture a young Wells, eager to see the world, to understand it. Four older brothers and a busy ranch operation that probably made him feel invisible.

"Anyway, it's not *technically* mine—the ranch belongs to all of us. But he kept his promise. I've never brought anyone here, either."

"Wait," I say, looking up at him. "This is part of the ranch?"

He nods. "That dirt road we turned down is ours."

"Wow," I breathe, impressed. I knew the Bennetts' ranch was big, but I didn't realize it was *this* big. We're miles and miles from where the main house must be. He looks down at me, the corner of his mouth quirking. "You never brought Jason?"

"Nope."

"I'm surprised."

He gives a half-hearted shrug. "I don't know . . . maybe it's selfish, but I've never had a lot that I could call wholly mine," he says. "And Jason . . . I don't know," he repeats. The tops of his ears tinge pink as he looks away.

"What?" I press.

He looks back at me, a quiet resolve settling over his brow. "He had so much."

Four simple words, and yet I recognize the deep confession in them. He watches me, bracing for my response, but I'm honestly not sure what to say because . . . he's right. Jason seemed to have everything: supportive parents, the natural gift of sharp athleticism, a community that supported and loved him. From the outside looking in, he lived a charmed life.

I look back toward the water, the truth of what this place means to Wells settling around us. Something wholly his. Sacred and secret. For him to bring *me* here . . .

"Are you ready to talk about it now?" he asks quietly.

I turn back to face him and find an intensity in his gaze— the full weight of his attention like a hook beneath my skin.

"It's just . . . everyone loves Jason," I start. "Everyone loves him so much, and I don't know how to keep absorbing that every time I leave my house. Because I loved him too, but I'm also really fucking *mad* at him, and I don't know how to hold that anger."

Wells keeps his expression neutral as he looks at me, giving me the space and patience to continue when I'm ready.

"I tried to do what you asked, Wells. I've tried to open up to other people, to find someone who understands what I'm going through, but nobody else gets it. You're the only one I feel like I can *breathe* around because I can be honest about the full spectrum of my feelings. I can tell you how sad I am, and how much I miss him. But also how *furious* and fucking devastated I am.

"Even if Jason felt the weight of the world on his shoulders, even if he was feeling really fucking lonely . . . he had *us*, Wells. He had us, and we were so damn good to him, you know? So forgiving and supportive. You didn't even *want* to play football, yet you gave all that time and energy to stand by him while he worked to reach his dreams.

"I know that him having us might not have been enough to erase the pain he was going through. He was suffering, and we may not have understood the full extent of it." The tears spill over freely now, but I can't stop. I *have* to get this out. "But dammit, Wells, we were there for him as much as we knew how to be. You can't blame yourself for falling short with something you had no idea about . . . Jason *had* us, and he still held it all in. He didn't give us a chance to do anything different, and—" I catch my breath just as a sob breaks through, my chest splintering apart right down the middle.

Wells steps forward, wrapping his arms around my shoulders and pulling me in close to his chest. Still, I have to finish.

"It's not our fault," I whisper into his gray shirt, now spotted with my tears. "It's *not* our fault."

"Shh," he soothes, a strong hand winding into my hair as he cradles my head, tucking me under his chin as my shoulders shake violently. His other palm sweeps down my back. "Layla," he breathes, and it cracks through me.

"I'm just . . ." I say through the fresh onslaught of tears. "I'm so mad, Wells. I'm so mad at him for making me feel like I wasn't good enough to help him." And there is it, my deepest shame. For as much as I tried to put my own needs aside to prioritize Jason and what he needed, it still wasn't enough.

"I know," he murmurs, pressing a kiss to my temple. "I know, sunshine."

I pull back from his chest, tilting up to face him. His eyes are sad, his lips twisted. But the way he looks at me . . . like I'm something precious and treasured to be careful with and cared for.

It's too much.

"Stop," I say, watching his brows pull together as the word wraps around him. His hands stop their movement along my body, but he doesn't yield his hold on me.

"What?" he asks.

The features of his face become nothing but a blur through watery eyes. "Stop looking at me like that," I whisper.

But he just shakes his head. "I can't."

And . . . *oh*. It feels like another confession. An aching reminder of a past life, a dark night and a crying girl on her doorstep, desperate to be enough.

A boy who may have wanted something that wasn't his to have.

I blink through my tears, feeling them glide down my cheek

as I watch his mouth part. He hesitates, eyes glimmering with a spark of something electric and new, and then he says it again: "I can't stop."

My heart pounds thunderously in my chest, matching the rhythm of his. His eyes drop down to my mouth, only inches from his own, as the air between us heats with our shared breath. "Oh," is all I can think to say before I reach up to press my fingertips against the rough stubble of his chin, dragging them lightly down the column of his throat.

The hand he holds against my back drifts down my spine before rising again to settle between my shoulder blades. On instinct, I arch into him, and when he lets out a low groan I revel in the sound.

"Layla," he whispers, his voice unsteady as his other hand skates against my cheek. I close my eyes, savoring the feeling of him right here, his warm and tender presence, a soft landing for every emotion pouring out of me.

How long? How long have you been looking at me like this?

I open my eyes again as he presses another kiss against my skin, just above my brow. His lips stay rooted there as he says, "I'm sorry." And then he pulls back.

"For what?" I ask, suddenly cold from the loss of him.

He takes a deep breath, shoulders sagging with its release. "I shouldn't . . ." he starts, then scrubs a hand across his jaw as his eyes pin me in place. "I shouldn't tell you things like that."

I can only stare at him until he finally breaks first, turning to face the rushing water beyond. A breeze kicks up, cold and biting as it winds through the rustling trees, like a bucket of ice thrown onto the heat of a moment, hell-bent on snuffing it out.

I wipe at my cheeks, feeling exhausted and yet . . . there's something *alive* building in my chest, crackling through the hollow corners that've ensnared me for weeks. I want to sink into the feeling, to be consumed by it.

Another gust blows through us, and a big fat rain droplet plops on my forehead.

"Oh shit," Wells says as he catches the movement of the water down my temple. The sky flashes with lightning, and then completely opens up.

It's a hard and unyielding downpour that soaks us both in seconds.

"Oh *shit*," Wells says again, awestruck as he looks up at the sky. I mirror him to look up too, but my sandals lose their battle with the now wet and slippery mud beneath me and I lose my balance, falling right on my ass.

A deep, roaring laugh spills out of me, so fierce it shakes my entire body. "Layla!" Wells shouts through the rain. He's on me in seconds, wiping water away from my face so he can get a better look at me. When he realizes I'm laughing his shoulders sag in relief, and then a smile blooms from his face. "You okay?" he asks.

"Yes," I nod. "More than okay." It's true—I feel lighter than I have in weeks. Years, even.

He stands and holds a hand out to help me get to my feet. The whole right side of my body is covered in mud and the sight of it sends me into another fit of laughter. But it dies when my eyes meet Wells's.

"Why did you bring me here?" I ask.

Small droplets cluster in his thick lashes. But he doesn't answer.

"Tell me," I demand softly.

"Because," he finally says. "Somebody needs to take care of

you. And . . . I want it to be me. I told you that you should find somebody else to lean on because I'm not sure I know how to stop myself from wanting you the way I do—the way I always have. I don't even think I fully comprehend how *fucked* it is for me to say that to you, Layla."

My mouth parts as the truth of his words crashes through me, but he continues before I can form a coherent thought. "Being around you is all I think about, and it's the last thing I should be asking you to make room for right now. But dammit, I want to be the one to hold you when you cry. I want to be the one you fall apart with. I want to spend the entire day figuring out how I can make you smile, because when you do it's like a drug, and I get so fucking *high* from it."

Lightning flashes again as the full weight of his words sinks into my heart. The realization of how much Wells *wants*, of how much he must have held himself back for so many years, careful to protect his friendship with Jason. How he's finally telling me here, in the only place he feels like he has any ownership.

I know Wells loves his family, but between Rhett and his father, there's plenty of drama to be overshadowed by. And Brooks has kids now . . . I can't help but wonder if there's been room for Wells in any of it, for the things he wants and needs. I don't think he'd have the heart to ask.

But he's doing it now, with me.

I step toward him until our bodies are flush. And then I reach up on tiptoes and press my mouth to his.

CHAPTER TWENTY-FOUR

THEN

The Mustangs make it into the playoffs to no one's surprise—they've been undefeated all season long and Jason is playing at his best. When Thanksgiving rolls around, he pulls away from our relationship completely to focus on football. His dad hires a private trainer to work with him after an already ramped-up schedule of practices at school. Sundays are his only days off, and he's usually so tired he sleeps it away, dead to the world. I'm lucky if I get a text back from him before dinnertime.

I distract myself by spending more and more time at the ranch. The Bennetts' farrier, Hank, has taught me how to pick out the horses' hooves during their morning grooming, and when Wells isn't around (also because of practice) Kasey graciously takes me under his wing and lets me shadow him. I keep my visits mostly under wraps from my mother, but at the very least she always believes I'm here with Jason.

She doesn't approve of me hanging around the Bennetts,

but every time she expresses her concern over the rumors surrounding the family, I remind her that I can't control who Jason chooses to be friends with, which seems to tamp down her judgment. I feel wrong for letting her believe I'm only friends with Wells because Jason is, even though I suppose it might be true. I'm not sure someone like him would want to be friends with someone like me in any other world. Still, regardless of how it happened, we *are* friends—at least, I think we still are.

When a wild colt is delivered to the ranch, Kasey teaches me how to bottle-feed him. He was born out of season, which is pretty rare for mustangs, and when he couldn't keep up with his herd, a local rancher from a few counties over stepped in to bring him here.

I go out to the ranch every morning before school to feed him knowing it'll help the Bennetts, but also because I learn that I love the rush of caring for something so young and vulnerable. By the next weekend, Kasey shows me how to transition him to bucket-feeding by letting him nurse on my finger and guiding him to the milk in the bucket. When he starts to do it on his own, I'm filled with so much pride I could burst.

Kasey lets me name him, and I don't hesitate to call him Lucky for ending up here with the Bennetts. I still don't understand the town's aversion to this family—aside from some occasional moodiness (it seems to run in the family), they've all been so kind in having me around. Mrs. Bennett is always quick to bring out a cool glass of lemonade, and while Brooks and Sawyer don't really talk much, they still acknowledge me with a hello when they see me.

Rhett's the only one who looks at me like I might be a toy to play with, but of all the Bennetts there's no doubt he's the wildest. More often than not he's got a beer in his hand, and Brooks and Kasey are constantly on him about his lack of respect toward . . . well, *anyone.*

The only Bennett I've yet to meet is Wells's father. I tried to ask about him once, but all he'd tell me was that his dad is sick and doesn't leave the house very often. I could tell by the way his ears tinged pink that it wasn't something he wanted to discuss further, so I dropped it. Sometimes I'm tempted to ask Jason what he knows, but then I worry that I'd be no better than anyone else in this town.

On the first Saturday of December, I eagerly watch Kasey and Wells turn Lucky out in the large corral with Lady. The hope is that by introducing Lucky to the older mare, her maternal instincts will take over and she'll eventually help him learn to socialize with the other horses. It's nerve-wracking, at first, to watch them cautiously approach each other. But when Lady gives Lucky an affectionate rub, I'm so happy it brings me to tears. It's the first time I think it, that *this* might be what I want to do with my life.

"You okay?" Wells asks from inside the corral, noticing me wipe my eyes.

"Yeah," I say, and I beam, clicking the shutter of the camera around my neck as I do my best to capture the moment.

The returning smile he throws is real, one of his rare natural ones, and I can't help it when my eyes burn with more tears. Despite calling a truce for Jason's sake a few months ago, Wells has kept his distance. I'm not sure of the reason and I've stopped trying to figure it out, but the smile he wears now is reassuring.

"What are you all up to today?"

I turn to find Melody walking up behind us. She's wearing

short black boots embroidered with what looks like bluebonnets that match her cobalt dress. She's gorgeous, her curly blonde hair bouncing with each step she takes, but her face is pale and distant, and I'm reminded of having the same thought the first time I met her.

"Oh, hey," Kasey says in greeting. "Just trying to help our new little orphan friend here." He's watching both horses carefully, looking for any signs of an issue, but Lucky follows behind Lady as she meanders around the confines of the corral.

Melody clicks her tongue. "Gosh, he's cute."

I smile, focusing back on her boots. "Did you make those, too?"

"Sure did! I stitched these ones last spring."

"I love them," I say.

She laughs, a small twinkling sound. "Thank you. I honestly don't get to do it as much these days, especially since James was born, but it's one of my favorite things to do. I used to sell them at the Foxborough fair."

"Melody, you ready?" Brooks calls from where he stands near the stalls, a frown on his face.

"Coming!" she hollers back. "Well, I better go—I have a doctor's appointment in town," she says to no one in particular. "Great job with the colt—you guys always know just what these horses need."

Kasey gives her a polite smile and tips his hat. Wells watches her with a curious expression, like he notices something might be off, too. But he doesn't say anything, and soon Brooks and Melody disappear around the building toward the main drive.

MY BIRTHDAY COMES FIVE DAYS INTO THE NEW YEAR, almost two weeks after Christmas and three weeks after the Saddlebrook High Mustangs win the Texas State Championship. Celebrating my birthday has always felt secondary on the heels of so many major holidays, and this year is no different with the added excitement over our state win. Jason and the rest of the team are beside themselves with joy and pride after prevailing in a rematch against the Mayfield Matadors. It was almost a complete shutout, but Mayfield was able to clinch a third-quarter field goal to get some points on the board.

This year, Jason kept his anxiety at bay and showed up to AT&T Stadium raring for a win. With every possession, the Mustangs drove hard against the Matador defense and pushed into the end zone three times. The town is still celebrating, and Jason has undoubtedly cemented himself as Saddlebrook Falls royalty. The spirit committee organized a parade (which was really just a caravan of a bunch of decorated cars and trucks) and kids from the local Pop Warner league stood in line to get autographs from Jason and the other players. Even Liam was a part of it, bragging to the other little kids that his Uncle Wells helped the Mustangs to win state.

Now that the season is over it feels like I have my boyfriend back. There are dozens of house parties thrown over the course of winter break, most of them focused on launching the football team on an even higher pedestal than they're already on, and I'm on Jason's arm at every single one of them.

We spend most afternoons, like today, at the ranch. Jason was taken aback when he realized how much I've been here over the last few months. Not that he didn't know—I always told him about what I was up to any time we had a chance to catch up. Even still, he was surprised to learn how integral I was in Lucky's transfer to the ranch, and even more surprised to learn how much Kasey has taught me.

When I groom and tack up Champ all by myself, Jason shakes his head in disbelief. "Dang, girl," he says. "Who is this cowgirl in front of me, and where did my cheerleader go?"

I laugh off the comment. "I'm still a cheerleader," I insist. "But I really like it here. I'd love to have a ranch like this one day."

"I don't know about that," he counters. "It's a lot of work, and I'll be away from home quite a bit." He watches as I glide the curry comb over Champ's back. "Plus I'll want you to travel to games with me, you know?"

I peel my eyes away from Champ to look at him, noting the eagerness in his expression. The desire to agree immediately flares, but something gives me pause . . . It's the first time I think I've ever shared a *want* for my future, but it goes against the natural progression of what being with Jason would mean.

I know I don't just want to be an NFL wife—I want to carve out something of my own, something that no one can ever take away from me. But, if Jason and I really are going to spend the rest of our lives together, I should probably find something to do that complements his dreams, not competes with them.

"Maybe after you retire, then," I say.

His eyes twinkle. "That sounds nice . . . a happy retirement with a big piece of Texas land to call ours."

See? He's not shutting me down completely, he's just being practical. I force a smile and turn my attention back to Champ.

Later, Jason comes to my door wearing a dark gray sports coat and matching pants, his white button-down open at the collar. And he looks *good*. "Wow," I say, a bit breathless. "I didn't realize it was a fancy occasion."

Jason looks down at the white dress with a flower pattern I'm wearing and smiles. "You look perfect, babe. Trust me." He leans in to press a kiss to my cheek, a warm hand wrapping lightly against my waist. The touch sends a current of electric heat through me, anticipation curling tight.

We still haven't had sex yet, but I've been feeling ready to take that step with him—especially now that the season is over. As he pulls away and smiles down at me, I wonder if tonight might be the night. "Ready?" he asks, his voice low.

I can only nod, grabbing my purse as my mom comes around the corner from the kitchen. "Hey, Jason! You guys heading out?"

"Yes, ma'am." Jason nods, standing straighter as he turns his gaze toward her. "Thank you for letting me steal Layla away tonight."

Mom's returning smile is as wide as a Cheshire Cat's. "I'm just happy she has such a darling young man who treats her so well," she says, eyes brightening.

Jason lets out a quiet chuckle. "Thank you, ma'am. I'll have her back in before eleven."

She waves a hand, shifting her focus to me. "Oh, don't rush home. You two just enjoy yourselves, all right, bug?"

I smile. "Thanks, Mom."

Jason drives us to Emiliano's, an Italian restaurant in the next town over. It's a gorgeous dinner with ivory table linens and pasta so rich and creamy I can't help but moan as I eat. Jason's blue eyes smolder in the flickering candlelight, and I'm struck with another wave of desire so strong I squirm in my seat.

"I have something for you," Jason says just as the waiter takes our plates.

"You do?" I look around the table—I didn't notice him bring anything in. "I thought dinner was my present."

He laughs softly. "You're worth more than just a dinner, Layla." When I give him a look that says, *Okay then where the hell is it?* his eyes flash with a heady mix of desire and excitement. "It's in the car."

The waiter returns to ask for our dessert order, but I shake my head. "None for me, thank you."

Jason's smile curves higher. "No dessert? Are you sure?"

"Yes," I say, *more* than sure.

Jason takes care of the bill and holds my hand on our way out. He drives us down a back road that winds parallel to the main highway, and when he parks within a cluster of tall trees my stomach flips. *This is it*, I think. *It's happening.*

But then Jason pulls a beautifully wrapped box from the back seat, adorned with a bright yellow bow. I stare at it with wide eyes and ask, "What's this?"

"Your gift," he murmurs, placing the box in my lap.

I carefully pull on the ribbon until the bow unfurls, and when I lift the lid, a loud gasp escapes me. "Oh my god!" I exclaim as I pull out a dark brown cowboy boot with ornate yellow daylilies embroidered along the front and back shaft. I know immediately that Melody made them—they look just like the ones she wears. "These are amazing! How did you know?"

His grin is shimmering and dripping with confidence. "I know how much you've been enjoying the horses, and I figured it was time for you to have some proper boots," he says.

This is the best present I've ever gotten in my life. Tucking it back in the box, I lean forward to untie the shoelaces of my Keds, then switch them for my new boots, thrilled that they're a perfect fit. "And you knew my size!" I exclaim.

Jason chuckles. "I asked your mom," he explains.

Joy bubbles through me, effervescent in the way it moves through my chest. For the third time tonight, I'm struck with the instinct that I'm ready to take things further. "I want to have sex." The words nearly burst out of my mouth, and I can't help but laugh at the absurdity of such a left turn in conversation.

Jason's eyes grow as wide as saucers. "What?" he rasps.

My smile stretches all the way to my ears. "I'm ready, Jay. I'm so crazy about you, and I thought it's what you meant about a gift in the car, and I feel dumb about that now but these boots are perfect and you're perfect and I'm just really ready—"

I'm cut off by Jason's mouth on mine, eager and hungry. His hands grip my waist as he tries to pull me closer, but my hip hits the gearshift with a loud thump. "Ow," I laugh again.

Jason's blue eyes have grown five shades darker. "Get in the back seat," he directs.

So I do.

He's slow and careful and yet so earnest in the way he touches me, like he really wants to make this count. I've never asked him how many girls he's done this with, but I'd guess there have been a few based on how he seems to know exactly what will make my head spin and my body tremble in anticipation.

"Are you sure?" he asks, his lips sucking at my collarbone.

I nod. "Mhmm."

He reaches to pull a foil wrapper from his wallet and makes quick work of taking off his slacks. I help him pull his jacket off, and he folds it over the headrest. When he's ready, he positions himself over me as his hands roam beneath my dress. "I love you, Layla," he says, like he can't believe this is happening. "I love you so much, and I swear I'm going to love you for the rest of my life."

"You better," I whisper. And then I gasp, because his fingers have found where I'm most sensitive, and I've never felt anything like this before. It's a wild current of electricity that sparks across every inch of my skin.

"I promise," he says as he pushes into me.

And I believe him.

CHAPTER TWENTY-FIVE

NOW

The first thought that comes to mind as my lips press against Wells is how warm he is, even in the middle of this mid-December Texan downpour. I can feel heat radiating off his skin like he's made of the sun, and I want to sink further into him.

The second thought is how this kiss is like nothing I've ever felt. It takes him only seconds to reach up and cup my face in his strong hands, tilting my head back for better access. I may have started this kiss, but he's making it his own, deepening it to something near-feral and wicked with desire.

When I slide my tongue against his, a low grunt escapes from his throat, and I *love* the sound. I lose all thoughts, my only focus becoming a one-tracked need to get him to make it again. His fingers wind into my hair as he grips the back of my neck and pulls me in closer—as if we could possibly *get* any closer—and when I arch my chest against his he makes the sound again, a rough and guttural groan straight from his lizard brain. It sets me on fire. Burns through me like kerosene.

A loud crash of thunder sounds from overhead, and Wells pulls away from me. He rests his forehead against mine as his breath fans across my neck. "We need to get out of here," he slurs, his focus moving from my mouth to my shoulder to my cheek.

I swallow down the need to kiss him again, forcing myself to nod. And then I'm caught completely off guard when he bends low and wraps his arms around my legs, hauling me over his shoulder as he stands. "Put me down!" I shriek.

"Not a chance!" he calls out, and then he starts the trek up the steep and muddy hill, carrying me like a ragdoll.

I can't help but laugh at the absurdity of the last few minutes. The sudden rain, the heated confessions, *kissing* Wells Bennett.

And it was a good kiss.

Halfway up the hill he slips, but he quickly catches his balance as he squeezes against my thighs. Like his instinct is to keep me bound to him, no matter the cost. At the top, I'm still breathless and laughing, but he still doesn't put me back down. He marches straight for where his truck is parked in the grassy meadow.

When I'm settled and shivering in the passenger seat, he climbs in, shaking the rain from the ends of his hair beneath his hat. "About time that thing got washed," I say, nodding at the dirt-smudged Wild Coyote logo on the front.

He smiles, and it nearly wrecks me. His eyes are blown wide with need, and it's all it takes for me to slide my right leg over his thighs and straddle him.

"Layla," he warns, as if I didn't already propel us over this line down by the river. His eyes drop to my mouth as I settle over his lap, and I love the way it makes me feel: bold and brave and *alive*. Somewhere deep inside my mind, I know how bad this is. I know there's a very real possibility that we'll both regret it the second we burst through the haze and drive back into town. But for now, surrounded by the outskirts of his family ranch where no one can find us, all I want is to savor the moment. To let it wash over me and bathe me in something new.

"What, cowboy?" I ask. There's a dare in my tone and I watch as he registers it, fascinated as it sparks a new wave of hunger in his molten brown eyes.

"Fuck," he murmurs. "You're so damn pretty like this." And this time he kisses me.

His hands grip my waist as he pulls me closer until there's no space between us and I can feel the way he shakes. I melt into him, my hands frantic as they take him in. Our rain-soaked shirts stick together, fabric dragging against fabric until he lifts mine over my head and drops it on the truck floor with a wet slap. His fingers trace along the edges of my bra strap as I reach for the hem of his shirt, eager to get to the warmth of his skin, and when I get it off, I can't help the moan that escapes as my need winds tight within me.

He's hard beneath his jeans, and I grind into him until he's sputtering for air. "Layla," he pleads, his hands like a vise as he holds me still. His eyes track along my body, along the shape of my breasts beneath lavender cotton, and he shakes his head. "We can't."

I move my mouth to his jaw, sucking and licking the column of his throat. "Why not?"

A whimper escapes his mouth when I bite into his skin,

and he shifts his hips up and into me. *A reward*, I think, for earning that sound. But then he's shaking his head again, gently moving me down his legs and away from where I want to touch him most. "Layla," he says again, firmer this time.

I sigh through a shaky exhale, and when I look at him, I know this is over.

"We can't," he insists. "Not like this."

Not like this. The words hit me all at once. I'm desperate to know when and how we *can* do this because god—I want to. "Okay," I whisper. "Yeah, we can . . . wait? I think." My brain feels frazzled, but my body is sharp with focus. The pressure of his mouth against my skin is on repeat, like a scratch on an old record. The heat in his eyes, his hands still wrapped tightly around my waist. I don't want it to stop.

It doesn't even scare me. Not like it seems to be scaring him.

He nods. And then his face stills. "Or not," he adds. "You know . . . if this—" He clears his throat. "If you change your mind."

I watch his mouth as they shape the words, but they lose meaning in the air between us. Rain continues to belt down against the roof, and with the sudden lack of movement, of delicious friction between our bodies, a chill rattles through me.

"Shit," Wells says on an exhale, swiping his thumb against the waistband of my shorts. "You're freezing."

I shake my head. "No, I'm good." But goosebumps give me away, and he gently scoots me off of his lap so he can start the truck and crank on the heat.

"Here." He reaches for my shirt from the footwell and hands it to me, his cheeks flushing pink as his eyes drop to my bra before quickly jumping back up to meet mine. "It's soaked . . . Hold it against the vent and let it dry a little before you put it back on."

I nod, my mouth growing dry as the reality of what just happened settles over me. I open my shirt and spread it over the side vent, holding it in place as Wells backs away from the trees.

He drives all the way back into town without a shirt on, and I swear I do my best not to look. But he catches me sneaking glances, and an unrestrained grin spreads over his face. It lights me up all over again.

"Do you need to go home?" he asks. I look at the time on his dash and see it's only four-thirty—still early enough to stay with Wells. The fact that he's even asking makes me think he's hoping I can.

"No," I say softly. "Not yet."

"Can I take you to the cabin?" His voice is even, but my heart somersaults all the same. When I don't answer, he turns to face me. "Not . . . not for that. I promise." His jaw jumps and his throat works around a hard swallow. I've never seen him so . . . affected. "I just want to make sure you warm up."

A flush crawls up my neck, and I wonder if he can see it. "Yes."

He nods, brown eyes assessing me. "You're okay?"

I can't help but smile. I'm *more* than okay.

I don't know how to explain how I feel right now, sitting shotgun in Wells's truck with my shirt off. But after weeks of hell and so much heartbreak, I finally feel alive again.

"I'm okay," I confirm, focusing back on the vent and my wet shirt.

Flames crack in the stone fireplace, warming the chill from my bones as Wells comes in from the kitchen with two mugs in hand. "I hope you like hot chocolate," he says as he sets one mug down on the table in front of me.

I'm sitting in the exact spot of the cozy green couch I was on that first night here, after finding out about Jason's affair with Emma. Only weeks have passed since then, yet it feels like a lifetime ago. I remember looking at Wells that night like he was a stranger, like everything in the last six years of my life had been a lie. But as I watch shadows from the light of the fire dance across his face, I realize that somewhere along the way he's become my lifeline. I'm anchored to his attention and care in ways that I know I shouldn't be . . . But I can't get enough.

"I love it." I smile, reaching for the mug. He sits down beside me as I take a long sip, relishing the heat it brings me. *Factually*, I know my body is cold. My still-damp shirt hangs heavily from my shoulders after I refused to take a dry one from him, and my skin is prickled with goosebumps that flare every time I shift in my seat.

Still, I don't *really* feel it. My heart and mind are busy replaying everything that's happened in the last hour, careful to slow down in all the right places. I chance a look at him and find his gaze lost somewhere in the hearth.

"Thank you," I say quietly. "For taking me with you today. For . . . all of it." For pulling me out of a weeks-long spiral with a kiss so perfect I felt like I could *breathe* again.

His eyes blaze as they catch mine. But then he seems to turn in on himself, picking up the mug and tracing the lip. "I'm on the losing end of my restraint, Layla—I always have been when it comes to you. I've tried to fight it for so long and never seem to get it right. But all of this is a terrible idea. I never should have let it happen."

I feel my stomach drop. He . . . he *regrets* it?

"We can't do that again."

I jump up to my feet, the need to put space between us becoming all-consuming. I march across the living room toward the fireplace and whip back around to face him. "You tell me how much you want me . . . that you've wanted me *all this time*. And now you're going to push me away?"

He stares at me with sad eyes and says nothing.

"What the hell is wrong with you, Wells?" I shout.

"What's *wrong* with me?" he retorts. "I fell for my best friend's girl. That's what's wrong with me." His jaw jumps as he sets his mug down. "Jason may have made mistakes, but he doesn't deserve this."

My eyes burn with tears. "He was fucking another girl for weeks, Wells. Maybe months! And she wasn't even the first. He didn't care about me, not like I needed him to. He only ever cared about himself."

"That's not true."

An incredulous laugh bursts out of my mouth. "Are you kidding me? He didn't care! He gave me pretty lies about a perfect future and promised to take care of me and love me forever. But he wouldn't have hurt me like that if he did."

"Layla, goddammit—I *know* you don't want this," he roars, pushing up to his feet. Red-hot anger mars his beautiful face, and I revel in it. "I may have too many feelings for a girl who's never been mine, but you've never looked at me like you looked at him. You're just sad and angry about what he was doing, and my feelings for you are a perfect opportunity for you to get your revenge."

I scoff. "*Revenge*? He's dead, Wells!" I can't help the tears that stream down my face, and I'm so *angry* that I'm crying again. "He's not here for me to bask in the glory of some pathetic revenge plan."

"I just have a hard time believing this would actually mean anything to you," he says, and it's like a knife to the heart.

"I guess you don't know me, then."

His face twists in frustration. "You think I don't know you?"

I don't know how long I stare at him, but it's long enough to lose all sense of time and space. "Wells," I breathe out, my hands shaking with the restraint not to reach out and touch him.

"I fucking know you, Layla. I know you by heart."

My thoughts slow down, growing sticky against the heat of his gaze.

"Tell me I'm wrong," he says, quietly now as he moves closer to me. "Tell me this isn't just about revenge for you."

"Maybe in the beginning . . . I didn't understand you. You were moody and quiet and you sure made it obvious that you didn't want me around. I thought you hated me, and I was worried about it—worried that Jason might dump the girl who didn't get along with his best friend.

"But then . . . you just kept showing up, Wells. You were there for me along the edges of so many moments that it made it hard to ignore. You saw me even when Jason didn't—and I never knew how to explain it, other than that I hoped it meant we were becoming real friends. I *wanted* to be friends with you.

"And then you almost kissed me after Jason broke up with me, and I woke up the next morning realizing I wished you *had*."

He stills, his eyes pinning me in place. "You remember that?"

I frown. "I might have had too much to drink, but I remember everything."

His eyes flash as understanding sinks in. "You wanted me to kiss you?"

"Yes," I confirm. "But then Jason and I got back together, and I refocused on my relationship with him. And you went back to being moody and distant again. I figured it was all a fluke."

"That's why I grew distant. Why I've *still* tried to be." Wells's jaw tightens, and on his face is a look so wild and starved it twists inside my stomach. "You sure knew how to fucking make me suffer, sunshine," he says quietly. And then he closes the distance between us and crashes his lips against mine.

He kisses me like he can't survive without me for another second. The muscles in his forearm dance beneath honeyed skin as he steadies his grip on me. It's clear he can't contain himself any better than I can.

"I've loved you every day since the first time I laid eyes on you, Layla Hayes," he murmurs into my lips. "And I hated you for it, too, because I loved Jason—" He squeezes his eyes shut —the words too painful, too unimaginable to let out. But then his eyes open and I watch as they sharpen on me. "I *loved* Jason, Layla. He was my best friend, my brother. I loved him with my whole heart. And I hated you because I loved you *more*."

A sob rips through me, guttural and loud. This is all too much—it's too damn much to bear. I don't know how to move forward from here.

He presses me against the wall and kisses me again, and my

body ignites at the feel of it. But my mind is too clouded by everything he's said, and I know we're both hanging on by a mere thread. It'd be a good idea to take a second to breathe. To come back to this conversation after a bit of a reset.

"I think you should take me home," I say as I wind my fingers through his hair, tugging lightly on the strands.

He nods, swiping a knuckle against my jaw. "Yeah," he rasps. "That's a good idea."

"But I'm not done talking about this," I say. "Okay?"

He lets out a low hum and steps back. "Okay," he says. And then, after blowing out a breath, he tilts his head toward the cabin's door. "Let's go."

CHAPTER TWENTY-SIX

THEN

It's the first Friday of June and the humidity is oppressive. If it weren't for the delicate breeze that caresses our sweat-slicked skin as it rolls in off the ocean, I don't think I'd have it in me to be here at the Senior Bondfire, even *if* it's to celebrate Jason's graduating class.

Truthfully, it's not just the thick air that's got me bothered. The buzzing of a brand-new anxiety has been rattling through me for weeks knowing all of this is coming: Jason has officially finished high school, and he'll be off to his first year as an Aggie at Texas A&M. I'll barely have a chance to prepare myself to be trapped in Saddlebrook Falls for another *two years* while my handsome and successful football-playing boyfriend is moving on with his life somewhere new and exciting. Somewhere that he gets an opportunity to start being whoever he wants to be and doesn't have to continue living up to the expectations set for the mayor's son or god's gift to our stifling town.

Needless to say, as happy as I am for him—truly, he

deserves that scholarship after how hard he's worked his whole life—I'm dreading the fact that he has to leave me to chase those dreams. I've spent most of the last two years molded in the space at Jay's side. We've not only grown in our love for each other, but in the easy friendship that continues to bloom so big and bright between us.

"You're in your head again," Jason murmurs as we trudge hand in hand through the soft sand toward his classmates, who are gathered near the shore. He knows enough about my headspace these days, and has been paying extra close attention to my emotions. And it's nice . . . even though it makes me feel like more of a sour puss raining sad puddles down instead of the happy and supportive girlfriend I'm trying like hell to be.

"I know," I say as I look up at him, watching a lock of his golden hair bounce on a long stride. "I'm sorry."

He squeezes my hand. "Hey, none of that. You have nothing to be sorry for. But we still have two months before I leave," he reminds me, *again*, and lets out a sigh. "Tonight is nothing more than a silly senior tradition. So let's try to have a little fun, okay?"

My temples pulse at his careful tone, a dose of shame radiating out into the space between us. I might be able to slip on a mask for most things in my life, but when it comes to Jason and my fear of losing everything we've built . . . It's a struggle.

It's not lost on me that I promised myself I'd never let a boy in so deep that I couldn't imagine a future without him—but that rule was based on my desire to leave this place and my refusal to let anyone change my mind. It's ironic, really, that the boy I fell for is the one now leaving *me* behind.

Up ahead, someone blows an air horn, and I'm lassoed

back into the moment. I force a smile on my face and nod. "Okay," I agree.

I'm able to shake myself out of my anxious haze as soon as we reach the rest of the group. Erin throws her arms around me when she sees me, and I say my hellos to Brad and Ethan. Jason pours beer into a plastic cup from a keg sitting in a kiddie pool of ice, and I dive into conversation with Matt and Haley who show up only minutes after we do.

I'm not the only non-senior here—Regan came with her older brother, Ian, a senior hockey player. Lizzie is here with her sister, Amanda, who's been president of the yearbook club for the last two years, and David is even here—though I'm not sure who he came with.

It's a large crowd of Mustangs, expanding beyond the social circles of the football team and cheerleaders, and it's a subtle reminder that life beyond our treasured football program does exist. A reminder that I'll find a new place within the layers of it all next year without Jason, that I'll be okay.

At least I'll still have cheer.

About an hour after we arrive, Wells shows up with a brunette on his arm that I've never seen before. She's wearing the red T-shirt that all the seniors have on to celebrate their class, but it's too big for her. I have a feeling she's not a senior, which means it must be Wells's shirt . . . and I'm not sure why but it bothers me that she's wearing it. That he'd let her parade around in something of his like that.

Not that it's my place to have an opinion where Wells Bennett is concerned. Frankly, he can do whatever—*whomever* —he wants. It's just . . . tonight is supposed to be about the seniors, about the end of their high school era. Even *I* feel slightly out of place here, but as Jason's girlfriend of almost two years, I'm intertwined with his life enough to warrant the right.

I guess I just wish Wells were more focused on celebrating this with his best friend and the rest of the team and less on using the event to get into a girl's pants. I have half a mind to scold him for it, to slip into our old routine of tossing light insults disguised as friendly banter, but I'm not sure I could get away with it anymore. Things have continued to feel splintered between Wells and me since last summer, and he's made it pretty clear that he doesn't care much about anything I might have to say.

I watch as he carelessly drops two folded beach chairs in the sand just outside the circle of bodies, reaching to greet some of the other football players with their usual handshakes and laughter. His date stands dutifully by his side, though he doesn't do much to include her or introduce her.

"You wanna play a little catch, babe?" Jason murmurs in my ear, wrapping his arms around me from behind. Goosebumps light up a trail down my spine, and my face splits into a warm grin.

"Sure," I say, playfully ducking out of his arms and running toward the water. I hear the thump of his feet in the sand behind me as he chases me, laughing. I pivot to the left to avoid him catching me and almost run right into Brad and Erin. "Shit," I squeal. "Sorry!"

It's enough of a distraction to pull me away from thoughts of Wells. It's not like there's really anything to think about, anyway—I'm just a bit hurt that we couldn't keep up with the friendship I *thought* we'd built last year. I miss the easy conversation, miss him teaching me things around the ranch. I don't go there at all anymore—at least not without Jason, and even that feels different.

Jason backtracks to the group to pull a football out of his bag. Even through the distance, I can see how his eyes glimmer with mischief as he also pulls a bottle of whiskey from it. A handful of people catch the movement and keep focus on him, like they know he's good for a good time as long as they stay in his orbit. He turns to walk back to me, oblivious to the attention he's getting from others. "Every time someone drops the ball, they have to take a shot," he declares.

Dread curls tight in my stomach as I think about the last time I drank whiskey. On instinct, my gaze jumps to the crowd of onlookers and lands on Wells. He's already watching me, like he knows exactly what I'm thinking. It's unnerving the way he can still do that, despite everything. I turn back to Jason. "That sounds like a quick way to get me drunk."

He laughs and shakes his head. "Nah, I'll go easy on you. Promise."

"How are we supposed to get home?" I ask.

"Ethan is going to drive us. I'll come back and get my car tomorrow."

I was standing right next to him when we got here, and I definitely didn't hear this come up in conversation with Ethan, which means . . . "You planned this," I say. It's not a question.

He shrugs. "Not a big deal."

It's not the first time he's pre-arranged a ride home for us from a party, so I'm not *exactly* surprised. But this is technically a school function. I mean, most of the people here already graduated last week and there aren't any school chaperones . . . but still, even if the school is mostly hands-off, the teachers are advocates of the Senior Bondfire and do what they can to support it happening.

Considering I still have two years left at Saddlebrook Falls High, the last thing I want is to get caught drinking. But I'm also distinctly aware that my time with Jason is fleeting, and I want to make the most of it before he leaves for school.

This is okay, right?

"Okay." I nod. "But you have to go easy on me."

He chuckles. "I already promised. Here—" He hands me the ball.

Turns out, Jason goes *very* easy on me. He also manages to drop the ball seven times in the first twenty minutes of playing, and the tension in my stomach grows taut as he takes long pulls from the bottle. I've only dropped it twice, and I'm not the one who plays this game seriously.

"I thought you were trying to go pro," I tease from where I stand.

His smile is wicked. "I'm a quarterback, babe," he says. "I'm not a receiver. Plus, you don't have the best aim."

I scoff, hiding my irritation behind a smile. I don't love it when Jason drinks like this, but who am I to tell him to cool it on a night that's supposed to be a celebration? He said Ethan would take us home, and Ethan's been nursing a bottle of water the whole time we've been here, so I decide I can let loose, too.

I make less of an effort to move to catch the ball, and each time it slips through my fingers and into the sand I saunter over to Jason to take shots of his whiskey. It doesn't take long before the buzz sets in, and as the sun begins to set and the sky ignites in a kaleidoscope of pinks bond oranges and blues, I realize I've forgotten why I was worried about anything at all.

"Hey, Layla!" someone shouts from farther up the beach. I turn and find Wells standing from his chair. He claps his hands and holds them out like he wants me to throw him the ball. I raise it up in question, and he nods, grinning.

The sight of his lips pulled high cracks something open in my chest. I feel myself lean toward him, like a flower eager for the sun. My own smile grows wide as I wind my arm back and send the ball flying.

My aim isn't great, but Wells carefully moves behind the chair his date sits in and jumps to catch it. "Hell yeah, nice job!" he shouts down to me, and my body winds tight from his praise. "Ready, Jay?"

Jason laughs. "Lay it on me, Bennett!"

Wells hurls the ball back down toward the shoreline, forcing Jason to run for it. And he does—he runs right into the water, feet splashing as he reaches to catch the ball. His hands wrap around it and pull it from the air, but he loses his balance from the momentum and falls to his knees. When he holds the ball up triumphantly, his smile is beaming.

Wells laughs from behind me and I feel the spark of the moment like a match struck. It may be fleeting, only existing here on this beach, but it was only a year ago when Wells was just as much my friend as Jason's. So I hold on to it, desperate to stretch it out, and realize it's not just Jason I'm going to miss when they inevitably leave for college.

Later, when the sunlight has disappeared and the sky is black, we sit around the bonfire under a blanket of stars. Jason and Wells are both drunk and happy, and Jason looks at Wells with so much love it brings me to tears.

"Promise me, Wells," Jason says suddenly, eyes fixed on his best friend.

Wells gives him a lopsided smile. "Promise you what?"

Jason's smile slips. "That we'll be best friends forever."

Wells's eyes soften but his smile doesn't waver. "*Brothers*, Jay. Forever."

Jason nods, and then he looks at me.

And I think . . . I think we might just be okay after all. As long as we hold on to this love, we can make it through anything.

CHAPTER TWENTY-SEVEN

NOW

Two days after the . . . *incident* with Wells, I feel like I'm climbing out of my skin. I haven't talked to him at all, though the urge to text him grows so strong I end up shutting my phone away in a drawer in my bedroom, as if hiding it under a silky pink pajama set might lessen the impulse.

It's not that I'm avoiding him—not really. I'm just not sure what to say, and I can't imagine a lame *Hey* through text would make me feel any less nervous about the state of our relationship.

Or . . . lack thereof.

Because technically, we shouldn't have one.

Jason's death and cheating have been the hardest things I've ever experienced, but this recent whirlwind with Wells is a third blow I'm not sure I can navigate without crumbling. I try to process how I'm feeling about what happened between us, and it's like the hardwiring of my heart is fried. I've always cared about Wells as a friend, enough that I've been hurt in the past when he's pulled away. But now knowing the feelings he's harbored all this time, the feelings that rushed through me as I kissed him down by the river, or when I straddled him in his truck . . .

I shudder as a flush crawls up my neck. There's no denying that my libido is in full working condition. And it wants Wells.

He's all I can think about, and even though my feelings are a mess right now, I know I want to be near him. These two days without him have felt like holding my breath underwater, waiting desperately to surface. It's what drove me to text Regan this morning, asking if she had plans tonight.

When she replied that she didn't, it felt like fate. Wells has been spending most evenings helping his brothers behind the bar at Wild Coyote, and I can't find a good reason that should stop Regan and me from casually popping in. Worst-case scenario he's not there, and Regan and I enjoy a drink and have another attempt at catching up where I *hopefully* don't cry. Best case? Wells *is* there, and . . . well, I'm not sure what that would mean.

My biggest insecurity is that he regrets everything that happened. I haven't reached out yet, but neither has he, and I can't help but mentally trip over why that might be. It would make sense for him to, since I've been his best friend's girl for five and a half years . . . but I know how incredible it felt to be with him like *that*, even for just a few fleeting moments, and there's no way he didn't feel it too.

The chemistry was undeniable.

Regan and I meet at the gazebo in the middle of the town square with plans to walk together to the bar. It's safe to assume we'll both have a few drinks, and aside from a handful of lifts Gus gives out in the mornings before Mustang's Pizza opens, rideshare apps don't exist in Saddlebrook Falls.

I get there first and try not to feel silly standing alone on the bright-green lawn. The skirt of my yellow dress sways in the breeze, and I close my jean jacket tight across my chest to block the chill. It's a night better suited for jeans and a sweater, but I felt compelled to wear my boots with the embroidered yellow flowers. I haven't worn them since I left for New York, and I forgot how much I love them.

When Regan spots me from the end of the street that leads to her neighborhood, I can feel her calculating my emotional state. I don't blame her—I wasn't exactly fine when I saw her earlier this week. Still, something within me has irrevocably changed, as if my very DNA has been rearranged.

"Hey!" she calls out from the edge of the lawn. I realize she's wearing heels—I don't think I've ever seen Regan in heels —and I walk to meet her so she doesn't have to step into the grass.

"Hi," I say back, smiling. "You look great!" I take in her slim-fitted jeans and beautiful ivory satin top beneath a tan blazer. She looks nothing like the girl who left home two years ago with ribbons in her hair. Tallahassee has been good for her.

"Thanks," she says coyly. "I actually have a date tonight."

My eyes widen. "I thought *we* were going out!"

She laughs. "We are. At least for a while—David is picking me up for karaoke in Williamson around nine."

"*David*?!" I squeal.

Her smile slips into something more bashful. "We've been . . . texting."

"Regan, he's been our friend since we were fourteen years old. We all text."

"Yeah but, I mean like, *texting*."

"Oh," I say. I'm . . . shocked. I never would have seen something like this coming, but I love Regan and David so much and would be thrilled if they found happiness in each other.

"It's super new," she insists. "And anyway, that's not what tonight is about." She shifts on her heels and looks to the ground, and I realize talking about this makes her nervous.

"Hey," I say quietly. When her eyes rise to meet mine, I give her a soft smile. "It's okay to be excited about a boy. I'm happy for you—I promise."

Her exhale is sharp, loosening her shoulders. "How are you doing?" she asks, cutting straight to the point.

My smile grows. I can't help it, even if it might not make sense to anyone else. I'm not ready to share what happened with Wells—I know how crazy it all sounds only weeks after losing Jason—but I know how sure I feel in my heart that what happened was *right*. "I'm okay," I say honestly. "It's been a hard few weeks, but I'm finally seeing a light at the end of the tunnel."

She tilts her head. "You seem lighter."

"I feel lighter," I agree.

She reaches a hand out to wrap around my shoulder in affection. "I'm glad, Layla."

My eyes sting with emotion, but for once it's not sadness.

We make our way down the block to Wild Coyote and find the lot already full of cars. I spot Wells's truck parked in the same corner he was in the night of Jason's funeral, and my heart takes a tumble. *He's here.*

Inside, the bar is dark. Without any windows, there's a perpetual feeling of night that feeds into the overall dungeon-like vibe of the place. It's what has the regulars squinting like raccoons being exposed by a midnight porch light when Regan holds the door open for me and I follow her in. Regan and I squint back, adjusting to the dark atmosphere as we look for open chairs.

Within moments of finding two open seats at the bar, Wells appears from the back. He looks like a dream under the neon lights, his olive skin glowing beneath his dark T-shirt and black cowboy hat. The line of his honeyed jaw jumps when he notices me sitting here, and I nearly fall out of my seat when he approaches.

I feel tipsy and I haven't even ordered a drink yet. My body sings under his attention, a spark in my chest igniting with a longing I can't explain. I'm not sure how long it's been there, but it's as real as the blood roaring to life beneath the surface of my skin.

His eyes bounce to Regan before they land on me again. "Enjoying your evening?" he asks, the corners of his mouth tugging into the smallest of smiles.

"We just got here," I clarify. "But that's the goal."

He hums, considering, taking a moment to scan the many faces around the bar before he continues. "It's busy here tonight—you two be careful, all right?"

I roll my eyes. Careful is the *last* thing I want to be. "You don't have to worry about us," I counter, sidestepping the authority in his voice with an attempt of my own.

His eyes narrow, the brown of them solidifying like stone. It's a look that drips in power, and it sends a shiver through me. "Layla," he warns. "You know how rough it can get in here."

It's true—most indecent and unruly behavior that erupts into gossip starts inside this very bar. With the Bennetts at the helm, it makes the establishment even more risqué. Town lore suggests Wells's grandfather, who founded the Wild Coyote in the 1930s amid the Great Depression, was as vile and mean as they came. His son, Wells's father, has instigated dozens of drunken bar fights here that have led to almost as many arrests. My eyes flick to Rhett behind the bar as he pours a beer from the tap into a pint glass, and I think of how he keeps that family reputation alive. Brooks has also had his fair share of fights and scandals, though he's calmed down over the years. But Wells . . . I'm not sure Wells has a mean bone in his beautiful body.

"You know, I figured that might be where the *Wild* comes into play in the name," I say with sass.

He ignores me and politely asks Regan, "Can I get you something to drink?"

Regan eyes the collection of liquor bottles that lines the bar's back wall, and then the three handles of beer on tap. "Do you serve martinis here?"

Wells's earthy eyes flash with amusement. "How about chilled bottom-shelf vodka in a regular glass with a wedge of lemon?"

Regan lets out a breathy laugh. "Sold."

He turns to me. "And for you, sunshine?"

I feel Regan stiffen at the nickname—for as much as Wells has called me that over the years, no one besides his brothers and Jason has ever heard it. I try to keep my voice casual as I answer. "Whiskey," I say. "Please."

He knows I only drink whiskey when I'm feeling reckless, and I want him to know that's exactly what I am tonight.

His throat rolls with a swallow. "Coming right up."

REGAN IS JUST ABOUT THREE SHEETS TO THE WIND off Wells's "martinis" when David arrives to pick her up for their karaoke date. If he were anyone else, I'd send him packing and get her home myself. But I trust David, and I recognize the warmth and delight in his eyes when he walks in and sees her— it's clear whatever is brewing between them is genuine.

When they leave, I turn back to the glass of bourbon I've been sipping on for the last hour. It's only my second one, but I know better than to rush whiskey. Plus, my body is already whirring from being in the same vicinity as Wells, and I don't want to overdo it and ruin any opportunities to get close to him again.

I steal a glance at the dark hallway that leads to the back office and I'm surprised to find him standing in the shadows. His arms are crossed over his chest, a shoulder leaning against the wall, and he's watching me with a level of reverence that steals the breath from my lungs.

He gives a small nod over his shoulder, beckoning me to follow him before he disappears around the corner.

My heart thunders, a wild pounding reaching my throat. I turn to find Rhett busy with customers at the other end of the bar, and a quick look around proves that the other patrons are engaged in their own conversations. It's all the encouragement I need to tip back the rest of my drink and slide off of my stool.

I find Wells in the open doorway to the office, a blue-lit sign that hangs from the hallway wall shining over him. It makes him look even more enticing, and I move toward him like a moth to a flame.

"You look good in neon." His eyes roam my face before they trail down my throat. And I feel it again: a dangerous pull for more.

It's what coaxes the question from my mouth. "How good?"

His eyes snap up to mine and I see how they change, how his pupils swallow his beautiful brown irises whole. And he must understand the dare in my bones, because he's suddenly standing taller, shoulders growing wider as he crowds into my space. He steps toward me so I'm forced to move until my back makes contact with the wall of the hallway behind me. The base of my skull disturbs a frame that hangs, but neither of us addresses it. "Layla," he breathes, the low timbre of his voice like the softest velvet.

His restraint is cracking, the splintered edges of his control fraying by the second. It feels like all the air's been sucked out of the narrow space around us. And I might be the world's biggest fool, but I *want* him to give in—it would be such a relief to all this restlessness in my heart.

So, emboldened by the tremble of his hand as it settles on my hip and the way I'm burning from the inside out, I decide I'm ready to face this fire head-on instead of running from it again. I brush my nose against his, inhaling the spice of his cologne and those familiar traces of wintergreen, and I say it. "Kiss me."

I feel the sharp breath he takes in, the way he holds it in his lungs as he looks at me with so much longing I'm not sure I can stand it.

And then he does.

His mouth moves against mine painfully slow, giving me so many chances to stop him, to stop this. But when I let out an eager whimper, his tenderness turns hungry. His hips pin mine against the wall, fingers pressing deep into my skin as he takes what he wants from my mouth. "Fuck, Layla," he whispers against my lips, darting his tongue out to part me open.

He glides his fingers up my jaw, where they settle possessively behind the nape of my neck as he pulls me closer, deepening the kiss. I wrap my arms around his neck and when a soft moan escapes me, he grunts and skates his teeth along my chin before his mouth presses hot against my throat.

My body practically sings under his touch, and it's . . . confusing. It's confusing and damn near terrifying and . . . oh my *god* his hands are rough and calloused as they whisper up my arms. "Wells," I plead, but I'm not sure what I'm begging for. He responds with a thrust, pressing his hips further into mine as he lifts my right leg up and over his waist. I nearly cry out as the skirt of my dress slips and bunches where his jeans meet my inner thigh, the buckle of his belt digging into my skin.

"I've been going out of my mind," he murmurs against my temple before leaning down to take my bottom lip between his teeth. "I've been fucking dying for this, Layla."

His confession is a match struck in a room full of kerosene, and I can only hope we're both not burned by the fire. He drags the stubble of his chin along my throat as I whisper, "I'm going to make a mess of this." I'm incapable of stopping what's happening, incapable of any restraint. But Wells deserves an out if he needs one.

"Make a mess of me, then," he insists, and I lose myself in him completely. His hips rock forward as his hand trails down my side to slip under my dress. Fingers ghost along my thigh, and my breath catches. "Can I go down on you?" he asks, his bee-stung lips slick from my mouth. "Please?"

My core pulses violently at the need in his voice, and when

I give him an eager nod, he immediately drops to his knees. "Will anyone find us?"

He shakes his head, lifting my raised leg over his shoulder. "It's just Rhett and me tonight, and he's busy out there."

Of all his brothers, Rhett is the *last* one I'd want to catch this. There's no telling what he'd do. But with Wells's impatient expression between my legs, my need for more outweighs all sanity. And when he tugs my panties to the side to expose my desire, I freeze in heady anticipation.

I look down to watch him in wonder. He keeps the cotton of my underwear pinned with one hand as his other traces my inner thigh. He's looking at my skin in awe, and it takes a moment to realize what he sees—the imprint of his buckle, where it was branded into my flesh. It takes the shape of a rodeo horse, outlined in red. He thumbs it softly, breath shaking as he whispers, "So fucking beautiful."

And when he turns his attention back to where I'm bared open for him, his eyes turn black. It takes only seconds for him to take me into his mouth, for his tongue to make contact where I want him most, and I nearly combust on the spot. He hums out a rattling breath and I feel it vibrate through my bones. There is nothing tender about the way he sucks against me, the way his teeth nip at swollen skin. There is only his hunger and my need, and we're both undone by it.

The impact is so intense that I squirm against his hot mouth, but a strong hand at the base of my spine holds me in place. His other hand disappears beneath him, and when he lets out a soft grunt, I realize he's touching himself. A wave of pleasure tips inside of me, crashing through every limb, and soon I'm on the precipice of completely unraveling. "I'm close," I whimper. "Fuck, Wells, I'm so close."

He groans out a guttural sound, and it's what takes me over the edge. I cover a hand over my mouth to stifle a cry as my mind blanks. The orgasm is a growing, blasting thing of light, and I don't know how to contain myself.

"Shh," he gently shushes from beneath me. But then his forehead presses into my stomach and he's trying like hell to smother his own groans, and I realize that *he's* coming. It takes me by surprise that this would be enough to get him off, too. A savage delight shakes through me. A feeling of power like I've never experienced before.

After a long breath, he tips his head back to look up at me, an almost shy smile on his slicked lips. He carefully positions my underwear back in place and smooths my dress back down before he rises.

But he doesn't back away. Those lips connect with mine, and I can taste myself on them. "Do you have anywhere else to be tonight?" His eyes are sharp and hopeful.

"No." I shake my head.

"Good," he says simply, adjusting himself through his pants. "I'm not done with you yet."

CHAPTER TWENTY-EIGHT

THEN

I consider myself a spiritual person, undoubtedly. There's a general magic to life that continues to foster my belief in some higher power or higher truth. A Texas sunset in the fall is so beautiful it can bring you to your knees, and getting lost in nature is a sure comfort.

That said, I don't consider myself to be religious. At least, it's a truth I hold inside myself, because to actually let it out would be my great undoing as far as my mother is concerned. The concept is almost comical to me since *she* didn't seem very religious until she met Barry—but that's not my judgment to make.

Even so, my family has attended the eight o'clock service at Blessed Harvest Church every single Sunday since Barry and my mother married, save for the one time in second grade when I was hit with the flu so bad I was allowed to stay home with my then-nanny, Brigitte. I've tried to get out of other services for various reasons but haven't been successful since.

It's not that I'm against the sermons—not exactly. I believe in much of what Pastor Brown imparts on our congregation, and I know it comes from a well-meaning place. It's more that I feel surrounded by the stifling presence of hypocrites and gossip mongers who leave each service to spread the good "word" of town dirt with each other in the courtyard before heading home—my mother included.

When Jason and I started dating, I learned he went to the same service every week with his parents, too, but they usually attended the one at nine-thirty. It took a little convincing on his part, but soon the Moores shifted to the earlier service, and Jason and I found an ounce of freedom in getting to sit together on our own—usually somewhere toward the back.

Now that he's gone, I'm forced to sit with my mother who chastises my posture and forces me to sing every hymn. Her expectation for Annie and I to be "good girls" only leads to resentment, because a performance by any eager parishioner has *nothing* to do with the level of good they exude in their life, as proven by the die-hard congregants who now surround me in this pew.

"Focus, bug," Mom murmurs from where she sits next to me, her string of pearls gliding along the floral dress she's wearing as she leans toward me. She has this uncanny ability to correct me without ever tearing her focus away from Pastor Brown.

I sigh, adjusting my gaze away from old lady Maeve's silver beehive hair and back toward the altar. We're only halfway through the hour-long service—it never fails to feel absolutely endless.

A loud crash sounds from the back of the room, and the full congregation turns in tandem. A lone figure in a dusty cowboy hat stumbles backward into the nave from the lobby, a familiar black leather jacket smeared with dirt.

Rhett.

"Oh my word," my mother whispers next to me as Barry groans out a sound of annoyance that matches others all around the room, and a soft murmuring ignites.

Rhett spins around, his face twisting into a burning anger unlike I've ever seen. It puts me on edge. "What!" he shouts. "What are you fuckers looking at, huh?!"

His words are slurred, and it's clear that he's drunk. He's probably been at it all night if I had to guess. Pastor Brown's voice sounds, a careful, "Are you okay, son?"

Rhett shoots a vicious glare at him. "I'm not your fucking son," he spits. "You know who my father is."

Pastor Brown simply nods, stone-faced. "Indeed I do."

Rhett squares up. His eyes are bloodshot, and even as he straightens, he's swaying on his feet. When he starts to march down the closest aisle like he's going to do something with all that hostility, I shoot out of my seat on instinct.

"*Layla*," Mom demands in a hushed voice, but I ignore her. I step right into Rhett's path and throw my hands out to stop him.

"Hey," I say gently. "What's wrong, Rhett?"

His gray eyes slide to me, glassy and unfocused. "Get out of the way, Layla."

I shake my head. "How about we go outside instead?" His chest heaves, probably with adrenaline, but he doesn't say anything. So I brave a handful of steps forward until he's just in reach, and then I wind my arm through his and carefully turn him around. I feel the sharp stares of every person in the room —it's so quiet that I can hear Nosy Maeve clear her throat from the other side, but I ignore it. "What happened?" I ask Rhett quietly.

It's enough of a distraction to loosen his shoulders. I keep my arm threaded through his, like this is nothing more than a casual walk between two people courting each other in some faraway kingdom. I know if I can get him back outside and away from all these people, we can avoid giving them all more to talk about.

He scrubs a hand over his face with his free hand, and I notice his knuckles are bloody and bruised. "It's been a long night," he says, his voice strained and gravelly like sandpaper. It's clear he's dehydrated; I can smell the stale liquor on his breath.

As soon as we clear the lobby and push through the stained-glass doors, the warm sun floods over our faces. I take a quick look around, but I don't see his motorcycle anywhere in the parking lot—thank god he didn't ride it here—so it's safe to assume he walked. The ranch is a few miles out of town, but if I have to walk him all the way, I will. "I'm a good listener, you know."

I feel him look at me, as if considering. Of all the Bennetts, I'm closest to Wells, and then probably Kasey from our time spent around the ranch last year. I'm around Rhett much more than Brooks or Sawyer—but I know him the least. He's also the one who intimidates me the most. Right now, though, I just want to make sure he's okay.

"Not interested," he mutters dryly.

I nod, letting it drop as we walk arm in arm along the side-walk. It's quiet out—still early for a Sunday. Only half of the shops will open today, and most not before eleven. The gazebo comes into view and I can't help but sneak a glance at Rhett.

We all know the rumors, and it usually seems to trigger him, but right now he's only focused on the road ahead.

The sound of a car approaches from behind us, and I find Gus behind the wheel of his white sedan, eyes glued to Rhett and me. It's almost comical, the way he stares so intensely. Like he's witnessing a crime.

"You don't have to walk with me," Rhett huffs out. He sounds dejected, and I can't help the worry that creeps in.

"What do you mean?"

His laugh is without humor. "You don't want to be seen with me."

"Says who?"

He looks at me, unconvinced. His eyes—even glazed from a night spent drinking—hold so much depth it's hard to look away.

Rhett's always been an asshole. He wears it like a badge of honor, something to be proud of. I've always thought it was all a bit attention-seeking, despite the obvious commitment to bully everyone away from him. But right now, I see the familiar traces of hurt and longing for something *more*, something *better*. And I realize, maybe he isn't as scary as he tries to be.

"No one wants to be caught associating with me, sweetheart. But you already know that, don't you?"

I shrug, thinking carefully about my next words. "I think people are pretty unfair in their thoughts toward your family," I clarify. "But I also think you don't help the situation."

He smirks. "Is that right?"

"Well . . . you're a bit of a troublemaker, you know."

He laughs again, and this time it sounds more genuine. "Yeah, I know."

"Maybe you could try . . . *not* being one?" I suggest.

"I could," he agrees. "But where's the fun in that?"

"Is that why you do it? For fun?"

He nearly trips over a patch of uneven concrete, leaning into me for balance. I look up at him, finding his expression has grown softer. He seems to have lost most of the fight in him, and it's a relief. Intervening at church was impulsive, but if Rhett *really* wanted to cause damage to something or, god forbid, someone, I'm not sure I'd be able to stop him.

His slate eyes catch mine. "None of this is ever fun, Layla." And there it is again, that detached melancholy. It knocks something loose in my chest, a kernel of unease that Rhett might need more help than an escort home. I think he needs a friend.

I wish Wells was home so I could encourage him to be a source of comfort. I make a mental note to bring it up to Jason next time we talk.

The sound of another car pulls our focus back to the street, and I recognize Kasey's black pickup. "Oh goody," Rhett mutters, his mask of indifference slipping back on.

Kasey pulls over and rolls the window down. "Where the fuck have you been, Rhett?" he demands.

"For fuck's sake, Kase. I don't need you up my ass all the time."

Kasey scoffs. "Look at you, drunk on a Sunday morning. And you wonder *why* I have to be up your ass?" He shakes his head. "I'm getting real sick of your shit. Bigger things are going on in the world than you and your fucking tantrums."

Rhett rolls his eyes, and all traces of their earlier depth are gone. "Thanks for the chit-chat," he says coolly, and pulls away from my side.

I cross my arms over my chest, feeling awkward to be witnessing all of this. "No problem," I say.

Rhett swings open the passenger door and gets in as Kasey mouths a quick *Thank you* over his shoulder. As soon as the door slams shut, Kasey peels the truck away from the curb and they take off toward the ranch.

I stare after them until they're nothing more than a black dot on the horizon of the open countryside ahead.

Back at the church, I decide not to go in—I don't want to cause another distraction, and there are only a few minutes left of the service anyway. Instead, I sit on a bench in the front courtyard and wait, lost in thought about the Bennetts and Rhett and the possibility that he's not actually a bad guy. That he's just suffering, and misunderstood.

When the service lets out, my mother is one of the first out of the building, traces of both panic and annoyance marring her beautiful face. "Layla," she breathes out when she sees me sitting here.

I stand and walk to meet her. "I'm sorry," I say. "I was just trying to . . ."

"I don't want you near that family anymore, you hear me?" she interjects. "With Jason and . . . his *friend* gone, there's no reason for you to interact with any of them."

I frown. "There's nothing wrong with the Bennetts," I say firmly. "I don't understand what the big deal is."

She sighs, a strand of her long brown hair blowing away from her face. "You know Bud Bennett was found passed out drunk in his wheelchair in the middle of the road in front of their god-awful bar yesterday morning?" she asks. "They're dangerous people—all of them. A bunch of law-bending alcoholics who don't care about anyone else. And you're too sweet of a young lady to get mixed up with them. I should have put my foot down a long time ago, but I'm doing it now." She straightens her spine before laying the final blow. "No more Bennetts, Layla—tell me you understand."

She seems genuinely worried that I'll be tainted just by being around them, as if their family is a disease to carve out of our environment. I can't help but think of Mrs. Bennett and her warm smile. Of Brooks and Melody and their beautiful boys, of Kasey and his dedication to the rescue horses and his patience in teaching me how to care for Lucky. Of Wells and his ability to always know how to help me, even when our friendship is on shaky ground.

"I don't understand," I say honestly. "Don't you think they deserve some of the same grace you like to pray for?" Her cheeks flush as her eyes widen in shock. You'd think I slapped her.

"There you are," Barry says as he comes up behind her, Annie's hand held in his. "You rushed out of there so quickly." His smile is nervous as he looks back and forth between us.

"We were just taking a moment to pray for the Bennett family," I say, my gaze still locked on my mother. "Weren't we?"

Her tight lips rise in a smile so forced it looks painful. "Yes," she says after a beat. "Of course."

I nod, satisfied.

And then I turn to walk to the car.

CHAPTER TWENTY-NINE

NOW

Wells drives me back to the ranch, one hand spread wide across my leg the whole twelve minutes it takes for us to get there. We wind up the long driveway and past the main house as he steers us toward his cabin, and my stomach flips in anticipation when it comes into view. My body is a live wire, my desire a tangible, violent thing that rocks through me.

He turns his headlights off as we approach, and the world around us disappears in the night. It takes four or five heartbeats for my eyes to adjust to the starlit slope of the cabin's roof, to the shadowed corners of the window in the front. My cheeks burn hot as I picture us inside, exploring each other and all the things we can do under the blanket of night, tucked away from the rest of the world.

When the truck rolls to a stop, he pulls his hand from my thigh, and my skin is cold in its absence. We look at each other across the cab, nothing but the sound of shallow breathing between us. Even in the cover of darkness, I see his want take shape in his eyes.

We barely make it through the front door before he's crowding me against the nearest wall. His hands tremble as he cups my face, thumb pressing roughly into my bottom lip. And then he pulls me in for a kiss that scorches me right to my core.

"Layla," he whispers urgently against my cheek. "What I said earlier, about making a mess of this . . . I think I need to take it back." I tilt my head back to look at him, *really* look at him. For the first time tonight, I see small traces of his fear. "If we do this, it's going to mean something to me." His eyes move across my face. "I need you to be sure."

His shirt bunches in my fists as I hold him tighter, desperate to make him feel as warm and shimmering and *good* as he's making me feel. "I'm sure," I breathe. "Please."

"Okay." He nods, slack-jawed. "Okay." And when he slants his mouth over mine again, it feels like home.

He tastes me like he's been deprived . . . like I'm his first meal in years. Our tongues slide together as I catch his groan in my throat. I press myself further into him, wind my arms around his neck and pull him in deeper—I want to coax another groan out of him so I can taste it again.

"Tell me how to do this." He drags his teeth across my jaw as his hand ghosts up my back, pulling a shiver out of my bones.

It's a soft demand that throbs through me. But I don't know how to articulate the ache that's winding tight enough to be just on the edge of pain. "I . . . I—" I can't *think*.

"Tell me what you like. Be selfish."

"Selfish?" I ask, mind spinning.

His eyes drop to my mouth, to my neck. "*So* selfish, Layla.

Please." He presses his lips to my mouth, less of a kiss and more of a fix. "Tell me how to please you." His hand spreads over my ribs as he not-so-gently pushes me further into the wall—he's coming undone, and it knocks me off my mental ledge. "Tell me how to make you feel good."

I nod. "Touch me."

He grunts, the hand on my ribs squeezing. "Where?"

I slide my palm over the back of his hand and guide it down to my thighs, slipping it beneath my dress and between my legs where he already had me with his mouth. "Here," I say, and then gasp as his fingers curl into me, pushing against my panties.

"Fuck." He kisses me hard as his fingers plunge a second time. "I want to make you come again," he murmurs. "Show me how you like this."

When I circle my fingers against myself, his focus sharpens. His gaze drops, and he lifts the hem of my dress to watch what I'm doing. It nearly sends me to the moon to see him look at me the way he does. "Like this," I force out.

"Hm," he hums. His eyes rise to meet mine, shining and steadfast. "My turn."

His hand replaces mine as he sucks against my neck, and I close my eyes in euphoria. The edges of my vision blur as his fingertips sink deeper into my skin. His teeth rake against my jaw as his hips pin mine to the wall, and I want him to leave a mark.

He looks at me with a reverence I've never seen before, and I know it for what it is: the secret that's been buried in the layers of his heart for so long. Everything he's been clutching so tight for his best friend's girl.

Wells keeps a perfect rhythm against me with his fingers,

and I know it won't be long before I'm collapsing at his feet. He reaches with his free hand to pull the strap of my dress down over my shoulder, exposing a sliver of my bare nipple, and goes utterly still when he sees it.

"Are you bare under this dress, Layla?" he asks, swiping his fingers roughly between my legs.

My hips buck from the sensation, and I can only nod as I reach up to brace myself against him—I feel my orgasm coming, like a building wave across the surface of the ocean, bigger and brighter than anything I've ever felt before.

It's a dizzying thought. The only other person I've been with was Jason . . . but it was nothing like this—I don't know what to make of it.

Wells forcibly pulls the top of my dress down further until my full breast is on display, and he's completely entranced, as if he's discovered a trove full of riches. "You're so beautiful."

There's an odd sensation behind my sternum, as if my ribcage is expanding beneath my very skin. I'm desperate for the man who's already pressed against me. It feels white-hot and dangerous, like it will destroy me if I let it.

He bends his head down to take my nipple into his mouth, his tongue hot as it flattens against the peak, and it's all I need to tip into the unyielding pool of pleasure. And this time when I cry out from the force of it, he does nothing to quiet me. Instead, he *beams*.

"That was so hot," he says, mouth curved high. He winds his fingers through my hair and tugs my head back, exposing my neck to him. "Can I have you like this?" He presses a soft kiss to the center of my throat as the hand beneath my dress glides across my hip to palm my ass. He rocks against me, and I feel him everywhere. "Please?"

"Yes," I pant, reaching for his belt—he can have whatever he wants. Right now, I'm willing to give him anything he asks for—my body . . . my heart. He's rock hard beneath his jeans, the shape of him almost unbelievable. I want to get him *out*, want to see him for myself.

As soon as I get past the clasp of his buckle and the button of his worn jeans, he helps me push them down his muscular legs—and my mouth goes dry at the sight of him. He's all hard angles and sharp edges, his thighs straining against the fit of his jeans where they're bunched halfway to his knees. He reaches over his shoulder to grab the neck of his T-shirt and pulls it over his head. For the second time tonight, my mind completely blanks.

His shy smile tells me he notices the effect he's having on me, but it slips as his eyes dip to my exposed chest. And once again, he's enraptured.

Moving to close the short distance between us, his hands wrap around the backs of my thighs behind the skirt of my dress as he lifts me, pinning me against the wall. He settles his hips between my legs, burying his face in a sensitive spot between my chin and collarbone that has me gasping for air. I feel every inch of him pressed firmly against me, and it winds me right back up again.

"Is this okay?" he rasps, fingertips digging into my hips.

"Yes," I hiss through the pain, loving the way it feels. Loving how much he seems to need this as much as I do.

"Tell me again," he murmurs, his lips against my jaw. "Tell me I can have you like this." His voice grows softer. "Tell me this is real."

I moan as he palms my breast, warmth radiating through my skin. I reach to press a hand to his jaw, forcing him to look at me. His need is obvious, but I can still see traces of his worry. Of a quiet shame in giving in to what he wants most—knowing what it means.

"Wells," I say firmly as I heave out a breath. "This is real," I insist, watching his molten eyes clear as he hangs on to every word. "I'm right here, in your arms, and there's nowhere else in the world I'd rather be." My eyes sting with the truth. I know this probably won't end well—how could it? But all I see is him. All I feel is his body against mine, anchoring me to something that feels a lot like hope, and I know with a newfound clarity that it's *always* been like this: Wells has put my needs first for so long, over and over and over again.

I lean forward to kiss him, and it's not long before we become a frenzied tangle of limbs and mouths and sticky heat.

"Can I fuck you bare?" he asks, winded. "I haven't . . . I haven't been with anyone in a long time."

The question sends a shiver through me, an electric edge of power. He's already positioned where I want him most, it would take only the smallest adjustment to make it count. "*Yes*," I breathe.

My body is pliant, especially after the two orgasms he's already pulled out of me. I feel loose and heavy, but he has no problem holding me up with his hefty thighs and strong arms. He reaches to shove the cotton of my underwear to the side and, despite his size, rocks into me with a single, blazing thrust.

Immediately, his eyes squeeze shut, one palm slapping the wall beside my head to steady himself. "*Fuuuck*," he whooshes out. He keeps his body completely still like he's in anguish.

My chest heaves as I stretch around him, burning and pulsing and at once utterly bent to his will. "Oh my god," I whisper, pressing my mouth to the notch at the center of his collarbone. Wells trembles around me, his quiet vulnerability shining like a beacon in the otherwise dark room.

I find him looking at me, his eyes a liquid pool of emotions: euphoria, anticipation, shame, and a palpable layer of grief that mirrors my own. Because we've done it—we've irrevocably crossed this line. It's a freefall plummet into the chasm of everything this could lead to—both good and bad—and neither of us is wearing a parachute.

Somehow, I'm struck by what a relief it is.

"This is real," I say again with clarity. And I'm grateful when it seems to wash most of that anxiousness away as he leans in to kiss me, open and raw.

And then he starts to move.

I become nothing but flesh and bones as an electric tendril of pleasure pulls taut. "I've wanted this for so long," he admits before biting into my shoulder, showing he's not quite in control. He keeps a hand braced against the wall, his thrusts brutal and vicious and so perfect in all the ways that light me up.

The sounds he makes are guttural, his heat blistering as he sinks further into me. His body cocoons around me, a temporary home that I never want to leave. I lose myself, pinned between the wall and the weight of him, a whole new wave of satisfaction scorching me from the inside out as my boots knock against his bunched jeans.

My mind spins as my body tenses, right on the cusp of losing it. His mouth is hot against my ear as he tells me over and over again how beautiful I am, how he never wants to let me go. It's when tells me all the ways he plans to fuck me on every surface inside the cabin that I finally launch over the edge. I come hard, so hard my vision blurs and stars seem to float around us. They're so captivating and beguiling that I almost don't hear him say it.

"Layla." His voice is low, frantic. "Fuck, Layla, should I—should I pull out?"

I shake my head, mind buzzing, body deliciously numb. And when I smile, he erupts, concealing his sounds in the crook of my neck. The sounds of his pleasure, of his undoing.

I plan all the ways I can keep them there, to save them for later.

When his eyes find mine, they're awestruck. "Do you see it, too?"

"See what?" I ask, breathless.

"The light," he says, so clearly. "All around us."

He doesn't wait for me to answer—just kisses me long and slow. But I can't help but wonder . . .

"The stars?" I ask, pulling my mouth away only enough to say the words.

"No." He smiles. "It was the sun."

CHAPTER THIRTY

THEN

Jason invites me to visit him at Texas A&M during the spring break of his freshman year. It's only a few months after his first season of college ball finishes, and he and Wells decide to stay on campus for the week-long holiday. I've been going crazy missing him at home, so it doesn't take much convincing for me to want to go.

It takes my mom and Barry a little more to agree, though. I suppose letting their seventeen-year-old daughter drive alone to visit her boyfriend at college is a little . . . *unbecoming*. Thankfully, my mother's love for Jason and her hope for our future together wins out, and she sends me off after I promise to check in with her every day.

The drive from Saddlebrook Falls to College Station is about two and a half hours, and I make it in good time. When I pull into the parking lot of Keahey Hall, the five-story building where Jason and Wells share a dorm together, I soak in the surroundings. The building looks like it's been here for over a hundred years. The luscious green lawn surrounding it is freshly manicured, and the concrete sidewalks look like they've been recently resurfaced. Despite its age, the grounds are well-kept, and I have no doubt plenty of money flows through it.

I check the ribbon tied around my ponytail in the rearview mirror of Mom's Mercedes before pulling my cheer duffle from the back seat. Pushing out the door, I send a quick text to Jason to let him know I'm here, and then make my way toward the hall's front entrance.

I enter the double doors to the front lobby just as Jason rounds the corner from the stairwell, a white Aggies T-shirt stretched across his chest, and I can't help but skip forward to close the distance between us.

"My girl," he murmurs into my hair as his arms wrap tightly around me. I've seen him twice since school started, for Thanksgiving weekend and soon after for Christmas break, but in the months that have passed since then, he's . . . changed. He's all angles and hard muscle, so much more the man of my future. "It's so good to see you. How was the drive?"

I nuzzle into his chest as his familiar smell of clean soap and woody aftershave wraps around me. "God, I've missed you," I confess, the truth of it hitting me harder than expected. I've been so lonely this year without Jason around, but to feel his body against mine like this ignites an ache I've buried deep. I only have five days here, and I'm already anxious about how quickly it'll go by. "The drive was good," I continue. "A little traffic going through Houston but overall not bad."

He gives me a quick squeeze before pulling away and grabbing the duffle from my hand. "Hope you don't mind climbing the stairs—the elevator's been out for a week."

I laugh, unable to contain my excitement. "I don't mind at all."

The stairwell is dark and narrow, the walls a beige-painted brick that glares against the fluorescent lights. Jason's dorm is on the fourth floor, and as we push through the swing door that leads to a long, carpeted hallway the smell of burnt popcorn overtakes us.

Most of the doors along the corridor are open. The few that are shut are adorned with pictures and streamers. Each door has a dry-erase board that lists two names at the top, and many have colorful notes scrawled in different handwriting.

I trail behind Jason as we maneuver between two girls leaning against opposite sides of the hall, and I try not to notice the way they both stare at me. I catch a glimpse of a shirtless boy with wild blond curls inside a dorm room to my left, sitting on the foot of a small bed. He's got one foot propped up as he strums quietly on an acoustic guitar and . . . he's *good* from what I can hear. His eyes pop up to look at me just as we clear the doorway.

A tall boy with a smattering of freckles and bright red hair flies across the hall from one room to another just as a small cheer erupts from within the first. It's a lively environment, and Jason nods a hello to everyone we see along the way. It hits me that these are his peers now, the people he sees every day and spends countless hours with, who he's inevitably built a life with.

"Here we are," Jason says as he veers toward a room on the right, the names JASON and WELLS marked at the top of the dry-erase board in sharp black marker. There's curvy red print in the bottom corner that says "Kimmy was here!" drawn with a heart that sends mine tripping over itself.

Jason opens the door, and I'm surprised to see the shared room is tidier than expected. Two beds rest against opposite walls, one with a navy comforter and one with gray. There's a desk at the foot of each bed that both look well used—good academics are a requirement for college athletes, so I imagine he and Wells spend a lot of *real* time studying. My eyes trace along the stacks of papers on each wooden surface, the Aggie zip-ups that hang from a hook near the door, the wide window that lets in a ton of natural light. "Wow," I say, my mind in overdrive as I take it all in.

"Yeah." Jason nods as he looks around, too. "It's not much but . . . it's home."

I reach for the side pocket of my duffle and pull out my camera—a DSLR I got for Christmas. Popping the cap off the front of the lens, I find Jason in the viewfinder and snap a picture.

He grins. "You're taking a photography class again?"

I shake my head. "It's mine. I had to find something to do without you at home." It was quickly becoming my favorite possession. I'd forgotten how much I loved capturing moments, and these days it was rare for me to *not* have the Canon hanging from my neck.

Replacing the cap back on the lens, I look around again. Wells has always been organized and tidy with his work around the ranch so I'm not surprised to find his space so clean. But Jason has *always* been messy. He must have spent some time sprucing up the place before I got here. "It looks good in here," I admit. "Nicer than I expected."

Jason narrows his eyes as the corner of his mouth tugs. "What did you expect?"

I shrug. "I don't know . . . forgotten food containers. Empty beer bottles. A general 'ass' smell."

Jason laughs. "Ouch. Ass, huh?" I nod, and he laughs again. "It's a small space, and we've learned through a little trial and error that we're both happier when it's clean. Plus, beer isn't *technically* allowed, so . . ." He leans in close, his mouth hovering close to my ear. "We keep the case of it tucked behind Wells's clothes in his closet."

I roll my eyes, smiling. "Where is he, anyway?"

He circles me, tosses my duffle on the floor by his bed—the one with the gray comforter—and bounds down on top of it, smirking. "I don't know, but he's not here, so . . ." He winks.

"Jason!" I gasp, turning around to face the still-open door. A girl with a shaved head casually walks by, her blue headphones covered in colorful cartoon stickers. I slide my focus back to Jason, brows arched. "There are, like, a *million* people out there."

Jason's smirk rises. "Trust me, there are ways to create privacy when you need it." He effortlessly rolls off the bed and shimmies past me, shutting the door gently with a light click. When he turns back around, his eyes have lost all trace of humor.

"Oh." I swallow as my stomach rolls in anticipation. "How convenient." The weight of the metal door drowns out most of the noise from the hallway, and it suddenly feels like it really *is* just me and Jason.

He hums as he saunters toward me. "Do you know how much I've missed you, Layla?"

My heart pounds as I pull my dry tongue from the roof of my mouth. "How much?" I ask.

He's inches from me in the span of a breath, and even

without a single inch of our bodies touching, I feel him *every-where*. Leaning forward to ghost his lips against mine, he whispers, "So. Fucking. Much." And then he drives his tongue into my parted mouth and pulls my body tight to him.

My hips press against his, and I feel how hard he already is beneath his shorts. He reaches to swipe a hand beneath my shirt, fingers skating across my ribs, but the metal door groans open, and sounds from the hall bleed back into the room. Jason snatches his hand back from under my shirt but makes no attempt to move away from me. "Wells," he says simply, looking at me as his eyes dim in frustration.

"Uh . . . hey," I hear Wells say awkwardly, though I can't see him behind Jason's wide shoulders. "Sorry." He clears his throat. "I can—"

"No, it's okay!" I nearly shout, standing on my tiptoes to look over Jason's shoulder and ignoring the way his face falls. "Hey, Wells."

His mouth quirks into a smile. "Hey, sunshine," he says lightly, dropping his black backpack onto his desk. He's got that old Wild Coyote hat on backward, and it stirs a longing inside of me. A yearning for the ranch, for Jason and Wells to be home. For the horses that I haven't seen in over a year. "I almost forgot you were coming today."

I snake around Jason to hug him, careful not to knock my camera against his shoulder. His arms are stiff as they wrap around me. "It's good to see you," I admit.

He nods once. "Yeah, you too." He quickly looks past me to where Jay stands. "Colton said he texted you about The Stampede?"

Jason snorts. "He's got his panties in a wad because I left him on read for forty-five minutes?"

Wells shrugs. "I think he's just trying to make plans."

"What's The Stampede?" I ask.

Wells's eyes flash back to me. "A bar."

My brows pinch. "You aren't old enough for a bar."

His lips curve, and he looks back at Jason. I turn to find Jason walking toward us, smiling. "We're not in Saddlebrook Falls anymore, babe," he teases. "Here, we're kings."

TURNS OUT JASON WAS A *LITTLE* OVERCONFIDENT about his self-acclaimed royalty status. The bouncer at The Stampede is a surly brute of a man, and Jason's charms do nothing to get us through the door—but we get lucky when a fight breaks out on the street in front of the bar, causing enough of a distraction with all the bouncers that all three of us can slip inside unnoticed.

A tall boy with a bright smile and a sleeve of colorful tattoos beneath a Red Wings T-shirt stands and waves from a booth in the far corner. Jason steers us toward him through an open dance floor in the middle of the bar. Two couples dance on opposite ends as "You Look So Good in Love" plays from the jukebox. It's a country bar, through and through, and I immediately love it.

"Nice to finally meet Jason's betrothed," Colton says when we're introduced.

My cheeks heat. "You too," I say.

Two girls are seated in the booth, and Colton fumbles through introductions. Apparently, he just met them today during a game of lawn bowling at their sorority house. Jason hooks his arm around me as we exchange hellos, and a zip of pride flashes in my chest at the gesture. But it doesn't seem to matter, because it quickly becomes obvious that both girls are *very* interested in Wells.

"I'm going to go get us some drinks," Jason says, his gaze already skimming across the bar. "Stay here with Wells, yeah?" When I give him a confused look, he continues. "You're seventeen, babe. We may have gotten in the door, but you need to lay low with the staff." He gives me a swift kiss on the cheek and pulls himself away before I can respond.

He didn't even ask me what I wanted.

I turn back to the rest of the group and find Wells watching me, amusement on his face. "What?" I ask, feeling a little out of my element.

"Shake the Frost" by Tyler Childers starts to play, and the corners of his lips tug higher. One of the girls in the booth says his name, but he doesn't seem to hear her. "Dance with me," he says.

I laugh, shaking my head. "No."

"No?" He makes a show of looking hurt. My shoulders tense in response. I'd almost forgotten what the effect of his approval felt like—or, in many cases, the lack of it. "What if I insist?"

Before I realize what's happening, he grabs my hand and pulls me toward him, using the momentum to swirl us right to the middle of the dance floor. "Wells!" I protest.

He turns to face me, winding an arm around my waist and pulling me close against him. "What?" he asks.

"We shouldn't . . ." I hesitate, looking toward the bar where Jason's giving an order to a stocky bartender with what looks like a barbed wire tattoo snaking up his arm.

"Shouldn't what?" He takes my right hand into his left, his brown eyes sparking with mischief. "Dance?"

"You know what I mean," I insist.

"Afraid I don't," he volleys. And then he begins to move.

If there was one thing I was sure about only a minute ago, it was that Wells *isn't* a two-step country dance kind of guy. But the easy confidence in his steps is shocking as much as it is intriguing.

"Where'd you learn to dance like this?"

He smirks. "Why, you like it?"

I shrug, clearly impressed, and he huffs a breathy laugh that curls around my neck. "Seriously, where'd you learn to do this?" I press after he spins me in two tight circles.

This time, his smile is soft. "At home," he says. "With my mom."

I smile, picturing it. "How is your mom?"

His head dips low. He traded his old ball cap for his black cowboy hat before we left the dorms, and now it creates a partition between us and everyone else. "She's good," he says. "My dad's back on the wagon, which helps."

I'm struck by the casual honesty of it. Everyone knows Bud Bennett has suffered from an alcohol problem for his entire adult life—but this is the first time Wells has ever addressed it directly. At least with me. "How long?" I ask.

"'Bout two months."

I'm reminded of Rhett's interruption at church, of my mother's words about the condition their father had been found in that weekend. I wonder if it's what eventually propelled him back into sobriety. "That's something!"

He pulls his head back to look at me, his smile growing. "Yeah." He nods. "It is." And then he pushes lightly against my waist, spinning me away from him before he winds me back in for a dip that has me gasping.

His eyes flare at the sound.

"Oh my god," I say, as a giggle bubbles out of my throat. "I did *not* see that coming."

But his smile changes into something more forced than natural. And after pulling me to an upright position, he takes a firm step back.

"Thanks," he says evenly. "For the dance."

"But the song isn't over . . . ?" It comes out more like a question than anything.

He shrugs. "You didn't want to dance anyway."

And then he leaves me standing alone on the dance floor as he makes his way back to the booth. My shoulders sag with uncertainty . . . *Did I say something wrong?*

When I get to the table, Wells is seated on one of the long bench seats talking animatedly with Colton and the girls. Jason waits for me with two beers in his hands.

He does *not* look happy.

"You're back," I say, stating the obvious.

"Yep," he says.

I frown. "Is something wrong?"

He shakes his head. "Just trying to figure out if I should be concerned about my best friend slow dancing with my girl," he says.

My frown deepens. "Concerned?" I repeat. "Jason, he just asked me to dance. I didn't even say yes . . . but, it was *just* a dance."

"You didn't say yes?" he asks, eyes sliding to Wells with an unfamiliar heat. Is he . . . *jealous* of Wells?

I reach my hands out to press against his shoulders,

grounding his attention back to me. "Jay," I say firmly. "He's my friend. He's your *best* friend. It's Wells . . . there is nothing to worry about."

It's a truth I'm confident in—but it doesn't explain the images that flash through my mind as I say it.

Wells's midnight eyes, shadowed from the moonlight by the awning of my doorstep, watching me cry with a pained expression.

His hands on my waist as he carefully hoists me from Champ's saddle, the pressure of his fingers buzzing through my shirt.

The steady look on his face as he watches me across a crowded room of some party, even when I can hardly get him to hold a conversation.

It's a seed of doubt that takes root, even as I force the calculated indifference on my face now.

Jason sighs. "I don't know," he mutters, looking back at me. A deep line slices between his brows. "I'm gonna go get some air. I'll be right back."

For the second time tonight, Jason walks away from me. And this time it burns a hole through my stomach.

"Where'd he go?" Wells asks, surprising me. I startle, whipping around to face him.

"I told you dancing was a bad idea," I say back, tears stinging my eyes. His eyes grow wide and worried as they flit back toward the door Jason just left through, and I rush to the bathroom.

CHAPTER THIRTY-ONE

NOW

Hours later, just as the early morning light begins to bleed in through the bedroom window, I watch Wells sleep. My eyes trace the dips and curves of his body, memorizing every angle and soft expanse of skin. His squared jaw and the stubble that runs across his cheek. His unkempt hair, tousled from my fingers. His broad chest as it rises and falls with his deep breathing.

We were up for most of the night, lost in each other. After he made slow and delicate work of cleaning me up in the living room, he gave me a change of clothes so I could get out of my ruined dress. But his focus snared on seeing me in his T-shirt and sweatpants, and it wasn't long before he was hurtling us both toward new waves of pleasure.

Every careful and tender touch tore me apart, limb by limb, until I was simply a bag of bones beneath him. And then he put me back together in the light of the moonlit window, warm traces of him everywhere inside of me, becoming all that I am and will ever want to be.

I loved every glorious second of it.

He finally fell asleep about an hour ago. Even in his unconsciousness, his need took hold: body tensing, flexing beneath warm skin, reaching. Wanting. He kept an arm and a leg wrapped firmly around me, tethering me to him. And I never felt more content.

Until the quiet corners of my mind began to wake, the groaning, yawning monsters of grief and destruction fighting to take hold.

I carefully shift my hips from beneath his wide thigh, turning onto my side and nuzzling deeper into the mattress as I try to shake off what I know is an impending emotional storm. *Not here*, I think, willing my mind to blank. *Not now.*

The last thing I want is for Wells to register a single ounce of panic in me, knowing damn well he'll take it as a sign of regret or discomfort about this whole situation—and that's *not* how I feel. He's too good, too intent on doing the right thing when it comes to this and us, and I know seeing me falter would send him into a self-sabotaging spiral.

It's just . . . trying to reconcile how much my life has changed in the last few weeks isn't an easy feat. It's an emotional clusterfuck, and in quiet moments like this, the ramifications of it all pierce into me.

I will myself to fall asleep, but thoughts of Jason flood my mind. I wonder if, wherever he might be, he somehow knows what's happened between Wells and me. What's been slowly blooming between us since I came home and found him at the bar that night. I wonder if Jason knows how deeply the entire trajectory of my life has changed because of him—because of his accident. Because of Emma.

A soft wave of humiliation flares at the memory of my vomit on her shoes. Of the moment I learned the man I loved could hurt me like that.

I wonder if he'd be sorry. If it would be genuine.

And then I wonder if it would change anything.

If he were still here, would I forgive him? Would Wells and I still have this . . . thing between us? This thing that feels a lot like *hope*?

A tear slides down the side of my face, dropping off my cheek and into the soft pillow. The truth is, I don't regret a single moment that led me here, wrapped up in Wells's arms. But I also don't know what to do from here.

What I said earlier, about making a mess of this . . . I think I need to take it back.

My eyes squeeze shut as another tear falls. Is that what I've done? Have I made a mess of this?

If we do this, it's going to mean something to me.

I feel him shift behind me, a warm hand flexing around my ribs as his mouth nestles on my nape. "You're up?" he softly murmurs against my skin, sending a riot of goosebumps over my shoulder and scalp.

I quickly wipe my face before I turn to face him. He's sleepy and swollen and my heart nearly bursts at the sight. He cracks a single eye open, barely a sliver, and his lips curve into a smile that punches right into me. "Yeah," I say back, cheeks pulled wide. And I feel the heavy haze of grief begin to dissipate.

He pulls me into his chest. "Did you get any sleep?"

I shake my head. "Not really," I admit.

He hums, his fingertips featherlight as they stroke down my bare back. "I have to leave soon," he says. "Kasey and I are taking a couple horses out to Williamson County."

"Are they being adopted?" I ask, looking up at him.

"Maybe." He smiles. He presses his thumb into my bottom lip, dragging it down and watching in fascination. "I can't bear to leave you like this."

"Then don't," I try, reaching to pull his shoulders into me.

He relents, letting me move his large frame over my body until he's caging me into the bed. Heat pools in his eyes. "Trust me, sunshine," he murmurs. "If I could lock you in this room and keep you here for months, I would."

"Why do you call me 'sunshine'?" I ask, my gaze fastened to his face. I've asked so many times over the years—I finally want to know.

He looks down at me with so much tenderness I almost can't stand it, his eyes bright and honest as he asks, "Isn't it obvious?"

I shake my head, and his smile grows wistful.

"I've always lived in the shadows . . . the shadows of my brothers, of Jason. I never felt as exposed as you made me feel the second you showed up in our lives. I knew you were Jason's girl, but . . . you saw me, too. You looked at me and found me hiding in my obscurity. Your light pulls me out of it, Layla. It shines over me in a way I've never known before."

Tears burn my eyes as he adjusts his weight over me, his hand winding into my hair. "Having you like this . . . it's like touching the sunrise. You might pull me in so deep that I burn to ashes, but I don't care. It's already worth it."

He kisses away my tears as they fall until we're both breathless. Until our fingers turn frantic and our mouths hot.

Sliding a hand down my body, he curls his fingers into my slick skin and groans, circling around me and making me come in mere minutes. It's obvious he's taken care and interest in learning the ways I like to be touched, and now he wields that power over me until I'm panting and writhing beneath him.

When I reach to touch him, to grab him beneath the sheets, he shudders and shakes his head, pulling away. "I can't," he breathes. "Or I won't leave this bed, and someone will come knocking."

I laugh, my skin electric as I come down from the high of him. "Okay," I say. "I'll get dressed."

"Stay," he insists. "I want to know you're here, warm in my bed. It'll be a few hours—go to sleep, get some rest, and I'll bring you home when I'm done." He presses a tender kiss to my temple. "Okay?"

I nod, pressing another kiss to his mouth. "Okay," I say. It's probably better anyway—I already didn't go home last night, and sneaking in at dawn feels more scandalous than walking in later.

My mother will be upset regardless.

He smiles, pleased. And it shatters my heart.

WELLS DROPS ME OFF LATE IN THE AFTERNOON, AFTER insisting on feeding me one of Mrs. Bennett's egg salad sandwiches at the cabin with sweet tea he pulled out from his fridge. It'd felt so ordinary, so normal to share lunch with him, that I couldn't deny the deep contentment that washed over me as we sat together at the tiny kitchen table.

The few hours of deep sleep after a night of incredible sex didn't hurt, either.

My dress, now soiled, lies in a hamper in Wells's closet. He brings me home in the black T-shirt and sweatpants he lent me last night, and as we both look out the window, it's obvious he's nervous for me to walk through the front door.

"You'll call me?" he asks. "If you need anything?"

I'm usually just as anxious to face my mom, but right now I feel like nothing could burst the bubble Wells and I have created around ourselves. I turn to give him an assured smile— I don't want him to worry. "Of course." I nod. "But I'll be okay, Wells. I promise."

He looks at me like he can't stand to let me go, and it makes my heart flip. "Can I see you tomorrow?" he asks. "Take you to dinner?"

My smile grows. "Yeah." I lean to kiss him on the cheek, feeling the bite of his stubble on my lips, and then turn to push out of the truck. Wells waits for me to get inside the house before he drives away.

"Layla Lynette Hayes," says my mother, her voice cold. It startles me, my limbs tensing as I find her in the entryway. Her eyes are sharp and narrow as she looks down, taking in the clothes I'm wearing. Realizing they're not mine. "What in god's name is going on with you and that boy?" she asks, her gaze horrified.

I straighten my posture. "Mom, please drop it."

She scoffs. "You didn't come home last night, didn't answer any of my calls or texts, and then you saunter in here in a man's clothes and ask me to *drop it*?"

I sigh. "I'm not a kid anymore, I—"

"You are still my daughter," she states firmly, her tone taking on that regal southerness I've always been afraid of.

But not today.

"It's not your business."

"Oh yes it is. You might enjoy the freedom that being in New York affords you, but in this house, you are *my* daughter and how you conduct yourself is my business."

"No," I clarify. "It's mine. You don't get to control my life anymore, Mom. I'm not your doll or your plaything."

"Do *not* disrespect me." Her fists are clenched at the sides of her house dress—I'm not sure I've ever seen her so angry. "You're supposed to be mourning the death of the man who was to be your future husband! Not gallivanting around with trash, walking into this house in his clothes like some *whore*."

The word feels like a slap in the face, and my own anger burns bright.

"I need you to tell me how deep this goes," she continues. "Tell me what is going on between you and that boy."

"That *boy* is Wells Bennett, and he treats me better than Jason ever did."

"That's preposterous," she counters. "Jason Moore had the means to give you the life you deserve. He took care of you, Layla. He was working hard to create a future that would have kept you safe."

"He was cheating on me!" I shout. "He was building a future for *himself*, not me. He wanted me to mold my life around him, to be someone I'm not, while he was taking what he wanted without any regard for me or my feelings. He was selfish, Mom. And Wells—"

"Do *not* say his name in this house again," she spits. "He will ruin you, Layla. He and his family of criminals who don't give a shit about anyone else. He will use you to get what he wants and then he will drop you like you never existed—I've seen those boys do it to too many young girls. If you have any hope of a good man wanting to marry you, you need to come to your senses and distance yourself from the Bennetts."

I shake my head, my body vibrating with exasperation. "I don't need to be taken care of, don't you see that?" I yell. "I don't need a man to give me the life that I deserve—I will *create* the life that I want on my own." I take a step forward, chest heaving. "And I'll surround myself with good people who care about me, about who I *am*. Not about what I can give to them, or what I'm willing to sacrifice."

She closes her eyes, and I almost feel sorry for her. For this archaic and flawed belief system she holds so tightly to, where a woman can't be successful without attaching herself to a man. So I press on, hopeful my words might make a difference. "Annie is almost fourteen," I say, keeping my tone level. "She'll be in high school next year. You have a chance to build her up in a way you never did with me. You can teach her that she can flourish in her life on her own. That she can strive for more than a nice house and children to raise. And Mom," I say, bracing myself. "I hope to *god* you do. For her sake."

I don't give her a chance to reply. Instead, I turn to walk up the stairs, eager to get to my room and into my bed where I can lie in the quiet and *really* process the last twenty-four hours, and what it all means.

CHAPTER THIRTY-TWO

THEN

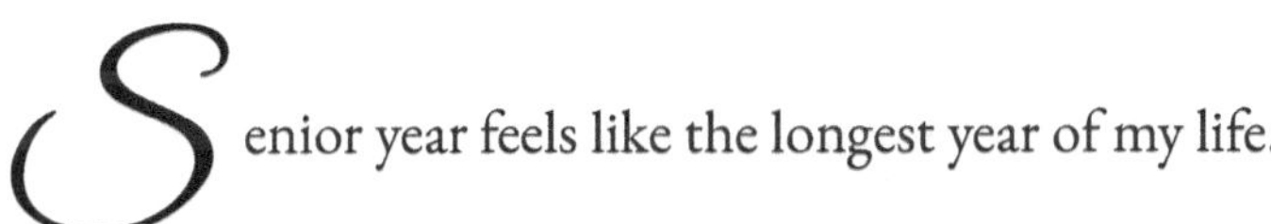

Senior year feels like the longest year of my life.

I can't help but count down the days until graduation. My class schedule is light since I was able to get ahead on some of my credits, so I get to leave campus a couple hours early every day. But for the first few months I don't have anything to fill the extra time with, and my boredom makes the days move slower than molasses.

By mid-fall, I've applied to a handful of colleges—*none* of them in Texas—but I know I won't hear back from them any time soon. I'm a little nervous about the whole process; as much as I still want to get out of dodge and see more of the world, I'm not sure how I'll feel once it all becomes official. I've lived in Saddlebrook Falls my entire life, and the idea of being somewhere else on my own is somewhat intimidating.

I *really* hope I'm accepted into NYU. I also applied to USC and Northwestern because they both have great journalism programs, but when I think about where I can experience the most during college, New York feels like the perfect place. I think my grades are good enough to get in, though I wish I'd taken the last few years of my academics more seriously. Thank god for my love of photography, because I was able to submit some samples alongside my application.

"Hey," Regan greets as she shuffles into a chair at the table I've been holding for the last twenty minutes. It's Saturday night, and though the Mustangs didn't win the game yesterday, Mustang's Pizza is still crowded with our classmates.

"Hi," I smile. "I already ordered us a pizza."

Regan shimmies with excitement. "Perfect." She looks around and waves at a handful of people before she settles her full attention on me. The corners of her mouth dip. "Uh oh."

"What?"

"You have that look."

"What look?"

"Like you're having an existential crisis."

I almost laugh. "I do *not*!" But she simply stares at me, leaning back in her chair as she crosses her arms over her chest. "Okay," I concede. "Maybe a small crisis."

"Mhmm."

I take a sip of my sweet tea. "Do you know what you want to study in college?"

Regan nods. "Criminal justice."

It's the ease in which she answers that causes my chest to tighten. I sigh. "I'm having a hard time figuring out what I want."

She tilts her head. "I thought you wanted to study journalism."

"I do," I say, nodding. "I just . . . I want to write about things that matter, like climate change or reproductive rights or wildlife conservation. Or, if writing doesn't work out, I could lean on photography to capture a story. But I guess I'm just not sure how a career like that fits with everything else."

"Fits?" she asks.

I feel my ears heat. "Jason wants me with him wherever he ends up. It kind of limits my options, not knowing where that'll be." It feels like an admission—the real source of my anxiety. The truth is, I'm terrified that my relationship with him goes against every belief I had before we started dating. As we all inch closer to adulthood, my life looks a lot like a version I never wanted. But I *do* want to be with Jason. I don't think I'm willing to give him up.

I would never admit it, but I almost understand my mom more now.

It's been a year and a half since Jason left for college, and I thought I'd use our time apart to really figure things out for myself. But instead, all I do is count down the days until he comes home for breaks from school. I get so excited for every opportunity we have to see each other that I forget to be selfish with this time to myself. He's so busy with classes and the toll of his second season as an Aggie, but he still makes time to call me every night. It's almost as if the distance has pushed us closer together somehow, like the way we miss each other is a living, breathing thing that yearns to be fed.

"What about what you want?" Regan asks, not unkindly.

Gus swings by to drop our pizza in the middle of the table, giving me the chance to think about how to respond. As soon as walks away, I shrug. "I don't know, Ray. I've always wanted to make something of myself . . . but if Jason makes it into the

NFL we could end up anywhere. It's not like I could traipse around the country to find the next burning social issue to write about. I *want* to be his wife, but I want more than that, too—I'm not sure how to realistically have it all."

Regan blows out a breath as she pulls a slice of cheesy pizza onto her small plate. "What does Jason think about it all?"

"I know he wants me to be happy, but he's been pretty vocal about wanting to get married after college." I take a bite of the scalding corner of my slice, having to move it around in my mouth so it doesn't burn my tongue before I continue. "For him, it's simple. He gets drafted, we go wherever that takes him, and we build a life and a family together while he lives out his dreams."

Regan eyes me. "Yeah but what about your dreams, Layla? They should matter just as much as his do, right?"

I feel my defenses rising, and I hate it. I thought talking this out would somehow make me feel better, but it's only shining a light on what I already know—I have *no* idea what I'm doing.

LATER, WHEN JASON CALLS, I STILL FEEL TENSE IN MY stomach.

"Do anything fun today?" he asks, his voice hushed like he's talking to me from the corner of his room. I can almost see him hunched around the phone from where he sits on his twin bed, his back to Wells.

After my first trip to visit him at college went south, I spent a long time trying to navigate the newfound jealousy dynamic of our trio. I haven't been back to College Station since then because of how nervous I became for something else to happen. I know Wells and I didn't do anything wrong, but I still think it's better to avoid tempting fate.

For as splintered as things felt between Jason and me after that trip, he and Wells didn't seem to skip a beat—at least from what I could tell. Even during visits home, after spending every day together at school, they still made plenty of plans together with each other and other friends from Saddlebrook Falls. I haven't had any direct contact with Wells in almost six months, and even though Jason says he's over it and that he believes me about nothing happening that night, I can't help but feel like he's keeping Wells and I apart.

"Um . . . I went to Mustang's Pizza with Regan and talked about college plans. But other than that it's been a pretty uneventful day," I laugh.

"Oh?" he asks. "Did you hear back from any of the schools?"

"No," I shake my head, as if he can see me through the phone. "I probably won't hear anything for a few months."

There's a pause from his side of the line. And then he asks, "Have you thought any more about Texas A&M?"

My stomach clenches tighter. "Jason," I whine. "You know I want to get out of Texas."

"I know, I know." He blows out a breath. "I just miss you, and I'd hate to lose the opportunity for us to be together after this year."

We've had this conversation a dozen times. Sometimes I wonder if he assumes I'll give in if he asks me enough, but it's the *one* thing I'm holding fast to, the one thing that ensures I'll get to have experiences that are simply for me after I graduate in the spring. "I watched your game this morning," I say, changing the subject.

"Well, I'd hope so!" He chuckles. "How'd I look?"

I roll my eyes, smiling. "Good, as always."

"I miss you cheering for me from the sidelines."

"Me too," I admit. Friday nights aren't the same here either, not without Jason on the field. I've loved cheerleading my entire life, but I'm ready to find new things to be passionate about. Thankfully, Texas A&M doesn't have an official cheerleading team since it originated as an all-male military school. If they did, I know Jason would push extra hard for me to go there with him.

I hear Wells say something in the background, the low tone of his voice at once so familiar and yet foreign. I can't hear what he says, but whatever it is prompts Jason to end our conversation. "All right babe, I gotta go get some things done over here. But I love you and I miss you—let's talk again tomorrow, yeah?"

My eyes find the digital clock on my nightstand, and I wonder what kinds of things he needs to get done at eight o'clock on a Saturday night. I would bet money that he's going to a party after the Aggies' win this morning—I'm not sure why he wouldn't just tell me. "Be safe," I say back, and then the phone disconnects.

Letting out a quick exhale, I plug my phone into the charger on my nightstand and pull my camera from where it lies on my dresser. Settling back in bed against my pillows, I put in an old memory card from two years ago and scroll through pictures of Jason and Wells at the ranch, of Ghost and Champ and Lady in different corrals, even a handful of shots of little Lucky before he was adopted. My heart begins to ache as I lose myself in the memories of a much simpler time, when it felt like I had everything I could ever want.

I know deep down that if I'm not careful about my choices this year, I may lose any chance of feeling as free and confident as I did back then, as the girl who was headstrong and brave about the things she wanted for her life. I think about Regan's words earlier and know she's right, that my dreams *are* just as important as anyone else's. I just hope I don't lose Jason in the process of finding my own way.

CHAPTER THIRTY-THREE

NOW

Wells pulls into one of the few open spaces between Sheriff Joe's patrol car and a black minivan that looks like it came right from a dealership. Dread coils uncomfortably against my ribs as I look around the full parking lot, at all the cars surrounding us.

"Doesn't look like it's a quiet night at June's," Wells murmurs, scanning the full lot.

"No," I agree with a sigh.

He looks at me, resolute. I feel it like a calming balm, settling my nerves. "Layla, we can have dinner," he says simply. His voice is low and patient with the smallest lilt of supplication. "We can go in there and sit in a booth together and enjoy a goddamn meal."

I meet his earnest gaze, and I know he's right. I try to muster some of the confidence that flooded through me when I faced Mom yesterday—but something about facing the whole town feels . . . bigger.

There's a radical shift occurring here in the static between Wells and me, and though it electrifies my skin and bones and the tempo of my heartbeat, it's not something anyone would see just from looking at us—not if we can maintain our composure. I've been inside June's Cafe hundreds of times, and just because Jason's dead it doesn't mean Wells and I can't share a dinner. Right?

I look back at the diner—the paint-chipped shutters and hanging red geraniums that sway in the evening breeze—and decide we might as well get this over with. It's not like Wells and I have anywhere else to go besides the cabin, but I'm not ready to go there again—not yet. I know it's also important that Wells doesn't think my nerves have anything to do with a desire to hide him, when it's *really* about hiding myself.

Whore.

I've tried so hard not to let my mother's words affect me, but they do. Facing her was a not-so-subtle reminder of the stifling haze that engulfs this town, of the people and the gossip and the *judgment*. I'm not sure anyone would understand how the late Jason Moore's perfect girlfriend could fall for his best friend—a *Bennett* at that.

And I honestly don't know what to do about it.

I wind my fingers through the ends of my hair, my foot tapping lightly against the mat.

"Look at me, Layla," Wells says gently. And I do. "No one else matters."

And I smile, because he's right. *Why do I care what anyone thinks?* Wells matters more to me than I ever intended for him to, and the way I feel about him is bigger and louder than some dirty secret.

He deserves to be seen. To know how much he means to me. And I can't let my mom's insults get in the way of what makes me happy.

"No one else matters," I repeat, my cheeks pulling wide. "Come on, let's go eat."

I walk close to him through the parking lot, my shoulder brushing against his. And when we get to the door of the diner, I reach to pull his hand in mine. His eyes flash to me, wide and surprised, and I love the way they hold and tell me I'm safe.

Inside, I ask Olivia for a table for two. She nods, grabbing two menus to take us to the only open table in the diner—right in the middle of the room—and halts when she sees our hands clasped together. Her gaze flies up, bounces between us, and then smiles at us in a way that feels real. "Follow me," she says, grinning.

As we trail her to the table, the soft murmuring of conversations around us dwindles and eventually comes to a screeching halt. I feel everyone's eyes on us, and it sends a flush crawling up my neck. But I don't let go of his hand, and he doesn't let go of mine.

"Wait," he urges as we reach the table, stepping past me to pull out my chair for me. It's a small gesture, but one that speaks volumes in this moment. *See*, I want to tell everyone. *See how respectful he is? How eager to do right by me?*

"Thank you," I smile, and I feel the soft brush of his fingers along my neck as he eases me in close to the table.

The room stays silent as we open our menus—as if we don't already know every option on it—but it doesn't take long for the whispering to begin.

"*. . . Layla Hayes and Wells Bennett . . .*"

"*. . . Jason's best friend?*"

"*. . . such a disgrace to his memory . . .*"

"*. . . going to call Lynette right now . . .*"

"Hey." Wells catches my eyes over the top of his menu. He smiles. "We got this."

I nod as I straighten my back.

"Evenin'," June greets, her expression warm. "You kids know what you want?"

"Yes ma'am," Wells answers politely, looking at me to go first.

"I'll have the cheeseburger and fries, please," I say. "And a lemonade."

"Mm," Wells hums. "That sounds perfect. I'll do the same." He hands June our menus and thanks her as she walks away.

"So," I say, ignoring everyone around us. "Tell me about your family. How have they been doing?"

"Good." He nods. "Real good. Sawyer is graduating this year. He's starting to apply to graduate programs for wildlife conservation. Rhett's been keeping his head down, working a lot at the bar with Kasey. Kasey and Brooks are really busy with the ranch. Melody's been fighting a lingering virus for the last few weeks so she's a little worn out. But the boys are good— Liam's learning to rope." He smiles. "Says he wants to compete."

The little boy who chased after Jason's ball all those years ago flashes in my mind, and I grin. "And your parents?"

"Dad's still sober." His smile grows, and then disappears. Like he's careful with how much emotion to show for it. "Mom's still proud."

June comes out with our drinks and, soon after, our burgers. We keep an easy rhythm of conversation as we eat, and by the end of the meal, things feel more normal than I thought possible. Risking a look around, I see Sheriff Joe in the corner with a deputy, both inhaling June's chicken pot pie like it's air. Maeve, circled by her three adult children in the corner booth, politely cuts her chicken into tiny pieces before placing each one in her mouth.

Plenty of people are still watching us, but I simply don't care.

Eventually, Olivia clears our plates and June brings the bill, which Wells insists on paying, and then we're back in the cold night air.

"You should've seen their faces on our way out." He laughs. "Cowards, all of them."

"You think so?"

He nods. "I know so. None of them would brazenly walk into that diner like you did tonight. Everyone in this town is so worried about what other people think. None of them are as brave as you, my sunshine girl."

He pulls me in for a kiss, pressing me against the side of his truck. I bask in the freedom of kissing him so openly, where anyone can see.

"Can I take you back to my place?" he asks, his body thrumming with an obvious desire as he grinds his hips into mine.

"Yes." I nod. "Please."

He buries his face in my neck, not quite ready to let me go, and I relish the heat pooling between us.

When we eventually make it to the cabin, he jumps out and says, "Wait here?" over his shoulder, a soft grin growing.

"Out here?" I ask, looking around at the dark ranch. When he nods, I say, "Okay."

He jogs toward the cabin and slips inside. It's less than two minutes before he's back out the door, a stack of thick blankets and pillows in hand. He leads me around the side of the cabin and out toward the mustang pasture, quietly pushing through the gate in the fence line. We keep walking for another fifty yards until he stops, looking around. "This'll do," he says to himself.

He lowers the stack of linens into the grass, taking the blanket from the top and spreading it open on the ground. He arranges both pillows and tells me to lie down. When I do, he covers me in the other thick blanket before crawling in next to me, wrapping me tightly in his arms.

"Look," he says softly, eyes on the sky.

I look up and see thousands of stars, all sparkling in the dark. "Wow," I say on an exhale. "Do you think he's up there?"

I don't even realize what I've asked until I do.

Wells stills, and then tightens his hold around me. "Yeah," he answers. "I do."

"Do you think he's mad at us?"

His chin swipes along the top of my scalp as he shakes his head. "No, sunshine," he murmurs. And I try to let that sink in.

"I hope not," I whisper.

"I think," he says, "that Jason isn't suffering anymore. That whatever struggles he had to bear during his life . . . they're gone now. He's at peace. And despite everything, I know he loved us both. So I like to think it would bring him some comfort to know we've found the same in each other."

I turn my head to face him, and he shifts onto his shoulder

to look down at me. "Do you think this is only happening because we miss him?" I dare to ask.

He stares at me for a long time before blowing out a soft breath. And then he shakes his head. "I can't speak for you. I— I don't know what your feelings are. You're going to have to find that answer for yourself, but . . ." He trails off, looking away. And I can sense it, the emotional distance he's creating between us. "I know how I feel."

The words he spoke only days ago crash back into me.

I've loved you every day since the first time I laid eyes on you, Layla Hayes.

I loved Jason. I loved him with my whole heart. And I hated you because I loved you more.

If we do this, it's going to mean something to me.

I watch his throat roll with a swallow as his eyes skim the trees in the distance. Do I love him? *Of course I do*, I tell myself. But . . . is it the kind of love that he's talking about? The kind that's all-consuming, body and soul? The kind that *really* means forever?

I want to tell him I'm not sure, that I still have so much to figure out about my life. I'm going back to New York in less than a week—a topic we've both been avoiding. I want to tell him that he'll always be important to me. That what he wants out of life *matters*.

I taste the words on my tongue, but before I have a chance to say any of them, Wells props himself up on an elbow. "Look," he says, pointing.

I push up too and follow the line of his extended finger, finding the silhouettes of four horses in the distance. Even under the blanket of night, I recognize the gleaming spots on her back. "Stardust," I whisper.

"She knows you're here," he says. And I wonder if it's true. If it's the same bone-deep understanding that lets him know Jason is, too.

I smile as I lean into his shoulder, breathing him in. And when he wraps his arm around me and pulls me in close, I realize that no matter what happens between us, we'll always have the love we share for them.

CHAPTER THIRTY-FOUR

THEN

I've never been one to make a New Year's resolution. I find the whole idea of it to be nothing more than a personal setup, a way to let yourself down when said resolution falls by the wayside. I've watched my mother make one every year for my whole life—promises to herself that she'll spend more time outside, more time with Annie and me. That she'll finally get around to planning a family vacation to Florida or California or Hawaii.

But every year her promises grow cold, fading into the background of her busy life. Always forgotten. If she ever remembers to be disappointed, she doesn't show it. But I know myself well enough to know that disappointment would run deep, so I avoid the whole thing altogether.

Jason, on the other hand, thinks resolutions are a chance to change what he *gets* out of the world around him. For instance, last year he'd made one to get laid more. Which, obviously with the logistics of his residence at Texas A&M and my big move to

New York City to attend NYU, meant he inevitably didn't get what he wanted.

But boy, did he try.

Don't get me wrong, I like sex for exactly what it is—a means of mutual pleasure, an opportunity to share something personal and vulnerable with someone you love. But to Jason . . . . I guess sometimes I feel like sex is a third party to our relationship, another entity to make considerations for and compromises with.

We all made our way home to Saddlebrook Falls over a week ago for Christmas break, and Jason and I still haven't found an opportunity for some . . . *alone* time. The days seem to go by in a flash—Annie is twelve now, and we spend nearly every day cuddled together on the couch in our festive pajamas, watching holiday rom-coms and eating Mom's famous Christmas cookies. She's growing up so fast, and being away from her during these formative years is a constant ache that never settles.

Jason calls one night during our third viewing of *The Family Stone*, and Annie pauses it while I answer, jumping off the couch to make a new bag of popcorn.

"Hey you," I say, smiling into the phone.

"Hey, babe." His warm voice vibrates back. "What are you doing right now?"

"Watching a movie with Annie," I say, eyes flicking to the TV screen.

He sighs. "Just curious if you could sneak away." The way he says it, I know what he wants. And while I wouldn't mind a spin in the back seat of his Mustang, we both know I'd never bail on Annie like that.

"Sorry," I say. "Maybe tomorrow?"

He chuckles. "I'll be in Foxborough with the boys. But, hey, do you have plans the night after?"

"New Year's Eve?" I clarify.

"Yeah."

I shake my head as if he can see me. "Nope!"

"I was thinking we could have a little camp out at the beach. With Wells?"

My heart does an involuntary flip. Camping at the beach? With Wells? For Jason to suggest this, it must be proof things are back to normal. Last summer, after I graduated and Jason and Wells finished their sophomore years at Texas A&M, things between the three of us felt better than they had the whole year prior. It almost felt like we were totally back to normal, but I still always felt an undercurrent of fear that Jason might interpret something between Wells and me as *too* friendly.

Thankfully, Wells also seemed to navigate carefully. I think we both understood that our pull-back from each other was a necessary sacrifice, a way to show Jason that he had nothing to worry about, but I'd be lying if I said I didn't miss him. All three of us spending the night together on the beach feels like the first clear indication that we might be back to how things used to be, and I'm thankful because I *do* care about my friendship with Wells, just like I know he cares about it, too.

"Oh," I say excitedly. "That sounds perfect."

I can hear his smile on the other end of the line. "Great. I'll pick you up around five."

Annie walks back into the room, a fresh bowl of popcorn in hand. "Sounds good," I tell Jason. "Can't wait. See you then!"

I hang up the phone and set it back on the coffee table, turning my attention to Annie. "Sorry about that," I say.

"Jason?" she asks, and I nod.

She smiles. "Are you going to marry him?"

I laugh, shrugging. "Do you think I should?"

"Mama says you will," she says simply before reaching for the remote and pressing play.

I settle back into the couch next to her, but I'm distracted. Something about her words digs uncomfortably in my mind. Marrying Jason feels likely at this point—it's something we always talk about as we discuss what life looks like after college. But I'm still wary of the collection of tiny cracks in our relationship, the proof that we may not be ready yet. That there might be some issues under the surface of *us* worth looking at a little more closely.

I only hope we figure it out before it's too late.

JASON RINGS THE DOORBELL JUST BEFORE FIVE ON New Year's Eve. Barry answers the door and shakes his hand before my mother cuts in to hug him so tight he grunts out a laugh. I kiss Annie goodbye, promising to be home by lunch the next day, and join him out on the porch.

Wells's truck is parked along the curb in front of the house, the two-toned white and red paint as familiar as my own front walkway. I didn't expect to see him yet—but I suppose it makes sense that we'd all drive out to Scorpion Bay together. I make quick work of getting into the back, squeezing in next to two stacked coolers, bags of groceries, and camping supplies. I spot a tent bag on the floor and silently pray there's more than one.

A thread of anxiety has been curling through me all morning in anticipation of this campout. It's not that I'm not happy to see Wells—I am. But after going to bed last night with thoughts of this whole excursion at the forefront of my mind, I realized my anxiety around it is born from a place rooted in Jason's insecurities, not from anything Wells or I have done wrong.

It helps relieve the small traces of guilt I've felt over this last year. But spending a night with Jason and Wells alone, camped out on a desolate beach with all the alcohol I'm sure is tucked into one or both of these coolers, feels like tempting a dragon.

Wells turns in his seat when I'm buckling myself in. "Hey," he says with warmth in his eyes.

"Hi," I say back. "Good to see you."

I sound almost formal, and I hate it. But if Wells notices, he doesn't show it. "You too," he says before turning back around. "Ready?" his gaze jumps to Jason, who's bouncing in his seat and adjusting the vents.

"Hell yeah!" Jason shouts, making me jump. Wells laughs and shifts the truck into drive.

It takes less than an hour to get to the wide-open bay, even less time to get our camp set up. I'm relieved to see two tents have made the trip, smoothing over some of the nerves still dancing in my chest.

For the most part, things feel like they were four years ago, when my world revolved around time spent with Jason and Wells. Jason seems relaxed and happy, and I can't help laughing at Wells's boy-like excitement at building a fire with nothing but his hands and any natural tools he finds in the tree-lined land just beyond the sand. Of course, he's able to get a fire roaring with no problem, and Jason pulls out packages of hot dogs to roast.

All things considered, the evening starts without a hitch.

Jason and Wells share stories from college and I find myself lost in them, leaning into each one with an eagerness that's bloomed from how much I've missed them. How much I've missed *this*. They pass a bottle of whiskey back and forth as they banter, and I'm not sure when it happens but at some point, I become part of the passing order, taking pulls from the bottle and letting the warmth of it sink deep in my belly.

The air is brisk tonight, and Jason covers me beneath a heavy blanket. But between our laughter and the whiskey, there's a contentment in my bones that the chill in the air couldn't possibly touch.

It's not until later, well after the sun has set and the crickets have started to chirp, well after I've gone from tipsy to drunk, that things begin to feel dangerous again.

What starts as an innocent drinking game of Never Have I Ever sours when Jason realizes that I've been living out my own college experience at NYU. When I take a swig of whiskey for having done a keg stand, he looks at me with confusion marring his otherwise happy expression. When I take another one for the time Chantal and I stripped naked with Leslie and Danielle and jumped in the Hudson River on a dare from Chantal's boyfriend (who *wasn't* present for the event itself), Jason's face twists into an unexpected anger that knocks me back.

"What the fuck, Layla?" His blue eyes darken, hazy in the way they narrow on me.

Adrenaline shoots through me at the sheer venom in his tone—I know he's been drinking a lot more than I have, and he's always been a little unpredictable when he's drunk. "What?" I ask gently. "It was with the girls—no one else was out there."

Wells straightens in his chair on the other side of Jason, who scoffs and shakes his head. "All right," he says after a beat. "You want to be some sort of bad girl?" He shoves the bottle of whiskey toward me. "Go ahead. Drink."

"Jay," Wells starts. But Jason ignores him. He just stares at me with a hard look, the bottle held out on the end of his long arm.

I know what he's doing—even through my buzz, I can see his insecurities on display. Our relationship has been long-distance for two and a half years now, and it hasn't been easy. But I've never given him a reason not to trust me, and I have every right to live my life in New York just like he's living his in Texas.

So I take the bottle from his hands. And I take a drink.

"Layla," Wells says, his tone careful.

This time, Jason turns to face him. "Leave her alone."

Wells's eyes flare. "She's had a lot to drink."

"So?" Jason retorts, his anger brewing. "Didn't you hear? She does whatever she wants."

I scoff. "Come on, Jason. That's unfair."

He sits back in his chair, turning his hard expression toward the dwindling fire.

My heart lurches and my mind spins—how did we go from laughing to *this* in a matter of minutes? I slide my gaze to Wells and find him thrumming with his own anger, and my stomach flips.

And then it flips again—and I realize I'm going to be sick.

I shoot out of my chair, knocking it over in the sand. Both Jason and Wells turn to look at me, wide-eyed, as I bolt for the ocean.

"Layla!" Jason shouts, but I ignore him. My stomach twists with a cramp, and my throat burns with acid.

I wonder if tomorrow, I'll remember the sensation of the freezing sea lapping against my shins, my body hunched over as waves of nausea rolled through me. And how, for a fleeting moment as my stomach emptied into the foamy water, I imagined the tide taking me with it.

CHAPTER THIRTY-FIVE

NOW

I spend the next few days at home, avoiding my mother as much as possible without giving Annie a reason to worry. It would seem I'm also avoiding Wells, because I haven't responded to the text he sent yesterday asking me how I'm feeling. I wasn't sure if he'd meant after our dinner at June's or the conversation we shared in the pasture. Either way, I don't know what to say about any of it.

Still, he's all I think about: in the early mornings as the sun heats up the sky; in the afternoons, when the cold winter air smells of earth and pine, wrapping around me as I walk through our neighborhood with Annie; at dusk, when the shadows of the fleeting sun whisper sweet nothings and beckon me in. For nearly six years, I was more than content with his place in my life. But now . . . it was so foolish to think that's where he'd stay.

My flight back to New York is in two days, and my anxiety about leaving grows with every passing minute. I know I need to be there, that the distance and space will be good for me as I process through both my grief and my budding feelings for Wells. School will be the perfect distraction. So will Chantal and my other friends. But despite all of that, I don't feel ready to go. So much of my life feels up in the air, and none of the pieces show any signs of coming back down.

I know I can't avoid Wells forever. We need to have an honest talk about everything that's happened and what it means for the future, and we're losing precious time. So I take a chance and ask Barry if I can borrow his old Lexus—the one that's been sitting in the garage, mostly untouched. I have a hunch he's saving it for Annie and likely won't say it because of what that means for me, but right now I don't care—I just know I can't ask my mom for her car after our fight.

Thankfully, he yields the keys to me without issue, and I head to the store to gather supplies before eventually pulling up in front of the cabin at the ranch. Wells isn't there—I figured he'd be working—but I let myself through the unlocked door anyway and get to work.

An hour later, the front door opens, and my body tenses in the awareness of him. But I keep my focus on the task at hand. "Layla?" I hear him ask.

I brave a turn and find Wells already moving toward me, pushed-up sleeves along tan forearms, brows slightly bunched as a bemused smile splashes across his sun-soaked face. He's been riding today; I can tell from his windblown hair and easy gait. He's found a little relief in the one thing he loves most. The one place he's wholly, viscerally himself. "Hi," I say, suddenly insecure. "I hope it's okay I let myself in."

His eyes roam around the room, taking in the empty brown grocery bags on the floor and the food on the stove.

And then his focus skims down my body, absorbing the simple cotton sweater and fitted jeans I'm wearing with my favorite embroidered boots. "Of course it is," he assures. "Are you cooking me food?" he asks. As if the possibility is so out of reach and yet . . . here I am.

"Chicken and dumplings," I confirm. "My mother's recipe—it's my favorite."

"That so?" he teases, humming appreciatively at the pan on the burner.

"Mhmm," I say back. My eyes catch on the way he looks at me, like I've just unlocked some new level of . . . *this* . . . so I busy myself with grabbing the salt and pepper to sprinkle over the gravy.

But he crowds into me, gently steering me back from the hot stove until my hips hit the island in the middle of the kitchen. He ducks his face down toward my neck and breathes me in. "Careful, sunshine," he murmurs low. "I might get used to this."

My blood thrums in response to how close he is, and I have to swallow the desire it's igniting. "I um . . ." I close my eyes, focusing on the words I need to say. "I did it to thank you," I force out. "For everything you've done for me."

I see how his body flinches, and he slowly pulls himself back to look at me. "Thank me?" he repeats, confused.

"Yes," I confirm.

The light in his eyes dims and he sucks down a deep breath. "Is that the kind of 'thank you' that comes right before a good-bye?" he asks, and my skin grows cold with the loss of the heat between us.

"My flight back to New York is coming up," I concede. "I leave early in the morning, the day after tomorrow."

A heavy disappointment splinters through his features, but he's quick to wipe it away. "Oh," he says, nodding like this doesn't wreck him. "Okay."

I set the wooden spoon I'm holding on the counter, and sigh. "It's just school, Wells. I can't *not* go back."

"I'd never want to stop you from going," he states firmly. "I think NYU is one of the best things you've done for yourself."

Surprise catches in my throat. "You do?"

He nods. "Yeah, I do."

I let that sink in. Everything it means to me.

Jason wanted me to follow him to Texas A&M, to shape my life outside of Saddlebrook Falls around him. And I can't help but think that if I'd done it, he might not have ever cheated on me. I know it's not a fair thought, that I can't blame myself for his choices. But it's one that's taken hold at some point over the last couple of weeks.

If I had followed him, maybe his life wouldn't have derailed.

Maybe he'd even still be alive.

But where would that've left me? Naively in the arms of a man who, at his core, would choose his own selfish tendencies over me?

And Wells . . . he'd still be harboring the weight of his secret. Suffering through so much, navigating a deep shame and a commitment to do the right thing.

"I'm not running from this," I say, anchoring back into the moment. "I don't want you to think that's what this is about."

His fingers reach to brush along my cheek before he pulls back, like a reflex he has to fight. "I wouldn't blame you if you were," he says honestly, and it stabs me right in the chest.

"I'm not," I say again with conviction. "But . . . I can't deny the space will be helpful." The admission flares brightly in my throat, uncomfortable and cramped. Because I know the implications of it.

If we do this, it's going to mean something to me.

He nods again, face tight.

"I'm sorry." The words spill out without warning—he needs to know this isn't about him. "I'm not saying it's the end of . . . this. Just that I need a second . . . I need to think—"

"Don't," he whispers. "Don't you dare apologize to me. You have nothing to be sorry for."

I close my eyes and lift my face, feeling the expanse of his jaw delicately slide along my cheek. "Do you regret it?" It's a question that's been burning on my tongue.

His eyes widen and then soften as he presses his thumb into my bottom lip. "No, of course not. Never in a million years would I regret what we did." Relief sinks deep in my chest. He takes a deep, grounding breath and continues. "I think your need for space is a good thing—there are a lot of emotions here. I—I think it'll be good for me, too. It's hard to put into words, but . . . you've always been his. Never mine. And I've been trying to figure out how to reconcile that."

I nod, knowing exactly what he means. A tectonic shift has taken place, one that changes everything. And we need a pause to come to some resolutions.

"Do you think we can really make this work?" I dare to ask. "Do you think we could . . . actually do this?"

My heartbeat skips when he smiles. "Layla," he whispers close to my cheek, his wintergreen breath curling around my ear. "I'm learning that when it comes to you, I don't know what I'm capable of. But I have to admit—I look forward to finding out."

I smile, too, and lean into his chest. He wraps his strong arms around me, and I can smell the horse he was on today. The field he rode in.

"You've already pushed me so far beyond my boundaries," he says into my hair. "At the beginning, I thought my attraction to you was just something physical. You were this gorgeous freshman who walked into my math class, and I . . . I had so many thoughts about all the ways I wanted to get to know you. And then you showed up to the ranch with Jay and I knew I had to back down—but the thoughts never stopped. They were always there, a low churning in the back of my mind that I could never get relief from.

"When you fainted after we lost state, I fucking lost my *mind*, Layla. I was beside myself, totally out of control, carrying you to the medic team—"

"Wait," I gasp. "*You* carried me off the field?"

His eyes sharpen. "You didn't know?"

I shake my head. "I thought it was Jason . . . my mom let me believe . . ." I trail off.

His eyes grow wistful. Almost sad. "It's okay. It was probably better that way. I acted inappropriately. I'm surprised Jason never came for me then, but he was so wrapped up in the loss—"

"No." I shake my head. "I've been lied to enough." A tendril of humiliation weaves through my gut, knowing all the ways Jason lied to me. The ways my mom manipulated me. "I want the truth. Always. Okay?"

"You'll always have it from me," he promises. "Actually," he adds, eyes bouncing to my boots, "there's something else that's always bothered me . . ."

"What?"

The right side of his mouth lifts, but his eyes grow wistful. "Those boots."

I exhale, already knowing where this is going. "Jason never knew I wanted them," I say. "But you did."

He nods once. "I asked Melody for them for your birthday . . . but then I chickened out." He lets out a humorless laugh. "I brought it up to Jason, told him Melody wanted you to have them, even told him he could say they were from him."

I shake my head. "Why would you do that?"

He shrugs. "I wanted you to have them, even if you never knew where they really came from. But every time you wear them . . . it's always been a little hard to swallow."

Tears well in my eyes and I pull him into a hug. His arms are warm and strong as they wrap around me—this tender man who's been hiding his feelings for so long, trying to protect the people he loves most.

I sigh into his shirt. "Let's enjoy the time we have left. Pretend that I'm not leaving?"

He pulls back, a small smile playing on his lips. "Anything you want."

I move back to the food, focusing on the gravy when I say, "Maybe I could stay here until I leave?"

He pauses. "Won't your family want to see you?"

I shrug. "I'll go back at some point to say goodbye to Annie, but . . . my mom and I got into a pretty big fight when you dropped me off the other morning. I don't really care to see her if I can avoid it."

"Shit," he mutters, coming up behind me, pressing a kiss to the top of my head. "How bad was it?

"She's worried you're corrupting me," I admit. "That

spending time with you will stamp away any potential I might have of being available to a more fitting suitor."

"Damn," he says, shaking his head. I turn just in time to catch the flicker of pain in his eyes. But then he wipes it away with a teasing smile. "Well, too bad for her, because ruining every other man's chance at you is exactly what I intend to do." There's an edge to the way he says it. When his eyes drop to his feet, I realize what it is: fear.

Like he still doesn't believe he could deserve this. Deserve *me*.

"I don't care what my mother says, Wells." I press my hand to his chest, right over his heart. "You know that. She doesn't know you like I do. She doesn't know that you're where I feel most like myself. Where I'm most at ease."

"I can't give you the life you may have had with Jason," he says carefully. "I already told you, the ranch is where I belong. I'm not going back to school."

I nod. "I know. That doesn't matter to me. Jason is the one who made success so specific."

Wells expels a breath, crossing his arms over his chest. "For what it's worth, that shit never sat right with me, Layla. His dreams were so big and important and . . ." He looks at me with a soft earnestness. "My dreams were always of you. It's what scares me the most, that it'll tear me apart when you go."

I stare at him until my eyes burn. Until a tear rolls down my cheek. He watches it trail down my face, his expression crestfallen. I turn back to the counter, pulling two plates toward the stove. "It's just a few months," I say. "I'll be back by summer."

I don't admit that I'm terrified to leave him, too. That he's already obliterated my heart.

"Come here," he murmurs as he gently pulls on my elbow, tethering me back into his chest. He turns us so that I'm backed against the island, and then he lifts me onto it, positioning himself between my legs. At this height we're eye level, and his are determined. "Promise me that when you leave, you do whatever you need to make yourself happy," he says, cupping my face. "Have fun, enjoy your friends . . . Promise me that you'll be selfish, and don't worry about anything or anyone else."

My chest squeezes so tight, I think it might burst. "I promise," I whisper.

He watches my mouth as I say the words. "Good." He nods. "But until you go, you're *mine*, sunshine." His hand moves to the back of my head as he pulls me in for a scorching kiss. I wind my fingers through his hair, memorizing the way he feels against me, the warmth he pours into me.

It doesn't take long before he's unzipping my jeans and reaching in, finding me wet enough to be embarrassed—but I'm not. Not with him. I yank on his belt loops until his hips are right between my thighs, making quick work of his button and zipper until I can feel his need heavy in my hands.

Soon he presses into me, and it feels like free falling. Like we've climbed to the top of the highest canyon and jumped off the edge with no regard for what comes next. Nothing matters except for the beat of our hearts and the feel of him moving inside of me as we chase the high that only this will bring. And when I come in a furious white-hot ecstasy that robs me of my breath, he sputters his release inside of me shortly after, and the truth crashes through me like a hurricane.

I love him.

I love him more than I've ever loved anything in my whole life.

CHAPTER THIRTY-SIX

NOW

The next day, we get up before sunrise.

Wells wants to take me on a long horseback ride, something I haven't done in years. Champ whinnies from his stall when he sees me, nuzzling his long nose against my shoulder, and I laugh. There's a sense of gratification in knowing that, even after all this time, he still remembers me.

We ride fifteen miles to Wells's secret spot by the river, draped by the trees that hide us from the rest of the world. As the horses get their fill of the cool water, he kisses me long and slow against a wide tree. He does a good job of not showing his panic, but I know it's there. I feel it in the way he licks into my mouth, savoring every taste. In the way his fingerprints mark my face and neck.

I do everything I can to stay present, trying not to let my impending departure ruin any second of our time together—but it's almost impossible. In twenty-four hours, I'll be over a thousand miles away, trying to sort through the mess of my life.

And Wells will be here, on this ranch that I love so much, forcing himself to give me the space that I've asked him for. That we both know we need.

Soon, we make the trek back, both of us near silent the whole ride home. By the end of it, my legs are sore and my knees ache, but there's an immeasurable contentment that I intend to hold on to for as long as possible. I kiss Champ on the nose before turning him back into his stall to rest, and my eyes well with tears as I walk back out of the barn and wait for Wells to finish turning in Lady.

He follows me to my house in his truck so I can return Barry's car and grab my suitcase—I packed it before I left yesterday. I tell Wells to wait before I run inside to find Annie.

Her eyes catch mine over the book she's reading, and she tosses it onto her nightstand. "You leave tomorrow," she says matter-of-factly.

I nod, forcing a watery smile. "Yeah."

She gets up from her bed and throws her arms around me. "Will you call me every day?" she asks. She must be able to sense that I'm not staying here tonight, and it makes me sad that things are so broken between me and Mom.

I kiss the top of her head and squeeze her to me. "I promise I will," I say. "I love you so much."

I find Barry in his home office and thank him for letting me borrow his car before heading out the door, not bothering to look back.

Back at the cabin, Wells sears two steaks in a cast-iron pan as I roast potatoes and green beans in the oven, and we eat under a blanket in the bed of his truck beneath the stars, drinking from an old bottle of wine he found in the cupboard.

As I lean back against him, I try to ease my racing heart.

It feels like everything is closing in, like the sky might fall on top of me and swallow me whole. It isn't long before my breaths saw out of me and the edges of my vision begin to blur.

Wells notices immediately and pushes our plates to the side. "Breathe, Layla," he orders gently, pulling me into his lap to face him, and I'm transported right back to that dark night only weeks ago when my entire world tilted on its axis for the second time in a matter of days. I try to fill my lungs with air, but my brain is moving too fast.

"Look at me," Wells says, cupping my face in his hands. I turn my focus to the slope of his jaw and the column of his throat. He pulls my hand over his chest, over his heart. "Feel that?" he asks. I nod, the pounding against my palm leveling my own pulse. "That's it," he praises. "Now breathe." He inhales deeply, his chest rising as it fills with air, and I close my eyes and do the same.

"No." His hands are back on my face. "Look at me." I do, and he breathes in again. This time, I focus on the golden flecks in his eyes as I pull air into my chest. Oxygen floods back through me, such a sweet relief, and I follow Wells's lead as he exhales and takes in another breath.

"Good girl." He smiles, kissing my cheek. "Keep going."

For the next five minutes, we watch each other as I breathe, the panic inside of me lessening in intensity but never leaving.

"I'm scared," I finally admit after my heart slows back to normal.

His brows pinch. "Of what?"

I chew the inside of my cheek. "Of losing you, too."

He shakes his head vehemently, sliding his hands to my waist and pulling me in closer so that my hips are flush with his. "I'm not going anywhere, Layla," he murmurs. "I'll wait here forever if I have to."

And when he leans in to capture my mouth, I'm enraptured by the feel of him all around me, enveloping me in so much love and care that I can't possibly walk away from this for good. Not when he's everything my heart craves, everything my soul needs to *feel* like this again.

"I have to leave first thing in the morning," I say as his fingers graze under my shirt.

"How about second thing?" he whispers, kissing me again, like our impending goodbye isn't clawing at him the way it is me. But I know he feels it.

When we move to his room neither of us sleeps, lost in the weight of each other and our mutual fear of what tomorrow brings. And when the morning light finally shines through the window, he makes good on his promise to distract me for as long as he can before we finally rip ourselves from his bed.

On the way to the airport, I ask him to drop me off at the curb—I can't bear to keep this going any longer. If he comes inside and walks me to the security checkpoint, I don't trust myself to go through it. It's obvious he wants to protest, but he holds himself back and relents.

For me.

His face is tight as he parks at the terminal, jumping out to grab my suitcase from the back. He meets me on the sidewalk and buries his face in the crook of my neck as a low, guttural sound escapes from somewhere in his chest.

I wind my fingers through his messy hair as my tears begin to fall. "We got this," I whisper, holding him close. "We can do this, Wells."

He pulls back to look at me, his eyes red-rimmed and lashes

damp, before disentangling himself from my arms. "Call me when you get there?" he asks as he shoves his hands into the pockets of his Carhartt jacket.

"Promise," I say, giving him one more smile before I turn to walk through the automatic doors.

And I cry the entire trip back.

CHAPTER THIRTY-SEVEN

FOUR MONTHS LATER

My appointment with Professor Zhang only takes twenty minutes.

I sit in the same worn leather chair I've sat in four times now, my shoulders vibrating with excitement as we plan out classes for my next semester at NYU. It's hard to sit still, hard not to beg him to just sign off on the damn paperwork so I can move on with my plan.

He looks at me from the other side of the mahogany desk, his eyes bouncing back and forth between my face and the piece of paper in front of him. "Are you sure about this?" he asks once more in his thick northeastern accent.

I turn to my copy of the paper—the same schedule he's looking at—and nod, certain. "Yes," I confirm. "More than sure."

His smile is friendly as he sits back in his leather chair, his tweed coat shifting over his chest. "Okay, then. You're all set, Miss Hayes. I'll check in with you at the start of the new year and make sure things are going well—but, I don't see any reason why they shouldn't be. You're a gifted student, and you're doing very well for yourself. Keep up the good work."

I beam. "Thank you so much . . . for everything." I reach out to shake his hand. And then I stand to leave, eager to get back to my shoebox of a dorm and keep moving all of this along, knowing what's waiting for me at the end.

Outside, the afternoon air is warmer than usual, and the smell of coffee wafts from all the cafés that line this part of campus. The street is crowded with students navigating to their last finals of the semester and there's a collective anticipation of summer break that I feel deep in my stomach. I finished my last final this morning—a two-hour assessment on the ethics and practice of investigative journalism—and now all I can think about is getting *out* of this city.

I hurry back to my building on the other side of campus, pushing the elevator button with a wave of impatience. *Sixteen more hours*, I think. *Only sixteen more hours until I board that plane home.* When the elevator still doesn't chime, likely caught in the traffic of students coming and going to make it to class, I exhale a frustrated breath and beeline for the stairs, taking them two at a time to the sixth floor.

By the time I reach it, I'm flushed and out of breath, but I don't care. I have fourteen hours to pack up my life here and say goodbye to the friends that have turned into family. My stomach flips at the thought, knowing how close I am. I ache for the dust and spring wildflowers, for the thundering sound of running horses.

Growing up in Saddlebrook Falls, I always felt homesick for a place I didn't yet know, desperate to make it somewhere else where I didn't have to try so hard to be something I'm not.

It's what eventually led me to New York. But now . . . now I crave the one place where I've ever felt truly like myself. Where I can be needy and messy and safely fall apart without feeling like I'll *lose* something in the process.

A place where a man with soft brown eyes waits for me, who never fails to remind me of all that I am and everything I'm capable of.

I've spent countless hours thinking about Wells over the last four months. I knew that leaving him would be hard, but I didn't realize the fundamental wreckage I'd have to endure. It took six weeks for me to find my footing again, to ease back into what it's like living in New York. I moved through my first two weeks of classes in a haze, unable to focus on anything around me. The anxiety I'd left Texas with continued to grow, and it was like trying to swim out of a riptide. It was exhausting, and I felt so helpless and alone.

When Chantal came home from class one day to find me on the floor in the middle of a brutal panic attack, she forced me to make an appointment with a therapist. It's what led me to Anika, a grief counseling specialist, who's been able to give me tools to manage my emotions. Those weekly online sessions have become my saving grace as I continue to work through healing the wounds I thought would rule my life forever.

I think the best part of therapy has been learning that I need to absolve myself of any blame for the things that have happened, and that the guilt I feel about my relationship with Wells is a normal byproduct of all the trauma I've experienced. It took *many* sessions to share the shame and anger I'd been holding tight to—the things that still flare up on the harder days—but with each new raw truth I handed over to Anika, she met me with patience and understanding. Eventually, I learned not to be so afraid of the process.

It breaks my heart that Jason never sought help for himself. That he never told anyone how hard he was struggling under the weight of pressure and expectation. I imagine it would've had an impact on him and the choices he made in the months leading up to his accident. But as much as I wish things had turned out differently—for all of us—I find comfort in knowing there's always a way forward, that while I'll always hold Jason close to my heart, I can still learn to let go of the disruptive and negative beliefs that bind me to his death.

There's no denying the impact that losing Jason has left on my life. Grief shapes us, it *changes* us. For me, it shifted the trajectory of my life in ways that forced me to rediscover who I am, to reexamine the things I want out of life. It's what shoved Wells and me back into each other's orbit. What led to the realization that he might not be just a small piece of my story—he might be what helps shape the rest of it.

When I was younger, I believed that to love someone meant giving up parts of myself. That I'd have to make concessions in exchange for loyalty and devotion. Jason had proven me right with everything he asked of me, and even though I'd never intended for it to happen, I'd played right into a game that I never wanted any part of.

Over time, it eroded much of the confidence I had in myself to make choices that put *my* needs first. It's what drove my feelings of betrayal when I learned about Emma, why I didn't trust the choices I was making with Wells.

Now, though, I can look back and see that Wells completely disrupts any notion that I need to give up important parts of myself to make room for love. He's championed my needs and encouraged me to be selfish about what I want for as long as I've known him . . . I just wish it didn't take me so long to see it. *And* I wish I never worried so much about everyone else and what they would think about my feelings for him.

When it comes to Wells, I know how things look. I know the impossibility of it all, that Jason's best friend and girlfriend would come together in grief and end up starting a fire together that burned as hot and bright as it did. To anyone, it might seem messy and irresponsible and a disgrace to the memory of Jason. But the truth of it feels a lot more like an awakening, a universal shift to a path that was there all along. In another life, maybe it would've been Wells from the start. Maybe we could have saved ourselves a lot of scrutiny and judgment from a town that thrives on both.

But I don't regret anything that's gotten me to where I am today. As flawed as all of this may seem, I would choose this path over and over and *over* again if it meant showing Wells how much he deserves this—because he does. He wants just like anyone else does, and after holding on to his secret for so long, I'm ready to love him out loud and in the open.

I unlock the door and walk in to find Chantal rolling a giant suitcase toward me, her magenta tennis dress a contrast to her dark skin. She finished her last final yesterday, putting her about twelve hours ahead of me on Operation Get Out of Dodge. "Hey," I say, looking at the duffle and tote bags on the floor by my feet.

She pulls the suitcase up next to them and pushes down the retractable handle. "How'd it go?" she asks.

I smile. "All set."

She squeals, pulling me in for a tight hug. "I'm going to miss you so much."

My heart flips—Chantal has been a lifeline for me here. "I'll miss you more," I confess. "But I know I'll see you soon, I promise."

She pulls back, eyes watery. "Come visit me over the summer? I'll take you to the Keys, it'll be so good."

I nod, smiling. "That sounds amazing."

Bending down to pick up her bags, she says, "Text me when you land in Texas?"

"Text me when you land in Florida," I parrot.

"You know I will."

"Do you need help getting all this down?"

She shakes her head, smirking. "Billy's on his way up with a cart for me." Billy, the security guard downstairs, has such an obvious thing for Chantal he'd probably carry her to JFK on his back if she let him.

I laugh, giving her another hug goodbye before I shut the door behind her and head to focus on my own packing.

Five minutes later, there's a soft knock on the door, and I look around wondering if Chantal's forgotten something. Or maybe it's Bernadette finally returning the curling iron I let her borrow over a month ago when she had a date with her TA. I pull open the heavy door, ready to tease whoever it is, but a loud gasp escapes my throat when I see Wells on the other side.

His hair is mussed, his eyes glowing like warm honey as they bounce between mine. "Hey, sunshine," he says.

"Oh my god," I say, throwing myself at him.

He wraps his strong arms around me and lifts me off the ground. "God it's good to see you," he whispers into my hair.

He smells so good—so much like him—and it breaks me apart.

"What are you doing here?" I force out through a wave of tears.

He sets me back down and says, "I was in West Virginia for a rodeo, and I just couldn't get on the plane home knowing I was only a few hundred miles from you." He looks past me into my dorm room and grins. "I figured if I made it in time, I could help you pack and fly home with you. Your roommate heard me ask the guard where I could find you and sent me up."

My heart nearly explodes. Wells has texted me every day since dropping me off at the airport in Texas, mostly to check in and see how I'm doing. To remind me that, even through the distance, he's there. That he's in my corner. It took me weeks before I finally started responding, after a few sessions with Anika when I'd finally begun to shed some of the guilt and shame I'd been carrying.

Since then, we've kept the conversation light. He sends me little updates on the horses and his family, and the occasional picture of things that remind him of me: a gorgeous sunrise over the ranch's quiet pasture, a glimpse of the river under the trees. Two and a half months ago, he was officially sponsored by a boot brand based in Texas that saw him compete at the rodeo in Dallas, and for the last several weeks he's been traveling in the professional rodeo circuit, competing in dozens of states. Our texts have been a little more infrequent as he travels, but he never misses a day.

"I've been counting down the hours to get back home to you," I admit as a tear falls from my jaw.

He wipes away my tears with his thumbs, both hands

cupped warmly around my face. "I've been looking forward to this since the day you left, Layla. Watching you walk away from me almost killed me." The confession splinters through the ache in my chest. I almost forgot what it's like to be at the center of his attention. The way he *sees* me in a way that feels real.

It's always felt so real.

"Is it okay that I'm here?" he asks, the line between his brow deepening. And it's one of my favorite things about him—how he's so eager to prioritize me. My needs. My emotions.

I give him a watery smile. So much has changed in the last four months and it's overwhelming that he's in front of me right now—but I've never been more sure about what I want. If I can hold fast to the grace and honor I'm showing myself, to this tender and honest thing of light blooming between us, I might somehow manage to have it all.

There's a sudden, burning need in my chest to tell him the words that I hope will smooth out the lines on his face.

"Wells," I breathe. "I—I have to show you something." I pull him in through the door, then turn to search for the paper from Professor Zhang. I find it on my desk and pick it up, handing it to him.

He takes it from me, mouth twisting, and reads.

"I've transferred my program," I explain. "Starting next year, I'll be enrolled in the online campus."

Wells looks up at me, brow dipping. "You won't be here?" he asks. "In New York?" I shake my head, smiling. But he still looks concerned. "Then . . . where will you be?"

I laugh. "Wherever you are, I hope."

The look on his face quickly morphs into disbelief. "With me?" he asks, his voice quiet.

I nod. "I know what I want, Wells. And it's you. It's the ranch and the rodeo, the horses . . . I want to be a part of it. I've started taking photos again. I want to build a brand for the ranch and showcase what your family is doing. Try to help bring in more resources. It's time people start understanding all the good you Bennetts do. I could travel with you to rodeos, or wait for you at home and help your brothers with the horses. I just . . ." I pause, nerves rolling through me at the look on his face, like he's frozen, with no indication of whether his feelings are good or bad.

"You brought me back to life, Wells. I was at my lowest point, and you were right there to lift me back up. *You* are where my heart belongs, where my home is. And I don't want to live for another moment without you knowing that I love you, too."

"Goddammit, Layla," he says quietly. Tears fill his eyes, and he wipes his hand over his face. And then his smile is so bright it catches fire in my heart.

I already can't wait for another.

"Are you *sure* this is what you want?" he asks, his voice still laced with uncertainty.

If we do this, it's going to mean something to me.

I need you to be sure.

I close the distance between us and wrap my arms around his waist, pressing my cheek to his chest. He snakes an arm around my back, winds his fingers through my hair. "Yes," I tell him. "I just needed time to heal some of my wounds. But I knew you'd be the one I wanted in the end." I reach to press a kiss to his lips and smile. "Take me home, Wells."

I look up from my textbook, squinting against a beam of sunlight that bends through the orange and yellow autumn leaves to watch Wells twist his body in tandem with the bucking horse beneath him. He's a new one, a large black mustang dropped off from somewhere in the Mojave Desert a couple of days ago, and he's got the willpower and strength of an entire herd. "How are you doing?" I call out.

Wells's face is tight in careful concentration as the horse bucks from the middle of the river. Water flows downstream, lapping along the expanse of his body, but the horse keeps bucking despite the resistance. Wells braves a look at me, a wild grin flashing on his face. "Good!" he yells back. "He's starting to tire out."

He's so handsome it steals my breath. I laugh, heart beaming, and turn back to my textbook. It's an afternoon spent like so many others—quiet and slow as he works with the horses and I work through my assignments. We've managed to figure out how to make it all possible while still spending most days together. When I'm not studying or navigating homework, I'm back to doing the things I used to do on the ranch: feeding, grooming, tacking, and other everyday chores. I even took charge of an orphaned filly that was dropped off during the summer.

It turns out I'm more of a country girl than I ever cared to admit—but I want to admit it now because being home with Wells is *everything*. Spending each day working alongside him and his brothers, knowing the impact they have on at-risk horses, has been fulfilling in a way I was never sure anything could be.

Years ago, I sat and watched Kasey try to break Stardust from her wild instincts. For years after, I watched Wells ride bucking horses in his pursuit of taming them, and it made me so sad that they'd inevitably lose the freedom they'd had since birth. That they'd been ripped from the prairies and deserts they came from.

But now, as I watch Wells wear down this new horse with the help of the flowing water, I realize the horses were never sad at all. One by one, they'd given their hearts to him—just like I have—and none of us are broken or trapped in having done so.

"Thatta boy," Wells murmurs, pulling me back into the moment. I turn my gaze back to him and find the mustang has stopped bucking. Wells runs a hand down the slope of his neck, giving him tender affection in exchange for his trust, and my heart thrums at witnessing such a beautiful moment.

As if Wells can read my thoughts, he smiles. "He gave me a solid run for my money," he jests, shaking his head.

"Good," I say. "You need the practice." It's been a few months since Wells competed, but there's a handful of rodeos he's scheduled for in November and December. We decided that I'd go with him, travel from one state to another, exploring landmarks along the way. I can't wait.

Wells laughs. "You in a good place for us to head back?"

I nod, closing my textbook and grabbing my notebook and highlighters spread around the flannel blanket. I tuck it all away in my backpack and amble toward Champ and Lady who rest in the shade. "Hey boy," I say softly as I stroke Champ's nose. "You ready to go home?" His ears flutter as he presses his mouth to my shoulder, and I can't help but giggle.

Wells comes up behind me in his bright-yellow waders and wraps his arms around my middle. "Hey!" I squeal as the back of my jeans soak from the water dripping down his legs. To add insult to injury, the new horse shakes the water off his body and sprays us all. Lady whinnies, and Wells chuckles.

He presses a kiss to the curve between my neck and shoulder. "Nothing wrong with getting you a little wet, is there?"

My cheeks heat. "Definitely not."

We make the long ride home, the black horse trailing behind Lady, tethered by the lead rope Wells holds with Champ and me taking up the back. Once the narrow trail through the denser part of the ranch opens up, I move to ride alongside Wells. We fall into an easy rhythm as the ranch spreads out around us, vast and majestic. I'm thankful I get to experience this every day—there's no denying it feels like home. And Wells . . . What we share together goes beyond words—it's a language all on its own.

When I look at him, I find him already watching me with a

heady mix of adoration and pride that nearly knocks me off the saddle. "What?" I ask, my throat squeezing around the word.

His mouth pulls up, and it's devastating. "You only smile like that when you're on a horse," he says simply.

No, I think to myself. *I smile like this because I'm with* you.

LATER THAT NIGHT, WELLS AND I MAKE DINNER together in the kitchen of our little cabin. I officially moved in at the end of summer after spending my first two months home with Annie during her break from school. It wasn't easy to navigate being back in my mother's house while things between us were still so broken, but Annie's fourteen and about to start high school. I know how important these years with her are, and I want to be a part of them as much as possible.

It's what led me to finally sit my mother down one night after Annie had gone to bed, to tell her what I had with Wells was serious and important to me. She didn't take it well, but something about the conversation was . . . different. I'm not sure if it was the confidence I'd been gaining through therapy or the clarity in my feelings for Wells, but even though she disagreed with me and insisted it was a phase, I could tell she was at least listening.

It was a start.

We've had many more conversations since then, especially later in the summer when I told her I was moving in with Wells. Logistically, it meant I'd be moving to Bennett Ranch, and that wasn't an easy conversation—but yet again, it felt like she really listened and tried to understand. I think she's waiting for the other shoe to drop, for me to have my heart broken by Wells in the way she was hurt by my biological father. But I know my story is different from hers, and someday she'll know it, too.

As much as the pain and grief of losing Jason shaped me, Wells changes the shape of me, too. He blurs all of my carefully drawn lines, and I've spent so much time trying to find the edges of them, to pinpoint the exact place where one of us ends and the other begins so that I can maintain some semblance of control. But now, as his eyes catch mine beneath the dim kitchen light of the cabin and an easy smile lifts from his beautiful mouth, it's so easy to admit the truth: this might be messy, but it's *real*.

It's realer than anything I've ever known, and how lucky am I to have a new set of firsts with him? A first kiss stolen in his secret place; the first dance in *our* cabin after I moved in, beneath the moonlight as the cicadas sang; a first leap into the unknown with the man who's loved me for so damn long.

I don't regret anything that's happened to get me here, my flower-stitched boots rooted firmly on the soil of this ranch, because I never knew how much I'd been missing until he showed me. Until I was reminded of the passion and delicious chaos of newness. I can't get enough of him. Of the temptation of him, my desperate want for him.

Maybe I'm a cowboy like him, meant to roam the world, to take from it just as much as I give. To live through the courage and pain of losing, through the glory of getting things right.

"What?" I ask as I watch his smile stretch.

He shakes his head, eyes sparking. "You."

It's the weight of everything we've been through, nestled inside a single word. My skin warms as he takes a step closer, his determination shining. He reaches to snake a large palm around my neck, tugging me to him for a long, slow kiss.

I lick into his mouth and he groans, pinning me to the edge of the counter with his hips. He's hard, and desire flares boldly inside me. "You'll burn the potatoes," I say, and I kiss him again.

"I don't care," he murmurs. "I'm going to fuck you right here, Layla." He looks down at my neck, at his fingers wrapped around the column of my throat, and his jaw rolls. "I'm going to fuck you until you scream and then I'm probably going to fuck you again because I already know I won't be able to stop." His dark eyes dart up to mine, his pupils blown with hunger. "That work for you?"

Even after months of living together, it's always like this with him: the desperation of his need. I arch into him as he slips a hand beneath my shirt, fingers spreading wide over my ribs.

"Promise me that this is forever," I whisper against his mouth. I don't think I could ever survive the loss of Wells—his fingerprints cover my heart and his fire burns in my soul.

He looks at me like I'm the only thing he's ever loved, and it nearly brings me to my knees.

Having you like this . . . it's like touching the sunrise.

"I promise, sunshine. I'm yours forever."

Suddenly, a loud pounding comes from the front door. Wells stills, then cranes his neck in confusion. Besides the occasional rouse from Kasey on the long mornings Wells tries to stretch even longer by keeping me wrapped around him, no one ever comes to our cabin.

"Wells!" a deep voice shouts from the other side.

Rhett.

"I'm going to fuck him up," Wells mutters as he adjusts my shirt back over my stomach and turns toward the door. I follow behind, an unmistakable sense of dread snapping tight in my chest. Something's wrong . . . I know it.

Wells opens the door with the force of his frustration, but whatever he intends to say dies in his throat at the sight of Rhett's stricken face. "What is it?" he asks, concern lancing through his features.

Rhett gives him a long look. "It's Melody," he says low. "Brooks just took her to the hospital, and Kasey followed with Mom. I need help with the boys."

"Melody?" I ask as fear thrums through me. "What happened to Melody?"

Wells turns to face me, eyes wide, before running to turn the stove off. He leaves the food in the pan as he grabs our jackets from the hook by the door and shuffles us outside.

"Wells?"

His knuckles brush my cheek—a reassuring touch—before he says, "I'll tell you everything later, I promise." He places his hand on the small of my back as we follow Rhett through the ranch's grounds, toward the bigger cabin that sits a few hundred yards away.

I wrap my jacket tight around my chest and try not to let my fear take control.

ACKNOWLEDGMENTS

Sunshine is my fourth (what!) book written, and it feels like with every story, I have more and more people to be thankful for.

To my team:

Britt: I would trust you with my life, at this point! Your commitment to helping me hone Sunshine into something worth sharing with the world is something I will always be thankful for. Thank you for pushing me to be a better writer. It's something I will always, always cherish.

Cindy: I meannnn . . . this cover??? You knocked my vision out of the park! I swear your talent knows no bounds, and I'm so thankful to have you in my creative corner to help me bring these characters to life.

Lauren and Amanda: Your early feedback (and excitement!) helped me navigate through some tough plot points. This was not the easiest story to write, but with you at the helm with me I always felt brave enough to push through. Maybe someday I'll write something fluffy and light and non-torturous? And we can just giggle and skip our way through it? Ha!

ARC readers: Thank you for your continued support and excitement with each project, and for always sharing such beautiful reviews. It's because of readers like you that I get to keep doing this, and words could never express how much you all mean to me. Thank you for being so feral for Sunshine content, and for shouting about this story from the rooftops. I may not always get to respond to every message, but please hear me when I say I see you, I feel you, and I love you.

Now . . . who's ready for the next one? 😉

xo, Michaela

ABOUT THE AUTHOR

Michaela is the author of heartwarming contemporary romance novels featuring diverse characters with strong emotional development. Don't worry - there's always a HEA (and plenty of spice).

When she's not reading or writing she's usually with her family and dogs, enjoying the desert in Arizona.

Stay tuned for exciting announcements at michaelajeantaylor.com

amazon.com/author/michaelajeantaylor

instagram.com/michaelajeanbooks

tiktok.com/@michaelajeanbooks

goodreads.com/michaelajeanbooks

facebook.com/michaelajeanbooks